The Art of Waiting

CHRISTOPHER JORY

Polygon

First published in hardback by Polygon in Great Britain in 2015.
This paperback edition published in 2016 by Polygon,
an imprint of Birlinn Ltd.

West Newington House
10 Newington Road
Edinburgh
EH9 1QS

www.polygonbooks.co.uk

Quotation by Georgi Litichevsky is from
The Meaning of Life (Time Inc. Magazine Company, 1991)

ISBN 978 1 84697 362 8
eBook ISBN 978 0 85790 839 1

British Library Cataloguing in Publication Data
A catalogue record for this book is available on request
from the British Library.

Typeset by 3btype.com

THE ART OF WAITING

Christopher Jory was born in 1968 in Newcastle-upon-Tyne. He spent his early childhood in Barbados, Venezuela and finally Oxfordshire. He did a degree in English Literature and Philosophy at Leicester University and then worked for the British Council and other organisations in Italy, Spain, Greece, Brazil and Venezuela. He is currently a Publisher at Cambridge University Press. His first book, *Lost in the Flames* (Matador, 2012), was a moving account of RAF Bomber Command airmen and their families.

Contents

Life means love. We are here for love. Only love is real, and everything is real thanks to love. We are nomads wandering through illusionary space. How to make it real? Only by destroying limits that separate us from others. No violence, no attempts at escape can help, only love. Too often love is more painful than joyful. The instances of love are much shorter than the periods during which we wait for love to emerge. The meaning of living is mastering the art of waiting.

Georgi Litichevsky, Ukrainian artist

For my wife, Lioudmila

Hope

Aldo Gardini stood behind barbed wire in the pale light of a Russian dawn, three hundred miles south-east of Moscow, the start of another desperate day as a prisoner of war. An insect – something small and dark, a butterfly or a moth – had perched itself on the wire a few feet away, its wings lifting up in the breeze. He looked at it longingly as it flew away, then rubbed his hands together for warmth, trying to get some life back into them after another freezing night spent down in his bunker. Tambov 188 had never been intended for human habitation, but needs must – there were just too many prisoners to know what to do with, so anywhere would do and who cared if they died. The prisoners slept underground, each bunker fifteen metres long, fifty men to each one, different nationalities all mixed in together – but Aldo would tell anyone who would listen that they had only one thing in common: they were all Stalin's enemies and all their leaders were stupid enough to think they could invade the Soviet Union and get away with it.

The roofs of the bunkers were made of branches and packed earth and the walls were solid concrete. There was no light and no ventilation, and when Aldo lay there at the end of each day and looked up into the pitch black, he felt as if he had been buried alive. The nights were hell – the cold and the damp, the lice, the jabbering of the men who had gone mad, the stink of the ones who were dying. Typhus did for most of them, a rampant epidemic, and in the morning you'd often wake up next to a dead man. That got the day off to a bad start, and it usually went downhill from there. Up at six, the door flung open by the guards, banging on it with hammers as they did so, shouting at you to get up, total darkness outside, a blast of cold air blowing in. Your first job was to separate the dead from the living. Farm carts and sleds pulled by mules trawled from bunker to bunker and you loaded the bodies on and took the cart out into the woods that encircled the camp. You'd light a huge fire to soften the ground six feet down, where the spring hadn't yet thawed it out, and then you'd dig a pit and throw them all in. Once you'd sorted out the dead, it was time to wash out the bunker, slopping it out like a barn. Then everyone would troop out into the cold and you'd strip so the guards could inspect you for lice. They dragged this out longer than necessary, of course, watching you shiver, and by the time you got your clothes on again, you were lucky if you ever warmed up. Then off you'd go to spend the day hard at work, as if you still had any strength left in you at all. Then back to the camp, a bowl of soup, something indescribable, a few grains of wheat at the bottom of it if you were lucky. Then an hour of 'rest' – political indoctrination – with some bastard in a uniform berating you for something you didn't believe in anyway, when all you wanted to do was sleep. Then finally back to your bunker, where you lay down in the dark at last and prayed.

Today's lice-checking routine had just finished. Aldo had flung on his clothes and was standing by the wire, waiting for the shouting to begin again, the order to set off for work. He thrust his hands into his pockets and rubbed his fingers against the little wooden fish he had carved for himself out of oak at the boatyard back in Venice a year or two before – a little piece of home, a good-luck charm he had carried with him through the war. He listened to the sounds of the camp around him, the dull buzz of deadened voices, thousands of them, as the prisoners gathered to wait for whatever miseries the day had in store for them. A plane flew in overhead, the first of the day, heading for the landing strip somewhere out of sight among the trees. Aldo often wondered who on earth was flying in. Who the hell would want to come here?

The noise of the plane faded and Aldo heard the sound of a beating going on behind him. It was a bit early in the day for a beating, he thought, especially one as bad as this one sounded. It was a bad sign – the sooner they started, the more they got a taste for it, and that was just the guards. Some of the other prisoners were almost as bad – Romanians, Hungarians, Croats, a few Germans thrown in for good measure, including some that were probably SS. And the thousands of Italians, of course, peasants and manual workers by and large before the war – at least Aldo could understand them, knew what made them tick, knew they would wish him no harm. The thumping stopped and he turned to look. The guards were dragging a body away by its feet. A group of prisoners stood by and watched. Then one of them – a Romanian, judging by the uniform, what was left of it – broke away from the pack, hands in pockets, slouching along as he followed the body. He caught up with it and let fly with his boot, kicking the man repeatedly in the head. The guards dropped the victim's feet and yelled at the man who'd been doing the kicking. He clearly couldn't understand what they were saying, but Aldo could.

'You're wasting your fucking time!' they were saying. 'You've killed him already!'

One of the guards fetched a spade. He chucked it at the Romanian.

'You'd better bury him now, hadn't you? But work starts at eight, so be done by then or we'll put you in the grave with him.'

The man just stood there, so they shouted at him again and pushed him towards the gate and around the edge of the fence to an area of bare ground outside. The man got the message. He took the spade and walked towards the gate, then out of it and around towards Aldo, followed by a guard. Aldo watched as the Romanian started digging. He was digging too slowly. The ground was too hard. He would never get it done in time and the guards knew it. Aldo called out to the man in Italian, warning him that his time was limited, but the man just stared at him and said something that must have been an oath.

Fuck you, then, thought Aldo, I was only trying to help.

He leant into the fence, feeling the barbs against his coat as he let it take his weight, testing its strength, daring the guards to react, but they ignored him – they usually did, and this only heightened the boredom, the isolation, even among all these thousands. He closed his eyes and tried to remember something good, from the time before the war. How long had he been away from home? Less than a year? And only a few weeks in this camp, after the hellish retreat from the Don. But less than a year had completely changed him, and he could make nothing good come to mind. So he forced his eyes open again and let reality back in. Oh God, he thought, it's still here, all of it, the whole damn lot: the barbed wire, the woods, the camp behind, all its smells and its sounds, and the Romanian in front of him digging grimly at the ground. So, eyes closed again, reach out, now, imagine you are anywhere, anywhere but here. But then the buzz of an insect, homing in on the smell of him.

'Fucking bugs,' he muttered, and he opened his eyes and looked at the sleeve of his muddy stinking coat, saw it there, something small and leggy that had blown in off the steppe, coming in to bite at him, to take another piece of him. He slapped at it, flailing, but he failed, the thing lifting up again and buzzing off behind him, then going quiet, setting itself down somewhere he couldn't see, just out of reach. They were cunning like that, he thought, never still unless the winter got them, always on the hunt for another bit of his blood. And there would never be an end to them, too many to count, more born every minute, hatching up all around him now that spring was here, thousands of these fucking Russian bugs. So, eyes closed again now, just the sound of the Romanian and his spade, and the guards shouting at someone behind – but then something else too, something soft and hesitant. Footsteps, right in front of him, and a sound like a breath, then a touch upon his hand, his eyelids snapping open as her hand withdrew its touch.

'I'm so sorry,' she said. 'I didn't mean to startle you.'

He looked at her face and into her eyes, and he saw it in them now, that look, the look he had always loved, an unexpected recognition, something hatching up from nothing, as if she already knew him, as if she always had, or perhaps he reminded her of a friend, somebody just like him, someone she had loved. There were people like that, capable of it – he had known that, back in the old days, before the war, and he remembered it still, despite it all. Suddenly her hand was in her pocket, digging around for something, then pulling it out, a rabbit from a hat for him, a little piece of magic, her small white hand holding a dark piece of bread. And what a trick it was, how it made him feel, how it filled his leaping heart.

'Have this,' she said, twisting her hand between the strands of wire, catching her skin on one of the barbs. Up rose a tiny sphere of blood, red on the white of her hand, like all the red he had seen on the snow in the depths of the winter just past.

'I'm so sorry,' he said, at the sight of the blood, as if he were somehow to blame.

'For what?' she said, wiping it away. 'You've done nothing wrong.'

The wind carried her words away across the steppe before he could cling to them.

'Go on, take it. It's not exactly fresh, but I'm sure it's better than what you get in there.'

Aldo reached out and took the gift. He lifted it to his lips, bit off a piece of it.

'Thank you,' he said at last.

Her lips moved, something uncertain, a kind of smile, as if she had remembered something again but wanted to keep it hidden. Aldo longed to speak, to tell her everything, but no more words would come, so they stood there, the two of them, on the edge of wilderness, and he was suddenly aware of the state of him, embarrassed by it, a feeling he had not known for months, a civilising reminder, almost a politeness, brought on by this girl, this reminder of what life had been, what it should always be, a thing of unexpected kindness.

'I might come and see you again tomorrow,' she said. 'If you want me to?'

'Oh,' he said, taken aback. 'Yes, I would like that very much.'

'Good,' she said. 'Then I'll do just that.' She turned to go, then stopped. 'You know, I feel so sorry for you,' she said, then paused. 'Well, I'll see you tomorrow.'

'Yes,' he said. 'Yes . . . but . . . what's your name?' Trying to detain her, every moment an unexpected joy now, until she went away.

'I'll tell you that tomorrow.'

'Tell me now. In case you don't come back.'

'Don't worry, I will come back.'

'Tell me anyway. Please. Just in case.'

She looked at him. 'Katerina,' she said.

'What a beautiful name,' he said, trying to keep her there with compliments, but she was turning away again. 'Katerina, wait!'

She turned again.

'Have this,' he said.

He was holding something in his hand and she reached out and took it. A little wooden fish.

'I carved it myself,' he said. 'A long time ago. When I was at home.'

'It's beautiful,' she said. 'I'll treasure it.'

'It's oak,' he said. 'It'll last forever, and it'll bring you luck.'

'Thank you.'

'Something to remember me by. In case you don't come back.'

'Don't worry,' she said. 'I told you I will, and I meant it.'

She turned away again and he watched her all the way down the path, her legs brushing against the grass as she went, and then he lost sight of her among the trees.

He turned his attention back to the Romanian. He was struggling now, only two feet into the ground and time was running out. If only he knew. Aldo shouted at him again, urging him to hurry, but the man just looked at him. Aldo could hear the sounds of the trucks behind as the prisoners were gathering for another long day of backbreaking work. He shouted again, but then there was a rough hand on his shoulder, a guard pulling him away from the fence, shoving him towards one of the trucks. He hauled himself up into it, already exhausted before the day had begun. A whistle blew and the trucks pulled away and as he was passing out through the gate, Aldo looked over to where the Romanian stood digging at the earth beneath the gaze of the guard. Then the guard looked at his watch and raised his rifle. The Romanian stopped digging and looked at the guard. There was the sound of a shot and the Romanian fell into the semi-dug grave.

Aldo spent the rest of the day chopping logs into bits, lifting the dead weight of his axe time after time, but all the while he thought of Katerina. What on earth had compelled her to come over to him, to risk herself for him? Why him out of all the others in the camp? And anyway, wasn't he the enemy? Shouldn't she be afraid of him? Shouldn't she hate his guts? As he dwelt on what she had done, he allowed himself to dream, that one day the world might be at peace and he and Katerina might meet again after the war, and she would come to visit him at his home in Venice, and he would show the most beautiful person in the world the most beautiful city that had ever existed. And they would be together there forever, that's how it would be.

He was still thinking of her late that night as he lay on the concrete floor of the bunker and listened to men all around him tormented in their sleep. And as he wondered if she really would come back to see him again, he was suddenly aware of it, that feeling again, something he had forgotten, something lighting up in him, something she had lit in him.

It was hope.

And he loved her for it.

PART ONE

Russia

Katerina

Leningrad, winter 1928

The little girl thrust her head up through the surface of the river and gulped at the freezing air. She opened her throat and let out a roar of extraordinary rage and volume as the water rushed into her mouth and her head dipped below the surface again. For a moment it looked as though she was giving up the fight, sinking down into the darkness of the River Neva, but then she beat her legs frantically once more and thrashed her arms and fists and pulled herself towards the surface. Her head emerged again into the fading afternoon light, the icy wind snatching at her skin, and she gasped, a spluttering, coughing, spraying exhalation. And then a strong hand took hold of her wrist with a certainty that sent death slinking back beneath the waves, back into its hole among the dark, inert and rusting things that littered the riverbed. The fisherman hauled the girl out of the water and deposited her on the quayside. The wet bundle sat and stared back at him in shock.

'What the hell are you doing falling into the water on a day like this? Or any day, for that matter? And you shouldn't be out and about on your own anyway, a little thing like you. Does your mother even know where you are?'

His tone was harsh and reproachful, and as she listened to his scolding, her wide eyes blinked slowly and dissolved into tears.

'Come on, you can't sit there like that. You'll freeze to death in no time. But don't think I'm going to carry you, all soaking wet like that.'

He picked her up, placed her on her feet, and hurried her along to the nearest building – a museum – chiding her as they went, his stride lengthening as he spoke. Her little steps quickened to keep up and she felt a warmth edging through her and her shivers became less violent in the dusk.

'I bet you, when I get back, someone will have taken all my fishing gear,' he said.

'Do you really think so?' she whispered, feeling guilty now for the trouble she was putting him to.

'Yes, I do. I honestly think so! You come along bothering me for fish every day, and then you go and fall in the river and now I . . . I don't know.'

'I'm sorry,' she said.

'And there's no point in you coming and asking me for fish any more, is there? Because I'm not going to have any, am I?'

'No?'

'No, not if someone goes and steals all my stuff! And they'll take the fish I caught too! They're probably half-way home with them now, all pleased with themselves, wondering if they're going to cook them nice and simple with a few potatoes and maybe a little dill and a nice bit of butter sauce, some onions . . . damn it. Or maybe they'll fry them up and have them with blinys.'

'I like blinys,' she said.

'Oh, really? Honestly, I've been there all day in the freezing cold and now I've got no food for this evening.'

He looked down at the girl. Her big eyes were watching him as she tripped and hurried along. She stopped and raised a clenched little fist, blotched blue and purple with the cold, and held it out towards him.

'For you,' she said, as she opened her hand.

A little fish lay in her palm, crushed and broken by her tenacious grip.

'No, I think that's your fish now,' the man said, smiling at last. 'You hold onto it.'

She closed her fingers around it once more. They went inside the museum and a clerk took the girl into an office where a fire burned in the grate and they sat her down next to it. The girl took off her wet coat and dried her hair with a towel, then watched the flames through her ragged fringe as someone brought her a mug of hot milk.

When she turned to look for the fisherman he had gone. A little later a woman came and spoke to her as she sipped the milk.

'Are you all right, my dear?'

The girl nodded.

'What's your name?'

'Katerina. Katerina Kuznetsova.'

'Well, Katerina. I think you've been very lucky today. If that man hadn't seen you, well, you wouldn't be here now, would you?'

'No. I'd have been with the fishes.'

The woman looked at her sternly. 'Yes. You'd have been with the fishes.'

Katerina opened her fist again and the woman saw the broken little silver thing in the palm of her hand.

'Where did you get that from?'

'The river. It was a present, from that man. But he doesn't have any fish now. Somebody stole them. And his fishing lines. He said he won't have any dinner now.'

'Don't worry, I'm sure he's got plenty of fishing lines . . . and fish. He was just giving you a telling off.'

'No. It's true. He hasn't got any fish now. Someone will have wandered off with them.'

'Who will?'

'I don't know, he didn't say. Thieves, I guess. Fish thieves.'

'Fish thieves?' The woman smiled at the thought.

'It's not funny, you know.'

'Well, don't worry, he'll catch some more fish tomorrow, I'm sure of that. Here, let me get rid of that smelly little thing for you.'

'No.' The firmness of the girl's voice took the woman aback. 'No,' she repeated, then added, 'It's a roach. They eat worms!'

The woman's expression hinted at a sudden waning of sympathy for the spiky little creature sitting in front of her. 'I think you're dry now. Where do you live, Katerina?'

'Not far from here. I can walk.'

'You shouldn't really go on your own. It's getting dark. Do you want me to get someone to walk you home?'

Katerina knew that the woman's tone was less than genuine. She had heard that tone before. 'No, thank you. I'll go on my own. I go everywhere on my own.' She stood up. 'Goodbye,' she said. 'Thank you for the milk.'

She walked out of the museum, turned towards the river, and went to look for the fisherman. She walked quickly to the spot near the Trinity Bridge where he had been, but the quay was deserted. She wandered along opposite the Fortress of Peter and Paul, towards the arsenal and the zoological gardens, but he was not there either, so she went back and sat at the end of the bridge and looked at the inky water of the River Neva as it swirled around the arches. Across the river, the long walls of the fortress, dusted by an early fall of snow, stretched around the perimeter of the island. The sun had set and Katerina watched as a waning moon crept low across the horizon. In the centre of the island, the body of Peter the Great lay somewhere beneath the long thin spire of the cathedral as it stitched constellations upon the sky with its needle point.

The cold finally forced Katerina up and she crossed the long bridge over the Neva and passed through the summer gardens, the trees now devoid of leaves, the red squirrels busying themselves with the last of their chores before the onset of winter's depths. No one paid any attention to the eight-year-old girl as she hurried up Nevski Prospekt and along the Griboedova Canal. A few minutes later she was in the familiar alley that led towards the small court-yard. The washing still hung from an upstairs window, the sheets stiff with ice. The girl banged on the door.

'It's me, Katerina! I'm home! Open the door!'

She banged again, then stepped back and looked up at the window, but the room beyond lay in darkness. She knocked again.

'It's me! I'm home!'

But no one came to the door. She sat on the step and rested her chin on her knees. Her clothes were still damp from the river and she felt the cold rising up through the glazed green tiles of the doorstep and into her bones. A freezing rain began to fall, irregularly at first, then steadily, the heavy drops exploding off the cobbles until the courtyard was covered in a layer of water that would soon turn to ice. Katerina looked at the fish that still lay in her hand. Its belly had split open and a grey sludge was slipping out. She raised it to her nose and sniffed, and then laid the fish on the step and swished her hand around in the puddle that had collected at her feet. Tiny silver scales swirled in the pool of water, glinting as they slipped into the gutter. Katerina stood up again and walked back down the alley, feeling a peculiar delight at the numbness in her feet, no longer aware of the ground beneath her as she walked.

A couple of streets away, a bell rattled dustily as Katerina pushed open the door of Anna Suvurova's general store. Rumours proliferated among the neighbourhood's children as to what Anna Suvurova kept in the back room of her shop. When the bell rang, she would emerge from the shadows and stand by the till and glower at whoever had disturbed her nefarious activities. Her nicknames were various, but the balance of opinion seemed to favour the most opaque. No one could quite remember why she had come to be known as the Mushroom Woman, but the name was lent thrilling substance by tales of her cultivating poisonous fungi on shelves in the back room for use against her enemies, which in her case meant most of the human race. The absence of mushroom-related deaths in the area somewhat undermined this theory, but it was still enough to terrify the local children.

Katerina looked towards the counter and saw the Mushroom Woman loom out of the darkness. She glared ferociously at the child who had dared to enter her lair unaccompanied. Katerina screwed up her face and glared back with fierce little eyes.

'What do you want, you little scumbag?' snapped the Mushroom Woman.

Katerina ignored her and ducked up the aisle, moving quickly to the far end of the shop. Out of sight, she looked quickly around the shelves. Where were they? She was sure she had seen them here the previous week, had picked one up and pushed one of the little hooks into the end of her finger to test its sharpness, licked the blood away and put the line back on the shelf. Yes, it was definitely this shelf. The Mushroom Woman had probably moved them up higher, just to stop her playing with them again. The witch! Now Katerina could hear the woman's footsteps tracing their way round the counter and towards the aisle. She knew that this in itself was a cause for concern, as the Mushroom Woman rarely ventured out from behind the tall worktop that housed the till, a fact which had led to ever more colourful rumours about her not having any feet, or even possessing more of them than she should. A boy from across the river swore that she did in fact have two feet – he had seen them with his very own eyes – but the Lord had put them on backwards as a sign that he had disowned her at birth. Or that she wasn't a Communist. Or something equally dreadful.

Katerina caught sight of one of the fishing lines, a nice one, a bit old and dusty – it had probably been here since before the Great War – but wound round a nice wooden holder and with a float, one of those round painted ones, and a weight and several small hooks. She reached up and grabbed it, then turned her back as the Mushroom Woman appeared at the end of the aisle. She tucked the fishing line up under her sweater, drew her coat around herself, and folded her arms tightly across her chest.

'What do you want?' hissed the Mushroom Woman.

'Nothing in particular. I'm just looking, thank you.'

Katerina looked down at the Mushroom Woman's feet, just to make sure.

'Get out! Get out!'

'I said I'm just looking. I haven't found what I want yet – I'll tell you when I do.'

The Mushroom Woman lunged at Katerina. The girl skipped backwards, then up another aisle, past the vegetables and dried apples and some sort of yellow fruit she had never seen before. Then she saw a shelf of small white cheeses and slipped one into her pocket, then ducked under the nearest rack of shelves and past the till. The Mushroom Woman was standing by the door.

'Turn out your pockets, you little wretch. Come on!'

Katerina drew one hand out of a pocket and opened it slowly, mockingly.

'See? Nothing.'

'And the other. Come on, show me, or I'll call the police.'

'They wouldn't come. Even the police are afraid of you! Even Comrade Stalin would be, you . . . you . . . you Mushroom Woman!'

'What did you say?'

'Mushroom Woman! Everyone knows your secret.'

'What on earth are you talking about? Show me what you've got in that pocket.'

Katerina drew her other fist from her pocket and held it up to the woman. 'Come and see . . .'

The Mushroom Woman edged towards the fist, stooping down until it was inches from her face. Her nose twitched. 'Open it!'

Katerina opened her fist and pushed the palm of her hand, still smelling of the guts of the dead fish, into the woman's face. Then she dashed past her and the bell clattered as the door slammed shut. She heard the Mushroom Woman howling some way behind as she ran through the narrow streets, her legs no longer numb, her little body lit up by adventure, and soon she was back in the courtyard outside her house where the sheets still hung solid and the water on the cobblestones had formed itself into a sheet of black ice. Katerina looked up at the window. A dim yellow light hung behind the condensation that coated the inside of the pane. Katerina banged on the door and a few seconds later it was thrown open.

'Come on, come on. In you come,' her mother scolded as she stumbled in. 'Where in heaven's name have you been all this time? I've been worried sick about you. And who said you could go out? I asked you to get the vegetables ready and put them in the bowl.'

'I've done the vegetables.'

'No, you haven't. You did the potatoes, some of the potatoes. I can't do everything, you know. Your dad's out at work all day, and . . .'

'He's not my dad. My dad's dead.'

Katerina's mother put her arm round her shoulders.

'Katerina, he *is* your dad now.'

'He isn't.'

'But, Katerina, he loves you just the same as the others. He loves you just the same.'

Katerina said nothing.

'You know that, don't you? He loves you just the same.'

'No, he doesn't. And I don't love him just the same, and neither should you. He's not my dad and you can't change that, and neither can he.'

'Come on now, Katerina, take your coat off, it's all wet. Go and change your clothes or you'll catch your death. I'll warm up some soup.'

'He's not my dad.'

Katerina walked slowly up the stairs and into the bedroom at the top. She took off her damp coat, laid it on the bed that was shared by her half-brother and half-sister, Vladimir and Svetlana, and sat down on her own bed. She pulled the spool of fishing line out from under her jumper and admired the float, its cork whittled to a perfect sphere, a quill thrust through its heart and out the other side. She thought of all the fish the fisherman would catch on the hooks that ran up the line in a string of dull silver, and then she tucked the spool under the mattress. She sat on the spot where the spool lay hidden, to check it was undetectable among the other lumps in the bed. She removed the rest of her damp clothes and replaced them with the first ones she found in her drawer. Then she gathered everything up to take downstairs to dry by the stove. She glanced back at the bed to check again that the fishing line wasn't visible, then stepped lightly onto the landing and went downstairs. Her mother was in the kitchen and she poured the soup into a *ghzel* bowl, the rim chipped but the blue-painted leaves and flowers still perfect on a white background and undimmed by time. Katerina shovelled the pale lumpy liquid into her mouth.

'What is it?'

'Don't you like it? It's mystery soup.'

'That means you don't want to say what's in it. It's not parsnip, is it? I hate parsnips. They're not like real carrots.'

'No, it's cauliflower.'

Katerina screwed up her face.

'And onion.'

'What's for dinner?'

'I don't know yet. Let's see what your dad brings home.'

'My stepdad . . .'

She ignored Katerina's comment.

'My stepdad.'

'Do you like the soup, then?'

'It's not bad, I suppose.'

Katerina suddenly jumped up and ran out of the room. Her mother heard the door open and slam shut again. Katerina reappeared. 'Where's my fish?'

'What fish?'

'My fish. I left it on the doorstep earlier.'

'Oh, that. I put it in the bin.'

'But I wanted it for dinner.'

'It was all dirty and battered. You couldn't eat a thing like that.'

'But you always cook them for me.'

'Yes, but Katerina, there was nothing left of it.'

'That doesn't matter.'

Katerina was already ferreting through the bin. She retrieved the little lump of silver from beneath the cauliflower leaves and the skins of the other vegetables, laid it on the table, and resumed her soup.

'Where did you get the fish from anyway?'

'From a fisherman, over by the fort.'

'What on earth were you doing all the way over there? How many times do I have to tell you not to go wandering around on your own? You never know who you might meet. There are some funny people around. Bad people.'

'He wasn't a bad person. He pulled me out of the river.'

'He what?'

'He pulled me out of the river. I fell in the river and he pulled me out and took me to the museum. They gave me some milk and the woman wanted to take the fish away, but I told her not to and she didn't like me any more after that, so I left. And my clothes were still wet and she pretended they weren't.'

'Katerina, listen to me. You are never to go to the river on your own again. Do you understand? It's too dangerous.'

'What do you expect me to do all day, then, when you're out? I can't stay at home all day. It's boring.'

'I'm not out all day.'

'You are.'

'I had to go out – and you weren't here when I came back. I was worried about you.'

'That's because you were late. I came home and the house was locked and I had to sit in the rain again, so I went to the Mushroom Woman's shop.'

'The Mushroom Woman?'

'I don't know her real name. The scary one.'

'Oh, yes. Anna Suvurova . . .'

'She's got two feet, you know, just like the rest of us.'

'Listen, shall I cook that little fish for you?'

Katerina nodded and smiled. Her mother poured a little oil into the base of a heavy black pan and fried the remains of the fish, doing her best to keep it from breaking into pieces. She placed the fish on a saucer and put it in front of Katerina.

'Do you want some, Mum?'

'I don't think there's enough for two of us. Wait, don't eat it yet . . . close your eyes. All right, open them.'

A lemon, small, blotched and imperfect, sat on the saucer next to the fish.

'An orange!'

'A lemon . . .'

'Wow, a lemon! Where did you get it?'

'From the Mushroom Woman's shop.'

'No!'

'Here, let me cut a piece of that off for you.' She cut the end off the lemon, and squeezed a few drops onto the fish. 'There, try it now.'

Katerina lifted the fish and looked into the empty hole where its eye had been.

'I'm sorry, little fish,' she said, and bit off its head. 'Delicious. Can I have the rest of the lemon? Please.'

Her mother nodded. 'So, are you looking forward to starting school next week?'

'No.'

'But it'll keep you away from that river.'

Later that evening, Katerina sat on her bed in the darkness and looked at Vladimir and Svetlana as they slept in the bed by the door. She reached under her mattress and felt for the fishing line. She pulled it out and ran her fingers along the wooden rim, feeling the rough edge. Then she picked at the line until she located the hooks, felt their cruel points in the darkness, rubbed her thumb against one of the barbs. She put the spool back under the mattress, placed the lemon next to it and went to sleep. The next morning, Katerina got up early to dress Vladimir and Svetlana while her mother prepared breakfast. Her stepfather left early for the engineering works and her mother then had to take the infants to their grandmother's before going to work at the factory.

'Why don't you come to your grandma's too?'

'No, thank you, I'll stay here.'

'Well, all right. But you know where she is – you can always go later. And no wandering today, Katerina!' she called out from the hall. 'I might come back at lunchtime to check on you. I've left that book you like on the chair in my room – the one about France.'

The door was pulled shut and her mother's footsteps faded away down the alleyway. Katerina took the spool and the lemon out from under the mattress, tucked the spool up her jumper, and went downstairs. She put on her coat, still a little damp, slipped the lemon into a pocket and left the house. Outside in the courtyard, she saw the boy from the house opposite looking out of the window, his face grey in the weak light that reached down between the tall houses. He looked at Katerina longingly.

'What are you looking at, stupid?' she said.

He continued to watch her, his passive face, mild and good, now overcome by some sort of ill-defined misery. Katerina remembered the lemon in her pocket.

'Look,' she said. 'Look, I've got a lemon.' She waved it at the boy, who stared back, unmoving. 'I've got a lemon.'

She put the lemon to her mouth and pretended to suck on it. The boy looked back at her from behind the glass, his sallow skin and hollow cheeks expressing the apparent emptiness of his existence. His deep sigh misted the pane, his face became blurred, and then he was gone.

Katerina went straight to Anna Suvurova's shop. 'Hello! Hello! Mushroom Woman? I'd like a lemon, please.'

She ran out of the shop, squealing with delight as the Mushroom Woman lurched at her from the darkness of the back room. She headed straight for Nevski Prospekt and the Summer Gardens, then across the bridge towards the fort. As she approached the far side of the river she saw the hunched figure by the quayside and her heart lifted. She hurried up to the man. 'Can I have a fish, please?'

He turned round. 'Not you again. I thought I told you not to come to the river on your own?'

'They didn't steal your fishing line, then?' She sounded disappointed.

'No, they didn't steal my fishing line.'

He looked back at the float as it bobbed in the water and was dragged under by the current.

'And did they steal your fish?'

'No. I had them for dinner. Very nice too.'

He didn't look back at her this time. She stood behind him watching the float. Several minutes passed.

'I think you had a bite there. I saw a fish next to the float.'

'No, the bait's down in the water, deeper down. So are the fish.'

'There, look, you had another bite.'

'It's just the current.'

Katerina stood next to the man for a while longer as he watched his float intently.

'Those fish thieves,' she said at last, 'I was hoping they'd stolen your line.'

'I rescue you from the river and you were hoping they'd stolen my line? Thanks a bunch.'

'Yes, I wish they'd stolen your line because I got this for you . . . but now it won't mean so much.'

The man turned round. Katerina had removed the spool from under her jumper and was holding it out towards him. 'For you,' she said.

The man's hard old face melted into a smile and he took the spool in a great swollen paw, red with cold, the skin round the knuckles cracked and raw. He ran his fingers around the rim of the spool, examining the float in great detail. 'It's very beautiful. Thank you.'

Katerina looked at him seriously. 'You're very welcome,' she said with studied gravitas, her chest swelling with pride at her achievement. 'Did you have your fish with blinys yesterday?'

'No, with potatoes.'

'Potatoes with butter sauce?'

'No. Potatoes with potatoes.'

'Just potatoes? I had fish for dinner yesterday too. With lemon.'

'Very nice.'

'I have something else for you.' She plucked the piece of lemon from her pocket. 'It's to have with your fish.'

The man took the lemon, scratched at the skin with a nail, and sniffed. For a moment he looked like a little boy. 'I tell you what,' he said. 'The next fish I catch is yours. A present for a present, all right?'

'All right.'

'And then you must promise to go home. Promise now?'

'Promise.'

A little later the float ducked under the water, the quill rose up again, then slid across the surface and slowly submerged, like the periscope of a departing submarine. The man pulled the line tight and it moved across the surface in irregular jags and pulls as the fish turned with the current and nodded a repeated acceptance of its fate.

'It's a big one,' he said.

'Really? How big?'

'Very big. A whale.'

'A whale's not a fish.'

'Very good – a whale is not a fish.'

He swung the fish up onto the quayside and it slapped around on the stones. He struck it across the head with the spanner he carried in his bag for that purpose and it lay still.

'Here, it's yours. Must be nearly a kilo.'

Katerina took the fish in both hands.

'It's a perch,' he said. 'Have you seen one before?'

'No. Is it good to eat?'

'Very good, especially fried with a little garlic. Take it home to your mother now. And watch the spines on its back – they're sharp.'

Katerina turned and went. On her way she stopped off at the museum. The woman from the previous day was behind a desk in the entrance hall. Katerina walked in with the fish in her hands. 'Hello,' she said.

The woman looked up. She regarded Katerina with studied reproach from behind her glasses, then raised a single arched brow. 'Yes?'

'Do you like my fish?'

The woman looked back down at her work.

'I said do you like my fish? It's nearly a kilo.'

'No, I don't like your fish.'

'That's because you're an idiot.'

Katerina turned and walked out and across the bridge again, heading towards home. As she turned the corner near her house she saw that the door of Mrs Ilieva's house lay wide open. She paused in the street outside and peered down the hall. A huddle of black shifted around the base of the stairs and then parted as the visitors began to move up towards the first-floor room where Mrs Ilieva's daughter lay in her wedding dress, her eyes closed. Katerina slipped in through the door as more figures in black arrived. She followed them up the stairs to the landing and peered through a gap to where Mrs Ilieva sat by a table in the middle of the room, the place suspended in a twilight of candles, their flames slowly dying in the small airless space. Mrs Ilieva looked towards the doorway and her son rose from his place beside her and ushered the newcomers in. They stood a respectful distance from the table and bowed their heads in silence. Someone nudged Katerina to the front. She stood clutching her fish in both hands and stared at the coffin. They had adorned it in the red cloth of the young and the dead and had dressed Nadia Ilieva in the bridal clothes she had never been able to wear in life. Her fiancé stood alone in the corner furthest from the door and watched in empathy as the flame of the candle struggled with its own existence. Then the pall-bearers arrived and they lifted the coffin and carried Nadia Ilieva down into the street. She stared through closed eyelids into the grey of the sky as the mourners followed her to the cemetery, passing between the headstones that lay among a riot of nettles and ivy. Katerina followed somewhere near the back and watched from one side as the coffin was placed next to the empty grave. The remnants of an earlier passing squall leapt from the lid as the nails were driven home, and then Nadia Ilieva was lowered into the ground. The mourners trailed back between the tombs, then out through the heavy iron gates and back along the sodden streets to Mrs Ilieva's house. Some time later, each of them left with a small wooden spoon and a handkerchief bearing the name of Nadia, so that they might remember her while they salted their soup with their tears.

Katerina arrived home as the rain began to fall again in the dark. She looked across to where the boy had been that morning, the window now dark and empty, impenetrable with condensation. She banged on the door of her house but no one came. She thought about visiting the Mushroom Woman, then laid the fish on the step next to her. It had stiffened during the course of the day and lay in a rigid curve, its mouth still open. She nudged its tail and it rocked gently back and forth. There was a noise from across the courtyard. She looked up to see the door closing. A cat had been put out in the rain. It stood watching the door indignantly for a second or two and then crouched, chin low to the ground, coughing up fur-balls. Then it scurried off. The door across the courtyard twitched ajar and Katerina saw a pale face watching her from within.

'Hey, stupid,' she called out. 'What are you looking at?'

The face didn't reply. The door closed slightly, then opened again, a little wider this time. The boy came out and walked tentatively across the courtyard to where Katerina sat on the doorstep of her home. 'What's that you've got there?' he asked.

'A fish.'

'I know that's a fish. That . . . there.'

'It's a spoon.'

'Oh.'

'Can't you see it's a spoon?'

'Yes.'

'So why did you ask me what it is? I got it at Mrs Ilieva's.'

'You got it at Mrs Ilieva's?'

'Is that all you do? Ask questions?'

'No.'

He was already half-way back to his door. He went inside and the door closed and Katerina sat in the rain. She got up and went to the Mushroom Woman's shop but it was shut. She came back and sat on the step. A little while later the door opened again and the boy poked his head outside.

'Why don't you go inside?'

Katerina considered the question beneath her dignity, too stupid to merit an answer.

'Why don't you go in?' he asked again. 'You'll get all wet there.'

'I *am* all wet.'

'Why don't you go in, then?'

'Because I haven't got a key, you idiot. Why do you think?'

The boy came outside again, not venturing quite so close this time. He stood in the rain and looked at Katerina. He was a little older than she'd first thought, maybe around ten.

'You've got teeth like a horse,' she said.

'I know.' He shrugged. 'What am I supposed to do about it? Anyway, you've got teeth like a rabbit.'

'No, I haven't!'

'Look in the mirror. Like a rabbit. I'm going inside. You can come in if you want.'

Katerina followed him in. She had never been in the house opposite before, not even when the Krilovs had lived there. Natalia Krilova had been a good friend of Katerina's mother, but the Krilovs had moved out a couple of months before and the boy's family had moved in. The other couple that lived in the house, the Ivanovs, had been there for years and were notorious in the neighbourhood. The husband, Vassili Ivanov, worked on ships and was away for months at a time. On his return, sales of vodka in the local shops and bars rose significantly and the ensuing disorder often woke the inhabitants of all the houses around the yard and required the assistance of the local officials to bring under control. It was because of incidents such as this that Mrs Krilova had never invited Katerina's mother to visit her at home.

'You wouldn't like the neighbours,' she'd say, and would then go home to the shared kitchen and listen to the sailor's wife's long monologues of lament about her absent husband. And later in the evening the wife of Vassili Ivanov would lie in bed and think how much better it was when her husband was afloat somewhere far away on the Atlantic or the Pacific or the Indian Ocean, and she would contemplate with a heavy heart the remoteness of the possibility that he would fall overboard and be consumed by passing sharks.

Katerina followed the boy into his hallway and noticed a greasy stale smell of cooking. Two women were talking in a room off to one side, their voices rising and falling rhythmically, each jostling with the other for space in the conversation.

'Oleg, is that you? Let the cat back in, will you?'

It was Oleg's mother.

'The cat's gone,' said Oleg.

'Oleg, let the cat back in, will you?' she repeated.

Oleg looked in through the kitchen doorway. 'The cat's gone.'

'Where's it gone? What do you mean *gone*?'

'I don't know. It's gone, wherever cats go.'

Mrs Ivanova was sitting fidgeting in the chair opposite Oleg's mother, picking continuously at her fingers. She periodically looked at the table top with her mad, quizzical eyes, as if it might hold the answer to her questions. Vassili Ivanov, sharks permitting, was due home that weekend, and the woman's torment had arrived even before the ship had drawn into sight of the Baltic.

Oleg's mother noticed Katerina standing just behind her son. 'Who's this, Oleg?'

'A friend. She lives across the yard. She was locked out in the rain.'

Oleg's mother looked askance at the girl in the doorway. 'What's a nice little girl like you doing locked out of her own house?' she asked, smiling less than sweetly. 'I'm sure your mother wouldn't be happy if she knew.'

'I'm not a nice little girl,' said Katerina. 'And my mother lets me out on my own whenever I want.'

'Does she really?'

Oleg's mother looked at Mrs Ivanova. Mrs Ivanova's twitching ceased momentarily and the two women silently communicated their disapproval of Mrs Kuznetsova's dereliction of parental duty.

'Dreadful,' muttered Oleg's mother, to reinforce the point.

'Utterly irresponsible,' concurred Mrs Ivanova, her fingers once more turning against themselves, working away at their own nails in a frenzy of neurotic jabbing.

'She isn't irrespons—' Katerina failed to negotiate the unfamiliar word. 'But she says you're a fucking whore.'

Mrs Ivanova's digits went into overdrive, like the claws of an overexcited, underfed fiddler crab. She launched herself up out of her seat, grabbed Katerina by the scruff of the neck, dragged her towards the door, flung it open, and threw the girl back out in the rain. Katerina picked herself up and went back to sit on her doorstep. She looked up at the window opposite and saw Oleg's pale shadow watching over her. He wiped the condensation from the glass and sat with her, separated from her only by the bleak walls of his home, the incessant rain and the darkness of the courtyard, until her mother returned with the infants and swept her inside.

The next morning, when her mother had left, Katerina looked out and saw the boy at his window again. She left the house and motioned for him to come outside. He quietly pulled the door ajar.

'Come out with me today,' she whispered to him through the gap.

He looked appalled.

'Come on, it'll be fun,' she said. 'You know, fun.'

The word meant nothing to him. 'My mum would kill me,' he said, swallowing hard.

'Come on, I dare you. You can't just sit in there all day with that madwoman Mrs Ivanova. Go on, get your coat.'

He nodded uncertainly. 'Well, perhaps . . .' He slipped out of the door and they dashed down the alley and into the street, Katerina striding out in front.

'Right, follow me,' she said. 'First I'm going to show you the Mushroom Woman's shop!'

But the shop was closed so they wandered along to the railway station and sat on a bench and watched the trains departing along the tracks.

'Vassili Ivanov is a bastard,' said Oleg.

Katerina didn't reply.

'It's terrible when he's around,' Oleg continued. 'The last time he was home, we didn't sleep all weekend, he was shouting all night. He'd been out drinking, as usual. He's just a bastard.'

'His wife's a whore, though.'

'She's all right.'

'I don't like her. I'm not surprised her husband drinks. And he's nice to me anyway – he even gave me sweets once.'

'He never gives anything to anyone, unless it's something awful.'

'Well, they weren't very nice sweets. He got them in England. I swapped them for a rabbit.'

'A rabbit?'

'Yes, a nice one. I called it Vassili.'

Oleg laughed.

'Don't laugh! Vassili escaped and a dog ate him.'

'Oh. It sounds like he should have stayed in his cage.'

'I didn't keep him in a cage. He wanted to be free.'

'It's your own bloody fault, then.'

'It wasn't my fault! It was the bloody dog that ate him.' She scowled at him and he edged away from her a bit. They sat there in silence until she decided she would speak to him again.

'Have you ever been on a train, Oleg?'

Oleg shook his head.

'Me neither. Let's get on the next one that comes.'

'What?' He screwed up his eyes to convey the idiocy of her suggestion.

'Let's get on the next train,' she repeated, as an engine drew into sight around the bend.

'What for?'

'We can go somewhere.'

'Oh yes, and where are we going to go?'

'Moscow, and then abroad.'

'Moscow is miles away. We can't go there. And abroad is probably even further.'

She stood up and moved with the crowd along the platform, Oleg following a few steps behind.

'Katerina, you can't go on the train.'

'Yes, I can.'

'You haven't got a ticket. And how do you know where it's going?'

'I don't.'

She stepped up into the carriage and found a seat by the window. She looked at Oleg through the glass and smiled. He looked around. The guard was at the other end of the platform. Oleg looked back at Katerina. She gestured to him to get on board. The whistle blew and the doors of the carriages were each in turn pushed shut by the guard as he advanced down the platform. The train began to tremble and Katerina mouthed urgently at Oleg through the window, 'Come on, Oleg!'

He stepped up into the carriage, and sat down next to her. They watched the platform slide past as the train left the station behind and trundled out of the city centre, through the industrial areas and out into the flat open countryside.

'How long till we get to Moscow?' asked Oleg.

'How should I know? I'm not an expert on everything, you know.'

'You're not an expert on anything.'

'What?'

A little later the guard came round and Katerina and Oleg were put off the train at Kolpino. They reached Leningrad again as dusk was falling and arrived home in the dark. Katerina sat on the step outside her empty house and listened as Oleg ventured inside his own. She heard the shrieks and squawks that ensued as Oleg's mother welcomed him home with a succession of cuffs and blows that sent him scurrying upstairs and past the room in which Mrs Ivanova sat in the darkness picking at her nails and muttering incomprehensibly in futile preparation for the return of Vassili Ivanov.

Vassili Ivanov

Leningrad, winter 1928

Vassili Ivanov had been at sea for several weeks, the last two without a break, and he was going to make the most of his first night back home – he and all the others. The vodka had come out long before they disembarked and, as they made their way through the dark streets and along the icy lengths of the Fontanka Canal, they were already itching for violence. They found the steps of the drinking den and stumbled down past the women who lingered on the stairs, Vassili in the lead, bellowing. He shoved past a group of men near the door, noticed their uniforms too late, swore at them anyway as he passed. He had come across them before, right here, in the very same place, the last time he was home. They had blocked his way then too, as if they had the right, just because of those uniforms. He rubbed his head as he entered the bar, smearing his hair back across his scalp, feeling the lumps and bulges beneath, the places where life had battered him. He took his usual table near the bar and the others crowded in, jostling for the stools. Vassili Ivanov sat and looked at his hands, ran a thumbnail across the tabletop. He looked at the black grime beneath the nail and scraped it out again with the corner of a tooth, rolled the knot of dirt across his tongue and spat it out onto the floor. Then he stood up and roared at the barman. He shoved past the men who were blocking his path. Then he saw their uniforms, inside the building now, waiting for him to make the mistake he had just made, one indiscretion too many, an obvious lack of respect. He swore at them again, pushed away the hand that tried to hold him, pushing his way along the bar now, shouting at the barman still. Then more hands were on his shoulder and he was near the door, the OGPU men shoving him out, out into the well of the stairs, down onto the ground as the women looked on and his mates still squabbled over the stools inside. Then a knife came out and it went into him and the OGPU men looked at each other.

'Look what you've gone and done,' one said.

'He deserved it.'

'Yes, who cares?' said the other.

'You'll care if the truth comes out.'

'Who's going to say anything? Them?' He glared at the women on the stairs. They turned away. 'Come on, let's go.'

They went up the stairs and along the canal.

'Have you got the knife? Chuck it in the canal.'

'I left it.'

'You what?'

'I left it. Back there.'

'You fucking idiot. Go back and get it. It's evidence, isn't it?'

The man hesitated.

'I said go! It's evidence!'

'He's right,' said the other. 'Go get it, bring it back and chuck it in the canal.'

He hurried off, avoiding the women's gaze as he stumbled down the stairs. He found the knife at the bottom, picked it up and hurried away.

'Here it is,' he said, as he got back to the others.

'So chuck it, then. Into the canal.'

He chucked it. It clattered across the ice.

'Fuck it,' he said. 'The water's fucking frozen.'

'What did you chuck it there for, then?'

'You told me to.'

'Not there, you idiot. At the edge, where the ice is thinner, right by the wall. They'll find it now, won't they, in daylight. Blood on it and everything. Fingerprints.'

'What now?'

'You'll have to go out and get it.'

'Get it? Are you joking?'

'Crawl out on the ice. Go slowly and you'll be all right.'

He looked at them. 'Are you sure?'

They looked back at him.

'Go. And that's an order, as if from Comrade Stalin himself.'

'All right, all right, I'll go.'

He clambered over the wall and onto the ice and gingerly lay flat. The ice creaked and groaned. He moved across it, a foot or two, then stopped. It groaned again, then split. Down he went.

'That's him gone,' said one.

'Stupid idiot,' said the other.

'The knife's still there.'

'Leave it. No one will bother with it.'

'What about him? What will we say?'

'Don't worry, I'll think of something. Some sort of accident. I know the right people. No questions asked.'

'A noble end, I suppose. Sacrificing himself like that, for the good of others.'

'Exactly, comrade. I couldn't have put it better myself.'

Katerina looked at the face of Vassili Ivanov as he lay in his coffin in the room above the kitchen in Oleg's house. They were alone in the room, accompanied only by the sound of Mrs Ivanova's voice drifting gaily up the stairs from the kitchen where she sat and trilled away, like a canary released from a lifetime down the coalmine, at Oleg's mother regarding the happy practicalities of the funeral. And no one really cared too much about the funeral. The next day, Vassili Ivanov would be transported to the gateway of the hereafter, leaving the dwellers of this earthly dimension in something a little nearer peace – and that was all anyone really cared about, except, if the truth be told, Katerina Kuznetsova. As she looked at the becalmed body, the dark shroud of his beard and the battered shaven skull, she thought of his blue eyes, how they had smiled at her as he gave her unpleasant-tasting sweets from distant lands, and she knew, though not at all on a conscious level, that she had lost some sort of kindred spirit, someone who had also recognised a part of himself in the girl on the step in the rain, and whose cold eyes had melted just a fraction when they alighted upon her because he had seen no fear in her face as she fixed her own stare upon him. Now she reached out towards the corpse and lifted an eyelid and saw a blue eye looking back at her, but he was gone now and she quickly closed the lid again and remembered how he had been when he was alive. And by all accounts he had been truly terrible, a living hell for almost anyone who crossed his path, but she had seen another side of him and that was the only side she could ever see.

'Bet you wouldn't have dared be alone in a room with him when he was alive.'

It was Oleg, standing in the doorway.

'Why not? I wasn't afraid of him, you know.'

'Should have been. Everyone else was.'

Katerina left the body in the room and went downstairs with Oleg.

'Are you going to his funeral?' she asked.

'Don't suppose so.'

'Suit yourself.'

The next day, Katerina followed the coffin through the streets and into the cemetery and between the brambles that suffocated that part of the graveyard. Mrs Ivanova's solitary tear was prompted by relief not grief, and her fingers rested calm and motionless around a pristine handkerchief. When they had finished, everyone soon went back about their business with nothing to remember Vassili Ivanov by but their brutal memories and their scars.

Katerina went back home and knocked on Oleg's door. 'Do you want to come out? We could go to the Mushroom Woman's shop.'

'I can't,' he said.

'Why not?'

'I'm busy.'

Katerina looked at him dubiously.

'Really, I'm busy. I'm going to my ballet class.'

'Your what? Ballet?'

'What's so funny about that?'

Katerina stopped laughing. 'I can't imagine you . . .' She laughed again. 'It's for girls, anyway.'

'No, it's not.'

'Yes, it is. And for queers.'

Oleg closed the door rather less gently than usual. Katerina sat on her step and waited a few minutes until Oleg emerged again.

'What are you looking at?'

'Nothing,' she replied.

He walked towards the alleyway, then turned round to face her.

'You can come with me, if you want.'

She considered the invitation for a moment, then jumped up and followed him along the alley towards the street.

'Where's your ballet school, then?' Katerina asked as they walked.

'Not far. Past the Mariinsky Theatre.'

'The Mariinsky! Are you really good, then?'

'I said *past* the Mariinsky. Do you think they'd let the likes of me dance there?'

'Oh,' she said.

A short time later they passed the Mariinsky and paused outside to look through the tall windows at the canvas pictures of dancers that hung from golden ropes in the foyer.

'That'll be you one day,' she said, pointing to a dancer in mid-flight.

He laughed.

'What are you laughing for?' She was annoyed now. 'Why shouldn't it be you?'

'Why *should* it be me?'

He looked at her and laughed again, an embarrassed disbelieving little laugh.

A few minutes later they stopped outside an old building. 'This is it,' said Oleg. 'My teacher's called Mrs Andropova. She's very beautiful, but also very fierce.'

Oleg pushed the door open and Katerina followed him up the stairs and into a large hall. Katerina sat on a bench by the window while Oleg and the other students began their warm-up, Mrs Andropova's voice pursuing them terrified around the room. Then she noticed Katerina sitting on the bench, watching from the sidelines.

'You, girl! What are you doing sitting there?'

Katerina looked up, petrified.

'Are you deaf as well as lazy? What are you doing sitting there on your own? Come on, join in, we've already started!'

'But I'm not . . .'

'What?'

'I haven't got the right clothes.'

'What? Speak up! I can't hear you if you don't open your mouth. Carry on, you lot!'

She marched over to Katerina.

'I haven't got the right clothes. I just came to watch my friend. Him over there. Oleg.'

'Nonsense! You can't just sit there watching. The others won't be able to concentrate, and if they can't concentrate, they can't dance and I can't teach.'

Katerina stood up and began to walk towards the door. Mrs Andropova watched her go.

'Wait! Girl! Wait! Come with me.'

She took Katerina into a side-room and began flustering about in a cupboard, muttering irritably to herself as she did so. 'Here, put these on, and come and join the others. Quickly now!'

She placed a bundle of clothes in Katerina's arms and went back into the hall which rang once more with her voice and the drumming of little feet on the wooden floor. Katerina felt the unfamiliar fine touch of the fabric of the tights and the heavy padded comfort of the socks and she looked at herself in the mirror. She put on a white sweater, smelling of dust and age, and edged back into the hall. Oleg caught her eye.

'Come on, hurry up!' called out Mrs Andropova.

Katerina scuttled across towards Oleg.

'Only for queers, is it?' he smiled.

She glared at him, then frowned, and concentrated on mimicking the movements of the others in the room, but she was always out of time, leaping as they fell, falling as they leapt.

An hour later Katerina and Oleg were passing the Mariinsky Theatre once more and they stopped again to look through the windows.

'Look, there you are again,' said Katerina, pointing at the dancer in the picture.

'And that's you there,' he whispered, stumbling over his words.

'Yes,' she said. 'You and me.' She looked for a moment at the ballerina, cast in hues of blue and grey in the stage lights, her face raised towards the sky, a pale slender arm reaching out to something unseen. They walked on a little further.

'Oleg, could you do me a favour?'

'It depends.'

'You see, Vassili Ivanov . . .'

'Hmm . . .'

'I'd like a photograph of him.'

'What are you asking me for? I haven't got one.'

'I know. But you live in the same house.'

'Not any more, I don't.'

They walked on in silence until they got to the courtyard.

'See you,' said Oleg.

Katerina didn't reply. Oleg went into his house and closed the door. Katerina sat on the step and waited. A few minutes later Oleg came back out and ushered her over to the alleyway. 'Close your eyes,' he said. 'All right, now open them.'

She looked at the photograph for several long seconds. 'Thank you, Oleg! Where did you find it?'

'Where I expected – in the bin. Your mum not back yet?'

'No,' she sighed.

'Come in, then. We can sit in the kitchen until she gets back. You'll be warmer in there.'

'Thank you, Oleg. You're my best friend.'

PART TWO

Italy

Isabella

Aldo Gardini watched dusk arrive, gradual and furtive, bringing with it a late-autumn mist that hovered in threads above the Rio della Sensa, a chill lifting up from the waters of the canal as the sun dipped behind the buildings of the ghetto. He wiped the condensation from the window with his sleeve, peered out at the people passing below in the dim glow of the streetlamps, and wondered if Isabella would really be there to meet him as she had promised. He could hardly believe what was on the cards, but could see no other reason for her invitation. Well, he would find out soon enough – he could hardly wait! He looked again at his watch. Time to go, no more waiting now, no more bated breath. He took the key from the table by his bed, pulled up the collar of his coat, and hurried downstairs. He could hear his parents talking in the kitchen, something about Fausto Pozzi. Mussolini's strident voice maintained its familiar steady rhythm in the background, intermittently cut short by the crackle and fuzz of poor reception, struggling to be heard above the insults that Luca, Aldo's father, hurled at the radio at regular intervals.

'Fucking delinquent!' he was shouting, the usual thing. 'Jumped-up bastard! War-mongering pig! Go fuck your mother! Go kiss Hitler's fat fascist arse!'

Then Aldo's mother's voice, quiet, reproachful, 'Calm yourself, Luca. The children might hear.'

Then Luca's voice again, quieter now, still muttering profanities. As Aldo walked through the hall he could hear his teenage sister, Elena, in the front room, singing something to herself, one of those songs she was always inventing about love, and the sound of their maternal grandmother snoring by the fire, the air rattling up out of her throat, dreaming of her native Ukraine again, no doubt, slipping ever closer to her past as her advancing years took her closer to death.

'Aldo, where are you going?'

It was his mother's voice again now. Damn it, he thought, not now! Not now that his time with Isabella was so close! His mother must have heard the creaking of the stairs as he descended.

'Dinner will be ready soon, Aldo!'

She emerged from the kitchen, a freshly plucked chicken in one hand, a filleting knife in the other. The family dog followed, turning its nose to the dead bird and tentatively licking the skin, ears pinned back in anticipation of the coming blow.

'Get off!' she said. 'Bloody dog!'

'I'm off out for a walk,' said Aldo. 'I'll be back soon . . .'

His mother's eyes narrowed, then she noticed the increasingly bold attention that the dog was paying to the principal ingredient of the evening meal. She struck the animal across the rump with the object of its desire, and as it scurried away Aldo slipped outside, breathed in the cool air, and hurried off along the quay. His mind buzzed with uncertainty as he made his way along Fondamenta della Sensa and down the shopping street of Strada Nuova, built by the practical Austrians during their time in charge, then on through the chaos of narrow alleyways and passages, dimly lit and damp, between San Marco and the Ponte di Rialto. Crossing Campo Santo Stefano, he passed the statue of Niccolò Tommaseo, who had led a popular revolt against those practical Austrians about whom Aldo had written a history essay in his final year at school – a schooling that had been a torment for him, desperate to get out, to free himself from its walls and do useful things, things with his hands, not with books. As he hurried on he saw a familiar shape heading his way from the other side of the square. It was Massimo, his best friend, walking in that fat, busy way of his.

'Hey, Aldo!' Massimo's voice was as full as his belly, each preceding the rest of him by a distance.

'Oh, hi there, Massimo. I'll see you tomorrow,' Aldo replied, all in a rush, as if keen to hurry on past. Massimo was a diverting companion, and they had spent so much of their youth together he was almost a brother, but any time spent chatting here would leave even less of it for Isabella – and whatever it was she had in mind for Aldo that evening.

'Wait, Aldo, wait. I was just on my way round to see you. I thought we could go down to the bar after dinner?'

Massimo had clearly had his dinner early. He usually did – that way there was always time for another one. He lifted his hand now in that habitual way of his, an involuntary motion, rubbing his chin with an open palm as if something edible might leap out of it and into his mouth. Aldo noticed the grime beneath his friend's nails, a crescent of slime from the fish he flung about in boats every day. Massimo was a fisherman's son, and his hands would always smell of them now, just as Aldo's would have done if Luca had not found a place for himself, and therefore his son, on dry land. And it occurred to Aldo now how important to this evening's events his own clean fingers might be. However little he knew about Isabella, he was quite sure she wouldn't want a fisherman's breamy hands upon her, a fisherman's stinking fingers in the perfumed waves of her hair. But he was getting well ahead of himself now, and he hauled himself back in and suddenly realised that Massimo's mouth was full again with words.

'So, how about it?' Massimo's question came again. 'Just a couple of drinks before bed?'

'Oh, I don't know, Massimo. I've got to be up early tomorrow, you see.'

'Come on, Aldo, don't be a bore.'

'Er, well . . .'

'Please, Aldo.'

Aldo thought again of Isabella, the look he had seen in her eyes. 'Look, I'm really sorry, Massimo. I'm on an errand, you see. I have to dash.'

'An errand? No problem, I'll come with you. I fancy a walk.'

Aldo looked at him, considered his options. 'No, really, er . . . look, Massimo, really it's . . . well . . . you see, it's a *private* errand.'

'A private errand?'

'Precisely.'

Massimo looked at him, then burst out laughing and punched him on the shoulder, almost knocking him over.

'Oh, I get it, Aldo, you little devil.' He laughed again. 'I thought you looked a bit too spruce. Scrub up well when you want to, don't you? Go on, then, who is she? Do I know her, the little minx?'

'Can't say. Sorry. Listen, got to go.'

'All right, all right, tell me all about it tomorrow. I'm only your best friend, after all. Don't forget, though!'

Aldo was hurrying away now, glancing back to check that Massimo was not coming after him on the sly. But his fat friend would not have been able to keep up with him anyway, not if he ran. And run he would. He would run miles for Isabella, he would cross the whole city just for the thought of her. He quickened his pace now, thrusting his hands deeper into his coat, warming them, the fingers of one hand closing once more around the heavy key, the other around the little fish he had carved for himself out of oak the previous week. He hurried across the wooden bridge at Accademia. From there it was just a short walk along the Rio di San Trovaso, past his father's trattoria – Casa Luca – to the boatyard where he now spent most of his days learning his new trade from a master. A fresh doubt sidled up and whispered in his ear: 'Might Antonio still be there?' He usually left the boatyard before dark but you could never be sure and no one would want to get on the wrong side of Antonio, least of all one of his young apprentices.

Antonio ate regularly at Casa Luca and it was six months earlier, over a jug of lunchtime wine, that Luca had first brought up the idea of Aldo helping out down at the yard. Aldo was nearly eighteen and needed to learn a proper trade. Fishing was always a possibility – the boy seemed to enjoy helping out on the boats and at the Rialto market in the holidays, and he had made innumerable crossings to and from the lagoon island of Burano – but Luca knew from experience what a hard life that would be. If Antonio would take him on, Aldo would work for virtually nothing for the first year, learning the basics, after which another arrangement could be made. This suited Antonio and so the two men cemented their agreement over plates of polenta and squid and another jug of wine.

Aldo began the following week. His first task as an apprentice was to learn to prepare Antonio's coffee just the way his new master liked it, an undertaking that required the best part of a week. In the interim, numerous offerings were pitched into the canal, much to the amusement of the other craftsmen who would chuckle at the newcomer while whittling their wood into intricate shapes.

'I can't drink that!' Antonio would bellow, startling passers-by on the other side of the canal and sending the neighbourhood's pigeons up into the air in fright. 'How can I teach you to build the most beautiful boats in the world when you can't even make me a decent cup of coffee? In this yard, only perfection will do, and don't you ever forget it! Go make me another!'

And the pigeons would settle back down as Aldo returned to the kitchen for another attempt. Finally mastering the art of the perfect espresso, Aldo then learned to clean the yard to Antonio's fastidious requirements. As the long, sleek, gently curving boats took embryonic shape upon the trestles – their three-month gestation a reflection of the paternal pride of the craftsmen – the resulting sawdust and chippings, in nearly a dozen different varieties, kept Aldo busy with the broom. If it wasn't the beech, pine, larch and elm that he swept up into bags, then it was the cherry, mahogany, walnut and oak. Every now and again Antonio would toss an offcut in Aldo's general direction, scattering a carefully gathered pile of sawdust.

'What sort of wood?' he would growl.

'Walnut?' Aldo would venture.

'Walnut?! Look at the grain.'

'Elm?'

'Elm?!' Antonio would rage, shoving it close up under Aldo's nose. 'Elm?! That's oak! Oak! Smell it! Touch it! Feel its weight! Go make me a coffee!'

Soon Aldo came to know each type of wood – initially by sight, then by smell, and finally, with his eyes lightly closed to heighten the sensation, by touch, his long fingers running gently up and down the lengths of wood, tripping across the grain which, as he came to know it more intimately, seemed to rise lightly up to meet his touch, revealing to him its true identity. Towards the end of each week Luca would pitch up, set a couple of sacks of mixed sawdust down in the bottom of his boat, and chug the short distance up San Trovaso to Casa Luca, the floor of which would subsequently boast the most upmarket sawdust in all the downmarket restaurants in Venice. After a few weeks, Antonio decided his apprentice could be permitted to touch the virgin wood, lifting it off the delivery barge with the nervous anticipation of a husband carrying his new bride across the threshold, stacking it in long racks and piles against the walls of the cavernous shed. In quieter moments, Aldo tried out the lathes, planes, chisels and saws that hung in orderly rows along the tar-stained wooden walls, cutting and scraping the scraps and offcuts that were kept in a pile by the quay. Soon he was allowed to repair small faults on the older gondolas, worn-out ladies of the canals who were brought into dry dock for new coats of black paint in a vain attempt to make them beautiful again. Finally, just a month before, with no explanation other than a grunt and a wink, Antonio had taken Aldo out in one of the older craft. They had been drifting in and out of side-canals for the best part of an hour when Antonio beckoned Aldo back towards the stern.

'Come on, then, let's see how you get on.'

Aldo clambered up from the bench in the middle of the boat and stumbled around on the rear platform, wielding the long oar to little effect, sending the boat around in slow circles as he maintained his precarious position upon the slippery deck. Since that first nervous attempt, Aldo had been out in the gondolas regularly and now considered himself sufficiently competent to risk an attempt at water-borne seduction. Of course, Antonio had not the slightest idea of Aldo's plans. When he had noticed before locking up for the night that the spare key to the yard was missing from its usual place, he never imagined that Aldo could have had the nerve to hatch such a plot. He was a spirited and determined youth, but he would certainly know the consequences of such an escapade if it ever came to Antonio's attention. And very little that happened in and around the boatyard ever went unnoticed by those steel-grey eyes, hard as the Dolomite hills in which their owner had been raised.

But Aldo wasn't thinking of Antonio now, he was thinking of Isabella. He crossed the little hump-backed bridge, next to Casa Luca, that led over the canal and past the church of San Trovaso. Just across the square from the church lay the boatyard. The mist had come down again in rapidly thickening drapes, stilling the night to silence. A solitary sound came to Aldo through the fog – a door slamming some way off in the night – and the square lay deserted but for figures that formed, morphed and disappeared as the denser patches of mist alternately communed and dispersed. The church bell sounded out, muffled by the fog. He could hear footsteps somewhere behind him, fading across the bridge on the other side of the square. He thought of Isabella waiting for him out there in the darkness and he took the key, turned the handle, and shoved the door of the boatyard open. Inside, all was quiet, the only living thing the tree that stood in the corner furthest from the canal, dripping autumn damp from black branches. The wooden buildings away to the left, fashioned in the alpine style with balconies running their full length, lay in darkness. Aldo knew which gondola he would take, one of the older ones that would forgive his amateurish technique. He swiftly found the boat in the darkness, lying on her side at the end of the row of upturned craft that lined the slipway. He struggled to right her, then dragged the heavy vessel to the lip of the canal, the gentle waves slapping her belly as he took an oar, and a couple of cushions for the bench, and pushed off into the night.

As he edged along the backwater that ran up from the Canale Grande towards Campo Santo Stefano, he saw Isabella waiting for him where they had hurriedly arranged. She was standing close to the wall by the water's edge, wisps of mist around her feet, a halo of light upon her from the streetlamp above, and for a moment Aldo had a vision of an angel suspended on clouds somewhere out in space. He steered the gondola in alongside the quay and she gave him that slow, assured smile, delicate lines around her eyes half-lost behind raven hair. He saw her offered hand and he clutched at it, too abruptly, brushing her fine white fingers as the gondola moved beneath his feet. He lost his fragile composure and his balance, took an inadvertent step backwards, and hauled Isabella unceremoniously off the quay and into the boat. He felt her collapse on top of him, an elegant heap, and the gondola rocked vigorously. She breathed in deeply, then out, her breath caressing his face with its fragrant warmth. He was simultaneously terrified and elated by the physicality of her presence and the ridiculous prospect of her lips lowering themselves to touch his own, fearing now that he would not be up to the challenge. She bowed her head as if considering whether to run the tip of her tongue slowly across his lips, then withdrew and looked him in the eye.

'Hello there, Aldo.'

'Hello.'

A stupid response, and he felt such a fool as he said it.

'Don't you think you should help me up now? That would be the gentlemanly thing to do.'

The sound of her voice made him jump again. 'Oh yes, of course, I'm so sorry.'

'Don't be so keen to apologise. It won't do you any good, you know.'

She eased herself aside and Aldo squeezed himself out from under her. He helped her to the bench and took the oar and began to turn the boat around.

'So, dear boy, where are you planning on taking me? Surprise me, now. I do so like surprises.'

'Er, well, let's see . . . well, I don't know, really. Where would you like to go? Any ideas?'

She clicked her tongue, shook her head, flashed him that wicked smile again. 'I must say I'm terribly disappointed, Aldo. Not at all a good start to the evening. I thought you'd have come better prepared. You've had nearly a week to think about it, after all. Haven't I been on your mind? Too many other things to think about? Too many other girls?'

'No, no, not at all. I mean, yes, on my mind, yes, of course. But no, not much else to think about. Nothing that could compare, anyway.'

She raised an eyebrow.

'San Marco, perhaps?' he said. 'It'll be nice down there at this time. Nice and quiet.'

If she replied, her voice was inaudible, so Aldo rowed on in silence, observing the side of her face, as pale and blank and beautiful as an alabaster mask, savouring the moment as one does when you know it to be a fleeting one. Another gondola slipped by, a lantern placed just behind the notched iron *ferro* that protected its bow, the passing gondolier calling out to Aldo as he disappeared into the gloom. The mist was lifting now and the two waterborne strangers watched the shadows of buildings drifting by, as if it were the houses that were moving, suspended on the water, and the boat that lay motionless. They passed the point of Dorsoduro, the domes of Santa Maria della Salute towering above, the darkness around them speckled up high by gulls, and as the boat moved beyond her protecting lee and into the broader expanse of the Canale di San Marco the waves took on more intimidating proportions. Aldo was suddenly aware again of his inexperience as an oarsman and, for the first time since catching sight of Isabella in the glow of the streetlight, he began to concentrate more on navigating the waters of the canal than the equally unfamiliar labyrinths of carnal intrigue. They drifted under a bridge into Rio del Palazzo, lowering their heads to avoid the low stone arch. To their left towered the back wall of the Palazzo Ducale, to the right the walls of the prison, and running directly overhead was the Bridge of Sighs, its name stolen from the laments of thieves and prisoners passing from their cells to the chamber of the state prosecutor and back again.

'I don't like it in here,' said Isabella. 'I feel like I'm being judged.'

'Who's judging you? I'm not.'

'Not yet.'

A little further along the Canale di San Marco, Isabella indicated an insignificant backwater. 'Up that way, just past that tower,' she said. 'Pull the boat over here, Aldo. There, just by that door. Tie it up to that jetty.'

'Tie it up?'

'Yes, tie it up. I want to get out.'

'You want to get out? Already?'

'Correct. I want to get out.'

Isabella had already stepped out onto the tiny landing stage and was turning the key in a nearby door. She pushed it open and slipped inside. Aldo hesitated, assuming this unexpected turn of events signalled an abrupt end to his evening.

'Well, aren't you going to come in?' Isabella whispered, suddenly furtive.

A moment later, Aldo was in the hall and Isabella was closing the door behind him. He felt her hand in his, then the tug of her as she led him up barely lit stairs. He was aware of grim portraits that glowered on the walls and a heavy chandelier hanging from the ceiling, its glass tears whispering together in an unexplained stirring of the air. On the landing lay a conspiracy of doors. One, slightly ajar, let in a pale light from across the canal and it streaked the floorboards with its watery beam. Isabella led Aldo down a dark passage and up a short flight of steps. She pushed open another door. In the half-light Aldo could make out a large bed and one or two heavy pieces of furniture, but the high-ceilinged room gave an impression of space. In the far wall, a window of gothic arches looked out on the thinning mist and the terracotta-tiled roofs of the buildings across the canal.

Isabella took off her coat. The dress beneath was simple and dark and resembled the one she was wearing the first time he had seen her, seated next to her husband at the concert in the church near the Ponte di Rialto the week before. Now she stepped towards him and once more he felt her breath on his face, then again, closer this time. Her lips parted and closed on his, just a brush at first, a glancing blow, then something firmer, more urgent. Her mouth opened wide now, an unhealed wound, pressing hard, the taste of her filling him. She lay down, drawing him onto the bed beside her.

'Touch me here, Aldo,' she said. 'Don't worry. You needn't be shy . . .' She guided him to her again. 'That's it, Aldo, yes. Yes, Aldo, don't worry, I'll show you how.'

She smiled one of her many smiles, a momentary suggestion of vulnerability, then quickly hid herself away again beneath her cloak of irony. 'Hold me the way you held your violin in the church last week. Run your bow across me gently now . . .' She giggled, a curious delighted little laugh.

Aldo could hear a boat now, out there beneath the darkened window, its sound fading as it slipped under the arch of a bridge, sending ripples pulsing across the water, gliding through the night and ever deeper into the heart of Venice. Isabella was all that mattered now, this world of hers, her body and his, locked together in the dark. And then the intruder, reality, separated time from space once more and Aldo and Isabella lay suddenly still on the bed, the heat of her body mingling with his own, then a chill on their skin as it shone pale in the night. She pulled him beneath the covers.

'Was that your first time, by any chance?' she asked, just as he was starting to feel comfortable, once more taking him off guard as his mind struggled to come to terms with what had occurred. He had stepped across a threshold, emerging into a parallel existence where everything was essentially the same yet nothing seemed quite as it had before. His bearings were all misaligned, his context changed, unfamiliar. He gave himself up to truth.

'Um, yes, it was,' he said, propping himself up on one elbow and looking at her.

'That's remarkably honest,' she said. 'I approve.'

He looked into her eyes but they hid themselves again in the darkness. 'What about you?' he asked.

'Oh, yes, me too.'

'You're pulling my leg'

'Of course. Just a little white lie.'

There was a strangely comfortable silence.

'Why did you arrange all this?' he said. 'I mean . . .'

She ran a hand across the lower reaches of his abdomen. 'Oh, Aldo, isn't that obvious?'

'Well, yes and no. You have a husband, this is your house here, you have a life . . .'

'I have a life? What do you know about my life?' Her voice was suddenly harsh. 'Are you so sure you really want to know about all that, about why you're here with me? Maybe you just got lucky and for a few hours I'm yours. It might never happen again. You'll leave this house and you'll never come back. Maybe you'll never even see me again. Didn't that occur to you?'

'I hadn't really thought.'

'No, of course not, you hadn't really thought. Listen, Aldo, as you're so interested in the truth, let's play a little game. I ask you a question, and you must answer truthfully. Whatever I ask, you have to answer, and it must be the truth. And then you ask me a question, and I'll answer truthfully, whatever the question. Anything goes.'

'But how do I know you'll be telling the truth?'

'Because those are the rules, so you'll just have to trust me. We'll start with an easy one, all right, until you get the hang of it. Which part of this sinking pile of a town do you call home?'

'Come on, that's a pretty uninspiring question.'

'Didn't I just tell you the rules? Do you need me to explain them to you again? They're not that hard.'

'No, I think I've got them.'

'Good. The questions will get more interesting later, I can assure you of that.'

'Cannaregio. Fondamenta della Sensa. About half-way along, opposite Ponte del Forno.'

'Never been there.'

'Near Tintoretto's house.'

'Tintoretto? Very nice. That's what I'll call you . . . my little Tintoretto. Now you. Ask me a question. And make it a good one.'

'Is this your room?'

She exhaled loudly. 'An equally uninspired question.'

'You made the rules.'

'Don't be so cheeky.' She pinched his thigh, not too hard, just a suggestion of control. 'Of course it's my room. Whose room do you think it is?'

'I mean is it where you usually sleep?'

'Yes, this is where I usually sleep. Any more stupid questions?'

'Where you both sleep?'

'Where we sleep, and make love, and argue, and all those other things.'

'Those other things?'

'Hey, Tintoretto, that's three questions. My turn now. Do you live with your mum and dad, over there at Tintoretto's house?'

'*Near* Tintoretto's house. Yes, with them . . .'

'Mummy's boy, eh?'

'. . . and with my dog and my sister.'

'In that order?'

'And my grandmother – she's from the Ukraine.'

'Tintoretski, eh? So you speak Russian?

'Ukrainian too.'

'And your dad?'

'From Burano.'

'Where the women make lace and the men make babies. A fisherman, is he? Boat-builder?'

'No, he has a restaurant, just a small one. Casa Luca, in Dorsoduro.'

'Casa Luca? Don't know it.'

'You wouldn't. It's not your kind of place.'

'What's that supposed to mean?'

'Nothing. It's just my dad's old mates who go there, really. My turn?'

'Wait, with all this excitement I'm dying for a cigarette.'

She got out of bed and padded across the floor and retrieved her cigarettes from a drawer. She stood at the foot of the bed, placed a cigarette between her lips, struck a match and sucked hard, drawing in the smoke in the light of the flame, enjoying his gaze.

'Want one?' she asked.

'A what?'

'A cigarette, stupid.'

'I don't smoke.'

'Go on, try one. I might as well corrupt you in as many ways as I can.' She threw the pack of cigarettes onto the bed. 'Go on, take one.'

'I'd rather choose my own vices.'

'Oh, you're the one in control now, are you?'

'I'd rather not.'

'Suit yourself.' She got back into bed, leant across to kiss him, and transferred the smoke from her mouth to his. 'Your turn, Tintoretto. Ask me a question. Make it a good one this time.'

'So, if this is also your husband's room, where's he now?'

'Why do you want to know that? He's not here, and he won't be back until tomorrow.'

'Those aren't the rules. I was honest with you.'

'He's in Rome.'

'Is that it? No further details?'

'No. Confidential information, I'm afraid.'

'What about the truth?'

'Temporary postponement of the rules.'

'How convenient.'

'Shut up, Aldo. My turn now. What's your favourite position?'

'My favourite position?'

'Yes, you know, for making love. For fucking. Oh, I'm sorry, I forgot – that's not a fair question, is it? For someone of your limited experience . . .'

'Well, I quite liked the first one we tried.'

'The first one?'

'Yes, you know, the first one.' He stumbled slightly over his words as she breathed out another lungful of smoke.

'Which one was that?' she asked, smirking slightly.

'What, you want me to describe it?'

'Yes, that might help.' She took an especially long drag on the cigarette, then stubbed it out in the marble ashtray she kept on the floor by the bed. 'Maybe we could try it again if you tell me.'

'When I was, you know, like this . . .'

'Oh yes, I like that one too. You can't really see who's there and you can imagine, well, anything, anyone. Sometimes, in the heat of the moment, I really do forget who's there.'

'You forget? Are there really so many . . . possibilities?'

'I suppose there must be.' She laughed and raised her hand to her mouth in mock embarrassment. 'It could be my husband, of course, although it would be difficult not to recognise his style. Or Pierino, or Vincenzo, or Alberto, or . . . what was his name? The Spanish one . . . I can't remember. I think he only came here once in the end. Such a shame.'

'You're joking with me.'

'Why would I be joking?' Her voice had lost a little of its playfulness. 'Aldo, did you really think you were the only one? Do you think a married woman who brings someone she hardly knows to her room and pulls him into bed barely before asking his name isn't likely to have done the same thing before, probably many, many times?'

'I hadn't really thought . . .'

'Poor Tintoretto. You don't think much, do you? Did you think it was something more than that? Did you really think it could have anything to do with, I don't know, feelings, any of that old romantic stuff?'

'No, but I thought perhaps you liked me.'

'I do like you, you're very pleasant company, but that's not important. I do the same with people I don't like. I just wouldn't waste my time talking to them afterwards.'

'But you must like them. At least a bit?'

'Why? Are those the rules? They're not the ones I live by. You can't like everyone, Aldo. In a lot of them there's nothing much to like. They serve my purposes, then they go.'

'And aren't you worried your husband will get to know?'

'What makes you think he doesn't know already? And I know for a fact he does the same. He says he has to go to Rome on business, but half the time I'm sure he's tucked up with some little whore in Trastevere. He doesn't get away as much now as he used to, with the war and all that, but I'm sure he still takes every opportunity he gets.'

'What's the point of it all, then?'

'The point?'

'In you being together.'

'I don't know. There's no point, I suppose. It's certainly not love, that's for sure. In fact, I'll tell you a little secret. Remember when you were a kid and at Christmas you believed in *la befana*, and you were so sure she existed because you found the presents she left for you at the bottom of your bed? And then remember how you felt when you found out none of it was true, that it was all one big lie? Well, here's a truth for you, Aldo – love's just the same.'

'What about the presents, though? They were there. Does it really matter if they weren't from the person you thought they were from?'

'Of course it does. The present isn't really the thing. What they're really giving you is a piece of themselves. So of course it matters who's giving it.'

'Strange you should say that. You don't seem too fussy who the gifts are from.'

'Well, they're not really giving anything, are they? Why should I worry who I get nothing from? It all adds up to nothing.' She snapped her fingers. 'Just like love, a fairytale, nothing more. We go for a walk in the woods, Aldo, and we find a house made from sweetness and cake, sunlight and air, and we can't believe our luck and we get carried away and eat so much of the walls that it makes us sick, and then the walls collapse because we've eaten them all away and we realise it was never really a house at all. Love doesn't exist, Aldo, believe me. It's just something people invent to describe feelings they can't put into any other category.'

'Maybe that's what makes it love? It can't be described as anything else.'

'Too clever by half. It's much simpler than that – it simply doesn't exist.'

'Maybe that's because you don't want it to?'

'You're right, I don't.'

'But if you gave it a chance . . .'

'Why should I give it a chance? I prefer life without it.'

'But if you prefer life without it, you must have felt it once, I mean, to make the comparison, to know you prefer to be without it.'

'I didn't say that.'

'But it makes sense, you must have . . .'

'Aldo, you know sometimes you can search so hard for an answer, and then you realise it just isn't there, that there is no answer, that nothing makes sense. Nothing makes sense, Aldo, nothing makes sense. Remember that, and you'll always be all right.' She stretched herself across him again. 'So shall we try that position again? Or do you want me to show you a better one?'

It was late, nearly nine, when night became day and Aldo woke for the first time in his life in unfamiliar surroundings. Isabella's room was very different in daylight. The autumn sun lit up the room and the voices of the delivery men in the canal echoed up from below. Aldo could still sense Isabella's presence, the hint of her scent, but when he turned to her the bed was empty. He slowed his breathing and listened. The house was quiet. He had to leave straight away – Antonio would have been waiting for him at the boatyard since eight – but he was suddenly anxious as to who or what he would find on his way out. He got up and slipped on his clothes. He thought about leaving a note but could not think what to write. He picked up his boots and crept out of the room, down the passageway and onto the landing. The doors were all firmly closed. He leant closer to the one that had lain ajar the night before. He heard breathing, a sigh, and then a man's voice speaking in low insistent tones. He was just about to turn away when he heard another sound – a woman laughing. Or was it a sob? His hand moved towards the handle of the door, but then he withdrew and moved off down the stairs. The chandelier hung motionless and mute as Aldo passed beneath the disapproving gaze of the portraits and down into the hall. It was only then that he remembered the gondola. He could not risk taking it out onto the canals in daylight, and he certainly couldn't take it back to the yard while Antonio was there. He would leave it where it was and come back for it later. He let himself out of the front door and into a small courtyard, wisteria climbing the walls, and walked quickly towards the arch that led into Calle degli Specchieri.

As he was about to disappear from view, something made him turn and look up. A figure was standing by a window, just far enough back for the face to be hidden from the light. Aldo turned quickly away and passed out of sight, troubled thoughts flocking around him as he waded through the pigeons on Piazza San Marco. Then a black dog snapped through the winged throng, sending the birds up into the air in a flurry of white feathers, and the white feathers floated down on Aldo like an early dusting of snow as he made his way towards Dorsoduro, Casa Luca and the boatyard.

When he got there, Antonio was in a rage. 'Some fucker stole one of the gondolas last night. That damned Giuseppe, I bet.'

'Giuseppe?' said Aldo. 'Yes, I wouldn't be surprised. Not exactly trustworthy. What on earth was he thinking?'

'Aldo, just you wait till I get my hands on the bastard! Just you wait and see!'

Aldo gulped, then went off to the kitchen to make Antonio his coffee.

Casa Luca

Casa Luca lay just a short distance off the beaten track, only a street or two back into Dorsoduro from the bridge at Accademia, but it had never attracted the hordes of tourists who streamed over the Ponte di Rialto and in and out of the bars and restaurants along the Riva del Vin. This had never bothered Luca Gardini very much – those who valued simple Venetian cooking at sensible prices knew where to find him. Rich tourists and celebrities, having lost themselves in the backstreets on their way to the hotels and restaurants around San Marco, would sometimes glance by chance through the door, stare for a moment, mutter something incomprehensible and depart. Luca could tell by the tone of their voices, even if he did not understand their myriad languages, that they would instantly forget the dim little trattoria that had confused and perhaps offended their refined and delicate senses with its multitude of unfamiliar stimuli. A peculiarly fragrant sawdust spread out across the floorboards, collecting in great drifts in the backwaters of the floor, mingling with the detritus of discarded crusts of bread, empty mussel shells, fish heads, and the occasional bone from one of the wild ducks that thrived among the reedbeds of the lagoon. For years the sawdust had been fighting a losing battle against the steady tide of wine that fell from careless lips or was brushed by rough hands from the stained old bar top on which elbows, heavy with work, rested a while as their owners engaged in animated conversation about the progress – or otherwise – of the war, the elevated price of eels, mullet, and bream, the diminishing wildfowl in the marshes around Torcello, or the problem of sediment building up, as ever, in the less frequented canals. Or perhaps they would simply prop themselves up and contemplate the coarse rosy-coloured wine, reminiscent of diluted blood, in their squat flat-bottomed glasses, rows of which Luca kept, like transparent headstones, on precarious shelves upon the facing wall.

Lunchtimes were always the most animated. Sometime after midday, the workers from the markets near the Ponte di Rialto cleared up for the day and made their way along the narrow alleys, sometimes bringing in old bags the fish they wanted Luca to prepare for them. There was no formal menu, just a hastily scribbled list of possibilities that was passed around the room as more hungry men arrived. As each dish ran out, it was crossed through until only one or two of the least popular choices remained for the late arrivals, perhaps meatballs in sauce or veal cutlet done in the Milanese style. And there was no price list at Casa Luca either. Unless you were a particular glutton, you paid the same as everyone else. Each meal would start with a dark green bottle of house wine, whether you wanted it or not, brought to the table freshly filled from the barrels in the back, and the customers would then choose from the hand-written list.

'You want that, do you?' Luca would say. 'Sorry. We haven't got it. Choose something else.'

'But it's on the list.'

'Yes, I know, but the list is wrong. The meatballs are very good today, though. Have those.'

'Hey, Luca, what does this say here?' someone else would enquire, indicating something indecipherable on the little notepad.

Luca would take a look. 'I don't know. I can't read that.'

'But Luca, you wrote it.'

'Yes, well, it's probably finished anyway.' And he would strike it through with a decisive flourish of his pen. 'But the veal's great. Have some of that.'

'Hey, Luca,' another voice, hoarse with cold and smoke, might call out from some dark corner of the room. 'Can you stick this in a pan for me?'

And Luca would take the fish from the man and take it into the kitchen where his wife, Maria, would cut off the head and the fins and shovel out the guts and fry it up, and the man would be charged an especially insignificant sum, and the next time he came he might bring half a dozen fish and eat two and leave the rest to be added to what passed for a menu.

Luca would drift between the tables, or busy himself behind the bar and pretend not to notice Elena flirting with the better-looking customers as she took them their plates of food, and as the men finished their meals he would wander around dispensing small plates of homemade biscuits and cakes while filling stubby little glasses with *amaro* or *grappa* or *limoncello*.

'How much are you going to give me today, then?' he would say.

'Whatever you say, Luca.'

'How about ...'

And Luca would hazard a particularly round figure, conservative by any measure, and the cash would be handed over, and the taxman would only receive what Luca felt to be his fair share, which varied with the seasons and with his mood but was always significantly less than the fiscal authorities would have wished had the decision been their own.

By two-thirty the din would start to abate as one by one the fishermen, market workers, boat-builders and gondoliers drifted back to their respective occupations or wandered home to pass the afternoon in heavy-limbed slumber, and by three o'clock the place would be virtually empty. It was no coincidence that Fausto Pozzi rarely put in an appearance before then. Well endowed though he was with self-importance, he knew better than to turn up while the regulars were still around. On the few occasions that he seriously misjudged his time of arrival, the room would fall silent as his hulking silhouette hesitated in the doorway, blocking out the light. There would be a brief but significant pause, and the noise would then erupt again as abruptly as it had ceased, the renewed tumult masking the various colourful oaths that questioned Fausto's parentage, sexual prowess and nocturnal preferences. Thrusting out his ample chest, Fausto would stride towards the bar as Luca took down the only tall-stemmed glass to be found on the premises, filled it with *pinot grigio*, then placed a plate of deep-fried whitebait, without lemon, next to it on the bar. A forced smile might be offered in welcome, which Fausto Pozzi would sometimes replicate, depending on the value of recent takings. Words would be exchanged, the conversation pregnant with brief and awkward silences. Often Aldo, on his lunch-break from the boatyard, would be busying himself behind the bar or ferrying plates of fish about the place, and Fausto would regard him with an odd mixture of pride and admiration which occasioned Luca to seriously contemplate Fausto's reputed sexual ambiguity.

'That's a fine boy you have there,' Fausto said one afternoon, dabbing at his thick moustache after polishing off his whitebait. 'He's got his mother's eyes . . . and his father's smile.' He grinned wickedly and Luca grimaced. 'Hey, Aldo, come over here. Where are you playing this evening? Maybe I'll come along this time. Best young violinist in Venice, you know, Luca. Best young violinist in Venice.'

Fausto patted Aldo heartily on the shoulder and Aldo smiled in genuine youthful pleasure and then shifted uneasily as he sensed Luca's disapproval. Fausto withdrew his fat paw and looked at the floor. Recovering his composure, he began to quiz Luca on the week's takings. Aldo excused himself and went into the kitchen. His mother, sweat upon her brow, was tending to hot pans of spitting fish, conscious of the low monotone of Fausto's voice but mercifully unaware of the attention he had been paying to her son.

'Fausto's here again, is he?' she asked.

'Yes, he's talking to Dad about money again. Same old story.'

'That bloody man! He's a blight on all our lives.'

She grabbed a lemon and placed it upon the chopping board and sliced it into rather more pieces than was strictly necessary.

'He's all right,' Aldo said. 'I don't know why you and Dad hate him so much. He's always nice to me. Who knows why, but he is.'

'Yes, who knows why,' Maria would mutter.

Back by the bar, Luca would usually try to ignore Fausto's

unwelcome interest in his son, but occasionally his irritation would manifest itself in a few barbed words. Fausto invariably bit his tongue and let them pass. There'd be plenty of time for confrontation later if it really had to come to that. Instead, he would ask politely after Maria, drain his glass, and mention something about coming back at a more convenient time. Dozens of eyes would fix on his back as he made his exit. Back outside on the quay, he would loudly exhale his exasperation, anger and relief. Then he would take a deep breath, his proud chest would re-inflate and he would float away across the bridge at Accademia and on towards San Marco.

These were highly embarrassing episodes for someone of Fausto Pozzi's exaggerated yet fragile self-esteem. Usually, just as the last of the regular customers were leaving, he would lumber across Campo Santo Stefano, pausing on Ponte dell'Accademia to contemplate the majesty of Santa Maria della Salute a little way along the canal in the direction of San Marco, its two domes illuminated by the sun falling across the back of Dorsoduro. He would then steel himself, make his way down off the wooden bridge, and as he approached the door of Casa Luca his jaw would tighten and his chin jut forward. With a prime location like this, Casa Luca could be – should be – one of the finest and most expensive restaurants in Venice. Tourists should be flocking to sit and eat fine food while looking past the nodding heads of gondolas and across the lapping waters of the canal to the church of San Trovaso.

Five years before, Fausto and Luca had made a deal. It was quite simple. Luca had the relative youth, energy and desire to leave behind his fishing nets and start up a small restaurant. Fausto had the capital and the contacts to secure a fine location for the business, arrange a suitably long-term lease, and purchase the necessary furniture and other paraphernalia. He would then allow Luca to get on with the serious business of making enough money for both of their needs. They had agreed to share the profits equally. This had seemed a little unfair to Luca, as he would be doing all the work, but as Fausto frequently pointed out, he did not have a great deal of choice. There was no way Luca could have arranged and financed any of this on his own and Fausto liked to think of it as a symbiotic relationship. The trattoria was now well known among the locals as a rare and valued place where basic fresh food could be had in down-to-earth surroundings at a price that reflected the spending power of the local working class rather than fancy-shoed, high-spending foreign visitors or more well-to-do Venetians. This was not quite what Fausto had had in mind at the outset. Of course he had been aware of Luca's obvious lack of ambition, but he trusted in human nature and felt sure that the younger man would sooner or later accede to the worldwide laws of business. The bottom line was king, however low you had to stoop to get your hands on it, or how vulnerable your posture while stooping.

Initially, Fausto allowed Luca to get on with organising the place as he wished. After all, it meant less work for him, and he had fulfilled his part of the bargain by arranging the finances and oiling the necessary cogs in the local political machinery. After a slow start, business picked up but profits never grew to the level Fausto had anticipated, and the onset of war had vastly reduced the number of foreign visitors. There had always been enough money to provide Luca with a little bit more than the bare necessities, which is all he really wanted, but Fausto needed considerably more than that. His other businesses did reasonably well, but a couple of shops in Cannaregio, an area frequented principally by locals, would never make him rich. Casa Luca was his one big hope, and as time passed and ever greater quantities of rough country wine flowed cheaply down the throats of Luca's friends and ex-workmates, it began to dawn on him that he had chosen the wrong man with whom to go into business.

At first he tried to persuade Luca through reasoned argument. A change of image, a refitted interior, a different menu, or indeed any menu at all, tables overlooking the canal with fine cloths and china, crystal flutes of *spumante* chiming away the early evening hours, waiters trained in the restaurants of Milan hovering attentively, perhaps the occasional violinist to serenade the honeymooners – these few simple alterations might change their fortunes forever.

Granted, Aldo could string together a cracking good tune on the violin, but rumbustuous drunken singing was decidedly not the ideal accompaniment to a romantic meal.

'But why would I want all that?' Luca had asked. 'I'm perfectly happy the way things are. I've got my house, my children are happy and well fed, and I enjoy my work. Why would I want to change anything?'

So Fausto resorted to implications of unpleasantness, and then to more direct threats, culminating in an attempt to dissolve the partnership and set up an alternative establishment, Antica Locanda Fausto, on the same premises. He had gone so far as to contract the signpainter to change the name above the door. Luca arrived one morning to find the poor workman perched precariously up a ladder, poised with his brush, having already painted over a part of the sign. Luca was a tall, broad-shouldered man, strong from years of manual work, and he had a Vesuvian temper when provoked. The unfortunate painter's equipment, ladder and all, was swiftly deposited in the canal, followed for good measure by the painter himself. Luca never bothered to have the sign repainted. Everyone knew where Casa Luca was and what it was called – it was only the uninformed who thought there was a dark little place, just a short distance from the bridge at Accademia, going under the name of Casa Lu.

Tipped off by his drenched and irate signpainter, Fausto had descended on Casa Luca somewhat earlier than was advisable. He paused outside, contemplating the view down the quay towards the Giudecca, picturing exotic visitors lining up to gild his pockets with their foreign gold. The noisy chatter from within was punctuated by a loud uninhibited belch, shattering his idyll. A couple of the regulars tumbled out, stinking of fish. Fausto Pozzi grizzled his nose and, although it was not yet one-thirty, walked decisively into the restaurant accompanied by his legal representative.

'Our agreement is terminated with immediate effect,' Fausto declared to Luca. 'My lawyer has prepared the necessary documentation. Please sign here. You have seven days in which to wind up your affairs. I will be maintaining the lease in my name, and shall henceforth manage this business in the manner in which I see fit.'

Luca observed him from a perspective somewhere between pity and contempt, but leaning towards the latter sentiment.

'I'll do no such thing. You know as well as I do that the lease is in both our names, and that one cannot strike the other off without the agreement of both parties.'

Fausto released a spluttering noise.

'That was the deal,' continued Luca. 'And that's why I've been doing all the work all these years. I'm not your employee, I'm your partner. And you also know that the contract between us states that I manage the business without interference, as long as we're making a profit. Now, if you'll excuse me, I still have work to do.'

Luca stood up and disappeared through the door that led into the kitchen, where Maria raised her eyes to the ceiling and shook her head.

'Stupid bastard,' said Luca, as the front door slammed shut.

He made himself an espresso, sweet and strong, and went outside. He sat at one of the pair of small wooden tables he kept outside on either side of the door. His customers rarely used them, preferring to be in the thick of the fug and gossip indoors, but Luca liked to sit outside, especially on warm evenings when the jasmine was in bloom, and watch the light fragmenting in the canal, the waves lapping at the quayside at his feet.

On summer evenings, when the door to the restaurant was cast wide open, a breeze would sometimes blow in off the lagoon, displacing the stagnant odours that seeped out of the canal. It would reach inside the dark interior, stir up the sawdust, and play idly with the lace curtains that hung across the windows. The curtains were from the island of Burano, an hour or so by boat across to the northern end of the lagoon. It was there, at the turn of the century, in a powder-blue house towards the southern tip of the island, behind the main square, that Luca was born. On childhood winter days he had accompanied his father on walks past the brightly coloured houses of fishermen and along the windblown shore. They would stop and sit, looking back down the lagoon in the direction of the island on which the city of Venice had emerged from the water and the mud.

'One day I'm going to live there, Dad,' Luca would say. 'I'm going to have my own restaurant, near San Marco, and you'll catch fish from the lagoon and bring them and we'll cook them and sell them to the tourists, and you'll eat for free whenever you want. And on special days you'll bring me the ducks that you shoot over there in the marshes, but the ducks will be just for us, not the tourists. You'd like that, wouldn't you, Dad?'

The man looked at his son and smiled. 'Yes, Luca, I'd like that very much.'

Some forty years later, Luca's father would look out, rheumy-eyed, across the lagoon towards Murano and Venice, observe flights of ducks coming over from the south, think of Luca lying in his grave on San Michele, and wonder what had really become of his grandson, Aldo, during the war. And he would occasionally, despite the weight of his years, drag his old boat down to the water, coax the outboard into some form of life, and lose himself among the reeds.

Wild pig

Venice, autumn 1941

Dawn was creeping over the rooftops as Aldo Gardini stumbled down the stairs bleary-eyed, still dressing himself. He could hear his dad outside, cursing as he scattered a jumble of gear about on the quay, flinging in the rods and the baskets and the pans and then laying down with great care a pair of rifles wrapped in oilskin in the well of the boat. Aldo pulled on his coat, poked his head around the living-room door to whisper a good-morning to his slumbering gran, then took the last of the bags and jumped aboard just as Luca was firing up the engine. They set off up the canal, the dog an animated yapping figurehead on the bow, stopping off after a few minutes to collect Massimo and his father Paolo from their home on the other side of Cannaregio. Of course Paolo and Massimo both ate at the same kitchen table, three times a day, and the shape of each body matched the other, reflecting the volume of their intake and the joy and duration of their mealtimes. Paolo's voice boomed up out of the depths of him, bursting into song at the slightest provocation, and he started into one now as Aldo poled the boat away from the quay, and soon the dog was howling again as Paolo and Luca and each of their sons sang their way across the lagoon towards Mestre. Aldo sat at the front with his back turned to the wind and winked at Luca as Paolo bawled out the lyrics of a tale of tragic lovers, his hair thick with the salt that blew in off the sea, his face now red in the morning chill. They reached Mestre and walked the short distance to the bus station. Paolo bought the tickets and handed them round. They dumped themselves down on the bench at the back and the bus rolled out of town and onto the broad Veneto plain.

'I tell you, Aldo, this weekend we're going to shoot the biggest boar you've ever seen,' Luca was saying as the bus pulled itself along the road. 'An extra special fat one for your first hunting trip!'

'That's right,' said Paolo. 'The biggest fucking beast in the whole damned forest. And then we'll roast it right there round a fire and . . .'

'. . . and eat the whole damned thing, no doubt!' shouted Luca. 'All in one sitting!'

Aldo smiled at Massimo and his friend smiled back guiltily.

'Well, maybe just a small morsel,' Massimo said quietly and patted his stomach. Aldo laughed and then looked past his friend through the window. It was a clear October day and beyond the plain Aldo could see the ground edging up at first, then the peaks lifting up behind. In the foot-hills, beside the fledgling River Piave, Luca rapped his knuckles on the hard wooden bench and the driver pulled over at the usual signal. The men and their boys tumbled along the aisle with their armfuls of gear and then out by the side of the road. They followed the path up a steep wooded slope, sunshine dappling the ground, and Paolo started to sing again as they walked. They reached the shelter where they would spend the night high up on the hillside, a rudimentary stone structure, windowless and with a heavy wooden door, a refuge for hunters or walkers or anyone lost in the mountains close to dark when the wolves were about. They unpacked the cooking pots, laid their blankets on the bare wooden bunks, and brewed a coffee.

'What's first, then?' asked Paolo. 'Trout or boar? Fish or flesh?'

'Trout,' said Luca. 'The boar will be tucked right away among the brambles until dusk.'

'True. Let's go up to the stream, pull out some trout for lunch, then go after the boar in the evening.'

By mid-afternoon they were tramping their way back down the slope towards the hut, several brown trout slipping around in a basket slung from Aldo's shoulder, sluggish autumn flies trying to work their way between the wicker strands. They spent the rest of the afternoon smoking the fish over a fire in the clearing by the hut, all the while filling then draining metal mugs of red wine that had come from the barrels at Casa Luca. Aldo knew the procedure well. He had heard Luca tell him all about it so many times over the years: how he would fill the bottles at the bar the night before and carry them home from Dorsoduro, through San Marco and around the long bend in the Canale Grande towards the family home in Cannaregio. He knew his father would almost certainly have made a detour to sit on the northern quays and looked across the waves towards the small island of San Michele, where the dead of Venice rested in the shadows of the long brick perimeter wall and the cypress trees stood solemn and black against the evening sky. Aldo could just imagine him now, sitting there in the twilight by the lapping lagoon, plucking out the cork with his teeth, lifting the bottle's weight to his lips, savouring the wine as it filled him with the life of the Veneto plain. Across the lagoon the wine had travelled in barrels made from the wood of Dolomite trees, in boats fashioned in the heart of Venice by the hands of mountain people, boats that carried the lifeblood of the city across the brackish lagoon, across the silting wilderness of water, weed, and mud. Luca, his son knew, would have watched the lagoon as the wine filled his mouth, an innate seam of melancholy binding him to his fragile city, narrowing the distinction between him, the water, the mud and the air to a casual difference in the arrangement of atoms.

As the last of the light turned the horizon a cool blue, Luca would have walked the rest of the way home to see if Aldo had made it back after his adventures of the previous day. Luca still did not know where his son had got to all night, and Aldo could sense both irritation and pride in his father's response. Everyone had to grow up, and Luca must have known that Aldo had gained new insight the previous evening even if he did not know quite what form it had taken or in whose company it had been acquired. But no harm had been done – Aldo had worried his mother half to death but had been back at work at the boatyard early enough in the morning not to put at risk his apprenticeship, and at lunchtime had gone round the corner to Casa Luca, taken his mother's scolding with good humour, and then sat at a table with a plate of meatballs in front of him and a faraway look in his eyes.

Luca was looking at Aldo again now as his son sat by the camp-fire in the fading afternoon light, pulling pink flesh from a trout. Aldo's hands bore a pattern of fresh scars, the legacy of cutting and shaping wood with unfamiliar instruments down at the boatyard in recent months. Luca looked at his own hands, large and heavy, scarred by the sawing action of fishing nets on cold days years before, in a time before he had met Fausto Pozzi and all the things that followed in his wake.

'We should get going,' said Luca, draining the last of his wine. 'It'll be pitch black in a couple of hours. We want to get at those boar while we can still see them, don't we, son?'

Aldo brushed remnants of trout from his lips and nodded. Luca disappeared into the hut with Paolo to get the guns. They showed Aldo and Massimo how to use them, how to flick the safety catches off and on, how to grip the gun and feel the butt tight against your shoulder as you aimed the thing. Then they set off. The forest was beginning to twitch around them as they walked and a squirrel bounced along a branch overhead, silhouetted against what was left of the day. Then Aldo heard the sound of something approaching from further down the hill.

'Well, look who it is,' whispered Luca as Fausto Pozzi appeared among the trees.

For a moment it looked as though he would not notice the group. Then the dog growled and Fausto stopped and turned.

'Hey, fancy bumping into you lot up here!' he called out as Luca uttered a sudden and violent profanity. 'A little bird told me you'd be here, Luca, so I thought I'd pop along and see if I could shoot myself a boar or two. You don't mind, do you?'

Luca spat at the ground and swore again.

'Anyway, shouldn't you be at the bar, Luca? It's Saturday night. We must make a profit, you know.'

'Come on, let's go,' said Luca to the others, but Fausto set off after them anyway, his ursine gait exaggerated by the setting. They left him behind as they quickened their pace, but Aldo could hear his footsteps padding some distance behind, dogged in his pursuit. Then his footsteps faded, and Aldo turned and Fausto was gone.

'Right, then,' said Luca. 'We should split into twos. Too many together and the boar will scarper.'

'You and me, then?' said Paolo.

'What, and the boys together?'

Paolo nodded.

'Well, I guess . . .' said Luca. 'Are you up to it, lads?'

'Course we are,' said Massimo. 'Aren't we, Aldo?'

'Of course.'

'Well, all right, I suppose it'll be good for you,' said Luca. 'Character-building, out and about in the dark without your old man.'

'Sure,' said Aldo, and off they set in their different directions.

Aldo and Massimo headed down into a glade, then into the trees on the other side. Aldo could hear their fathers' progress through the trees maybe a hundred yards away. It was hard to tell distances at night, especially when you were unaccustomed to the tricks the night could play on you. Massimo's stomach suddenly rumbled, long and loud in the quiet dusk.

'Fucking hell. Can't you shut that thing up? You made me bloody jump.'

'Sorry, Aldo.' Massimo let out a noisy belch.

'Jesus Christ, there'll be no animals left in the forest if you carry on like that.'

They carried on down the path, Massimo a few paces behind, panting like a beast. God, Aldo thought, we've got no chance this evening. Then Massimo tripped and fell and dead branches strewn about by summer storms cracked noisily under his weight.

'For fuck's sake!' said Aldo, out loud now, all hope of furtive stalking now gone.

But then a snort and a scuffle, and shapes moving between the trees in front of them, a line of black shadows. A mother and her young.

'Quick,' said Massimo. 'Let's shoot the fuckers.'

But as he pulled up his rifle the shapes crashed away into the undergrowth and Aldo sighed as he heard the sound of them receding into the forest.

'Come on, you fat bastard,' he whispered. 'Let's get after them.'

And he hared off, Massimo wheezing along after him. Suddenly Aldo stopped, a noise in front of him again, then a shape. Then he heard the voice. Fausto Pozzi.

'Who's that?' Fausto said.

'Me.'

'Aldo?'

'And Massimo.'

Massimo was standing at Aldo's shoulder now.

'Why were you two making such a racket?' said Fausto. 'I could hear you a mile off.'

'It wasn't us,' said Massimo. 'It was the boar. Loads of them.'

'Yes, I heard them too. You'll learn to tell the difference.'

'They'll be miles away now,' said Aldo.

'Not necessarily,' said Fausto. 'Sometimes they go to ground. Especially if they have young ones with them.'

'Oh they did,' said Massimo. 'Lots of young ones, little babies. Didn't they, Aldo?'

Aldo nodded.

'Good,' said Fausto. 'Let's wait here for a while, then. If they've gone to ground, they're bound to move again before too long.'

'If Massimo keeps quiet, that is,' said Aldo.

'Sorry,' said Massimo, and his stomach rumbled again. 'Must be nerves.'

'If they move,' said Fausto, 'then we wait, we listen, we assess their direction. If necessary, we follow, silently. Then we shoot. All right?'

'Yes,' said Aldo.

'Sure,' said Massimo. 'Whatever you say, you're the boss.'

Fausto grunted his approval.

'Aldo, you have the first shot,' he said. 'Let's see how good you are, see if you're as good as your dad.'

Then another noise, something in the trees, down in the

direction the wild pigs had gone. Fausto moved off silently and the boys followed. There was a shadow among the trees again, and a shape, maybe more than one, something darker than the night, and Fausto turned momentarily, pausing. Then a crack and a scuff as something heavy pushed its way through the branches, and a heavy breath or a snort, then rustling.

'Listen, Aldo. Can you hear it?'

There was an excitement in Fausto Pozzi's voice and Aldo felt the excitement welling up in him too. The boar were back! He wanted to cry out, to release the unbearable tension. The noise came again, something indefinable and heavy, moving slowly, too ponderous for a wolf, too substantial to be some kind of wildfowl, almost too big for a boar. It must be a huge one! What a prize for your first night as a hunter. How it would look, its head mounted on an oak board in Casa Luca, for everyone to admire. And how proud Luca would be of his son, first time out, bagging the biggest beast in the forest, just as Luca had said he would, shooting the biggest fucking boar any of them had ever seen. And his mother cooking up the meat, the men at Casa Luca feasting for weeks on it, thinking of Aldo every time they sat down and chewed. Even for Massimo it would be a notable meal! Aldo felt a sudden upwards pressure on the barrel of his gun, Fausto leaning his hand up into it, then leaning in to Aldo's ear and whispering his instructions.

'I'm just going over there, Aldo, to cover their escape. When I whistle, you shoot, understand?'

'Yes,' said Aldo, and out of the corner of his eye he saw Fausto moving away, now just a shadow among the trees.

The beast was passing directly in front of him now, deep in the undergrowth, just yards away. Aldo raised his rifle and pressed the stock into his shoulder. He swallowed hard. Then he heard Fausto's whistle. He hesitated for a moment and the whistle came again. His finger tightened and there was the flash and the bang of his gun and an instant later an echo of equal resonance, almost as if someone had let off both barrels at once. Something fell in a great splintering of branches. A dog was barking. A man howled, then began choking out barely intelligible words. Another man began to shout and swear, his curses deafening.

Fausto Pozzi came and stared at Aldo, his eyes now bright and clear, burning in the night. 'Oh my God, Aldo. What have you done?'

'What's going on?' Aldo was saying. Then just, 'Fuck, fuck, fuck . . .'

Massimo was looking at him, not laughing now, belching out a jumble of words. Fausto was over in the undergrowth now and Aldo hurried after him. Paolo was frantic in the chaos of torch beams, clasping Luca in his short stocky arms, holding him tight to his chest as Fausto tried to prop up Luca's lolling head, Luca's eyes barely open, eyelids flickering, blood coursing in a dark incessant stream from his mouth and his lips gibbering away frantically in a futile attempt at words.

Aldo leant down and his words spilled out, a tumbling confusion of apology and denial. 'Dad, Dad, I'm sorry, I'm so sorry.' Then turning to the others, and shouting at them, 'There was another shot, there was, I tell you! Didn't you hear it?'

Then back again to Luca, Aldo's hands pulling at his father's shirt, blood on his hands now, and blood still pouring from Luca's mouth, then Luca coughing, a choking sound and his eyes wild and then nothing, a sudden blankness, all bleak and gone, and the body limp and more shouting from the others and Fausto putting a heavy arm around Aldo's shoulder and saying something in his ear again. 'Not your fault. An accident. You mustn't blame yourself.' And Aldo pushing his hand away, yelling at him, 'You're a liar! There was a second shot, I heard it.'

'An echo.'

'No, not an echo! It was real!'

And Paolo putting his arms around Aldo too now, hugging him, saying nothing, and Massimo staring at Aldo over Paolo's shoulder and Aldo shouting at his fat friend, 'Massimo, you heard it, didn't you? You must have. You were standing right next to me, you must have heard what I heard!'

And Paolo, 'Is it true, Massimo? What did you hear?'

'I don't know. I couldn't say. It sounded like an echo, I think. I'm not sure.'

'Massimo! Massimo! Back me up on this, please! It wasn't me, it was someone else! There was another shot!'

'But who, Aldo? Who?'

'Fausto Pozzi!'

And then Aldo was on his knees beside the body, sobbing and begging forgiveness again and the confusion of the world fell in on him.

The police got involved the following day. They questioned Aldo and all the others, but they found nothing to support his denials, nothing to prove his accusations, no evidence or testimony that a second shot had been fired, nor any indication of where it could have come from or who would have fired it.

'Fausto Pozzi,' said Aldo. 'It must've been him. Firing simultan-eously, so no one would know. He's clever like that.'

'No, there was no second shot,' said Massimo, when pushed. 'I'm sure I would have heard it if it had been so close.'

'Call yourself a friend?'

The police tested the gun anyway, the Chief Inspector, no less, taking personal charge, seeing to it that the tests were carried out in just the right way.

'Conclusive evidence,' he whispered, under his breath, when he came to give Aldo's mother the news. 'Fausto Pozzi's gun shows no sign at all of having been fired for a period of at least several weeks. And the bullet – ballistics have confirmed – the rifle from which it was fired. I'm sorry, but it's your boy who did it. A dreadful mistake. A genuine tragedy. He will need his mother's love more than ever now.'

And Aldo standing quietly in the hall outside and listening to the Chief Inspector's words, like a judge reading out a verdict, and his mother's silence in response. Then the sound of the Chief Inspector lifting himself up out of the chair and pacing across the floor and into the hall, and his hand on Aldo's shoulder, a hard bony hand, and looking Aldo in the eye, a knowing look, then the Chief Inspector turning away and walking down the hall and out into the street, the door pulled shut behind him. And Aldo silent in the hall, and his mother silent on the sofa in the living room, each out of sight of the other, both of them like that for what seemed like hours, neither of them able to speak.

And then Aldo went upstairs and closed the bedroom door and lay on his bed and closed his eyes upon the world.

They buried Luca Gardini on a grey October Friday, a large black gondola carrying the coffin the short distance across the lagoon from Cannaregio to the island of San Michele. Luca lay in his box beneath a gilded awning as the oarsmen pulled their long poles through the green water. Aldo sat beside his mother next to the coffin and fought off a desire to rip open the lid and shake the corpse, to wake Luca from his sleep, to tell him he was not really dead and must come back to her, must tell the oarsmen to stop rowing and take the vessel back to the house on Fondamenta della Sensa, where they would sit at dinner and forget the whole thing had ever happened. But instead she sat motionless and watched the bow of the boat as it cut through the drizzle, the brass eagle on the prow coated with fine drops that slid across its outstretched wings and slipped one by one onto the waves of the lagoon. And she thought of Luca's barrel chest and how, when she had first lain next to him in the house on Burano, her head resting on the mattress beside him, he had towered above her like a protecting mountain, a wall that would keep out all the bad in the world for the rest of their life together. But now the mountain had gone and she lay open to the wild creatures that roamed the plains and she would have to create her own refuge again.

The gondola hugged the outer wall of the cemetery as it moved up the western side of the island. It drew alongside the jetty near the north-west point, where the cypress trees stood, dark sentinels against the sky, the small dome of the church of San Michele in Isola, so white when the sun shone, now grey and indistinguishable from the clouds and the rain. The pall-bearers carried Luca into the cemetery, through the lines of vertical tombs and the silent corridors of graves. Many were ornate, others simple, some well tended, fresh flowers in the holders, others uncared for and colourless, and Aldo noted that it was not necessarily the simplest that were the least cherished or the most ornate that bore the freshest flowers. He listened as the priest spoke the eloquent words that Luca had not been able to say in life, and then his father's body was passed over to the land of the dead. He stood beside his mother, looking around at the faces, the occasional glance in his direction, that questioning look, the one he had seen so many times since the shooting, sympathy and accusation rolled into one, and the blood drained from his face whenever he saw their eyes. His face was thinner than ever now, grey as wet ashes, his eyes as blank as the sodden sky. The name of Fausto Pozzi seeped like an illness from his mind, out of his mouth in a silent obsessive flow. The man himself stood a little further back, not welcome, as ever, barely tolerated but still going through the appropriate motions of sorrow. No one had turned him away and so there he was, hanging over Luca in death as he had done in life. A tragic accident, he had said. The poor boy, shooting his father dead, of course he would want to distance himself from blame, deny to everyone, including himself, what he had done. But it was Aldo who had fired the gun, of that the police, who had been most helpful in the matter, had provided conclusive proof. So everyone concurred: poor boy, what must he be feeling now? And how uncharacteristically reasonable it was of Fausto Pozzi to bear the boy's accusations with such good grace, to be so generous in his forgiveness of the slandering of his name. Yet Aldo persisted, he swore to everyone that he would not forgive, that he would prove one day that though he had also pulled his trigger, it was Fausto Pozzi who had killed his father. 'Poor boy, he cannot forgive himself, and so he seeks another culprit,' they said, but Aldo knew his own truth and he knew that one day, somehow, he would reveal it to them all and Fausto Pozzi would pay the price for what he had done.

The wake was held at Casa Luca. They drank the wine and ate

the food and talked of Luca and tried to remember the good times, but the atmosphere was heavy and oppressive and the mourners drifted away empty and unfulfilled under a teeming rain. As Aldo watched each of them leave through the door of Casa Luca, the wind blew in and lifted the sawdust, the lace curtains shifted imperceptibly and then settled, and the door slammed shut in his face.

Aldo Gardini found the house, just as it had been described to him, in the depths of a dead-end alley, the walls dark and green with moss where water streamed down the walls from broken gutters overhead. Nice door, he thought, once upon a time, centuries before: solid oak, rotting around the edges now, gone all old and grey. He looked around, almost had second thoughts, stopped himself, then hammered on the door so hard that the rough wood drove a dusting of splinters into his knuckles. He called out to the man inside, wanting to get it over with, wanting to get it done.

'Hey, it's me! We have an appointment, remember? Open up!'

'Yes, yes, yes, patience, patience. I'm coming.'

Then footsteps and the door swung open and Aldo was looking down at a grim facial arrangement upon the body of a dwarf. He looked at the man's eyes, his clothes, their creases edged with grime, then back up to the twisted face. How appropriate, he thought. An ugly man for an ugly task.

'Aldo? It *is* Aldo, I assume?'

'Yes, Aldo. Who else?'

'Come in. You're letting in the damp.'

The man set off, his metal-tipped heels echoing down the hall. He led Aldo down a staircase into a basement, an oil lamp burning in the corner, another propped up on a table by the far wall. A fire flickered in the grate, casting red and black shapes around the room. Aldo sniffed. The place stank.

'Are you sure there's enough light in here for you to work?' Aldo said, uncertain again.

'Every artist has his method,' the man replied, the candlelight revealing an awful smile. Not really a smile at all, thought Aldo, more of a threat.

'Sit down,' the man said. He hooked his foot around the leg of a stool and pulled it out from under the table. 'I said *sit*.'

Aldo hesitated and the man's smile threatened him again.

'Look, you made contact with me. If you want luxury, you'll have to go elsewhere.'

Aldo sat down.

'So what was it you wanted?'

'A pig.'

'A *pig*?'

'Yes, a pig. A wild pig. You know, a boar. Just the head. Really ugly. Here, where I can see it easily.' He rolled up his sleeve and placed his forearm on the table. 'Just here. About this size.' He clenched his other fist and placed it on his arm.

The man opened a cupboard and exhumed an oil-cloth bag and a dark bottle topped with a cork. He unfurled the bag, removed his instruments with the care of a surgeon, placed them on the table, extracted the cork with his teeth. The needle caught the light of the fire as the man rubbed Aldo's forearm with the noxious contents of the bottle. Then the man set to work and Aldo watched as the animal's face took gradual shape upon his arm, first the outline, then the heavy jaws, the teeth, the tusks, the wrinkled moustached snout. And then the eyes.

'Fiercer than that,' said Aldo. He knew exactly what he wanted now. 'Make them angry-looking. Furious. Evil.'

The needle worked away, the man occasionally wiping the image down with the stinging liquid from the bottle. Aldo gritted his teeth and swallowed the pain and held it in his stomach, staring all the while at the face that was forming on his arm. The man paid special attention to the expression of the eyes, working at the corners, increasing the depth, his digging and scraping bringing blood welling up out of the skin. Aldo wiped it away and urged the man on.

'Dig a little deeper. I don't want it to fade.'

'It won't fade.'

'Dig a little deeper anyway.'

Finally, it was done, the skin angry and sore, and the man wiped it down again with the fiery liquid and Aldo bit his lip and handed over the money and made for the stairs.

'Can't say I've done one of those before,' said the man. 'Any particular reason for it?'

'To remind me of someone. Of something I have to do. It's a part of me now.'

And he walked up the stairs, a new companion on his arm, and in his head was the image of a pig, the name of a man with a moustache, a hole in his soul, and the shadow of an echo in his heart.

After Luca

Venice, autumn 1941

Aldo arrived early at the market just along from the Ponte di Rialto. The fishermen watched him as he went by, one or two calling out their commiserations.

'See you at lunchtime,' said one to Aldo as he passed. Aldo ignored him, not really meaning to, just too late to acknowledge the greeting by the time it had hit him. Just being nice to him, as they all had been, trying their best to get him over it, the thing that he had done. Fuck the lot of them, Aldo thought, they think I did it. They are wrong. He collected the bags of fish from the usual place, paid the man, feigned a smile, and headed for Casa Luca. He unlocked the door and shoved it open. The smell of the past struck him in the face, that Casa Luca smell, without its Luca now, its name suddenly meaningless, just a memory of what Luca had been and what he had built here. The room was dark, the stale odour of yesterday's wine heavy in the air. Aldo put the bags of fish in the sink behind the bar and rested his hands on the top, rubbing the wood, feeling the grain. Chestnut, got it in one. Antonio would be proud of me. Sure he would. He thought of Antonio at the boatyard just over the canal, of the apprenticeship he would have to give up now, so soon after he had perfected his coffee-making, able now to recognise the various woods, permitted even to repair some of the older boats, those that belonged to the least demanding customers. But all that was finished, all that would have to end if Casa Luca was to remain as Luca would have wished rather than as Fausto Pozzi had always wanted. Aldo's mother could not do it all on her own and Aldo would have to fill the unfillable void that Luca had made when he left them. Aldo looked at the sawdust on the wooden floor, picked up a handful and nosed the different scents. He cast it back down, scuffed at it with his foot, flicked on the lights and opened the door, letting in the fresh, cool morning air, clearing out something of the past. He cleared away last night's dirty glasses from the tables where the customers had left them, breaking one against the sink as he tumbled them into it. Then he wiped down the tables and set about sweeping away the old sawdust and replacing it from the sack in the far corner, under the shelf where the money was kept in a locked wooden box. He rearranged the tables and chairs, pulled the door to and set off over the arched bridge towards the boatyard. He knocked as he entered and passed the bench where the lathe sat under the corrugated canopy of the shed, then went out onto the slipway. He found Antonio crouched under a curved black hull, poking at a small imperfection with his stubby fingers. He hauled himself out at the sound of Aldo's footsteps.

'Hello there, Aldo. How are things?'

Aldo shrugged.

'Yes, of course. Stupid of me to ask. Here, let me show you this heap of old timber.'

He led Aldo to the far side of the yard where an ageing gondola rested on trestles. He began to pick at a hole near the stern. 'See this, Aldo? Here, look. Whoever did this last time missed a bit and the water's got in. How can you miss the same bit with every coat? Can't have been done here, that's for sure. Must have been those idiots in Castello.'

He continued to pick at the hole, making small exasperated noises as he did so.

'Fancy a coffee?' asked Aldo, a spare part here now. He knew it, Antonio knew it too.

'Coffee? Sure, why not?'

Aldo went into the kitchen, in the corner by the tree, filled a blackened pan with water and set it on the stove. When the coffee was ready he took it to Antonio and they sat at the water's edge.

'Not bad,' Antonio said, as he sipped the hot dark liquid. 'Remember that first cup you made me?'

'How could I forget it?'

'How could *you* forget it? It was me that had to drink it.'

'I don't recall you drinking it. Didn't it end up in the canal?'

'Probably. Like all the others,' he grinned.

They sat in silence for a few moments, sipping their coffee and watching an elderly couple amble arm in arm along the quay on the far side of the canal. A whole life together, thought Aldo. The luck of it.

'Have you had a chance to think about things, Aldo? About your apprenticeship?'

'Yes,' he said, removing his gaze from the old couple. 'I'm sorry. I haven't really got any choice.'

'Yes, I suppose your mum will need you at the trattoria.'

'She can't do it all on her own, that's for sure.'

'I understand, Aldo, I really do. Come down here at the weekends if you want. Keep your hand in.'

'Thanks. I'll pop along when I can. And I'd still like to come for the sawdust, if that's all right?'

'Of course, every Friday, just like Luca did. Casa Luca wouldn't be the same without it.'

Aldo looked at him. It wouldn't be the same anyway now, old man, truth be told. Not now, not ever.

'Here, take some of it now. There's a sack over there.'

'Thanks, Antonio. See you at lunchtime?'

'Of course. What's on the menu today?'

'I don't know. Mum hadn't arrived when I left. Fish, anyway, I got it on my way in.'

'Yes, fish. Sure to be.'

'See you later, then.'

'See you later, Aldo. Keep your chin up, son.'

'Sure.'

He picked up the sack and walked out of the boatyard and towards Casa Luca. His mother had arrived now with Elena and was in the kitchen chopping onions, big purple ones. Tears were rolling down her cheeks.

'It's just the onions,' she said as Aldo looked at her doubtfully.

Elena shrugged.

'The tables need putting out the front,' his mother said firmly, and resumed her chopping.

Aldo put a couple of tables outside and sat and watched the waters of the canal as his father used to do, but he couldn't stand it for long. Then he went back inside and helped to get things ready for opening time. By midday, everything was done and the first of the regulars began to arrive. They nodded at him as they approached the bar. Aldo took down the squat glasses from the shelves behind him, poured the wine, and they drank. As the restaurant filled, the noise increased, and it almost seemed as if nothing had changed as Elena ferried plates piled high with food to tables where hungry men sat and ate and filled their stomachs to the brim with wine. But then they looked across towards the unfamiliar figure behind the bar and reality shoved its head back in through the door. The only blessing was that Fausto Pozzi did not put in an appearance that day.

When the men had gone and the restaurant had fallen quiet, Aldo took his violin case from the shelf in the back room. He laid it on the desk, cluttered with unpaid bills and unanswered letters, flicked back the catches, lifted the lid. He took the violin in his hands, picked up the bow and ran it gently across the strings. He thought of Isabella, the shape of her, the sounds she had made, almost singing up at him, her body humming as he touched her. He had not seen her since that night they had spent together, a week ago, or was it more? He had lost track of time in the interim. He had hoped to see her again, under the pretence of recovering the gondola, but the hunting accident and everything that had followed had put paid to all of that. As Aldo played, he glimpsed his mother through the open door, sitting at the kitchen table, listening. Aldo played a last, discordant note, placed the instrument back on its red velvet bed and gently closed the lid, as an undertaker might close the lid of a coffin.

As Aldo hurried into the church near the Rialto that evening, he could hear the other musicians already tuning up their instruments in a side-room.

'Come on, Aldo. You're late,' scolded Bruno, a rotund jovial man in his forties who had been playing recitals in the churches and music rooms of Venice for more than half his life.

Aldo quickly tuned his violin as the others waited and then they came out together and stepped up onto the marble platform, took their seats in front of the altar, and the music began. The audience sat in the half-light and watched the rhythmic movements of the musicians' elbows, or cocked their heads at odd angles, tuning their ears to the music. One member of the audience sat motionless but for the occasional lift and fall of her eyes. She listened, but mainly she watched, staring at Aldo as he played. She observed his alternating expressions of furious concentration and desperation, strained to pick out the notes of his violin, sought to distinguish it from the other beautiful sounds that filled the air. At the end, when the church was silent and the lights had been put out and everyone else had gone, she was still in her seat and she stood up as Aldo approached her along the aisle.

'Aldo, will you walk with me a while?'

He followed her out of the church and they walked through Campo Santo Stefano and on towards San Marco.

'I heard about your dad, Aldo. I'm so sorry. You must feel terrible. I've been thinking about you, how you must be feeling.'

'Thank you, Isabella. That's kind of you.'

'I wanted to see you sooner, you know, but I thought better of it. Not the right time, perhaps.'

'No, it hasn't been good.'

'Well, it's good to see you now, anyway.'

'Yes?'

'Yes, Aldo.'

'I wasn't really expecting to see you again. You know, what you said, not really bothering with people more than once.'

'Did I say that?'

'It sounded that way.'

'But you left a part of you behind.'

He looked at her.

'The gondola . . .'

'Ah, yes, of course. But it's not really mine.'

'Will you take me out in it again sometime? In fact, why don't you take me out in it now?'

They walked unobstructed across Piazza San Marco, its tide of pigeons having ebbed away earlier with the fading hours, then up Calle degli Specchieri and under the low arch that led into the courtyard. Aldo remembered now the figure at the window that morning as he had sneaked away like a thief from the scene of a crime, snatching away something that didn't belong to him.

'Did you watch me leave that morning, Isabella?'

She looked puzzled, shook her head.

'But there was somebody at the window.'

'Not me.'

'But I heard voices when I was leaving.'

She raised a finger to her lips and turned the key in the lock. They slipped through the unlit hall, past the foot of the stairs, then out through the back door and onto the jetty, the gondola nodding on the gentle waves. Aldo stepped aboard, Isabella following, her entrance more dignified than that first time when his nerves had nearly overwhelmed him and he had hauled her aboard. She sat on the cushion on the black wooden bench and leant back as Aldo took up the oar, set it in its rest, and pushed them out into the canal.

'Where to?' he asked.

'The lagoon.'

'There's not much to see out there at night.'

'We can look at the stars.'

Aldo looked up at the sky. 'On a cloudy night?'

'Yes, Aldo. The stars are always there, even if you can't see them.'

'How romantic . . .'

'I was just being ironic.'

'Of course.'

But he wondered. Something hadn't rung true in the way she

had said it, just an inflection. They headed out towards the eastern end of the island. As Aldo tired, the boat slowed and they began to drift in the dark.

'We should really have a light on the prow, you know. There are collisions sometimes.'

'Don't worry, Aldo, just look at the stars.'

He looked up again. The clouds had parted above them now and beyond hung the velvet black of the sky, dotted here and there with crystal light. He sat on the stern and watched as distant suns were alternately buried and exhumed by banks of passing cloud. A fine drizzle began to descend.

'I'm cold,' said Isabella suddenly. 'Take me home.'

He turned the boat and pushed the oar against the current. His arms ached as they approached the Riva degli Schiavoni. Several times he nearly lost the oar to the pull of the water but finally he guided the gondola under the low bridge and into the side-canal that led to Isabella's house. Once more, Aldo found himself in the hall, Isabella's hand around his own, guiding him up the darkened stairs beneath the chandelier and the portraits, then past the doors on the landing and along the passageway to the room at the end. Her room, Isabella's room, no matter who else had been here. It was exactly as it had been that first night, the big bed, the arched windows, the ceiling in the darkness high above, and Isabella clutching him to her again and again. They lay together and listened to the humming of the night and she felt the burning face of the pig, its hot fetid breath where Aldo's arm curled around her. She rubbed her hand along his arm, felt the raised and wounded flesh, soothed it with her fingertips, caressed it with her tender lips.

'It still hurts you?'

'It'll hurt me forever,' he replied. 'It'll be with me wherever I go. Even if I go to the war it'll be with me.'

'The war . . . Your papers still haven't come through?'

He shook his head.

'Thank goodness,' she said.

'But I'm expecting the call any day now.'

'The longer they make you wait, the better.'

'Most of my friends have already gone off for training.'

'Maybe someone's protecting you.'

'I doubt it.'

'But it happens sometimes. The right contacts, a word or two in an influential ear.'

'I wish. But who would do that for me? Who could? I don't know those types. They'll call me soon enough.'

'So then, Aldo darling, make the most of me while you can.'

There was a noise from somewhere, the creak of floorboards along the corridor.

'Isabella, who's that?' whispered Aldo, his voice suddenly urgent, the darkness no longer a sheltering friend but an accomplice to whoever was outside the room.

'Ssh, Aldo. Don't worry. It's nothing. Really nothing.'

'But there's someone there. Who is it?' he whispered back.

'Aldo, I told you, don't worry.'

He got up and began to dress, fumbling around noisily in the dark for his clothes. The footsteps receded at the noise.

'Don't go, Aldo, it's nothing. Please trust me. Please stay, I want you here with me now.'

But he shook his head and stepped into the inky passage and as he started down the stairs he saw a figure behind him on the landing.

'Who are you?' Aldo said, his voice brittle now.

'Who am I?' said the man. 'Who am I? You've got a nerve. Who the fuck are *you*?'

Isabella hurried along the passageway, clasping a robe in front of her.

'Aldo, I'm so sorry,' she said. 'Oh, God, why must it always be like this? Listen, Aldo, it's best if you go now. Please go.'

'But, Isabella, will you be all right?'

She laughed, something small and dark in her laughter. Something wrong.

'Yes, of course. I'll be just fine. Go now. Please. It'll be better that way.'

Aldo hurried down the stairs, stopped, turned, changed his mind again, stepped out into the courtyard. He walked slowly home through the narrow streets, regretting every foolish step, leaving his gondola again where he should have been, still lashed firmly to Isabella's jetty.

The next day, when the lunchtime regulars had left and he had wiped down the bar and rearranged the tables, removed the scraps of food from the floor and sprinkled it with fresh sawdust, Aldo left Casa Luca. He saw her as he was closing the door, leaning against the arch of the bridge, her long dark hair upon the velvet blue of her coat.

'Aldo,' she said, and at the sound of his name, of her voice, his irritation at the way things had ended the night before fell away.

'I'm sorry about last night,' she said, but really she needn't have, he had forgiven her already.

'Isabella, it's fine, really it is. It's not as if I should have been there anyway. It's hardly the place for me, is it?'

'But I wanted you there. You should have stayed. You will next time, won't you?'

Next time, he thought. So there will be a next time after all? He had been wondering. And now his heart lifted and he felt a growing warmth towards her, and a warmth coming back the other way as she stood there smiling, sweeping her hair back with a hand he wanted to take in his own now, but dare not, not yet at least. Later, yes, the next time: she'd just said so, hadn't she?

'Were you all right when I left, Isabella?'

'Yes, I said I would be. Didn't you believe me?'

'I wasn't sure, that's all. I regretted leaving, thought about going back. I was kicking myself all the way home.'

'Poor you. Listen, Aldo, can we walk for a while? I'd like to explain.'

'There's no need.'

'Oh, but I must,' she said, her hand on his arm now as she spoke. They walked the short distance to the quayside of the Zattere, the long promenade lining the southern edge of Dorsoduro. They sat at a table in the sun outside one of the cafés that punctuated the waterside. A waiter brought the drinks and Isabella paid him. They sat in silence and sipped their coffees and looked across the water to the island of Giudecca, where Byron had swum in the days when the water was still clean. The church of Il Redentore, visited by the doges each year in centuries past, their entourage crossing the Canale della Giudecca on a bridge of shifting boats, stood ephemeral in the afternoon light. Aldo watched Isabella as her eyes fell upon it, as thousands of eyes had done before in search of redemption across the long years.

'I suppose you know who the man was last night?' she said at last.

'I suppose I do. I assume it wasn't the Spanish one, anyway.'

'It wouldn't have been a problem if you'd stayed in the room.'

Aldo turned to look at her. 'But, Isabella, I couldn't really have stayed this time, shouldn't have, anyway. My mother would have been worried to death. I can't do that to her so soon, with my father not being around any more. It was best that I went when I did.'

'But I wanted you to stay.'

'With him creeping around outside like that?'

'He wouldn't have come in. He never does. He just listens.'

'Clearly a gentleman.'

'He was, once upon a time. When he still thought he needed me.'

'Have things been this way for long?'

'For long? Yes, for too long, for far too long. We've been married seven years, nearly eight. I was only twenty. At the beginning I had such high hopes. You know how it is when you're young.'

She did not look at Aldo as she spoke, her gaze fixed still on Il Redentore across the way, as if she were talking to the building itself, as if it were able, in its age and wisdom, to understand the pain of a soliloquoy she had rehearsed a thousand times but never spoken.

'It happened gradually, I suppose. And when we realised what was happening, it was already too late. We tried and we tried, and at first he blamed himself, but it's not him, it seems, it's me. And when the doctor confirmed things, well, he just lost interest. Can you imagine how that felt, Aldo, how it feels? I'd have been a good mother. Maybe not the best in the world, but I wanted it, you know. I'd always assumed it would just happen, I'd have two or three kids, they'd grow up and then they'd have their own, and I'd learn how to bake big beautiful cakes on all their birthdays. Or something just about edible, anyway.' She laughed. 'But then it was gone, the hope, and there was nothing I could do about it and it seemed, from one day to the next, that I was different, completely different. He even looked at me differently, something subtle, something hidden in the eyes. Everyone did, his family, his friends. You know, that look? Just different.'

'Oh yes,' he said. 'I know that look. That sudden difference.'

She looked at him.

'Since the hunting accident,' he said. 'That difference, that look, I see it in nearly everyone now.'

'*Nearly* everyone?'

'Not in you,' he said.

'No,' she said. 'I would hope not.'

'Really,' he said. 'And that makes you special.'

'Oh,' she said, suddenly flustered, then snapping herself away from it again, back to what she'd been saying. 'Anyway,' she said. 'That look. He had it, has it still. I hated him for it at first, hated them all. If only he'd put his arms around me and told me he still felt the same, that nothing had changed, that I hadn't changed. But of course he didn't, and even if he had, his eyes would have told me his lies, and anyway, everything *had* changed, and there was nothing he or I could do about it. Not his fault really, I suppose.'

'Not yours either.'

She took out a handkerchief and blew her nose, then twisted and turned the lace between her fingers. The deep yellow light of late afternoon lifted off the waves and kissed her face with its warmth, glistening the tears that streamed down her face.

'Oh, I've been so stupid, Aldo. I've made so many mistakes. You wouldn't know about that, you haven't had a chance to make yours yet, but one day you'll know what I mean. Maybe he never really loved me, even at the beginning, but there was this invisible third person then, this future person, binding us together. But then that person was gone, before they had even arrived, and so it was always just going to be the two of us. The thing is, it might have been all right if there'd been a reason for it, if I'd known why I couldn't have a child. But that would have been too easy, wouldn't it? Too logical. So anyway, that was that. I took to sleeping in the spare room, another piece of furniture, another piece of wood.'

She rapped her knuckles hard on the table.

'And we arrived at a sort of unspoken agreement. He does what he wants, and I do my own thing, and we get by. I offered him a divorce, in fact I insisted, but the church and everything . . . It means a lot to him, and so he couldn't bring himself to do it, said it would turn us into sinners.'

She laughed again.

'Isabella, I really don't know what to say.'

'Then just say something, anything . . . anything would be better than nothing. I've had enough silence from others to last me a lifetime.'

'I'm so sorry, Isabella. I really can't imagine what it must be like – how you manage, how you cope.'

'Well, I suppose you can get used to anything if you have to.'

They stood up and walked along the Zattere. At Accademia they parted.

'Come and get your gondola sometime, take me out. If you want . . .'

'Yes, I'd like that, Isabella.'

'Tonight?'

He nodded.

'Good,' she said. 'Meet me in front of Caffé Florian at eight.'

She touched him gently as she turned away, and he felt her touch remain on his arm until they met again that evening, until they lay again together in the darkness of her room in the silence of the night.

PART THREE

Russia and Ukraine

Train to nowhere

Brescia, July 1942

Aldo looked down at his uniform, the rough green cloth, stiffer than any he'd ever worn as a civilian, the badges and the belts and the buckles and his clean black boots, as if all this might make him ready for war. He looked around at the other men – Gianni, Luigi, Sergeant Tancredi, all the others. Most of them had joined the division at the same time as him, shortly after it was formed in March '42 – the 277th Infantry Regiment of the 156th Vicenza Division, based in Brescia on the edge of the northern plain between Venice and Milan. What was it with the Army, Aldo thought, all these bloody numbers? They had spent their months of training learning the drill. This is how you walk, this is how you talk, this is how you fold your clothes and this is what you eat. And don't you bloody forget it. Oh, and this is how you wear your hair. He recalled that last day in town, out with Gianni and Luigi on a two-hour pass, looking for girls – but all they found was the sergeant. The sergeant had a thing about haircuts – Aldo suspected it was because he was going prematurely bald. Nice and short, the sergeant always said, just a little bit longer on top if you must. On the way back to the barracks that day they had passed a barber's and the sergeant had pushed them inside. The sergeant went first, taking the lead, setting an example, just as he'd been taught. Aldo watched as the barber shaved the sergeant's head, and he exchanged glances with Gianni, as if about to make for the door – but instead they just sat there and waited their turn, and the barber took away what was left of their civilian life, the right to wear their hair in the way that they preferred.

'You'll be better off that way,' said the sergeant as they left. 'Less chance of fleas. And the girls love a tidy man.'

'Not the girls I like to be with,' said Luigi.

'As if you'd know . . .' said the sergeant.

That had been two days ago. Aldo took off his cap now as he waited for the train. He rubbed his hand across the back of his head, felt the stubble, rough against his hand.

Fucking sergeant, he thought. Bald as a fucking egg.

He gazed at the hundreds of soldiers who were crowded onto the station platform. Numerous flags hung from the walls and the crowd that had gathered to see the men off waved dozens more, all red and white and green, an excited buzz spreading throughout the station, the occasional patriotic song starting up and then fading before it could really gather momentum. It struck Aldo that most of the noise was coming from the crowd. The soldiers were largely silent – disciplined or contemplative, depending on your point of view.

Gianni looked at his watch repeatedly and tutted. 'Call this military efficiency?' he muttered. 'I thought the fascists were supposed to know what they were doing. If they can't even get us there on time, how on earth will they ever get us home?'

'Shut up,' said the sergeant. 'Who said you were coming home anyway? This is a major undertaking. It's just a minor hitch. They'll be getting the train nice and ready for us, fit for kings.'

Aldo turned his attention away from the bickering. There was too much on his mind, too much he was missing already, too many people he needed to see. His family, of course, and Isabella, and Fausto Pozzi, always with him now, keeping him company, along with that memory of the forest and everything that had happened there. And now Aldo was here, on this damned platform, heading off in completely the wrong direction, away from life, away from what his life should have been. When would he be coming back? He had no idea. And would he even make it home? No idea about that either, but he didn't like the odds, didn't like the look of them. Oh yes, of course the papers said otherwise, a straightforward fascist victory, even against the great mass of Russia. Russia! How could they ever win against all that? His gran had told him so – Russia, her native Ukraine, the whole damned Soviet Union? Little Italy was going to make war with that lot, along with her German chums? You'll be like ants on a map, son, waiting to be stepped on. Thanks, Gran, that's really reassuring, as if I had a choice. Luca, he would have said the same, Aldo was sure of that – don't trust *Il Duce*, that fascist bastard, always kissing Hitler's arse, sending away the likes of Aldo, off over the horizon, somewhere they'd never seen, somewhere they should never be. But here he was, here they were, waiting for their train, and off they'd go, him and all the other poor bastards. So they waited – Aldo, Gianni, Luigi, Sergeant Tancredi, all the hundreds of others, the sergeant eager in his ignorance to be off towards a fate you couldn't imagine. The sergeant had tried to clarify things for them the other day, to tell them what victory would mean.

'So, let me get this straight,' Gianni had said. 'We're going to Russia to defeat the Russians?'

'Yes, the Russians – the Soviets, the whole damn lot of them,' said the sergeant.

'And why would that be?'

'Because they're the enemy.'

'The enemy?'

'Communists. The very worst.'

'Ah, I see.'

'It'll be a glorious victory,' the sergeant continued. 'The start of a new empire. Future generations will thank us for it.'

'And this glorious victory,' said Aldo, chipping in where Gianni had left off. 'What will it look like? Just so I know it when I see it.'

'You'll know it when the fighting stops. A few months from now, I expect.'

'And then what?'

'Well, then we'll come home, I suppose.'

'Oh, right,' said Aldo, and Gianni laughed. 'So why go there in the first place? Just to come back home again? Why don't we just stay put?'

'Look,' said the sergeant. 'There are important things in play here, big things, politics and stuff, things you lot don't understand.'

'You're right about that,' said Aldo, and Gianni laughed again and the sergeant told them to shut up and went back to shining the buttons on his tunic.

Well, thought Aldo now, as he waited for the train – at least the sooner you go, the sooner you might come back. Or something like that, even if none of it made sense. *Nothing makes sense, Aldo, nothing makes sense. Remember that, and you'll always be all right.* That's what she'd said, Isabella, that first time, and he realised now that she was right. He slapped at a fly as it landed on his face, picking at the sweat of him, one of the last of them as evening drew in and swallows swooped low across the tracks. Then a train's whistle sounded, silencing the crowd. The whistle came again, long and melancholy, closer this time. Aldo saw the smoke of the engine before the train came into view, twenty or thirty wooden cars in all, almost more than you could count. The huge dark engine, its brakes screaming against locked wheels, came to a halt beside the platform. The crowds of civilians cheered and waved their flags. The military police blew their whistles and the numbers of units were called out amid the din. Aldo pulled on his pack and his helmet, his water bottle and his spade and his gun and all the other things, and he looked at the other men doing the same. He pulled himself up into the carriage, then turned and helped Gianni and Luigi as they struggled to do the same. He choked on the dust that billowed up in clouds as he threw down his pack, Gianni and Luigi coughing up dust beside him too.

'What was that you said, sergeant?' said Aldo. 'A train fit for kings?'

Aldo slumped down, resting his head against the wooden wall of the carriage. Oak, he thought, then he coughed again and closed his eyes, relieved at last to have found a place to rest, a small space he could call his own, if only for a few days on the long journey into Stalin's empire and all that it meant. He heard more pushing and shoving as more and more men climbed aboard, then he opened his eyes and watched as one of the men in his platoon – a man whose name he would soon forget and never really knew – vigorously cursed the Virgin Mary and jumped back down onto the station platform where he said he'd left his gun, feeling such a fool, telling himself out loud that he was, and before the man could return, the carriage door was slammed shut. So who's the fool now, thought Aldo. Go home, you happy fool, pretend you never came here, let all us other fools go instead, packed in like sardines, packed off to die. Go home, brother, leave your gun, spend the war in front of your fire, drunk on wine, with your woman, or your mother. Forget about us, forget about *Il Duce* and his fat fascist arse.

Aldo stood up and leant against the carriage wall as the train lurched its way out of the station. He watched through a crack in the wood as the lights of the town faded and the countryside darkened behind him, and his mind eased open the door again for Fausto Pozzi and let him in and allowed him to look around his thoughts, and every mile the train travelled was another mile away from Fausto Pozzi, another mile from the truth, another mile from what Aldo knew should be his fate – Fausto's too – and the dimmer the lights of home became, the brighter burned the flame of revenge. It was only when Aldo finally slept that Fausto slipped out of sight, appearing again at intervals in his dreams as Aldo's head bibbed and bobbed to the rhythm of the wheels on the tracks, the nodding of a man resigned to his fate now, but the wrong fate all the same.

When Aldo woke, his mind turned to that evening in May when he had left what remained of his family at the door of their home in Cannaregio, when he had caught the boat to Mestre and then the train to Brescia. Everyone had been worried and he had put on a brave face. The news about Massimo didn't help, coming when it did, two days before. He had hardly set foot in Russia before they killed him. That's all anyone knew – no detail, killed in action, that was all. That was Massimo – dead for the honour of Italy, for *Il Duce* and his fat fascist arse. Well, Aldo wouldn't be dying for *Il Duce*, he was bloody sure of that.

'Please don't worry on my account,' Aldo had said as he was leaving. 'I'll be just fine, you'll see. The angels will keep me from harm.'

'There are no angels where you're going, Aldo,' his mother had said. 'Only Russians. So you just look after yourself instead.'

She prodded him in the chest with a finger as she spoke, as if pushing the words into him where he'd remember them.

'Really, don't worry,' he said. 'I'll be back – you know me, you know I will. And I'll write to you all whenever I get the chance, every day if I can.'

He embraced his mother one last time. Then he hugged his grandmother too, to whose country he was being sent to fight, not in its defence, but in the aid of those who were invading her. And then, bending down, he whispered in Elena's ear, 'Don't worry, little one, I'll be back – I promise you I will.'

But she began to cry and Aldo turned and left them so they would not see his tears, three hunched figures and a small black dog by a bridge beneath a perfect evening sky. At Piazza dei Mori, beside Tintoretto's house, he thought again of Isabella. He had seen her the day before. Her husband had been at home but he had left them in peace in the room at the end of the passage and then he had watched from the window as usual as Aldo departed, probably wondering which one it was this time, walking under the arch into Calle degli Specchieri and out of Isabella's life again, perhaps forever this time. On the bleak jetties of Fondamente Nuove, Aldo had waited an age for the boat to come and take him away and more than once he had turned to walk back home. Would anyone really notice if one young man, barely more than a boy, did not come, if he just ignored *Il Duce*, ignored the order to go and fight, somehow forgot to turn up where and when they had told him to? Maybe he could go and live in the marshes, or hide away at his grandfather's house on Burano and only come out at night to spend the dark hours lying beneath the beamed ceiling of Isabella's room, wrapped in her arms, listening to the sound of her breathing and the boats passing beneath her window in the night. Looking out across the waters of the lagoon at the silhouette of the church on the island of San Michele, in whose cemetery they had buried his father the previous autumn in the rain, he remembered for the hundred-thousandth time how he had come to be there among the graves that day, how Fausto Pozzi had joined the mourners at the burial, Aldo's outrage at this deceit, and the terrible scandal that followed, the scandal of his repeated accusations. And he remembered yet again his father as he used to stand, rolled-up sleeves revealing thick strong forearms, grinning broadly behind the bar, his bar, at Casa Luca. And then the boat arrived and Aldo got on board, and when he looked again the lights of Venice were small and distant in the night, and then they disappeared altogether.

The train crossed out of Italy the next day, into central Europe and then on into the Ukraine. Aldo watched the countryside grow harsh and unfamiliar as the train pulled him east, the comforting and familiar landscapes of northern Italy replaced by wide open spaces flecked with forests of birch. Flatbed cars loaded with artillery were coupled to the train and Aldo and the others took it in turns to stand guard in the fresh air that night brought with it. One night the train was rolling through a scrubby stretch of birch forest, Aldo standing guard with Gianni, both of them leaning against a tarpaulin, cupping their hands to shield the glow of their cigarettes from the eyes in the woods. Aldo could feel something hard and uncomfortable pressing into him as he leant on it, a piece of a field gun, a sinister piece of metal only fit for use at the front, only fit for killing people or making you uncomfortable if you leant into it on a lurching train somewhere in the depths of nowhere. He shifted his position but the thing jagged into him again. He pulled up the tarpaulin, saw the dull metal, black and ugly. He covered it up again.

They continued their largely uninformed conversation about the relative merits of the girls of Venice and Milan, Gianni bursting out laughing at something Aldo claimed to have done, sucking hard on his cigarette, throwing his head back and blowing smoke straight up into the air.

'Shut up!' said Aldo suddenly. 'And put out that cigarette.'

Gianni stubbed it out against the tarpaulin and followed Aldo's gaze. Figures were running alongside the train, five or six of them, dark shapes against the pale summer grass. Aldo couldn't see their faces, couldn't even tell if the running figures were men yet or boys.

'What should we do?' whispered Aldo.

'Fuck knows. What are they saying?'

'They're not saying anything. They're laughing.'

'Laughing? Let's shoot the fuckers, then.'

Let's shoot the fuckers. Just what Massimo had said, when they saw the wild pigs, out there in the forest, that night. *That* night. No, let's *not* shoot the fuckers, thought Aldo. Let's not shoot *anyone*.

'Wait,' he said, pressing down on the barrel of Gianni's gun as it was lifted. 'They're only young.'

'I'm only young too. They'll soon be shooting at me.'

'Put your gun down, Gianni.'

The figures ran alongside for some time as Aldo and Gianni watched them, their laughter turning to shouts, calling out over and over again, their youthful voices rising and falling as the train lurched and screeched. Aldo stood and watched, looked at Gianni in the darkness, wondered how he should react. Did they constitute a threat? Perhaps Gianni was right and they should shoot them. But was he really expected to fire upon laughing boys running beside a train? This wasn't how he had imagined his enemy to be and so he fidgeted with his gun and looked again at Gianni and Gianni shrugged and they did nothing. Then rocks smacked into the tarpaulin and one caught Gianni in the face. He raised his gun again but Aldo pushed it back down and the figures veered away towards the edge of the forest, still shouting, jubilant, seemingly devoid of fear, their noise receding into the trees.

'Bastards,' said Gianni, rubbing the spot where the stone had struck him. 'We should have shot them after all.'

'What would be the point?'

'What were they saying, anyway? You know their bloody lingo.'

'Germans,' said Aldo. 'Something about the Germans. I didn't catch the rest.'

They stood again in silence, then Aldo lit another cigarette and leant back into the tarpaulin. The metal of the field gun poked at him again.

'Can I ask you a question, Aldo?'

'Sure.'

'Is it just me, or are you scared too? Just a bit, I mean? No one ever mentions it.'

'Of course I'm scared. Isn't everyone?'

And Aldo thought about how afraid he was that he might never make it home, and that Fausto Pozzi might therefore get away with the terrible thing that he had done.

'But, Gianni, my friend, stick with me and you'll be just fine. I'm definitely going to make it home. I've got unfinished business there.'

'But Aldo, we've all got unfinished business back at home. We've all got lives to live.'

Sunflowers

Near Rostov-on-Don, August 1942

The sunflowers wilted for weeks, the heat of summer killing off flowers while the war killed off men, and the Soviets pulled back towards the River Don. The sun blazed down on Aldo and the others as they came to yet another village lost in the endless expanse of corn and flowers that covered the steppe. The transport situation had worsened and they had been marching for days. Gianni grumbled constantly now about the blisters on his feet where his boots had rubbed them raw and he was grumbling now as they entered the deserted village in the silence of the afternoon. The doors of all the *izbas* were firmly shut and the only thing moving was the dust, blowing up in breaths of wind that whispered in across the steppe. The sergeant called out to the stragglers to hurry up behind. Gianni cursed the sergeant under his breath and Aldo smiled and then Gianni went on cursing his blisters again.

'Right, split into threes,' said the sergeant. 'One hut to a group. You know the drill.'

'Threes?' said Gianni. 'Again?'

'Yes, threes,' said the sergeant.

'Why always threes?'

'Father, Son, and Holy Ghost.'

'What about the Virgin Mary?' someone said. 'Can't she be with us too?'

'She was totally fictional,' said the sergeant. 'Have you ever met a virgin?'

'I've met several,' said Gianni.

'And I bet they were still that way after you left them,' said the sergeant.

'Sure were, I was talking about my sisters. All good Catholic girls. Just like your mother . . .'

'All right, that's enough. Shut the fuck up now and concentrate. This stuff is serious.'

They split into threes and spread out through the village. Aldo went with Gianni and Luigi. The sergeant hurried up behind them.

'I thought you said threes?' said Aldo.

'Odd man out,' said the sergeant.

'Virgin Mary, number four,' muttered Gianni.

'You'll regret that when I get my hands on you later,' said the sergeant and he kicked open the door of the first *izba*. An old man was sitting at a table in front of a range and he tilted his head back and observed the intruders with contempt. In the corner furthest from the door hung a small mirror, the sullen reflection of a woman looking out at them from among the folds of a scarf as she sat out of sight in a back room. Aldo started searching the kitchen for food but there was nothing except the lump of bread that the old man held in his sun-blotched hands. The sergeant tugged it from his grasp and put it in his pocket.

'Why don't you leave that for the old man?' said Aldo.

'Because I'm hungry, that's why. And they're sure to have a whole stash hidden away somewhere. Where's the rest of it, eh?' he shouted at the man.

The man jutted his jaw out even further and glared.

'He looks like he hasn't eaten for a month. Let him keep his bread,' said Aldo. 'Have a heart.'

'Fuck you, pig boy,' said the sergeant. 'And fuck your stupid conscience. How many times do I have to tell you lot? Look after yourself and your mates out here or you won't last long. When you find food, take it, eat it, find some more. And to hell with everyone else.'

They followed the sergeant to the next *izba*. Gianni found a sack of dried apples and tipped them onto the floor. They all piled in,

Aldo using one hand to stuff his pockets while he ate with the other. All he could hear was scuffling and chewing as they wolfed the things down. Then the sound of their chewing was cut short by a sudden eruption of machine-gun fire outside, a hard dry sound, the devil spitting up stones as the men spat out what was left of their mouthfuls of apple, the sergeant squeezing a flurry of instructions out past his departing food. Then more shots, first to the right, then the left, then somewhere just outside their *izba*, then something smacking into the walls, like someone was hurling hard apples back at them. Then bullets coming through the windows, glass all over the place, and shouts amid the gunfire, hard Russian words, and the wind blowing dust in through the windows. Aldo followed the sergeant into the hall. He looked outside and ducked back in as bullets splintered the wall of the house around him. He saw crouching figures running between houses across the square and he followed the sergeant and the others to the back door. Outside, a small plot of land, half-garden, half-vegetable patch, was bordered by a low undernourished hedge, and beyond the hedge a dirt track, then an ocean of sunflowers stretching away as far as the eye could see.

Dozens of Russians in their brown uniforms were running now among the buildings and gardens, kicking in the doors of the *izbas*. A group of them hurtled through a garden to the left, one of them falling as he ran, collapsing into the dry earth, his neck almost folding under his own weight as he ploughed up the ground with his head. Aldo hovered just inside the door. He saw the rolling, staring eyes of the others, the pulsing veins on the sides of their sweating skulls. The sergeant moved out into the garden and they followed. A grenade exploded beside them, then a burst of gunfire. Gianni was down behind a pile of logs, shouting.

Aldo was on the ground now, his head spinning, and he looked up at the sun as it burned down on him. More bullets smacked into the side of the *izba*, ripping up the earth around him. An incessant vicious hum assailed his ears. He could still see Gianni, shouting at him now, then he felt someone dragging him to his feet and he looked up and saw the sergeant, and they stood up and stumbled past the hedge, across the dirt track and into the field of yellow flowers, Gianni and Luigi hurrying up behind. Aldo heard the gunfire spark up again and then die as he crawled between the stalks, staring at the earth as he followed the sergeant deeper into the field, Gianni panting like a dog behind them and Luigi chucking out Hail Marys ten to the dozen.

The sergeant stopped and, seeing him, so did Aldo. As he looked up, he saw why. The woman and old man from the first *izba* were just ahead of them, sitting there, the yellow glow of flowers upon them like gold upon the heads of icons. Time stood still between them. The woman sighed, looked at the ground, looked at the men. Aldo saw options flickering across her eyes. At last, she raised a finger to her lips and motioned them deeper into the flowers. Aldo crawled past, whispering his thanks, and as he crawled away he could hear the woman and the old man pushing their way back through the flowers in the opposite direction until the sound of them had gone. Aldo and the others remained there for the rest of the afternoon, the sunflowers slowly turning their wilting heads above them, turning away from the scene in the village as the sun inched across the sky.

When darkness came the men began to move, slowly at first, creeping to the edge of the field, then skirting the village, lit now by a swollen orange moon hanging low in the sky. They slipped into a field of wheat, the sergeant in the lead as always, the wheat parting as he walked, the sound of it sweeping against his legs as the others followed. At first they used the dimming lights of the village to guide them, and when the lights were gone they followed the stars, just as Aldo had done for years on the lagoon. They found the dirt track that would lead them back towards the west and they walked for hours.

Near dawn, Aldo sensed something close behind him in the darkness as he brought up the rear. He turned and saw a black shape, something indistinct, some way back along the track. Perhaps it was nothing, nothing really there. Tiredness distorts the senses, plays tricks on you. He watched it for several seconds, whatever it was, then took a step or two towards it, hesitated, then turned and set off after the others again, glancing back, the shadow still there, maintaining a constant distance. Aldo blinked, unsure still, quickened his pace and suddenly spun round. The thing was nearly upon him. They stood considering each other for a moment, Aldo and the beast, and then it snuffled about in the dust and squealed. Aldo turned and ran to catch up with the others. He did not look back for a long time, and when he did the creature was gone. For good, he hoped, whatever the hell it was.

As the light of dawn seeped over the eastern horizon at their backs, the men came upon a mixed column of Italians and Germans with light tanks heading east, and they fell in with them and turned around and marched back the way they had just come. Aldo found himself trudging again for a whole day through the powdery dust of the track until he approached again the place where the fighting had been the previous day, the *izbas* barely visible at first, isolated specks in the distance. Scouts were sent out, orders were given, instructions as to how the attack would proceed.

'Let's hope this is brief,' said Aldo.

'It will be,' said the sergeant. 'We've got tanks. They haven't.'

'Still, you never really know.'

Aldo rolled his sleeves up a fold or two higher, spat out a ball of dusty phlegm, and entered the village for the second time in two days. He knew the Russians would have heard the Panzers coming long before they saw them, their grim din descending upon the village, and they would be ready for them, as ready as the could be. The guns opened up, pounding the village. Aldo and Gianni and Luigi and the sergeant followed in the lee of a tank through the field and into the village, the *izbas* already ablaze now in the dusk, their dry wood sending columns of sparks spiralling into a thinning evening sky. The fighting was soon over, the Russians outnumbered, hurrying away, no NKVD men at their backs in an outpost like this, free to retreat without getting a shot in the back from the commissars. When the fighting died away, the few remaining inhabitants of the village, mainly women and their children, stood and watched their houses burn. Aldo walked to the edge of the sunflower field where he had cowered the previous day. He smeared away the sweat and the tears that covered his face and he saw the woman and the old man from the *izba* of the previous day, their *izba* now burning bright like all the others.

Away to one side, a few Russian partisans who had not made their escape through the fields were being herded along the track between the gardens and the fields. The women of the village were following behind them, shrieking and grabbing at the sleeves of the German soldiers who lingered around the edge of the group. Aldo saw the procession stop and a German officer, his face filthy, took one of the partisans to the edge of the field. There were no grand gestures, no set-piece drama, no firing squad, just a gathering of bodies in a ditch, a cold and ugly extinguishing of life administered by a middle-aged man who perhaps had once attended the opera in Berlin and now stalked the Russian countryside in a dirty grey uniform that stank of blood and sweat and shit and death. The German's expression sat somewhere between distaste and disinterest as his heavily veined hand, brown from the summer sun, took each man by the hair and pulled back his head, then with eyes closed pressed the barrel of the pistol up against the nape of the neck and fired. Each body sagged as the German maintained his grip on the hair, the grubby brown fingers now covered with bright splashes of blood. One by one, the men were taken down to the edge of the field and the officer's dirty bloody hand became redder and stickier with the blood of peasants, and the ditch began to fill with the blood from their wounds. The last partisan to die was a boy, like Aldo, in his late teens.

The German turned to the villagers and his gaze wandered across the watching faces, then alighted on the small group of Italians. It lingered for a moment upon Aldo, and for a moment Aldo felt panic amid his disgust and he feared he might lose control of himself, but then the gaze continued on its way and it stopped at the old man from the *izba*. The German strode across the garden and the old woman moved across to block him but he pushed her aside, slapping her down when she persisted. He dragged the old man across the garden to the ditch as the woman followed, and she tried to get hold of a scrap of clothing or a trailing limb, but the German, tiring of these difficulties, raised his gun and shot the man in the face. He fired again and the man lay still. He levelled the gun at the woman as she screamed her abuse. The officer's bloody finger tensed, trembled, then tightened against the trigger. But no bullet came. The gun was empty. The German did not smile ironically. He did not shout or scream or kick the woman in frustration, for he too must have been exhausted now and empty. He just walked away, behind the burning *izba*, and from where he stood Aldo could see the German stop and lean against a wall and bend down. It looked like he was throwing up, then wiping something off his trousers, standing upright again, running that bloody hand through his hair.

The woman was kneeling beside the old man now as the other women of the village knelt beside the pile of bodies in the ditch, lifting an arm, cradling a head, wailing in the glow of the fires that raged all around them. Aldo stared blankly ahead. His eyes met those of the woman, still on her knees by the old man. She spoke, her words inaudible amid the crackle of the fires and the wailing of the other women and the sound of the wooden walls of the *izbas* collapsing in on themselves all around them in the heat. Then her words grew louder, a vortex of misery that rose and spiralled from her throat, swarming all over Aldo, and he turned to where Gianni, Luigi and the sergeant stood beside him.

'What a bloody racket,' said the sergeant.

Aldo looked at him.

'What?' said the sergeant.

'You understand the lingo, Aldo,' said Gianni. 'What the fuck's she saying?'

'What do you think she's saying?' said Aldo. 'Why didn't you stop him? That's what she's fucking saying.'

The sergeant scuffed his feet and looked away.

'What could we have done?' he said. 'All this is way out of our hands.'

'Totally out of control,' confirmed Luigi.

Gianni nodded.

'What are you fucking nodding for?' said Aldo. 'I thought you were better than that.'

'Are *you*?' said Gianni, angry now.

'Yeah, what did you fucking do?' said Luigi, backing Gianni up, chucking back the guilt.

'Fuck you,' said Aldo, but he knew that they were right.

'Look, everyone,' said the sergeant. 'We do whatever we have to, and we just keep going. Look after yourselves and look after each other, until we make it home, that's all.'

'But don't you ever get that feeling?' said Luigi. 'That we'll never make it home?'

'Shut the fuck up,' said the sergeant.

'Yes, shut the fuck up,' said Aldo. 'Shut the fuck up. We have to be strong.'

'And what if we're not strong?' said Luigi. 'What then?'

'Then just fucking pretend that you are.'

'But we know we're all cowards now,' said Gianni. 'Not just today. Yesterday too. We didn't do anything, did we? We just hid in a field.'

'What could we have done?' said the sergeant. 'Try to be heroes? What's the point? Do that and you'll never see your home again, I promise you that.'

After dark they moved out of the village, now just a collection of dying embers among the blackened remains of the *izbas*, surrounded by fields of crushed and burning flowers. A small gaggle of women followed the soldiers along the track, one of them pleading with Aldo for help, begging him not to leave them among the ruins of the village with no shelter, no food, nothing but the clothes on their backs and the bodies of their men. Aldo stopped and was about to speak when the sergeant pushed himself between them.

'Leave her,' he said. 'She's not your fucking problem.'

And he pulled Aldo away and they rejoined the column and the column kept going, a weary line of shadows moving east, the dark shapes of German tanks roaring past, Panzer grenadiers upon the hulls, their cigarettes glowing orange flecks like fireflies in the night as they passed, looking down upon the tramping soldiers who stirred up the dust in the sudden cool of the night. And then a blood-red moon rose out of the field and lingered low over the horizon. It coated everything in the same subdued orange light: the dead and the living, the flowers in the fields, and the barren dusty track that was carrying them all away over the eastern horizon again. But this time there was no black shadow stalking Aldo, because the black shadow was within him now.

The Angel

Aldo was freezing to death, lying in the dark in a shallow depression in no-man's land beside the frozen banks of the River Don. In late afternoon, as the last of the light died away, his platoon had been sent out on patrol towards the Russian lines and they had been caught by the flares and the shells. Aldo fell to the ground and hadn't moved a muscle since. Move and a sniper's bullet would get you in the head – that was the usual way. But if he didn't move soon, he would die all the same from the cold, just more slowly. He looked now at the stars, the same stars, he thought, that would be shining over Venice, far away to the west, whichever way that was. He had plenty of time to think now, parts of him long-since numb, and his thoughts turned to those he had left back home that summer and he wondered what they might be doing, if they too were outside in the freezing air, his mother walking home in the moonlight from Casa Luca, or in Isabella's case, expertly navigating her tides of passion in the company of some new cabin boy before drawing him in for a shared cigarette. Tufts of coarse steppe grass speared the snow around Aldo, and by the banks of the river the remnants of reeds were bent double in the wind that was picking up again now. Thick ice covered the river and deep snow covered the ice, and the snow was still coming down heavily, falling upon the earth in a million goose-down flakes. Here and there the river-ice jagged and jutted in angular slabs where shells sent over by the artillery had split it open in an attempt to impede the Russian attacks, but the river froze so hard and so fast that the Russians always attacked anyway and the dark shapes of bodies littered the slope on either side. A disembodied voice rose and fell again, as it had done for hours, one of the lingering wounded. It was impossible to make out the man's words or the side for which he had been fighting when he fell.

Aldo heard the Russian guns starting up again, shells singing overhead, coming down on the Italian lines. There was movement around the Russian trenches too, white-clad figures moving down the slope towards the river, onto the ice, then across it. Then gunfire started up from both sides, the usual thing. Italian mortar shells were falling here and there, splitting the river, rafts of ice breaking free and drifting around in patches of open water as men clung to their slippery edges and tried to haul themselves out. But the river was wide and there were enough passages across its frozen surface, and soon Aldo saw Russian boots as they rushed past his face, kicking up the snow as they ran. He heard the shouts of the enemy and their cries as they fell. He heard the sound of the bullets as they buzzed and burrowed about and the explosions of the mortars that burst all around, but the chill had penetrated deeper now and an unexpected liberation swept over him, a sense of disembodiment, lifting him so that he began to feel as if he were floating above the ground, hovering there, suddenly only vaguely aware of the shouts and the violence that came to him through the night as if from another dimension. He lay insulated by cold and detached from the world, like a hibernating animal that would sleep through the long dark winter to wake again one bright heavenly day when the only sounds would be those of the breeze among young leaves, the unfolding of spring flowers, and an orchestra of birds hailing the rebirth of the world.

As Aldo lay semi-conscious in the midst of chaos he saw a great winged creature as it passed over the desolate scene, and he watched its slow trajectory as it illuminated the dying. He looked into its eyes and he understood now the meaning of things. It had revealed itself to him as he clung to the threshold between life and death, a moment of clarity, one that he would always remember, a fragment of insight from the depths of a dream, the essence of which remains beyond the comprehension of a normal consciousness. He would only know that he had once been shown the answer, that it does exist, and that it is as obvious and yet as intangible as the blue of the sky. Then he closed his eyes and the roar of battle grew more distant, like the sounds of a petty argument passing through the wall from a neighbouring room, and he lay somehow in sunshine, in some other place.

Water stretched out before him, reaching across a bay to steep wooded slopes that dropped into the blue-green of a lake. Shadowy fish rose up in the water and dappled the surface with their kisses, rings rippling out from where their rubbery lips sipped down insects that chanced upon the water. And away to one side a figure stood on an outcrop of rock, lit up by the sun, and she dived into the water, sending a giant wave rolling towards the place where Aldo sat naked in the grass, and the wave that she had created washed over him and he lay back and felt the sun drink the cool clean water from his weary flesh.

But then Aldo heard Italian voices again, close by now, and he snapped back to reality, to the dark and the cold and the snow. The attack must have foundered as it reached the Italian trenches: they usually did. Then he felt someone leaning over him, and an accent he recognised, a Milanese leaning in with a fragment of mirror, holding it to Aldo's mouth, waiting to see if it misted over with breath. And it did, so he hauled him up and dragged him back towards the Italian lines. In the smoky fug of a dugout they laid Aldo in front of a stove, rubbed him vigorously, shook him until he finally spoke, then filled his mouth with warm polenta, covered him with the grease that they used to protect the guns from the cold, and in this way they lured him back into what might pass for a normal state of consciousness.

'I saw an angel,' said Aldo when he was fully conscious again, his first words to the watching faces in the gloom.

'What the hell!' laughed the sergeant. 'You saw an angel? In this fucking place?'

'That's right. An angel. An angel in the snow.'

'Mother of God, that's all we need,' said the sergeant. 'Another fucking nutcase.'

'I promise you, it was an angel, all wings and light. And that look.'

'That look?'

'Yes, you know, that Jesus look.'

'Like you get in statues?' said Gianni, perking up suddenly from the back of the dugout, sitting there doubled up to retain some warmth.

'Yes, like you get in statues,' said Aldo. 'But it wasn't a statue, it was an angel.'

'Don't worry, my friend, I believe you,' said Gianni. 'I want to believe in angels too.'

The Retreat

Pavlovsk, near Rostov-on-Don, January 1943

Two weeks after New Year, the retreat began. In a brief lull between one Russian attack and the next, the 156th Vicenza Division – and the Tridentina and Cuneense, dug in on either side of them – abandoned their trenches just after dusk. Aldo pulled on his pack and tugged his scarf tight around his throat, and he followed the others up the steps towards the rear, leaving the network of trenches behind him empty, little sign of recent human habitation but for the footprints in the snow and the frozen contents of the latrines and, pinned to a wooden post and flapping in the wind, a photo of a girl on a beach on a sunny summer's day.

'The long road home starts here,' said the sergeant.

'The long road home started the day we came to this godforsaken country,' said Gianni. 'How did we ever think we could win against all this?'

He looked at the surrounding countryside, bleak and white and unending.

'And the Russians never stop coming, do they?' he said. 'Old Mother Russia must be a fertile old bitch, churning out all her millions of sons.'

'A heartless bitch too,' said Aldo. 'Chucking them all away with such haste. And *Il Duce* isn't much better.'

'Don't speak ill of your father,' said the sergeant.

'He's not my father. My father's dead. I told you that.'

'Oh yes,' the sergeant laughed. 'The hunting accident . . .'

'It wasn't a fucking accident. He killed him.'

'He?'

'Fausto Pozzi. Fausto Pozzi killed him. I told you that too,' said Aldo, and he felt that itch again on his arm, in that place with the tattoo, as if the pig were stirring, reminding him it was there.

'I still don't see why,' said the sergeant.

'Why what?'

'Why he would kill him.'

'Business, of course. Money. I told you that too. Christ, sergeant, have you got no fucking memory?'

'I'll remember what you've just said, if that's what you mean.'

'Money,' said Gianni, chipping in late as usual. 'The root of all evil. My priest always used to tell us that.'

'But, Gianni, we're the root of all evil,' said Aldo. 'Didn't your fucking priest ever tell you that? Haven't you seen enough here to realise it?'

'All right, Aldo. Calm down, I was just saying.'

'Well, don't say, don't just say. And tell that fucking priest of yours how things really are. If you ever make it home . . .'

They retreated for the whole of January, sniped at by pursuing troops, machine-gunned by planes that swept in out of clear blue skies, hunted down by partisans who gnawed at the flanks of the column as it snaked its way home. The unrelenting cold cloaked them in inertia. The wind swept cold death in all around them and then blew in blizzards to shield them from the eyes of Russian pilots high above, allowing them to lie a while in peace, curled up by the side of the track where some would lie down to rest, close their eyes, and sleep themselves to death if it were not for the sharp and brotherly prod in the ribs with which they kept each other awake and alive. When the sky cleared they continued their long march through the snow, an unbroken line of diminished figures that stretched from one edge of the horizon to the other, anonymous ants upon the map, waiting to be stepped on, time stretching into infinity in all directions, leaving them so far from home that even if they marched for a thousand years they would still be in the middle of this vast and empty white plain.

One morning, after the night had lifted the clouds and the sky hung huge and pale and clear, Aldo saw three specks high up to the east. He watched the dark specks swell to spots and then the hum of engines come sweeping in, the Russian Yaks coming down in a screaming dive. The column of men panicked and broke apart. Aldo and Gianni and Luigi and the sergeant ran for their lives as the planes shrieked low above their heads, their cannons leaving red furrows in the snow where men had been. Aldo threw himself down, trying to burrow into the snow with his hands. He could see men here and there firing wildly into the air as the planes climbed and turned and descended again. They came back again and again, and each time Aldo picked himself up and hurried further off into the emptiness of the steppe, and each time fewer men were running beside him and more men lay dead in the bloody snow. And then, as suddenly as they had arrived, the planes hummed away into the distance, the sound of their engines fading at last to nothing. Aldo picked himself up and looked around. He saw Luigi stumbling about, tripping over a broken body and falling into the snow. Luigi remained there on his hands and knees, head down, and as Aldo reached him he heard him whimpering.

'My eyes, my eyes,' Luigi was saying, his fingers pushing and probing around the edges of the sockets. 'God, I can't see. Help me. Help me.'

'Look at me Luigi, look at me,' Aldo shouted.

'How can I fucking look at you, you fucking idiot?' Luigi said as he lifted his head, and Aldo saw that his eyes had gone and his cheeks ran with blood, black specks embedded all over his face.

'Help me, Aldo. You will help me, won't you? How am I ever going to make it home when I can't even see where I'm going?'

Aldo wiped Luigi's blood away with handfuls of snow but the eyes overflowed again, so he found a dirty bandage and wound it around Luigi's head, then took a length of rope from the pack of a dead man and tied one end around Luigi's waist and the other around his own, and he led him off to find Gianni and the sergeant.

In the interminable depths of another night on the steppe the shapes of *izbas* came to them through the blizzard. The sergeant strode towards the huts, head down, a stubborn bull in a field. No stopping him, it seemed, and Aldo followed in his steps, Luigi trailing at the end of the rope, Gianni bringing up the rear. The sergeant banged on the door of the first *izba* and the door inched ajar. Through the crack Aldo saw a helmet with the proud cockerel feathers of the Bersaglieri, a pair of eyes peering out from under it.

'Fuck off, no room in here,' came the voice. 'We're already packed in like sardines. Try the houses further down.'

The door slammed shut and they moved on. The scene repeated itself again and again, only the expletives varying. Finally Aldo hammered on the door of the last hut, set back from the others at the end of the village, then kicked it open and tumbled in, Luigi following him at the end of the rope, smacking his head on the doorframe as he went in, and the sergeant pushing past Gianni and Gianni swearing and trying to pull the door closed behind them. Aldo looked around at the small kitchen, smoke from a black stove in the corner thickening the air. There were no Italians here. Three figures sat around a table in the middle of the room, two men and a woman, the woman looking over her shoulder towards the new arrivals, a look of surprise on her face; the other two, Russian soldiers, sat in their white winter coats, one still wearing his helmet, the other holding a spoon between bowl and mouth. An iron pot steamed in the middle of the table. Fuck me, thought Aldo, here we go. This is it. But then he saw the Russians' guns, propped together against the far wall, out of reach. Oh God, what now? Let's shoot the fuckers, Massimo had said, Gianni too. But no, let's not shoot anyone, Aldo. Calm yourself now. He saw the Russians looking at him, at his rifle, and he could hear the wind behind him, blowing great flakes of snow into the room.

'Well, if you're coming in, then shut the fucking door,' said one of the Russians, resuming his meal as the orange light of the stove set his face ablaze. An Asian face, Aldo thought, like so many he had seen, dead ones, usually, no other way to get this close to them. Until now.

'And if you're not coming in, then fuck off and shut the door on your way out,' said the other, a younger man, his face like an angel's but his eyes black and cold like the coal eyes of a snowman.

Aldo carefully propped his rifle against the wall and Gianni pulled the door shut and the sergeant looked more nervous than Aldo had ever seen him. The woman offered them chairs and they sat down, Luigi still holding on to his rope.

'Funny place to be taking a dog for a walk,' said one of the Russians, pointing at the rope. 'Woof, woof!' And he laughed.

'What's he saying, Aldo?'

'Nothing, Luigi. Nothing at all.'

The woman ladled soup into a bowl, placed it in front of them, and fetched four more spoons. Aldo breathed in the cabbage aroma. He lifted a spoon towards Luigi's mouth, then took a spoonful for himself. The woman passed him a cup, beautifully clean, blue flowers on white. She motioned him to fill it with soup and pass it to Luigi.

'*Spasiba*,' said Aldo.

'You speak Russian?' said the man with the Asiatic features.

Aldo nodded.

'You speak Russian but you wear an Italian uniform? I'd call that an unnatural combination.'

'I'm Italian. What sort of uniform do you want me to wear?'

The younger Russian looked at the intruders with his snowman's eyes.

'You know,' he said with sudden venom. 'I saw something one night, back home in Leningrad, before the war. I was walking through a park one night and there were these stray dogs, big rough ones, almost wild, like wolves. And they'd found this cat, cornered it in the bushes, and they got it between them and they shook it to pieces, ripped it apart, like this . . .'

The Russian growled and bared his teeth, took his hand in his mouth and shook it, bits of soup flying about as he re-enacted the cat's demise.

'And when they'd killed it they just left it there and went on their way, to look for another one, no doubt. You know what dogs are like when they're together. And every day after that for a month I walked through the park and I saw that cat's body, and every day it had changed. Every day it had shrunk just a bit, rotted just a little bit more. And that's what's happening to you, isn't it? Every day a little bit more. We take you and shake you, rip you to pieces, and every day you are less and we are more, and one day there will be nothing left of you but a stain on the ground where we left you. But we won't be able to just go on our way again like those dogs, because when we've pushed you all out of the Motherland, we'll take your country and we'll tear it to pieces too, and every day you'll walk past what used to be your home and you'll see it slowly disappear, smaller and smaller every day in front of your eyes, and there'll be nothing at all you can do about it. And then, when it's all gone, and you have nothing left to lose, then you'll know you should never have come here.'

'Nice story,' said Aldo.

The man hurled his spoon across the table at Aldo.

'Oh, ignore him,' said the other Russian. 'He's just upset because he got shot yesterday. Come on, Aleksandr, don't be shy. Show them your wound.'

The younger Russian lifted his arm and placed his hand on the table. He peeled back the grubby bandage and Aldo saw the bloody mess beneath.

'Two fingers I lost,' said the Russian. 'I've got them in my pocket. They're still fucking frozen. Do you want to see them?'

He took out a little bundle stained red and brown with blood. He pulled it open and two grey stubby lumps, black grime beneath the nails, tumbled out onto the table.

'Look at those fucking things!' he yelled, and he picked them up and hurled them one after the other at Aldo.

'Come on, that's no way to behave at the table,' said the older man.

'Fuck that! Look at my fucking hand!'

The woman went over and picked the fingers up off the floor and put them back on the table beside the young Russian.

'Put them back in your pocket, now,' she said. 'Stop talking rubbish and eat your soup.'

'Fuck my soup!' he yelled.

'My bowl's empty,' said the older man.

She refilled their bowls and suddenly there was silence as they ate.

'Maybe we should go and find somewhere else to sleep,' said Aldo when they had finished.

'Where are you going to find room now?' said the older man. 'All the other *izbas* will be packed full of your pals. You'll die out there in the cold. Stay here. There's plenty of room for us all.'

'Yes, and we'll slit your throats while you sleep,' said the younger man. 'Here, listen, listen, let me read you this.' He pulled a tattered page, torn from an old edition of *Red Star*, from his tunic. 'Listen, listen. Do not count days; do not count miles. Count only the number of Germans you have killed! Kill the German – this is your mother's prayer! Kill the German – this is the cry of your Russian earth! Do not waiver! Do not let up! Kill!'

'Yes,' said Aldo, 'but we're Italian.'

The older Russian laughed out loud, a raucous rumbling rolling laugh. The woman raised a cautious eyebrow.

'Do you think I give a fuck? Italians, Germans, you're all the fucking same!' yelled the younger man, hammering the tabletop with his wounded hand, sending the severed fingers leaping into the air again. He howled with pain and grabbed the fingers and hurled them one by one into the stove and banged his forehead up and down on the table and wept deep noisy sobs as the woman put her arms around him and whispered futile consolations in his ear.

'Seriously, though. Stay here for the night,' said the older Russian. 'Let's take a pause from the war, just for a few hours.'

So they stayed. The kitchen was the warmest room in the house and they slept on the rug on the floor, beneath the table, as close to the stove as they could get, the older Russian nearest the source of the heat, then the younger one, then the woman laying herself down between the men, a civilising buffer to stop the bloodshed, not wanting to mop men's blood from her floor again in the night, then Aldo and Luigi and Gianni and the sergeant. They lay in the darkness, seven bodies sharing each other's warmth, while the last embers of the fire fought back the cold that slipped in under the door. Several times in the night Aldo felt movement beside him, but it was just the woman rising to place another piece of wood in the stove, then lying down again quickly between the men as they slept. And in the silence outside, the snow continued to fall and the rest of the column continued to struggle through the night beyond the far end of the village, unaware of the *izbas* that lay just out of sight in the blizzard. When Aldo woke, dragged cold and aching from the brief refuge of sleep, the Russians had gone and the woman was heating milk.

'When did they leave?' he asked.

'Before dawn. The young one really did want to cut your throats, you know. It's only the older one that stopped him.'

'And you?'

'There's been enough blood spilt in this house already. Now drink your milk, boys, and take your guns and go. And don't ever come back.'

So they drank their milk and they took their guns and they left. The snow had stopped and the sky had cleared. They walked up through the village in the half-light of dawn and they rejoined the column and trudged again towards home under an endless dome of frozen sky.

On a dark and foggy night in February the Russians came at them in a vast swathe of tanks and men. Aldo ran and ran as the tanks hammered through and he found himself alone in the eerie night, the sound of the fighting some way behind him now. The rope hung limp from his waist, severed by something he hadn't seen.

'Luigi!' he shouted. 'Luigi! Where are you?'

'Shut the fuck up!' came the immediate response, the sergeant somewhere nearby in the fog. 'Shut the fuck up or you'll get us all killed!'

Aldo called out again.

'Shut up, damn you! You won't find him now.'

'Fuck! Fuck!' shouted Aldo, and he tore off what remained of the rope.

Then Gianni's voice, coming nearer. 'Which way from here, sergeant?'

'Fuck knows,' said the sergeant, as Aldo and Gianni made their way to him. 'Anyone got a compass?'

No one had a compass.

'I don't believe it, stuck out here in this fucking fog and we don't even know which way we're meant to be going.'

They walked for hours, seemingly in a straight line but probably around in circles. Aldo followed the sergeant, watching his back in the gloom, step after step into the night, then looking down at his own feet for a while, kicking up the snow as he walked. Occasionally in the distance he heard the sound of an engine or a burst of gunfire or the plaintive roar of a tank in the night answered by a scream, but he couldn't tell from which direction any of it was coming. Then he heard a tank's gears grinding in the fog. He crouched down with the others and silently prayed. The noise grew until it seemed that the tank must be nearly upon them and then it passed just yards away and began to disappear again into the gloom. The sergeant stood up and ran after it, looking over his shoulder and yelling back at the others, 'Come on, you two! It's a Panzer!'

Aldo stood up and ran after him, stumbling and slipping over the frozen ground, desperate for a free ride to somewhere else, anywhere but here, anything preferable to wandering through the night just waiting to be picked off by a Russian patrol. The hatch on the hull of the tank was flung open and a head rose up like a skull from a tomb. The skull began to shout at them in German, gesturing them up onto the back of the beast, and they hurried after it and pulled themselves aboard. They spent the rest of the night huddled together upon its freezing hull, and as daylight dispersed the fog, Aldo saw the interminable white steppe stretching out all around him, looking as if it could swallow the world.

'Where are we going, sergeant?' asked Gianni.

'Fuck knows,' said the sergeant. He looked up at the pale sun. 'But we're heading west, boys. We're heading towards home.'

In mid-afternoon their tank met up with a column of German armour.

'Izium? Izium?' said the tank commander to the men crouched on the hull.

'Do we want to go to Izium?' said Aldo.

'Where the fuck's Izium?' said Gianni.

'Fuck knows,' said the sergeant. 'But what the hell, let's all go to Izium. It's sure to be a laugh.'

Towards the end of the day the Panzer left Aldo and Gianni and the sergeant somewhere in the outskirts of Izium, where hundreds of Germans were setting up a defensive line. A man in a filthy uniform came over and started shouting at them. They looked at each other, then back at the German's beetroot face. Eventually he left them, still shouting to himself as he walked away.

'What the hell did he want?' said Gianni.

'Who cares? We don't take orders from bloody Germans,' said the sergeant. 'We're Italian, so I give the orders round here.'

'All right, then, so where now, sergeant?' said Aldo.

'Fucked if I know,' said the sergeant, and they laughed.

'Seriously, sergeant, what are we going to do now? There'll be fighting here soon. Do we really want to join in again with all that?'

'Yes,' said Gianni. 'What on earth are we doing here? We should never have left the column.'

'What column?' said the sergeant. 'There is no bloody column, not now, not after last night.'

'But what about all the others? They must still be out there somewhere.'

'Sure they are. The dead ones. And the prisoners. Come on, let's find some food. There are bound to be more like us round here somewhere.'

Aldo looked at the gutted buildings and the blackened brick chimneys as they walked. Then he heard music and as they turned a corner he saw a group of Germans in the ruins of a building, huddled around an upright piano covered in dust, its top strewn with stone and brick. A medic was sweetening the air with the sounds of Chopin, Mahler and Brahms as others stood around him and stole back a few minutes of their lives. Aldo listened, his eyes lost in a far-off personal place, the music transporting him back home to Venice, and in this way the doctor cured, if just for a few moments, a small part of the pain that had built up inside him. Aldo looked at the man's hands as he played, long fine fingers, delicate hands, not so much those of a soldier as a surgeon, and he thought about how, when the shells rained back down, the doctor would go down again into the cellars, down among the rats to repair the broken bodies of men, and up on the surface of the earth a shell might fall close beside the piano and it would disintegrate in a shower of keys and wood and wire, and its final note would be one of jarring and conflict drowned out by the noise of the bombs and the dying.

And sure enough, the attack soon came, and Aldo and the others fell straight in with the Germans. The nights were punctuated with bright white and orange flares and when the sun rose over the buildings, soldiers who had spent the night hunting down Russian patrols slid back to their positions among the ruins. They resumed their patrols when night returned, when everything was dark and confused and the crack of gunfire echoed around the wasteland. And then, eerily close, Aldo heard the roar of a tank and then the artillery started up, the Russian shells landing in waves that swept across the lines and sent the cowardly and the brave alike diving into shell-holes, wide-eyed with fear, a pushing, shoving herd, and when the bombardment finally stopped, the Russian tanks were there, the dark shapes of men all around them. The shattered defenders flung themselves once more in desperation at their guns and amid the chaos and the noise a tank was hit, then another, blocking the advance, and at last Aldo saw the Russians pulling back and he slipped where he lay into something like sleep, only to be prodded awake again by an irate man lying next to him, shouting something at him that he did not understand. So Aldo sneaked away into a cellar and lay down there with the dead and the dying until he was woken again by the skeletal hand of someone hungry for his own temporary oblivion, telling him to get up and take his place out there in the world, and so he went back out again and looked out to where the fires still burned and some lost soul still groaned his life away in no-man's land.

It went on that way for what seemed like ages, and then the Germans pulled out and Aldo was left among hundreds of men trapped in a pocket on the edge of town. In the watery light of a February dawn the Russian tanks reached them and Aldo and Gianni and the sergeant cast aside their weapons and the last of their hope. As he scrambled out of the trench that had been fashioned out of rubble, Aldo saw the Russians close up for the first time since that night in the *izba* in the snow, but this time there was no sharing of soup, no civilising influence of a peasant and her stove, just the hard eyes of men who had been fighting too long. He saw the red stars on their caps, the padded jackets of their uniforms, insulating them from the cold in a way his worn-out coat could no longer do, and the blue-black metal shine of the barrels of their guns and a man with a bayonet as long as his arm. The man shoved his rifle butt into Gianni and then into the sergeant and he was about to do the same to Aldo when Aldo shouted something at him in Russian.

'What did you say?' the man said. 'You a *hiwi*? We shoot traitors here!'

And he lifted his rifle and pressed the tip of the bayonet against Aldo's chest, holding it there, and there was fear in Aldo's mouth, a sudden taste of iron filings.

'I'm no traitor,' he shouted back. 'I'm Italian! Italian!'

And he heard the sergeant shouting at him too, then Gianni, a torrent of words. He snapped back at them, desperate, not knowing what to say, and the Italian words tumbling from his mouth saved him, the Russian withdrawing the bayonet and hitting him instead with the rifle butt. Aldo got up and stumbled back, falling several yards away, and the sergeant and Gianni were around him and the Russian's attention was distracted by another scuffle away to one side.

They hurried away towards a larger group: safety in numbers. Blend in with the others, Aldo thought. This is the last place on earth you'd want to stand out from the crowd. The prisoners shoaled together and stood around waiting, the hours dragging by until the long march back east started up, the long march home in reverse, retracing the steps of the previous weeks, and with each step Aldo felt the whole panorama of pain, not just the bruises where they had hit him but also the ache of exhaustion, and the hunger and the cold, and the agony of hopelessness where previously some faint hope had been.

They walked in long lines, the guards constantly urging them forward with 'Davai! Davai!', Aldo walking behind the sergeant, then Gianni behind Aldo, almost out of habit, their usual formation, watching the motion of the boots of the one in front, and the occasional sound of someone nearby collapsing in the snow, a soft thumping noise of a man too weak to go on, who no doubt would lie there in the wilderness until the animals spread his bones across the steppe. At night they were allowed to stop and rest, but there was no shelter, no *izbas*, no hope, nothing but the snow and the ice and the wind. The ice froze so hard and so brittle that Aldo heard it split like glass, puncturing the night with the sharp crack of its breaking. To lie down would be to die, so the men stood together like horses in a field, sleeping on their feet, each propped up by those around him. Those on the inside of the huddle stole most of the shared warmth and each night someone who had been clinging to the outside of the group would topple over and in the morning they would see him lying frozen and stiff as a board on the ground.

The Russian spring came early that year, and the snow turned to rain and the ice turned to mud and the land became a great mire of water, but the prisoners continued their march, ever slower in the quagmire, and one morning it was the sergeant – and his glorious victory, the start of a new empire – whom Aldo saw lying cold and dead and heavy in the mud. As Aldo and Gianni set off again a heavy rain fell and when Aldo looked back the sergeant's body was just one more muddy contour on the surface of the earth, and when he turned again he couldn't even tell which of the contours was the sergeant.

As he trudged on, Aldo dwelt on how one day some peasant might till the earth and find the sergeant's bones, and one day probably Aldo's too, and as bones bear neither flag nor uniform, the *muzhik* would not know whether to curse them or consecrate them, and so instead he would consider them for a moment and then cast them aside and continue to sow the seeds that would tide him through another endless winter on the steppe.

They came to the outskirts of a small town where thousands of men stood in the mud, penned into barbed-wire enclosures. Aldo could no longer distinguish between the nationalities of the prisoners – Italians, Hungarians, Romanians, mostly Germans – as their uniforms were all caked with the same filth that lay for hundreds of miles around them and they hid themselves beneath whatever extra clothing they had been able to steal during the retreat, swathing their heads in rags wrapped like shrouds. Aldo and Gianni sat in the mud and waited. Aldo watched as a man took a fragment of mirror from the pocket of his tunic and tried to reflect the weak sunlight onto his face, magnifying the sun's feeble rays, then turning away as if disgusted at his own reflection. Aldo turned to a small group of Italians a few feet away. One man sat leaning forward, his arms hooked around his knees, his chin resting on his wrists. He was staring at Aldo.

'He's dead, of course,' said another man. 'Can't you tell just by looking at him? He was talking to me just now, and he stopped right bang in the middle of a sentence. See, his mouth is still half open.'

'Oh, yes, you're right,' said Aldo. 'He's certainly dead.'

'You know what the last thing he said was?' said the man. 'We were sitting here in all this mud, and you know what he said?'

'What did he say?' said Gianni.

'He said . . . you'll never believe this . . . he said the most beautiful thing he ever saw was the Pantheon in a snowstorm. Can you believe that? He spends all winter out here in the snow, and the most beautiful thing he's ever seen is the Pantheon in a snowstorm. Isn't that just fucking nuts? I mean, how often does it snow in Rome anyway?'

'I used to live right next to the Pantheon,' said Gianni. 'My mum and dad still have a little flat right next to it, just down from that statue of the elephant, you know, the one they built with its arse pointing towards the church. When it rained I used to look out and watch the water pouring off the walls, floods of it, and all the people below hurrying to get out of the rain, their ice cream falling into the road, all pinks and whites and yellows, and sometimes that pale-orange melon flavour, you know the one? All washed away in the rain . . .'

The man shivered at the thought of it, then smiled wistfully. 'I'm Pietro, by the way,' he said, and they shook hands, pressing their bones against each other.

'It's a pleasure,' said Aldo. 'Well, you know what I mean . . .'

'After the war,' Pietro went on, 'after the war, the two of you must come to my house, all right? In Umbria. And I'll show you what a good Umbrian girl can do when she's in the mood.'

'I can't wait,' said Gianni.

'I was a postman, you know,' said Pietro. 'Back home in Umbria. A decent job, something you could look up to. A uniform and everything.'

'Who wants a fucking uniform?' said Gianni. 'After all this.'

'Well, I did then,' said Pietro. 'And I looked great in it, the colour really suited me. I used to get all these looks. And it had the nicest buttons! And, lucky me, I used to deliver to the farms and there was this girl, she had the best smile you ever saw. Used to give me milk. Warm it was, straight from the pail. Then one day she took me into a field of poppies, and she popped open those buttons and we popped ourselves out of our clothes, you know, as you do . . .'

'Yes, as you do,' said Aldo, and he was suddenly thinking of Isabella.

'Yes, just as nature intended, and we lay there all day in the sun, in the grass, told each other jokes and stupid stories. And her beautiful white skin, lying beside me in the sun . . .'

And Aldo dwelt on the thought of Isabella, of her lying there beside him in her bed, the warmth of her, in the darkness of her room in the silence of the night.

'. . . and this girl, in the sunshine, just looking at me, and the poppies and those little yellow flowers, the ones you get in spring-time. I can still smell her hands, warm milk and cows' udders.'

He sniffed his filth-caked hands and tears welled up in his bloodshot eyes. 'We got married last year.'

'Congratulations,' said Aldo.

'Thank you,' said Pietro, pulling back his tears.

'Any little ones?'

'One on the way when I left. A boy, as it turns out. I had a photo. Looks just like his dad, the wife says.'

'Must be a good-looking devil,' said Aldo.

'Oh yes, I guess he must be.' Pietro laughed, tears all over his face now as he wiped at them with muddy hands. There was mud all over his face too now, but it seemed that he hardly noticed it, and why on earth would he care? They all looked the same now anyway. He just sat there, looking glum, looking away towards the horizon, looking towards the west. Most people usually looked that way round here, thought Aldo, given the choice.

They sat in the mud for the rest of the day and every so often more prisoners blew in with the rain that came in off the steppe in squalls. During the night they heard the whistle of a train, then again, and then the sound of its engine again as it drew off into the night with its haul of men. Finally it was their turn and they stood together in the mud beside the track. The doors of the cattle trucks were pulled back and they clambered in, grey-faced commuters off to the suburbs of hell. The doors were slammed shut, and Aldo, Gianni and Pietro stood pressed up together, no space to sit down, each man standing in his square foot of space, leaning against the shoulder of another who in turn leant against the next, and the last one leant against the wooden wall of the train, and the train moved off and the men swayed. No one spoke and no one slept and time slipped by on endless rails and Aldo's legs went numb. After a day and a night the train slowed and then stopped, and Aldo stumbled out and fell to the ground and shook life back into his limbs. In the distance, to the east, always east, he could see a large village and then the confused line of the horizon, the steppe merging into a dark blur of forest beneath a watercolour sky. Aldo found Gianni and Pietro and helped them to their feet, and the three of them stood leaning against each other again in the watery sunshine of spring. Then the guards came round and shoved at them and the column gathered again and began to inch its way towards the forest and the barbed wire and the watchtowers that awaited them.

The Prisoner

Aldo lay on the concrete floor of the bunker, his stomach aching and empty, his body wracked with cramps. He stared up towards the ceiling but it was too dark to see it. No light would get in until the guards hurled the door open at six, and the ceiling wasn't much to write home about anyway – just branches and packed earth. But you certainly wouldn't worry about the craftsmanship, Aldo thought, not from his perspective now, down here on the floor, staring up at it, just wanting to sleep. A roof over his head, that was all, and at least it was that. And he certainly didn't care what wood it was, not now, not these days. He couldn't care less. Probably some fucking Russian wood, he thought, birch or larch or something like that. Rough bunks lined every wall but even with three or four men to each rotten mattress there was never enough room and the floor was covered with sleeping bodies, piled together for warmth. Aldo sniffed, then regretted it. You didn't want to go breathing in too deeply here, not this pungent rot – vomit and dysentery and the smell of feet that had been too long in damp and mud-filled boots. You couldn't leave the bunkers during the hours of darkness, so you just had to breathe it in, just had to live with it, and the smell was strongest towards dawn when you could hardly bear it any longer. When the bunker door was finally unlocked, Aldo would be the first out, gulping down the air that blew in from the Urals, looking around him as he did so at the other prisoners who were doing the same, grey ghosts loitering on the fringes of existence, their eyes hungry and raw. Aldo had eaten nothing for a week now and it felt as if his stomach had shrunk to the size of a walnut. It ached constantly.

He and Gianni and Pietro had survived on the rainwater that collected in a barrel under a downpipe. They spent the few minutes before work began sitting on the ground outside in the sun doing nothing, saying little. When they spoke, it was usually to bitch about the other prisoners, or the guards.

'The Hungarians are the worst,' said Gianni, drawing out his words, tiredness elongating them, the growing weakness that Aldo had noticed in Gianni's speech since they arrived at the camp. Soon he would be nodding off again, unannounced and sudden, just like yesterday and the day before that.

'The Hungarians?' said Pietro. 'What about the Germans? It's their fucking fault we're here in the first place.'

'It's *Il Duce*'s fucking fault we're here,' said Aldo. 'Don't you hate him most of all?'

'Didn't use to. Do now.'

'Snap,' said Gianni.

'Or the Russians,' said Pietro. 'The fucking guards. Why can't they bring us some food? I could eat a horse, and I'm not bloody exaggerating.'

'I'd eat anything,' said Gianni. 'A rat, even.'

'Or a hedgehog?' said Pietro.

'Definitely. Spines and all.'

'And a mole?'

'Of course. I'd eat one raw, no problem at all. I'd even eat worms if I could find any of the fuckers.'

'I'd eat the hand off the end of my wrist,' said Aldo. 'And then I'd eat my arm.'

He glanced over towards a group of men sitting nearby, the ones who had been in the camp since the beginning, who had claimed the top bunks where the body heat of others drifted up in the cold of the night. There was something about them, something he hadn't been able to put his finger on. But now he saw it – oh yes, he saw it now, they'd eat the hand off the end of your wrist, and then they'd eat your arm – and he recognised them for what they were, saw it for what it was, that subtly different look, a spark glinting in their eyes, eyes that were as desperate and crazed as all the others, but somewhere in their depths was the worm of stolen hope and he could see it now and it twitched and it squirmed. He'd noticed them in the burial area, always eager to usher away the dead ones, preparing them, seeing to it that they had a burial but exacting a price for it, a price of which the dead knew nothing and from which the living averted their eyes. Until now. Aldo had seen it; their cheeks were blushing a confession. He stood up and took a pace or two towards them.

'I know what you're up to!' he yelled at them. 'Keep away from me, you bastards! Keep away from me. And from my friends!'

They looked at him, threatening, nothing too much, just an obvious confidence in what they could do to him if no one stopped them. And no one would. He hurried back to where Gianni and Pietro were sitting. Gianni's eyes were closed now, tripping around the edges of sleep. They would want him soon if he carried on like this. They would have him. He shoved Gianni's arm and Gianni woke up and then his eyes slipped shut again. Pietro was staring into the distance now, turning away from reality again, wanting none of it. Every day he got worse, more sudden lapses into gibberish, and he was raving now, in a whisper, and Aldo was going to snap him out of it, snap him back into the world.

'Pietro, listen! We have to keep an eye on Gianni.'

'Yes, I know. Keep an eye on Gianni. We must keep an eye on Gianni. Keep an eye on Gianni.'

'No, listen, Pietro! Listen to me!'

'What?'

'I mean we have to keep a good eye on him.'

'Oh, yes, we do. I know.'

'He's too weak, Pietro. They might take him.'

'Yes, they might take him. They might take him. Who might take him?'

'Haven't you noticed?'

'Yes, I've noticed. Noticed what?'

'Look at that lot over there. Look at their faces. Don't you see?'

'Yes, I see.'

'What do you see, Pietro? What do you see? Look at them closely.'

'Yes, I see.'

'What do you see, damn it?'

'Come on, Aldo, don't shout at me. I'm tired.'

'Look at them, damn you! Can't you see they're not dying? Can't you see it? Why aren't they dying?'

'Why aren't they dying?'

'Yes, why aren't they dying?'

'They aren't dying? Why the fuck not?'

'Because they're eating them.'

'Them?'

'The dead. They're eating the dead.'

'No.'

'Look at the colour in their cheeks. Where do you think they get that from?'

'Please don't shout at me, Aldo.' Pietro turned his head away.

'Do you know what goes on in the other bunkers, Pietro? Have you been in them? Have you seen the dead being buried, up close?'

'Not recently.'

'I mean here, not out there, not before. Here, here at the camp.'

Pietro shook his head.

'So how do you know they bury the whole body? Maybe they take a piece first, slice a bit off, here and there, cover it up, bury the evidence. Or eat it!'

'No, no, I haven't heard anyone mention anything like that. Nothing at all.'

'But who would tell us? They probably all know what's going on.'

'No, no, impossible, ridiculous. I was a postman in Umbria, you know.'

Aldo stood up and began to shout, 'Cannibals, fucking cannibals!'

He walked across to the group of men again. 'Who did you have for dinner last night? Taste good, did he? Taste good, you sick bastards?'

A guard walked over and pushed Aldo away, and he went back to Gianni and Pietro and forced them up and pulled them a few yards away, behind a maintenance hut, and sat them down there and watched as they closed their eyes, and then he shut his own and breathed in the air and listened as Pietro talked nonsense about Umbria. *Nothing makes sense, Aldo, nothing makes sense. Remember that, and you'll always be all right.* How right she had been, he thought, wise old Isabella. If only he could be with her now, that would help, it certainly would. But he would never see her again, not now. He was sure of that, not a chance. Make the most of me while you can, she had said, but he hadn't, not really. Too many thoughts getting in the way when he was with her, too many moments wasted. If he ever got the chance again he would remember that, he would make sure he made the most of his time with her, every second of it.

That night he lay closer than usual to Gianni and listened to the sound of his breathing, irregular and hoarse, imagining it was Isabella's heart that rose and fell beneath him, his head on Gianni's chest in the dark as it rose and fell in time with his breathing, and he recalled the waves of Venice and its lagoon and the boats of his life rising on swells and sinking into troughs: his grandfather's fishing boat; the launch that took him and Luca and Massimo and his dad to Mestre for that last hunting trip; and the one that carried Luca to the cemetery on San Michele in the rain; the gondola nodding its approval beneath the arched windows of Isabella's room; the *vaporetto* that stole him away to war; and the fishing boats of the carefree years of his youth, now down in the silt that life left behind as it washed everything away downstream. He listened to the sound of Gianni's heart until its rhythmic beating filled his head and became the only sound in the universe, wiping away the grunts and moans of the weak and dying men who lay all around him in the shallow grave of sleep. The next night Gianni's heart beat more faintly still and by morning he was dead. The vultures of the camp had gathered, alerted by some dark instinct, and when Aldo flicked open his eyes he saw them perched on an adjacent bunk.

'He's gone,' one of them said when he saw Aldo looking. 'Let us take him and bury him.'

'He's my friend, not yours,' said Aldo, guessing what they meant.

'But you're too weak.'

And then Aldo really woke up and he threw himself at them, thrashing at them with his arms. The vultures flapped about, backed away towards the door, but others came in from behind and hauled up Gianni's limp body as Aldo wheeled around, striking out, held from behind by someone as they carried Gianni outside.

'Stop! Stop!' Aldo screamed, and he saw Pietro slumped in the corner, staring out through wide vacant eyes.

'I was a postman in Umbria,' he was saying. 'I was a postman in Umbria. And what a uniform, what buttons I had!'

'Pietro! Wake up! Help me! They've taken Gianni.'

'I was a postman in Umbria, you know. A person of dignity.'

Aldo stumbled outside but there was no sign of Gianni now. He crashed in through the door of the nearest bunker. 'Where is he? Where have they taken him?'

The men looked back at him in the half-light, passive as a flock of sheep. He rushed into the next bunker, then the next, and then he found one with its door wedged shut and he banged and yelled and bestial voices bellowed back at him from inside. The guards, hearing the noise, hurried up and dragged Aldo away as he screamed out his accusations in Russian.

'Not again!' said one of the guards. 'Animals.'

'Pigs,' said another.

They hammered down the door and dragged the cannibals out, leaving Gianni's body stretched out like a banquet on the floor, knife wounds in his thighs, toothmarks on his arms, his blood running in streams across the concrete floor. The guards took the guilty men out through the gate and to a patch of bare earth and ordered them to dig a pit in the ground. The men looked at Aldo as he dug Gianni's grave beside them and he was afraid they would lift their spades high and split his head open in a final futile act of barbarism, but the guards were standing close and the vultures were not yet certain enough of their own fate to act, and when they were finally certain, it was too late, because when the men had dug a hole that the guards deemed large enough, they shot the men and kicked their bodies in. Aldo continued to dig Gianni's grave and a guard stood and watched him digging, and then the guard helped him to lower Gianni into the ground.

'Was he a good friend?' asked the Russian.

'The only one I had left,' said Aldo.

'A good one, then.'

They walked back into the camp together, the guard locking the gate behind them.

'Couldn't you just leave that gate open for me one day? Just for a moment? Turn a blind eye, let me go.'

The guard looked at him, uncertain. For a moment it almost looked as if he was considering it. 'But they'd shoot me too if I did that,' he said. 'I'm just as much a prisoner here as you.'

That night Aldo lay down in a small space on the floor and pressed his ear to the ground. The concrete lay silent and cold beneath him. He pulled back his sleeve and looked into the eyes of the pig on his arm, its eyes burning bright in the night, and he seized it in his teeth and shook it until it bled and then he wiped its bloody tears away, and all he heard was a humming in his head as the spinning earth spun him into a black sleep.

Two days later, food began to arrive at the camp. Too late for Gianni, Aldo thought. Sod the lot of them, why couldn't they have sorted things out sooner? Bloody bureaucrats, somewhere comfortable behind the lines with their requisition sheets and their systems. At first there was just bread, stale crusts and offcuts, barely more than a mosaics of green spores. Aldo chiselled it down with yellowing teeth until the pain of it stopped him, then he softened it in the barrel of water beneath the downpipe and cursed the crumbs that broke away and lost themselves in the water. He spent long hours now by the perimeter fence, staring out at the woods, taking his lump of bread and sucking at the corners, savouring the taste, rolling the hard lumps around in his mouth until they disintegrated on his tongue, sucking at the grit and the dust, ignoring the mould, letting his mind carry him away over the horizon. He spoke to no one now. He didn't understand the Germans or the Hungarians or the

Romanians, or whatever the hell they were, and the guards ignored him. He couldn't be bothered to get to know any of the other Italians now – there were thousands of them, but what was the point? They'd all be dead soon anyway. And Pietro spent his days curled up in a corner facing the wall, chucking out random utterances in Umbrian dialect, so Aldo's conversation was limited to brief exchanges of views with the tattooed thing that lived on his arm. As Aldo looked out past the wire, unblinking, the world lost itself behind a film of images that rolled before his eyes, and occasionally he would almost smile at the sight of a fond memory from what seemed like another lifetime. Towards dark he would return to his place on the floor of the bunker, where he closed his eyes and tried to conjure up the images again, but in the dark oppressive confines, among the groans and the moans and the bodies, his mind could not see beyond the darkness and instead he thought of Fausto Pozzi, and his greatest fear was suddenly that he would never see the bloody man again, but then the wild pig that the war had almost purged from his mind winked at him in the night and Aldo winked back, and they quietly reconsummated their love in the blackest corner of his heart, the only part of him that still had the strength to carry on.

Hope

Katerina stood in the sunlight of a Russian spring and watched the man behind the wire. She had seen him the other day for the first time, then again yesterday, leaning against the wire as if testing its strength. She glanced up at the guards standing in their watchtower and wondered if they might react. But they seemed happy to ignore him. She was glad about that, at least – you never knew what they might do, she had heard the rumours about what went on in there. And then it occurred to her, the thought that had been welling up in her since the first time she saw him – she might save him, somehow. One good deed, one person to another, something he might always remember her by. She took a couple of steps forward, tentative, keeping an eye out for the guards again. Poor man, she thought, as she saw him up close now, a bit off to the side still. What a mess, standing there, eyes closed, as if in a dream. Then his eyelids snapped open and for some reason she flinched. But he didn't seem to notice her, just went on staring, out towards the woods. She heard the sound of someone digging at the ground behind her, breathing hard, hacking at the ground with a spade. Then the sound of a fly buzzing in past her, homing in on the smell of the man behind the wire, no doubt. She saw him flap at it, flailing, but he failed, the thing lifting up again and buzzing off behind him, then going quiet, setting itself down somewhere she could not see, out of his reach now. They were clever like that, she thought, these bugs, and too many of them to count – there would never be an end to them. Different bugs, these ones, more hungry than the ones back home in Leningrad. His eyes were closing again now and she stepped towards him again, soft and hesitant, the sound of her footsteps right in front of him now, then a breath from her as she reached out to him and touched his hand. His eyes opened wide and she withdrew her touch.

'I'm so sorry,' she said. 'I didn't mean to startle you.'

She looked into his eyes and she saw it in them now, that look, the look she had always loved, an unexpected recognition, something hatching up from nothing, as if he already knew her, as if he always had, or perhaps she reminded him of a friend, somebody just like her, someone he had loved.

Suddenly her hand was in her pocket, digging around for something, then pulling it out, a rabbit from a hat for him, a little piece of magic, her small white hand holding a dark piece of bread. And what a trick it was, how it made her feel, how it filled her leaping heart to be here, helping him, saving him, giving him a part of her.

'Have this,' she said, twisting her hand between the strands of wire, catching her skin on one of the barbs. Up rose a tiny sphere of blood, red on the white of her hand.

'I'm so sorry,' he said, at the sight of the blood, it seemed, as if he were somehow to blame for wounding her.

'For what?' she said, wiping it away. 'You've done nothing wrong.'

The wind carried her words away across the steppe.

'Go on, take it. It's not exactly fresh, but I'm sure it's better than what you get in there.'

He reached out and took the gift, lifted it to his lips, bit off a piece of it.

'Thank you,' he said at last.

She moved her lips, something uncertain, a kind of smile, remembering something she wanted to keep hidden. They stood there, the two of them, on the edge of wilderness.

'I might come and see you again tomorrow,' she said. 'If you want me to?'

'Oh,' he said. 'Yes, I would like that very much.'

'Good,' she said. 'Then I'll do just that.'

She turned to go, then stopped. 'You know, I feel so sorry for you,' she said, then paused. 'Well, I'll see you tomorrow.'

'Yes,' he said. 'Yes . . . but . . . what's your name?'

'I'll tell you that tomorrow.'

'Tell me now. In case you don't come back.'

'Don't worry, I will come back.'

'Tell me anyway. Please. Just in case.'

She looked at him. 'Katerina,' she said.

'What a beautiful name,' he said, but she was turning away again. 'Katerina, wait!'

She turned again.

'Have this,' he said.

He was holding something in his hand and she reached out and took it. A little wooden fish.

'I carved it myself,' he said. 'A long time ago. When I was at home.'

'It's beautiful,' she said. 'I'll treasure it.'

'It's oak,' he said. 'It'll last forever, and it'll bring you luck.'

'Thank you.'

'Something to remember me by. In case you don't come back.'

'Don't worry,' she said. 'I told you I will, and I meant it.'

She went away down the path, her feet sending insects up out of the grass as she walked, and soon she was into the trees. At first she kept to the path, humming as she walked. She trailed her hand across the top of the long grass and bees buzzed up into the spring air. The sun cast dusty shards through the gaps in the leaves, the air noticeably cooler in the shadows, the path soft underfoot, the damp earth silently accepting her footfalls as she padded lightly into the green-lit depths. She was young – she felt young too, bursting with it – and her pace was steady and relentless. The path dipped between large rocks and opened out into a small clearing, a stream emerging from a tunnel of trees, burbling over mossy stones as it disappeared into the forest again. Katerina crouched down and dipped her chin into the stream, letting the icy water gush around in her mouth until her teeth hurt and her lips and her chin went numb, then she stood up and followed the path up a gentle rise, heavy dew soaking her feet. She reached the top of a small hill. She could see the edge of the forest a mile or so behind her now, and in the forest the prison camp, and some distance beyond a cluster of houses, smoke rising from the chimneys. In one of these modest houses Katerina knew her aunt would be peeling potatoes or feeding the chickens or filling the samovar for tea. She wondered if she would be back in time. Perhaps not – it would depend on what she got up to in the meantime. She turned and set off again down the opposite slope, into a deep wooded valley cragged with rocks. There was no path to follow now but Katerina knew the way.

She came to the shore of a lake, blue-green water stretching out flat as glass to the far bank. She stood in the long grass that bordered the lake and looked out across the sparkling water, then began to skirt around the shore and up onto a rocky outcrop high above the lake. She looked straight down into the depths and watched as shadowy fish dimpled the surface here and there, sipping down insects that chanced upon the water. She removed her coat and her shoes and dived straight in. Rising to the surface, she stretched herself out, her body long and thin as an eel, feeling the goosebumps rise as she ducked under again and swam down through the water and touched the lakebed with her hands, and she crouched there, holding onto lengths of green weed bright in the sunlight, then pushed off and felt herself fly up, weightless as a leaping dancer, emerging again into the air a long way out from the shore. She looked around. A cove of grey sand lay fifty yards away and over to one side, beyond a jutting spit of land, she could just make out Viktor Belanov's house.

She had come across Viktor's house by chance the previous year, on one of her first excursions into the woods, sometime during the hot summer of 1942. She had found the little beach then, and the day had been especially warm, so she slipped into the water and out towards the island in the middle of the lake. She was strong as well as young and the long swim to the island was easy for her. She had swum round to the far side and pulled herself out onto the rocks. She was removing her dress to dry herself in the sun when she heard the slapping of oars and saw a rowing boat sliding into view from behind the trees. The old man in the boat averted his eyes as she looked up.

'Oh, I'm sorry,' he cried out.

'So you should be!' she called back, quickly pulling on her dress.

'I wasn't spying on you,' he said, still looking away, covering his eyes with a hand as if he had just seen something awful.

'Oh yes you were! Until I saw you, that is!'

He removed the hand from his eyes and turned to look at her as the boat drifted in.

'Is that your lunch?' she said, pointing at the little pile of trout that gleamed in the bottom of the boat.

'I suppose so,' he said. 'But one's for the cat.'

'They look very good. Too good for a cat.'

'Not too good for *my* cat,' he said. 'What's your name anyway?'

'Katerina.'

'Well, Katerina, little mermaid, you can join the cat and me for lunch if you like. But you must swear you'll keep this place a secret.'

'You're not a pervert, are you?' she said, but then she looked into his eyes and decided she would trust him. 'All right,' she said. 'You and your cat will get fat if you eat all those fish by yourselves.'

She clambered into the boat and the old man rowed them back to the shore, with surprising vigour, she thought, for someone his age. Must be all the fish. A small wooden house stood just back from the treeline, the wooded slope rising up directly behind.

'You're my first visitor in three years,' he said as Katerina followed him into a large room with whitewashed wooden walls and a window in each of its sides. There was a rough table in the middle of the room and three rickety chairs.

'Don't sit on that one,' he said. 'The last person who sat in it broke it. It's only here now because I can't bear to part with it.'

A woodburner stood by the far wall, the heaped ash of winter fires still in it. To the other side of the room stood a large sideboard, picture frames and jars of pickled vegetables, greens and yellows and reds, arranged upon its shelves.

'Sit down. Please, sit down. Oh, I'm sorry, I haven't introduced myself, have I? I've been out here so long I've forgotten my manners. I'm Viktor. And this is Koshka, my lovely cat.'

'Hello, Koshka, you are lovely indeed. And a funny name, you have. Rather literal, perhaps.'

'Easy for me to remember,' said Viktor. 'I'm an old man now, after all.'

'You're only as old as you feel.'

'And I do feel old. As old as the woods all around us.'

'Do you play?' she said, gesturing towards the pair of violins that shared a shelf with the pickles.

'A bit. But mostly I make them.'

'You *make* them? Wow! That's a special talent.'

He picked one up and plucked at a string, then damped the note down. 'It doesn't sound too bad, I suppose,' he said. 'But who's ever going to play them out here except me, and I'm no musician really. It's difficult to get hold of the right wood now, with the war and everything. I just use what I find in the forest, the same wood I use for the fire. Not the best, but better than nothing.'

They ate their trout as Koshka sat in the broken chair and ate hers straight off the table beside them. Then they drank a spirit with a hint of honey from small squat glasses etched with the patterns of leaves, and they talked about their lives: Viktor about the first war and the revolution and the sons he had lost to the commissars; Katerina about her life in Leningrad.

'I came here in the summer of 1941,' she said. 'When the Germans invaded, my mother put me straight on a train to Moscow, and then out here to stay with my aunt. Everyone thought it was highly irregular, that I'd never make it here without being stopped and sent back. But I was lucky.'

'You certainly were. You'll be safe here. The Germans will never make it this far, we'll stop them long before then. You must miss your home, though?'

'Oh, yes, yes, I do. Whatever's left of it. I think about it every day. And my mum, and my friends, my best friend, Oleg. And my ballet, of course! Oh, my ballet! Sometimes I feel I'll die without it. There were times I really could have died on stage and not minded. They were just small theatres, but it was the only place I wanted to be. I'd go home after the show and cry because I knew it would be a whole week before I could dance in front of an audience again.'

'I can understand that,' he said. 'I can imagine what it must have been like.'

When they finished eating, Viktor showed her the easiest way back to the beach where her shoes still lay warm in the sun, and she retraced her steps through the woods, passing the spot where she would first notice the prison camp the following winter, and where she would one day observe Aldo's bent figure standing day after day on the other side of the wire.

The day after that first lunch with Viktor, Katerina scrambled again down the secret path to his house and he let her in and as she sat at the table he picked up a violin.

'This one's my favourite,' he said. 'I made it the year that my first son was born.'

He tripped the bow across the strings, sat down in front of his audience – Katerina and the cat and a shelf of pickled vegetables – and he closed his eyes as he played. He was still playing that evening as Katerina danced on the beach for him, and she imagined that his face was just one of many and that his solitary violin was a whole orchestra lifting her skywards, and she felt again the ecstasy of momentary flight, and she imagined her dress trailing behind her like the pale tail of a comet on a dark and starry night.

Aldo stood in his usual place by the wire as early-evening thunderheads swept dusk in from the east. Lightning flickered across the horizon and the steppe grass whispered in the gathering breeze. Then the wind lifted its voice and the first drops of rain came down, spitting up the dust at his feet. Thunderclaps rolled overhead and a sudden curtain of water washed away the horizon, smudging the edge of the forest into a blur. Aldo stood in the downpour and looked around him as the other prisoners hurried away to the refuge of the bunkers. No fucking imagination, he thought. A drop or two of rain and off they run, back into the mess of their bunkers when it's so beautiful out here, out here alone in the air, fresh and clean, almost like being a free man again. Then he looked towards the guards huddled beneath their capes in the watchtowers. His eyes fell upon the main gate, left inexplicably open in the storm. Could the guard really have done that for him, another unexpected kindness, risking his own life in doing so? Well, whatever, freedom was just yards away. A short walk to the gate, a dash through the long wet grass, then into the trees. Then he would run so fast not even the dogs could catch him. Freedom, unexpected and beautiful! He must grasp it now, or he would die here, he knew that now more clearly than he had ever known anything. He willed his feet to move, wrenched one of them out of the muddying earth, took a step, looking up at the guards, huddled still beneath their capes, then another step. He paused and looked around, then forward again, slowly, steadily, deliberately, not quite sure if it could really be true. And then he reached the open gate. He turned and looked back and saw a stooping figure in the place where he had been, its face towards the eastern horizon, and he turned his back on the figure, turned his back on the wire, and he ran as fast as he could from the camp, lunging forward with his arms, desperately reaching out for the trees. Then the green canopy was suddenly above him, the rain slapping down on young leaves, and he crashed into the depths of the forest, listening out for the barking of dogs, but the barking never came and he ran until he could run no further and he lay down in the sopping grass and wept himself to sleep. He woke in daylight. The storm had blown over and morning slumbered under a thin mist. The sweet smell of damp earth overwhelmed him. Running water tickled his ears with its gentle rhythm. He opened his eyes and saw a stream inches in front of him.

'You're awake,' said a voice.

He was unsure if it was a question or an affirmation.

'You're awake. Come with me. You can't stay here. They might be looking for you.'

He looked up and saw Katerina sitting on the ground in front of him.

She stood up. 'Come on. We really have to go.'

Aldo stood up and followed her deeper into the forest. He paused often to rest but she chided him, urged him to walk faster. Then she took his hand and led him down to the shore of a lake. They reached a beach, hidden by rocks, and he lay down in the long grass by the shore.

'Stay here,' she said. 'I'll be back soon. No one will find you here.'

Aldo looked out across the water and he watched as she clambered over the rocks. He removed his coat and walked down to the edge of the lake. He got down on all fours and thrust his head into the cool water and then he stretched out in the grass and let the sun dry the water from his face. Then he fell asleep and dreamed that a wave had engulfed him, washing him clean. He woke with a start. Katerina had returned with Viktor and they helped Aldo over the rocks and down the hidden path to the house.

'You have to sleep,' said Viktor. 'But first you must wash and eat. A guest must not sleep on an empty stomach. Especially if he has fleas.'

He plucked one of the creatures from Aldo's hair and flicked it away.

'I'll get you some soap and some clothes,' said Katerina and when she came back she showed him a place behind the rocks at the far end of the beach where he could wash. She passed him a jar of treacly liquid that smelt of the forest.

'Here, look. First use this on your head. It'll get rid of those beasts you've got living on you.' Then she gave him some soap. 'And use this for the rest.'

Aldo took the soap and Katerina left him to wash. He removed his heavy coat, still thick with the mud and the grime of winter misery, then the shirt beneath, a rotten mess of rags that fell apart in his hands. He reached down to his boots and tried to remove them but his feet were swollen and the skin was stuck to the inside, so he sat on a rock and contemplated what to do about it, but his mind kept wandering and eventually he lay down on the rock and fell asleep. After a while Viktor came to find him.

'Haven't you finished yet?'

No answer, so Viktor climbed across and shook Aldo awake. 'Come on, you can sleep soon enough, but you have to get yourself tidied up a bit first.'

'But my feet are stuck,' Aldo said. 'I can't get them out.'

'Nonsense. Wait there.'

Viktor came back with a knife but Aldo was asleep again so Viktor set to work with the blade, sliding it inside each boot in turn and sawing away at the rotten leather.

'Soak your feet for a few minutes first, let the skin soften up a bit. Then you can take those things off. And when you've finished, leave everything here – I'll burn it later. No point in infesting the house with your fleas.'

His feet, when free of their boots, were red and raw and blood ran from them in steady little streams into the lake. He removed what remained of his clothes and for the first time in months looked at his naked body. He did not recognise himself. He was ruined. He had always been pale but his skin now was silver-grey, translucent, just like the dead fish he used to pick up at the Rialto market for the lunchtime menu at Casa Luca. His veins were twisted blue rivers, his whole body covered in scabs, and sores marked the spots where parasites had fed on his flesh all through the winter. He rubbed his arm, looked at the tattoo of the wild pig, the first time in months he had seen it in full sunlight. It had lost none of its strength, as stark and ugly as ever, if anything stronger and fiercer after its hibernation, shocking to look at after so long without it, and as he looked at it, the pig allowed him to imagine a day when a little strength might return to him too.

When he had finished washing, he put on the clothes and the boots that Viktor had left for him and he walked up to the house. He sat at the table and consumed everything they put in front of him, his stomach protesting at the unaccustomed load. As he ate, he saw the violins on the sideboard. He attempted a smile but all he could manage was an odd contorted grimace that caused the soup to dribble from the side of his mouth, though his eyes were smiling as Katerina wiped the soup away with her sleeve. They put him in the bed in the back room and he slept. He did not wake for two days, and when he did, he looked out of the window, instinctively searching for the horizon, but instead he saw the rise and fall of the hills and the waves on the lake. He turned to where Katerina sat in a chair by the door and he looked again into her eyes. There was a gentle silence between them. Aldo raised his head from the sack of clothes that served as a pillow. He looked around at the bare wooden walls, then back at Katerina.

'You're an angel,' he said.

She smiled and looked at him, that Jesus look, the one you find on statues, the one you get in books. Then a cobweb in the corner caught his eye and Aldo closed his eyes and sleep slipped its web around him once more. When he woke he heard Katerina's voice from somewhere outside. He sat up and looked through the window and saw her, so he walked out of the house and down to the shore of the lake. Katerina and Viktor were tying tiny barbed hooks to gossamer lines that Viktor would trail later for trout over the side of his boat. Aldo squinted as the sun ignited the lake with sparks and splinters, Viktor and Katerina mere silhouettes now, sunlight brilliant on the waves behind them. Aldo turned away. So they're just another illusion, he thought. Another bloody trick of the light, something he never should have believed in. He closed his eyes and saw again the wire of the prison camp and the forest beyond, the glassy-eyed prisoners and the mud that stretched away into the trees, and he turned to walk back to the bunker, but when he looked up it was no longer there and in its place was the house at the base of the hill and when he turned around again the two figures still sat by the lakeside tying hooks to their lines. He sat beside them, saw their faces looking into his own, and he willed them to reel him in. He stretched out his skeletal hand and touched Katerina's shoulder. He felt her skin and the flesh beneath, her body warm and soft and luxuriant, softer than Isabella's somehow. Then he spoke in a sudden jumble of quiet and unspecific words.

'What's up with you?' said Viktor. 'Haven't you seen a woman before?'

Aldo withdrew his hand.

'I'm sorry. I just wasn't sure,' said Aldo. 'I wanted to be sure.'

'Where are you from, anyway?' said Viktor. 'German, are you?'

'He's not German,' said Katerina. 'Does he look like a German?'

'I don't know what he looks like. Romanian, then? Well, he's not Russian, is he? The way he speaks, that accent.'

'What's your name?' said Katerina.

'Aldo.'

'Where are you from, Aldo, dear?' she asked.

'Venice.'

'Never heard of it,' said Viktor.

'It's in Italy, Viktor. Don't you know anything?' said Katerina. 'Are you still hungry, Aldo?'

He nodded.

'Well, we'll cook you another fish supper later,' said Viktor. 'I bet you'd like that, wouldn't you?'

Aldo nodded.

'I'd better go and catch us some fish, then.'

'Remember to get one for Koshka,' Katerina called out as Viktor pushed off in the boat with his baited lines, the oars slapping down the waves.

'Koshka?' said Aldo.

'Viktor's cat.'

'Oh, yes. She was sleeping on the bed next to me when I woke.'

'Cats cure people,' she said. 'They know.'

'Do they?'

She looked at him. He was watching Viktor as he rowed off into the lake.

'Do you remember my name?' she asked. 'From the other day?'

'Of course. Katerina.'

She liked the way he said it, like it meant something to him already.

'It's a lovely name,' he said. 'The same as my grandmother's.'

'Is she from Venice too? Your grandmother?'

'No, from Ukraine. But she's lived so long in Italy she's almost more Italian than I am. My grandfather's ship stopped off at Odessa and she was selling lace and he bought a tablecloth and went back a year later and she was still there.'

'So he bought another?'

'Exactly. How did you guess?'

'And they fell in love . . .'

'Yes, I suppose.'

'They're very lucky,' she said. 'To be the owners of such a beautiful story.'

'The owners? Doesn't the story own them?'

'No, Aldo. I don't believe in fate. You make your own luck. Your life is your own, it is what you make of it.'

'I've seen things over the last few months that would make you think otherwise.'

'Hey, Aldo,' she said brightly. 'How about a swim? I'll show you a beautiful spot out by the island there, where the water drops down deeper than those hills. You swim and look down and the water's so clear it feels like you're flying.'

'I'm not sure I'm ready for that.'

'Of course you are. The water will do you good.'

Aldo felt Katerina's hand in his and they stepped into the water together and the lakebed fell away beneath their feet. Katerina swam a couple of strokes ahead of him and then she dipped below the surface, the water rippling and flattening where she had submerged, and then he too slipped beneath the water and as he did so he was almost smiling.

Summer came, and Aldo was strong enough to take the long path around the lake and through the woods, and he followed Katerina through the trees at dusk. They passed through the small clearing where Aldo had woken on that first morning of freedom, after the gate of the camp had been left wide open and the storm had set him free.

'I need to go back to the camp,' he said suddenly. 'Just to take a look.'

She looked at him.

'Just to take a look, to see if it was real.'

'It was real, Aldo, I promise you that. And you don't want to go back there, I promise you that too.'

'So if that was real, maybe this is just a dream? How can two such different things exist together, in the same place, almost at the same time?'

'The world turns, Aldo. Things change.'

'Do they? Do they really?'

'Aldo, come here,' she said. 'Hold me.'

He embraced her in the gathering darkness.

'No, I mean hold me like you really mean it,' she said. 'Like you never want to let me go.'

And he squeezed her as tightly as his returning strength would allow and he held on to her until she spoke.

'Do I feel real to you now?' she asked at last.

He nodded.

'So I'm real, then. And even if this were all a dream, if it feels real, then what's the difference?'

'Because I'm afraid I'll wake up and you'll be gone.'

'Well, if that happens, then sleep again and you'll dream once more, and you'll find your way back to me that way.'

She smiled and ran her fingers through his hair. 'A wave always finds its way to the shore, Aldo. My friend Vassili Ivanov told me that, years ago, when I was just a little girl – and he was a sailor, so he should know.'

They skirted the edge of the forest and looked out from the last of the trees and Aldo saw again the guard tower thirty yards away, the barbed wire running in long lines around the bunkers where the prisoners lay and then Aldo saw a bent figure standing in darkness by the wire and his fear returned. He pinched his arm and bit his lip, and he held Katerina tightly in his arms again, but when he looked up again the figure was still there and now it had turned to face him, and he saw it looking back at him and it set him off running, out of her arms again, back into the forest, Katerina running after him. She caught up with him and grabbed his arm.

'Aldo, Aldo! What's wrong?'

'I won't go back, you know. And don't ever let them take me back, not ever. Promise me you won't let them.'

'I promise, Aldo. I promise. They'll never take you back. Never.'

That night they lay side by side, barely touching at first, only their eyes converging, then their lips met late in the night and they lay together until dawn and listened to the sound of early morning, the wooden beams creaking in the roof, the warming breeze rustling the leaves in the trees, and Viktor tramping back down the path to the house and quietly opening the door after a night in the woods. They rose late and went to the lake and swam out to the island and spent the morning beneath the swaying boughs as the sun brushed the tops of the clouds with yellow.

'Tell me about Venice,' she said after dinner that evening.

'Let me see,' he said. 'Pass me that bit of paper.'

He sketched a rough map of the lagoon, the island in the shape of a fish, an arrow towards his home on Fondamenta della Sensa, just back from the northern quays.

'This is where my house is,' he said as he scribbled the address. 'Promise you'll come and visit me there when I finally make it home.'

She laughed. 'That's ridiculous, Aldo. How could that ever come true?'

'A wave will always find its way to the shore, you said. Your life is what you make of it.'

'Well, all right, then,' she said, filling their glasses to the brim again. 'To us, in Venice, one day.'

'To us . . . in Venice . . . one day.'

They downed the spirit in one wholehearted swallow, then sat back and looked at each other in their chairs.

'Oh my, look at the moon,' said Katerina suddenly. 'Let's go out to the beach – it'll be beautiful out there now. And bring a violin.'

They went to the beach and Aldo began to play, the notes of the violin skimming like stones across the darkened waves, out towards the woods where they might fall upon the ears of the night's hidden creatures or the ears of a Russian patrol. But love is deaf as well as blind and Aldo played on and Katerina leapt and danced to the music as it lifted her higher, and finally she took the violin from Aldo's arms and replaced it with herself and she led him back to the house, to the room where the spider had hung its sticky web again, and Koshka already slept on the bed, and Aldo and Katerina slipped beneath the covers and into each other's arms.

In the morning, when they woke, they lay in silence, listening to Viktor going about his chores in the other rooms.

'Katerina,' Aldo said at last. 'You know, don't you? That I love you?'

He felt her head move against his chest in acknowledgement. He waited, to see if she would reciprocate.

'Might you also love me, Katerina? One day, if not now?'

'Aldo, it's when you tell people you love them that they get taken away from you. So I'd rather not say . . .'

'Perhaps you'll be able tell me one day,' he said.

'Perhaps,' she said. 'When you're safe. After the war.'

When they got up, they found Viktor standing by the sink in the far corner of the house, skinning rabbits, ready for cooking that day.

'I heard your violin last night, Aldo,' he said. 'A beautiful sound, but dangerous too. It was a clear night, very clear, too clear to be playing music outside. Even if you are in love . . .'

'Oh, Viktor, don't be a bore. It was such a beautiful night,' said Katerina.

'Beautiful nights are the most dangerous. The air is too thin and sound travels too far and you never know who might be around. If there's a patrol they'll hear the violin and they'll find this place and then we'll all be in for it. I could lose my home and all of us could lose our lives.'

'Lose our lives?' she said. 'For what?'

'For sheltering him. He is the enemy, after all.'

Viktor's words struck Aldo like a bullet, taking out a piece of him, just like the bullets he had seen taking away chunks of so many men around him, before he had found this place, before he had come here where he thought that he was safe, where it seemed he could be someone again, the man he used to be. But the war had suddenly caught up with him again – Viktor's words had brought it back. He *was* the enemy. He hated the thought of it, but facts are facts and there was no changing it. Katerina was trying to change it anyway, raging at Viktor, reproaching him for what he had said.

'Well,' said Viktor, 'enemy or not, he won't be playing the violin at night round here any more. I won't lose my home on account of him.'

Two nights later a patrol was waiting for Katerina and Aldo as they walked among the trees. Within an hour, Aldo was back in the prison camp and Katerina was back at Viktor's house, spilling out her heart. Aldo trudged into his old bunker and found a space on the floor. He curled himself up into a black-and-blue ball, beaten half to death by the guards, his punishment for being human, for wanting to be free. He listened to the sounds of the snoring prisoners, moaning and babbling in their sleep, and he thought of Viktor and how he must have betrayed him, the enemy after all, Viktor's patriotic duty done, seeing to one more bastard enemy of Mother Russia. Then a desperate thought brought tears to Aldo's eyes – the certainty that you couldn't trust anyone, not out here, not after everything that had gone on in this godforsaken war. Then he pulled up his sleeve and looked again into the eyes of his inky pig.

'Oh, pig, still there, are you?' he whispered bitterly. 'A wave will always find its way to the shore, eh? There's just no escaping you, is there?'

And as the pig's triumphant rage crashed over him again, he heard a familiar voice from the bunk above his head, Pietro's broken mind still churning out memories of his golden days in the sun.

'I was a postman in Umbria,' he was saying. 'I was a postman in Umbria . . .'

Aldo closed his eyes and untied the rope that moored him to reality, and as he drifted away, it came to him, with absolute certainty, despite it all, a sudden miracle – there *was* someone he could trust, just one, and he knew she would be out there, thinking of him still, and he knew that she would come. Yes, she would come, he was sure of it.

Back at Viktor's cottage, Katerina collapsed into bed, dived into the depths of sleep and dwelt like a stone at the bottom of a cold dark lifeless river. She was back at the camp as dawn peeked over the horizon. A short distance away, just behind the wire, she saw a stooping figure, his back towards her, his face towards the east. She ran towards him, around the angles of the perimeter fence, not hearing the shouts of the guards in the watchtowers, oblivious to the eyes of the other prisoners as she ran, and then she was in front of him and she saw that look, that longing in the eyes, as if he had never left the camp, as if they had never spent the last few weeks together in an unexpected heaven. Then she saw the bruises.

'Oh my God, Aldo! What have the bastards done to you?'

He averted his gaze as tears welled up in his eyes.

'Aldo, Aldo, look at me! Look at me, please!'

He looked at her.

'Aldo, don't cry, my darling.'

But she was crying too. She reached inside her pocket but she had nothing to give him this time. She twisted a hand through the wire all the same, then the other, then the full length of her arms, and she hauled him in towards her and she held him in her arms and tried to kiss his face through the wire, but the wire between them pushed its sharp points through their clothes, puncturing their skin, jabbing at them until they bled. Then the guards rushed up and pulled them from each other's arms, disentangling Aldo from the wire that bound them together, dragging him away, and the last glimpse that Aldo caught of her was her face pressed hard against the wire, and that was the moment she told him that she loved him.

Katerina returned to the camp the following day but there was no figure behind the wire, nor was there the next day, or the one after that.

'He's gone,' said one of the guards. 'They've sent him away.'

'Away? What do you mean away? Where to? The east?'

'I can't tell you.'

'Tell me, please. I beg you. I've never begged anyone for anything in my whole life but I'm begging you now.'

'Yes, to the east, I guess. The gulags.'

'Siberia?'

'I suppose. He could be anywhere. He should never have tried to escape, you know. Listen, do yourself a favour, love – forget about him. He's a dead man now, you can be sure of that. And you'll get yourself into all sorts of trouble if you come here again.'

She didn't budge.

'Really, love, you'll never find him, not now. Just accept it, move on.'

She turned and walked away.

Oleg

Leningrad, July 1944

It was never the same between Katerina and Viktor after that. He swore on his life he hadn't tipped off the guards, but Katerina never really believed him. When she finally said goodbye to him the following summer, and turned her back for the last time on his house by the lake in the woods, she did so without much regret.

She travelled first to Moscow, then boarded a train for Leningrad, where the siege had finally ended. She was unable to find a seat, the train crowded with soldiers and refugees and commissars and old women who sighed as they clasped and unclasped their hands in their laps. The train pulled into Leningrad through the bombed-out suburbs, then the passengers tumbled out onto the platform. The streets were dusty and warm in the early summer heat. An evening squall passed overhead, the raindrops gone as soon as they touched the street, the isolated cloud continuing on its way, leaving behind the scent of summer rain. Katerina walked briskly up the alleyway and into the courtyard where she had spent so many long childhood hours on her doorstep in the rain. Despite all the bombs that had fallen on the city during the siege, the house was intact. She stood on the step and banged on the door and waited. She knocked again but no one came so she sat on the step and looked across the courtyard at the window in which she had first seen Oleg's pallid little face all those years before. She thought of the last time she had seen him, in the early summer of 1941, both of them little more than twenty years old. It had been a beautiful May evening, but four weeks later the German army would seep out of the birch forests of Poland and Prussia and cross the border into the Soviet Union, the start of a long weary road that led not to Moscow but Berlin. In May 1941 the war had been far from their minds as Katerina and Oleg made their way along the busy avenues towards the Mariinsky. They spent the evening watching from the cheapest seats as the stars of the ballet company – their company – lit up the night with joy. Later they had returned home together via the long route, stopping at a coffee-house, staying there for hours, then ambling back to their neighbouring homes, walking so close to each other that their hips rubbed together. Oleg had turned to wave as he opened his door, beaming at Katerina as he stepped inside. He had been called up a week later, and before the summer was out Katerina had left Leningrad for her aunt's village in the countryside hundreds of miles to the south-east, and all the while the Germans burned their way across the Russian countryside and Katerina heard no news of Oleg. She had heard no news of him since.

But now the siege had finally lifted and Katerina was home, and she stood up from where she had been sitting and she knocked on the door of Oleg's house. Mrs Ivanova opened it, her canary song long gone. The war had piled the years upon her. She looked at Katerina for several long seconds.

'Well?' she said at last.

'Well what?' said Katerina.

'Well, look who it is.'

Katerina knew their relationship could never be repaired, not since that day in 1928 when she had called the woman a fucking whore and she had thrown the little girl out into the rain.

'Is he in?' Katerina asked, resisting the urge to use similar expletives again now.

'Is who in?'

'Who do you think? Oleg, of course.'

'Of course he's in. He's always in.'

Katerina's heart leapt. 'Well, aren't you going to let me in to see him?'

'I might.'

Katerina pushed her way past Mrs Ivanova and hurried up the stairs two at a time. 'Oleg! Oleg! Where are you?'

She heard his voice, quiet and changed, reaching out to her from the end of the hall, from the room where he had slept as a child. She rushed past the room in which the body of Vassili Ivanov had reposed in its coffin and she burst into Oleg's room, ready to embrace him in arms made heavy with waiting, but the curtains were drawn, the room was in darkness, and no one rushed over to greet her. Instead she heard his plaintive voice again. 'I'm here,' he whispered. 'Over here.'

Then she saw him, the strange chair in which he sat, and it all hit her in a rush. She dashed over and hugged him, reaching her arms out to him as he sat in the wheelchair and stretched his arms awkwardly around her, and her hair fell across his face and she smelt the familiar smell of his skin and a momentary happiness fluttered up in her.

'Oleg, Oleg. Oh, I'm so happy to see you. I can't believe it.' She grabbed him by the shoulders and shook him. 'I really thought you'd gone forever.'

'Perhaps it would have been better if I had,' he said softly.

'Don't say that, Oleg. Please don't say that.'

She felt his tears on her cheek and she wiped them away with her sleeve, first from her face, then from his. 'When did you get back?'

'A few months ago. After the siege was lifted, they sent me home. Before that I was in a hospital in Moscow, and before that I was in a hospital in Voronezh, a hospital in Saratov, a hospital in . . . well, I forget all the names. Seen one hospital, seen them all. It's two years since I walked, you know. There's a lot I don't remember, but I'll never forget that last step.'

He slumped further down in the chair as he talked, then stiffened slightly. 'I'm sorry. That's not much of a hello, is it? I saw you sitting on the step. I was watching you out of the window.'

'Why didn't you call me up to see you, then?

'What, like this? Surely not like this?'

'Oleg, don't be stupid. I don't care what you look like.'

'But, Katerina, I wanted you to remember me the way I was.

Remember how I was? I was magnificent, wasn't I?' He laughed. 'Well, maybe not, but you know what I mean. And now look at me. What a fucking mess.'

He slapped his leg hard and Katerina took his hand in hers and held it still.

'Don't do that to yourself.'

'Look at it,' he said. 'I can't move it, can I?'

She squeezed his hand and didn't know what to say. 'Been up to much since you got back?' she asked, awkwardly trying to lighten the tone. 'I bet you've been having a great time . . .'

'Oh yes, I've been out dancing almost every night.' He leant back in his chair and closed his eyes, screwing them tight, wrinkling his face with pain. 'What have I been up to?' he said. 'Now, let me see. Um, nothing. Less than nothing. Nothing but listening to fucking Mrs Ivanova wittering on all day. I sit here all day and I wait and I look at these curtains and sometimes I look out the window and then I close the curtains again. And that's about all. You know how often I've been out since I got back, Katerina? You know how often, in six months? Twice! Once when the building next door caught fire and they thought we'd better all get out before we burned, and the other was the day one of Mrs Ivanova's fancy men hauled me out and wheeled me around the streets like some sort of trophy. A hero returned from the front, he told everyone, shot to bits doing his duty for Mother Russia, and they all crowded round and had a bit of a gawp and a mutter about how brave I must have been, but I know half of them were thinking, "So what, another poor bastard who got his legs shot to bits, but at least he's not dead like all the poor dead bastards." And then they all went on their way to drink and fight and fuck themselves into oblivion and Mrs Ivanova's fancy man heaved me around for half the night, one flea-pit to another, and he tipped me out of my chair more than once, he was so out of his mind on vodka or diesel or whatever the hell it was he was drinking, and then eventually he got me home but he was too weak from drink to get me up the stairs so he left me in the kitchen all night and I froze half to death and pissed myself and had to listen to him and Mrs Ivanova testing out the springs in the bed above my head until dawn. And those are the two occasions – both highly memorable, you'll agree – on which I've been outside this house in the last six months.'

'Well, I'm taking you out now, then.'

'No, you're not.'

'Who's going to stop me? You?'

'Katerina, don't you dare! I don't want those bastards staring at me like I'm a freak.'

'You're not a freak, Oleg, you're the gentlest, most beautiful person I've ever known and I'm not going to let you sit here and rot just because you can't move your legs any more.'

She pulled the curtain open but Oleg pushed it back. They struggled back and forth with it until Katerina relented and the curtain once more covered the window.

'Oleg! You're coming out with me, do you hear?'

'Katerina, you don't understand. I'm not the person you knew. I'm not the same old Oleg. You probably won't even like me any more.'

'Of course I will. And we're going out whether you like it or not.'

She drew the curtain back again and it stayed there.

'See. There's still a bit of daylight out there. It'll be light for a while. I'll take you down to the river.'

'You and that river, Katerina. Always you and that bloody river . . .'

Katerina took the arms of the wheelchair and pushed Oleg along the landing, bringing him and his contraption to a clumsy halt at the top of the stairs.

'Katerina, are you trying to bloody kill me?'

'Oleg, you'll have to get out.'

'I can't.'

'Hey, witch!' Katerina yelled down the stairs. 'Come here!'

Mrs Ivanova appeared at the foot of the stairs.

'Help me with Oleg.'

'No, he has to stay in. The doctors have said so.'

'Have they? Well, the doctors can go fuck themselves, because we're going out, and you're going to help me. You're going to help me lift Oleg out of this chair or I'll bloody well tip him out.'

'Tip him out, then. Suit your stupid self.'

Mrs Ivanova disappeared back into the kitchen.

'Sorry, Oleg, but I'm going to have to do this on my own.'

She tried to tip the chair to one side but she wasn't strong enough to shift his dead weight, so she wedged herself between one of the wheels and the banister and rocked backwards and forwards until she tipped the chair over sideways and Oleg lay in a heap at the top of the stairs. He looked at her glumly.

'Oleg, you're going to have to go down the stairs on your arse.'

He was soon outside in the chair in the street. Katerina went back into the house and into the kitchen where Mrs Ivanova sat at the table drinking tea. Katerina marched over and kicked the chair out from under her.

'Next time you'll bloody help us,' she said, and strode out of the room.

She pushed Oleg out into the street. The wheels bumped and jarred across the cobbles and Oleg stared at the lumps of his knees and held the blanket over himself as if hiding a dirty secret from public gaze.

'Where to, Oleg?'

'Oh, anywhere, Katerina. You decide.'

'No, you decide. This is your third day out in six months. You get to choose.'

'And this is your first day back after . . . after how long away?'

'Nearly three years.'

'After three years away. Don't you want to see the sights?'

'The sights? Is that what you'd call them? This place is a mess.'

'Of course it is, after what the Germans did to us.'

They stopped in the square outside the Mariinsky Theatre and talked.

'So, what happened, Oleg? Do you want to tell me?'

'No,' he said firmly.

'I'm your friend. Remember that. Whenever you need me, I'm here for you.'

'I know.'

'I remember when I broke my ankle,' she said suddenly. 'When I was just little, just four or five. I'd been messing about down at the market and slipped on the ice. It was wintertime and I always wanted to be out – you know what I'm like – so my dad used to put me on the sledge every day and we'd go out in the snow and he'd pull me along and sometimes he'd take me fishing and I'd sit there in the freezing cold and my feet would go numb, but I always wanted to go with him all the same. Until that last time. I told you about that, didn't I? When he was fishing on the ice, and I looked up . . .'

'Yes, you told me.'

'. . . and I looked up and . . .'

'You told me.'

'. . . and he wasn't there any more. And there was a hole in the ice where he'd been, and I couldn't stand up, with my broken ankle and everything, I couldn't go over to see if I could save him. And I sat there until somebody came and helped me, and by then the hole in the ice had frozen over, and of course they never found him.' There were tears in her eyes now. 'So don't go all fucking morose on me, Oleg. You're still here, and I'm still here, and I'll look after you. I'll take you out and I'll wheel you around. I'll even put you on a sledge and pull you around when it snows if you want me to. But just don't get down on yourself, all right?'

'All right, Katerina. I'll try.'

They returned to the courtyard and Oleg's mother was there and she helped Katerina get him back up the stairs. Katerina sat on the side of the bed until his eyes closed and his breathing slowed into the steady rhythm of sleep and then she left and sat on the doorstep outside her house again and waited but no one came, so she stood up and walked back into the streets and she passed the Mushroom Woman's shop, now just a bombed-out shell. She came back an hour later and banged on the door of her home again. This time she heard footsteps and the door was flung open and Katerina saw an old woman who had rapidly aged and the woman held her in an iron embrace and whispered in her ear.

'Katerina, my daughter, Katerina. I'm so sorry. I'll never make you wait again.'

Katerina and Oleg sat by the River Neva, opposite the Fortress of Peter and Paul. Oleg's eyes were blank and cold as he recalled the day in October '42 when he emerged at first light from the train in the marshalling yard next to the burning banks of the Volga and saw for the first time the panorama of Stalingrad spread out in front of him, fear draining his face white as he gazed at the flames on the far side of the river. He dashed through the mud and the din in the scramble for the boats, the NKVD guns at his back in case he should turn and question the wisdom of crossing the water to the hell that awaited him. Under the screaming dives of the Stukas he boarded a barge as the Volga burned bright with oil from sunken boats and men leapt overboard in fright and were shot by the commissars.

'I was drenched in the blood of others. The Stukas kept turning and diving, again and again, and I saw my best friend ripped apart by a shell, standing right next to me, and when the boat reached the far bank I was somehow still alive and he was dead, and the last I saw of him was a mess beneath a blanket on the riverbank. And that was how his story ended, Katerina. At the end of that day I was alive and he was dead, and I'm still alive and he's still dead, and that's all there is to it. They herded us inland, among the rubble and the brick and buildings that looked like they were melting. The next night I found myself near the tractor plant and at dusk starving dogs came creeping out of the buildings, down to the riverbank, wanting to get across the river, I suppose, or drown in the attempt. I remember thinking that those dogs were a hundred times luckier than me because the dogs had a choice and I didn't. What chance did we have, flesh and bone among all that fire and stone and metal? And then it happened and they put me on a boat back across the Volga and all I remember is the motion of the waves and a dog licking the blood from my face. And then I was just one of hundreds in a field hospital. I tried to stand, to get out of bed, but my legs wouldn't move. The doctors told me I was lucky to be alive, and I wondered for a long time exactly what they meant, and I still don't really know. And now we're both back here again, looking at this bloody river. Do you remember, Katerina, when we were children, how we used to come down here and tell each other all the things we were going to do with our lives?'

'Yes, Oleg. And we've done a lot of them.'

'Yes, we *did* a lot of them. We *did*. But what are we talking about now? The past, the things that went wrong, the things that now we'll never do.'

'We have to keep looking forward.'

'Easy for you to say.'

'There's always a future.'

'No, Katerina. There is not always a future.'

'Come on, Oleg. You're depressing me.'

'Oh, poor dear! I'm depressing you, am I?'

'Fuck you, Oleg. Fuck you!'

Katerina screwed her hands up into fists and punched the top of his legs repeatedly.

'There's no point in hitting me there. You know I can't feel a thing.'

She put her arms around him and rested her forehead on his shoulder and wished he could grip her around the waist and lift her high as he had done so many times in the past on a stage, but instead she felt the arm of the wheelchair where it dug her in the ribs and the bony shoulder that had replaced the muscle, and the hard little pebbles that dug into her knees as she knelt.

'So what does this bright future hold for you, Katerina?' Oleg finally said.

'The same as it always did.'

'And what if they won't take you back?'

'But they will. Of course they will. I was one of the bright young things, remember?'

'I hope it works out for you, Katerina. I really do.' His voice tailed away and they watched the river turn a limpid blue in the evening light.

'You know, I fell in the river over there once, by the fort,' she said. 'Did I ever tell you that story?'

'You and your river stories . . .'

'I was about seven or eight and it was winter and there was ice floating around all over the place, and I just sort of fell in.'

'You just sort of fell in?'

'Yes, I just leant over and let myself go. It wasn't like I really wanted to do it, I guess, I just didn't bother stopping. And once I was in the water I went through the motions – you know, struggling a bit, trying to swim – but then I let the river take me, let myself go. And I was really going and I wasn't coming back. And then for some reason, when I was almost gone, I started to fight, and I only just got my head above the surface and I screamed and I screamed and I was going under again, swallowing down water and about to give up, when this big fisherman reached down and pulled me out of the water and dumped me on the quay. He took me to a building over there and they sat me in front of a fire and when I turned to look for him he had gone. He hadn't even waited for me to thank him. He just went back to where he'd left his gear and his fish, as if he'd done nothing.'

'And why are you telling me this now?'

'Because you're the one who's drowning now, and I can see you don't really want to swim. But I won't let you do it. I'll keep picking you out of the water and putting you on the quay until you finally get up and walk away from the river. But you have to help me do it. You have to start to struggle and fight or you'll go under and you'll sink out of reach and I won't be able to lift you out no matter how much I want to.'

'And would you be happy if I didn't thank you for saving me? Like you didn't thank the fisherman?'

'I did thank him, in the end. I stole a reel for him from the Mushroom Woman's shop.'

'The Mushroom Woman!' Oleg laughed. 'Wasn't she strange! Her house took a direct hit last year, you know. They never found her. Must have turned to vapour in the blast.'

'Poor Mushroom Woman,' said Katerina. 'I never really liked her anyway.'

Two years later, Oleg wheeled himself along the riverbank. He found the spot that he had been looking for, and he leant back in his chair and looked at the stars. He closed his eyes and thought of Katerina, of the night's performance, his pride at having finally seen his best friend on stage in a major production, the thrill of her achievement and his continuing crushing despair at his own fate. He had seen her briefly afterwards, congratulated her sincerely, shared her quiet delight, and had then attempted to take his leave.

'Stay, Oleg,' she had said. 'We can go to the coffee-house later. I'll be out of here in a few minutes.'

'No, really, Katerina, I'm tired. I'll see you tomorrow.'

'No, no, wait, I'll get you a drink. Stay there a minute.'

But she had been distracted by well-wishers and when she returned he had gone. He wheeled his way through the streets, lingering over each personal landmark with a fondness that almost broke his resolve, but each time his memories sliced him both ways with their double-edged sword, and so he pushed on until he came to the spot with the steep bank and the sudden unprotected drop where the handrail ended. He sat there beneath a warm black starry sky and he focused on one distant star and imagined it was a tiny hole in the fabric of the universe through which the clean bright light of another dimension strove to illuminate the world. He knew the time had come for him to seek out the source of that light. So he released the brake of his wheelchair, removed the walls of his prison, the wheels beneath him slowly turning, their motion like the liberating revolution of a key in a door that has never been opened, and he moved forward down the slope, gathering speed, and then the chair tipped over the lip of the bank and he felt again, for the last time, the joy of momentary flight that had ruled over him since he was ten years old, and his eyes were still somehow fixed on the bright distant star as he entered the water, and then the dark blanket of the river blocked out the sky and he held tight to the heavy chair as he floated down into the depths, gripping its cold wet metal in the dark, and he was carried away by the current, and the deeper he went so the nearer he was to the star in the sky, the hole in the universe, the light, the door.

PART FOUR

Italy

Homecoming

Milan, July 1950

Aldo passed his ticket to the inspector. The inspector looked him up and down, looked back at the ticket and frowned. 'Where did you get on?'

'Brescia.'

'Brescia?'

'Eight years ago.'

The inspector shrugged, clipped the ticket and handed it back. He moved off down the carriage, muttering to himself.

Fucking inspectors, Aldo thought, and he turned again to look through the window at the plains of northern Italy, the land dotted with small farms set among clusters of poplar and oak. Fat pigs rooted about in their pens beneath the trees, feeding on the acorns the farmers had left for them, while the pig on Aldo's arm, grown wild and hungry and impatient during long years on the steppe, raged beneath his sleeve, causing him to clench and unclench his fists in a manner that made the old lady opposite shift uneasily in her seat, as if she were contemplating moving to a different carriage. Five years in the gulag had cut Aldo off from the norms of civilian life. He closed his eyes and thought of the places he had been, the sights he had seen, the strange mental landscapes he had endured in the eight years since he caught a boat away from Venice and a train to Brescia. Through all those days, weeks, months and years of waiting, he had longed for the moment that was now approaching, the moment of homecoming, a reunion with the people and the places, the sights and smells and sounds that he had kept tucked away in his heart, but now the moment was arriving with undue haste and he felt desperately unprepared. And he felt another kind of longing now: for the wilderness he had left behind, for the person he had become in the intervening years, a person no longer comfortable in this benign environment, a person perhaps only fit for the life of a beast. And so, as the Italian countryside reached out to hold its long-lost son to its abundant breast, he shrank back and longed to be anywhere other than this land of apparent calm and serenity and beauty grown fat on endless spring and summer. The feeling had crept up on him gradually during the long journey home. The further the train crawled west across the steppe, the more the longing and the loss inverted themselves, the more the Russian emptiness seemed like home, and the greater became his anxiety at what he might find when he got back to Italy. His stomach bumped along sick and empty as the train steamed on and Russia slipped away, the last of its birch trees sinking out of sight beneath the horizon, like the masts of a stricken ship sinking out of sight beneath the waves. And Aldo sank ever deeper into doubt as the train rolled on, and then there was a spell in a camp before he could be released for repatriation. Finally he boarded another train and crossed into Italy and got off as instructed in Milan. He followed the directions he'd been given and pitched up outside an office door at the allotted time, nine o'clock sharp. He waited an hour before someone turned up. He followed the man inside and sat beside the desk as the man busied himself with the necessary paperwork. Then he took an envelope from the desk drawer and carefully counted out the notes.

'Here you go. Fifty thousand lire. You'll need it for lodging and sustenance, a new suit and shoes, perhaps, and your ticket home. When it's gone, you're on your own – sort things out as best you can. Sign here, and *arrivederci*.'

Aldo signed, took the money, and left. Fifty thousand lire! He'd never seen so much money. He went to the station, bought his ticket for Venice, and went to wait on the platform. He looked around him. How different it all seemed to that day in Brescia with the flags and the crowds with their tangible sense of adventure and his own tangible sense of dread. Well, he'd certainly been right about that.

But now he was back, just him and his suitcase, alone on the platform. He watched as a group of pigeons scrapped over something on the ground. Then he heard footsteps and voices behind him. He heard a heavy bag thumping down onto the platform, then laughter. He turned to look at the group of young men in sunglasses who stood by the far wall. He noted their frivolity, the backslapping and the horseplay, and suddenly he felt crushed and old. They must be, he thought, only a few years his junior, but those few years had made all the difference. They had grown up just too late to be called up and he looked upon them now as a completely different generation, almost another species. Who was left now among those who might understand what it was to be twenty-seven years old and already broken on the wheels of life? Gianni lay cannibalised in the Russian soil outside the prison camp, the sergeant decomposed in the mud of the steppe, Luigi had wandered off blind among the tanks in the night, and Pietro Lombardo probably still believed he was a postman in Umbria. And Katerina? What of Katerina, his unexpected angel? She had been swept away from him by the same tides that washed him up on the lost island of the gulag. Aldo took out the photograph that she had given him, that he had kept wrapped in a cloth in his breast pocket throughout the intervening years. He held it delicately in his long thin fingers and looked at the face that smiled out at him now from the hall of the ballet school, the face that had smiled at him in the photo throughout his time in the gulag, the face that was now slowly cracking and flaking as the fabric of the paper gave way to time, a process of decay accelerated by the kiss he placed on the photo at the start and the end of every day. He thought of the night at the house by the lake when he had drawn Katerina the map of his hometown, had scrawled his address at the end of an arrow, and their toast to the hope of meeting in Venice one day, and he almost allowed himself to believe the one thing he had not allowed himself in all the time since he had last seen her, that when he arrived home on Fondamenta della Sensa there would be a bundle of Katerina's letters, that his mother would have kept them bound by a pale pink ribbon in a safe place for when he returned. But now he looked again at the railway tracks, two parallel lines running side by side into infinity, and his hope was crushed before it had even been formed, and so he unbuttoned his cuff and rolled up his sleeve and looked into the eyes of his demon pig, his only eternal companion, and he saw that its eyes were still undimmed by time, still blazing, stronger than ever, and he smiled and stroked its face, pinched the skin hard until he winced with pain.

Oh pig, my faithful pig. The only one who has stood by me all these years, the only one. Where would I be without you, if you hadn't carried me all these years, if you hadn't stood strong for me, hadn't spoken to me every night in the moments before I slept, hadn't understood me, hadn't promised me that if I only waited long enough you would bring me home and it would all be worth the wait? What big ears you have, pig, all the better to hear me with. And what big, bright, burning eyes, all the better to see me through the long dark night. And soon we'll meet again for real, dear pig, in the flesh, and we'll see who's stronger then. I'll make you admit it, you'll see, all that you did wrong. You thought I'd gone away forever, didn't you, that I was out of your life for good, but I'm coming back now, pig, you've brought me back, you've helped me more than you can know, and now you're going to get what's coming to you.

He rolled down the sleeve again and tears would have run down his cheeks but the pig was a thirsty companion and had drunk him dry years before, and so he simply sat and blinked and wrinkled his nose and looked again at the tracks. Then there was an announcement over the tannoy. His train would be delayed. He had three more hours to kill. He stood around for a while, purely out of habit, unaccustomed to the freedom he now had, only vaguely aware that he was free to leave the station and go for a walk around the town, to stop for a coffee somewhere, maybe even strike up a conversation with someone in a bar, buy a newspaper and read about the triumphs and troubles of others. So he stood there for an hour, walked up and down the platform several times, and then finally stepped out into the street. The town was busy and he drew back from the cars and buses and the people that criss-crossed the streets and pavements.

He passed through the market, the fruit and vegetables dazzling him with their waxy brightness. He bought an apple and a peach and ate them as he walked, wiping away the juice that dripped from his chin. He stopped to buy a newspaper at a kiosk on a corner near a bar. The bar was dark and noisy, the wooden floor and large old bar top reminiscent of Casa Luca before the war. Aldo went in and rubbed his fingertips lightly across the wood. It was a good heavy wood, probably oak. He opened the paper and looked at the headlines. Most of the news was bad. The barman came over and Aldo ordered a coffee and a sandwich and sat at the end of the bar on a stool. The barman brought them over to him.

'How much?!' Aldo said, when he saw the bill.

'That's the going rate these days. You did ask for ham *and* cheese. Most people have one or the other.'

Aldo took out his wad of notes and paid him. My God, he thought, fifty thousand lire won't go far. He started to fret about money as he ate, flicking through the paper as he did so. He read about the migration from the south to the north, from the country to the cities, about the thousands in search of work and the aid programmes and the government and the problems with the communists.

'Is it true what they say in the papers?' he asked the barman. 'About the unemployment and everything?'

'Sure it's true. Been living under a stone, have you?'

'I've been away.'

'Oh, really?'

'But I'm on my way home now.'

'Lucky you. Everybody wants to go home. I've got another six hours here before I clock off.'

'I haven't been home for eight years.'

'Oh, is that right?'

The barman poured a bag of beans into the coffee grinder and switched it on.

'I've been in Russia.'

The machine clattered on.

'In Russia, I said.'

'Why on earth did you go there?'

'The war.'

'But the war finished five years ago,' said the barman, switching off the grinder. 'You been away all that time? In Russia, you say?'

'All that time.'

'But most of you lot came home in '45 or '46. Even the last of the top brass are back now, Battisti and the others. There was something about them in the paper just the other month.'

'Well, I guess I got lost in the system. I escaped, and when they got me back they sent me to Siberia. Then you just disappear.'

Aldo was suddenly aware of someone at his shoulder. He turned to look. It was a woman, around thirty years old. She was looking at him with a vague sort of longing.

'Excuse me,' she said. 'But I couldn't help overhearing. Did you say you were in Russia?'

He nodded.

'With the Eighth Army? I don't suppose you knew my husband? I haven't heard a single word from him since the start of '43.'

He looked at her, not knowing what to say.

'I don't think we would have met, *signora*. There were an awful lot of us over there.'

'Yes, but . . . I just thought, perhaps . . . He was in the Alpini, the Tridentina Division. His name was Marconi. Carlo Marconi.'

'I'm sorry, *signora*, but I was in the Vicenza Division. We were closer to the Cuneense – the Tridentina were some way along the line from us and then everything went to pot. I'm sure I wouldn't have met him.'

'Oh,' she said. 'That's such a shame . . . Um, I also heard you say you've just come home?'

'That's right.'

'Perhaps Carlito will come home too, then, one day? Do you think that's possible?'

'It's definitely not out of the question, *signora*.'

'Thank you, er . . . oh, I'm so sorry, I haven't even asked you your name. I'm Lucia. Lucia Marconi.'

'Gardini. Aldo Gardini.'

'Well, Aldo, thank you,' she said, suddenly smiling. Something had lit up in her since they'd been speaking – he could see it in her eyes, and he remembered the feeling well. 'Thank you, Aldo,' she repeated, 'for giving me hope.'

'It's my pleasure,' he said. 'Consider it a debt repaid.'

She looked confused.

'It's a long story.'

'Listen,' she said. 'Would you mind if I gave you my name and address, just in case something comes to mind? Memories come back sometimes. Or you might hear news of him somehow, you never know. Would you mind that?'

'No, Lucia. I wouldn't mind that at all.'

She wrote her address on a scrap of paper and she pushed it into Aldo's hand. 'Thank you, Aldo,' she said again, resting her hand on his shoulder as she did so. Then she walked out of the bar and into the street and Aldo lost sight of her among the cars.

'She's always in here,' said the barman. 'Always talking about that bloody husband of hers, as if he'd just gone away yesterday.'

'Is that so surprising?'

'He really was a fascist, you know, down to the bone. We're better off without his sort. This country's moved on.'

'Moved on? What on earth do you mean by that?'

'If you want to get on, get in with the communists.'

'The communists? I've had enough of them to last me a lifetime. And I know more about them than you could ever imagine – they tried drilling it into me for years.'

'And it still didn't stick?'

'In one ear, out the other. Just as it should be.'

'See, I knew you were a fascist. But the communists get things done. Half the partisans were communists, you know, organised by the Russians behind the scenes. They know how to run things properly, a proper society, where everyone has their place.'

'The Russians couldn't even run a prison camp properly, so how could they run a society?'

'Get the system right and everything follows.'

'Fuck the system. What about the individual? It's the individual that suffers, mate, whatever system you care to choose.'

'I tell you, if I'd got the call, I'd have told them where to stick it. There's no way I'd have helped those fascist bastards.'

'If they called you, you went. You had to.'

'I know plenty of people who didn't.'

'We had no choice!'

Aldo was gritting his teeth now and he slammed his cup down on the saucer, causing the spoon to bounce noisily onto the floor.

'Hey,' said the barman. 'You're not the only one who's been in a war, you know. Plenty of people suffered here too. And *you* chose to go.'

'I had no fucking choice! None of us did!'

'Take it easy, will you? This is a respectable joint. And watch your mouth – even if you are some sort of hero back from the war!'

'Fuck you!'

Aldo turned away and walked towards the door. The barman put down his cloth and ran out from behind the bar and caught Aldo and dragged him into the street. Aldo swung a punch at him but the barman was bigger and stronger, better fed all these years, and he pushed Aldo to the ground. Aldo got to his feet and swung again with one fist, then the other, but the man dodged easily out of the way and Aldo overbalanced and fell to the ground. He stood up and swung again and this time the man knocked him down with a punch to the mouth. Aldo stood up and slipped away, blood streaming down his chin now as the crowd buffeted and barged him as he made his way along the street towards the station. When he got there the young men in sunglasses had gone and he sat and waited for his train, but he felt suddenly unable to take the last of a million steps towards home. After so long in its company, longing had become such a part of him that he was now merely a small and insignificant part of a greater suffering that existed independently of him, all the things he had felt, all the things he had seen, and he feared that if the longing disappeared there would be nothing left of him at all. And so when his train finally arrived he remained on the bench as the other passengers got on board and the doors closed and the train departed without him, then another, and he walked out of the station and back into the street and he skulked around for another hour or two. Then he went back to the station and finally another train arrived and he got on board and found a seat by a window and he wished the train would carry him well away from here, back over the horizon, back to where he could lose himself again. He watched through the window, his reflection in the glass a pale ghost in the sunlight, imprinted upon the countryside that was speeding by outside. Then the train went into a tunnel and his face was suddenly a shocking presence in the darkened glass and the noise and confusion and darkness of the tunnel reflected the noise and confusion of his thoughts and the gathering darkness of his heart.

The train reached Mestre late that evening and it rolled onto the causeway and over the lagoon to the island of Venice. In the distance, away to the left beyond Cannaregio, Aldo could make out the Renaissance church of San Michele, its blanched face of Istrian stone turning pale orange in the fire of the setting sun, and at the sight of it his doubts began to fall away. He stepped down onto the platform and stood there for a moment, savouring his moment of homecoming as the other passengers pushed past him. Outside the station he came to the bridge that led across the Canale Grande to Santa Croce. Somewhere over the bridge to the right lay Casa Luca with its bittersweet memories and its promise of a confrontation with Fausto Pozzi. To the left, the streets of Cannaregio and home. For years he had ruminated on this moment, had never really known which route he would take, which path would tug at him most strongly, but now that he was living the moment for real, and not for the umpteenth time in his dreams, there was only one option. He turned for home. The business with Fausto Pozzi would have to wait. Familiar sights and sounds lightened his step, the sense of anticlimax dissipating now, and he felt a curious sensation, a rising excitement, even happiness, as each step took him closer to the end of his road. He walked as quickly as he could towards the house on

Fondamenta della Sensa, a home he had last seen eight years before, that he had given up all hope of ever seeing again, and as he walked he imagined everything as it had been, his grandmother by the fire, his sister, Elena, playing with the dog beside her, his mother busy in the kitchen, and his father . . . and his father, at least in the land of imagination and dreams, still seated at the table and cursing Fausto Pozzi.

As he approached along Fondamenta della Sensa, Aldo could see the small arched bridge opposite his house, fifty yards away, the silhouette of a familiar figure standing upon it, a small dog by her side. He quickened his pace in expectation, but as he rushed towards the woman she turned away. He arrived at the house just as the door was being closed in his face.

'Mamma,' he called out. 'Mamma, it's me, Aldo. I'm home.'

He heard shuffling inside the hall as he banged on the door. The dog began to bark. The door opened a fraction and a man looked out.

'What do you want?'

'Who are you?' said Aldo. 'Let me in.'

'I'm sorry, but I think you've got the wrong house.'

'No, I haven't got the wrong house. It's you that's in the wrong house.'

Aldo leant against the door as the man tried to push it shut.

'Look, if you don't go away I'll fetch the police.'

'But where is everyone? Maria Gardini, don't you know her? I'm her son, Aldo.'

The man opened the door a little more. 'Listen, we've been here for two years. Signora Gardini went away, she went to live elsewhere.'

'But that can't be true.'

'Look, we didn't really know her. We bought the place, she moved out, we moved in, that's all.'

'Didn't she leave a forwarding address? For when I got back?'

'Aldo, you say? Her son?'

'That's right.'

'Well, I think she thought you were dead, everyone did. Look, I'm really sorry . . .' He began to close the door again.

'And what about the restaurant?' Aldo said hurriedly.

'What restaurant?'

'Casa Luca, what about Casa Luca?'

'Listen, like I said, I don't know the details. I'm sorry,' and he closed the door in Aldo's face.

Aldo headed straight for Casa Luca, stumbling as he walked, bumping into people who were coming the other way along Strada Nuova. He crossed the bridge at Accademia and hurried up the Rio di San Trovaso. He saw the bridge just ahead and Casa Luca beside it, but something about the place was wrong. Many things were wrong. The lights were brighter than before and there were people seated at the tables outside. He saw a waiter emerge from within, a silver tray on his outstretched arm bearing an array of tall glasses of gently fizzing liquids with lumps of ice and cocktail cherries and little paper umbrellas, and small plates of bourgeois snacks, olives stuffed with overworked delicacies, anchovies pierced on cocktail sticks and unnaturally wedded to delicate little silverskin onions and gherkins that had been plucked too soon from their bush and plunged into vinegar. And then he saw the hulking presence in the doorway. Aldo glanced up at the sign above the door. And then he looked again. Oh my God, there it was, just as he had feared all these years, the hated name painted in large bold letters, ANTICA LOCANDA FAUSTO. He stared hard at the figure in the doorway. Fausto Pozzi hadn't noticed him yet – he was too busy admonishing a waiter for the sloppy delivery of a plate of *frutti di mare*. The trailing claw of a lobster had upended a glass of *prosecco* into a diner's delicate lap and she cried out loudly in a language that would never have been heard in Casa Luca before the war. Aldo stood by the bridge and watched the spectacle. He looked back at Fausto Pozzi and the furtive porcine little eyes wandered across his own, moved on, then looked instantly back. The dark mouth beneath the moustache fell open and for a moment Aldo saw something like fear in his face. Then Fausto hurried across and took Aldo by the arm and tried to lead him away from the bridge, away from the tables that nestled beside it in the glow of red candles. Aldo shook the outstretched hand violently away.

'Aldo, Aldo, but what a surprise!'

Aldo stared at him.

'It is Aldo, isn't it?'

'Of course it's me. Don't play your stupid games with me, Fausto.'

'But, Aldo, you've changed.'

'Of course I've fucking changed.'

'I mean I barely recognised you.'

'Well, I fucking recognised you. Which is more than I can say for this place.'

'Keep your voice down, Aldo. And watch your language too.'

'I'll say what I fucking like. What have you done to this place? What's all this shit? And where's Mum? Jesus Christ, I can't believe she's allowed this to happen! Look, even the bar's gone. That was chestnut, you know. Chestnut! Do you know how many elbows leant on that bar over the years, real elbows, real people's elbows, not like that lot you've got sitting over there now?'

'Aldo, look, you're not making much sense. Are you drunk?'

'Of course I'm not fucking drunk.'

'Well, have a drink, then, on me. Wait here. I'll go and get you something.'

'Don't bother. Is Mum in the kitchen?'

Fausto paused. 'No. No, she isn't, I'm afraid,' and Aldo thought he saw a fleeting sadness in Fausto's eyes.

'Well, where is she, then?'

'Aldo, listen. She's not here any more. She's moved away.'

'I don't believe you. She would never have left this place.'

'She wanted to, believe me. She couldn't manage it on her own. It would have closed anyway. I mean, it was closed for such a long time during the war, it was really going to ruin, and then she tried again but, you know how it is, it was so difficult for her. So I helped her out. As a friend. She wanted to sell up.'

'Liar.'

'She wanted to. No one else would have the place.'

'Liar!'

'So I helped her out. She was grateful. It meant, with the money from the house too, she could move to Rome.'

'To Rome?'

'Yes, Aldo.'

'You're a fucking liar!'

'It's true.'

'Why on earth would she go and live in Rome?'

'Because of your sister, Elena. Her husband's from Rome. He has a business there.'

'Her husband?'

'Well, I assume he's her husband now. They didn't have much choice, if you know what I mean.'

'You're a lying bastard.'

'Come on, Aldo, calm down. Let's sit down and have a chat. Do you need help? Do you need a job? Maybe I can sort something out for you here, a few hours in the kitchen, perhaps.'

'I'd never accept any help from you, not even if I was dying.'

He pushed his way past Fausto Pozzi and past a waiter and into the restaurant. He looked around at the tables covered in fine pink cloths and the empty space where the bar had been and the violinist serenading a couple in the far corner.

'Who the fuck are you? Who the fuck are all of you?'

He gripped the edge of the nearest table, lifted it up and turned it over, then moved on to the next and then the next, and he strode across to the violinist and snatched the instrument from his hands and smashed it against the wall and crushed it with his feet. The place was in uproar, the customers all up on their feet, Fausto Pozzi standing open-mouthed just inside the doorway.

'This isn't the last you'll be seeing of me,' Aldo shouted as he pushed his way past him and out onto the quay. He seized the nearest table and dragged it into the canal. It floated there, legs upturned, the pink tablecloth drifting away under the bridge and sinking out of sight. He strode off down the other side of the canal towards the boatyard, calling back at Fausto Pozzi as he went.

'This isn't the last you'll be seeing of me, I promise you that!

Not by a long way, you lying bastard! I'll be back. I've waited long enough. I'll be back. I'll be fucking back!'

Inside Casa Luca, a man with a high domed forehead, a pair of gold teeth in his lower jaw, and hair slightly too long for his profession, took Fausto Pozzi to one side and spoke to him in a voice barely audible amid the haughty din of offended diners.

'He's going to be a problem, that one. Let me sort him out.'

'No,' said Fausto. 'Leave it to me. I'll deal with him.'

'I think we're better equipped for that,' the man said. 'If you know what I mean.'

Fausto cast a glance at the ceiling. 'No, I said I'll deal with him.'

The man appeared unmoved.

'Please. Please let me deal with this,' repeated Fausto. 'You know it's important to me. Please.'

'All right,' said the man after a suitably authoritative pause. 'But make sure you do, or I'll certainly do it myself.'

Outside by the canal, Aldo walked past the eastern wall of the church of San Trovaso and into the square beyond. He pushed against the door of the boatyard. It creaked but would not open.

'Antonio? Antonio, open up! It's me, Aldo.'

But no one came to the door. It was nearly dark now and Antonio had probably left two or three hours before, so Aldo walked along the Zattere and stopped at one of the cafés overlooking the Canale della Giudecca and Il Redentore, the same café where he had sat with Isabella as she told him about the breakdown of her marriage, where they had drunk red wine before rushing back to her room and straight into bed.

He set off again now for Isabella's house, just behind the Basilica of San Marco. He walked under the arch and into the small courtyard beneath Isabella's window. He rapped on the door. A man in his fifties opened it.

'What do you want?'

Aldo recognised the voice, the one he had heard that night at the top of the stairs.

'I'm looking for Isabella,' Aldo said.

'She's not here. Who are you, anyway?'

'Do you know when she'll be back?'

'Are you one of them? You won't find her here any more. She won't be coming back.' Aldo could feel spittle on his face as the man chucked out his bitter words. 'The last I heard she was living in the ghetto somewhere,' he went on. 'And no, I don't have the address. But if you hang around long enough in the streets you might spot her. I'm not sure you'd recognise her, though. She's changed a bit since, well, since when? When was it you knew her?'

He looked Aldo up and down. 'You must have been one of her later ones. Her taste went downhill towards the end.'

Aldo was already walking away, too exhausted for further conflict that evening.

'As I said,' the man called out, 'look for her in the ghetto, in the streets somewhere. In the gutter.'

Aldo walked the streets for the rest of the night but he saw no one he knew and towards dawn, as the first light of another July day, his first morning back in Venice after eight years away, began to inch itself up behind San Giorgio Maggiore, he found himself in the public gardens towards Sant'Elena. He lay on a bench beneath a tree and listened to the waves of the lagoon until they washed him up on the rocks of broken sleep. When he woke he pondered where to go next and set off back towards the house in Cannaregio, with no particular idea of why he was going there, other than that he could not think of anywhere else. He thought about knocking on the door but instead he walked up onto the arched bridge opposite. He saw the woman from the previous evening in an upstairs window and he opened his mouth and began to raise his hand, but she closed the shutters before he could speak. He walked on towards the railway station and thought about getting back on a train, but where could he go? This was no longer home, but nor was anywhere else, and what he really wanted was to be taken back into the past, to a wooden house beside a Russian lake in the spring of 1943. He walked back through Santa Croce and Dorsoduro to Antica Locanda Fausto. The door was locked and bolted now, the shutters closed, the tables absent from the quayside, so he kicked hard on the door a couple of times, shoved his nose up against the wood, examined the grain, decided it was oak, yelled a few obscenities through the gap between the door and the frame, and walked on towards the boatyard. He heard the church bell strike nine. At this time of the morning Antonio would certainly be around. Aldo pictured him hunched beneath an upturned hull, muttering away to himself at the shoddy quality of someone else's workmanship, and he imagined the old man's surprise at the welcome return of his former apprentice. He might even offer him some paid work or allow him to resume his training, or possibly even both. It would be a foothold at least, something to build on. The door of the boatyard was open. Aldo went inside and sure enough he saw the hunched figure beneath the hull of a boat. He walked quietly up behind him, wanting to surprise the old man.

'Hey, Antonio, how about a coffee?'

A voice came back at him. 'Eh?'

'Can I get you a coffee? A good one, just like I used to make.'

The figure shuffled round and a head poked out from under the boat. 'What the bloody hell are you talking about?'

'Oh, I'm so sorry. I thought you were Antonio.'

The man looked at Aldo as if he were an idiot. 'Antonio hasn't been here for years! Hadn't you heard?'

'Don't tell me. He's gone away?'

'Gone away? Hell, no. They shot him in '44.'

'Oh my God! Who on earth would shoot Antonio?'

'The communists. They said he'd been helping the Germans. He hadn't, of course, but they shot him all the same. Some sort of vendetta, from long before the war.'

Aldo walked the streets aimlessly for the rest of the day and towards evening found himself on Fondamente Nuove. He took a *vaporetto* to Burano, passing the cemetery of San Michele and stopping at Murano before carrying on towards Burano, the small island at the northern end of the lagoon where his grandfather had his house. Aldo got off the boat and walked the short distance from the quay to the centre of the village, passing the fishermen's houses all painted pastel shades of blue and red and yellow to guide the fishermen home. Tourists stood around and examined the lace that the women of the island had eked out of barren winters past. At the far end of the island, on a scruffy plot of land that served as a garden, one side bordered by a stagnant canal, the other by the lagoon, Aldo's grandfather's house, its walls daubed a deep powder-blue, stood beside a pair of stunted trees. The blue paint was flaking off the walls, lumps of plaster gouged out by the fingertips of time, and several windowpanes were broken or missing. Aldo looked around the garden, overgrown with wild flowers and weeds. His grandfather's boat was still tied up at the end of the canal but it held a slough of green water. The door of the house was open. Aldo went inside and looked around. Most of the furniture was still there as he remembered it, but his grandfather had always kept it neat and orderly and now it was strewn around the room. Sunlight shone down from the bedroom above, passing through the holes in the ceiling. The stone floor of the kitchen was barely visible beneath lumps of plaster and clumps of grass and dirt that something had dragged in from the garden. Aldo sniffed. The room smelt of animals. He heard the ruminant chewing of the goat before he saw its insouciant eyes. It was standing half-concealed in the cupboard beneath the stairs. He ignored it and went upstairs. Another one stood by the window, nosing the air through the broken pane, then chewing at the edges of the glass. Aldo went downstairs and out into the garden and he knocked on the neighbours' door.

'Hello,' he said.

They looked at him. He saw that look in their eyes again, that subtly different look, the one Isabella had told him she'd seen in others who looked at her that way for very different reasons, but the same look all the same – that knowing look, as if they were well-informed, when really they were mistaken, the look he had seen before the war, when he could read people's thoughts, when he could tell they were thinking about Luca and what Aldo had done to him, out there in the woods. Well, fuck them, he thought. Fuck them then, fuck them now, they really haven't changed.

'Hello, Aldo,' said the neighbours. 'We thought you were dead.'

You weren't the only ones, he thought. Bet you wish I was, using the house as a stable.

'Well,' he said, 'you were wrong.'

'Yes. Well, it's good to see you.'

They had never liked his grandfather. It was the usual thing, neighbours on the wrong end of each other's misunderstandings, digging in, entrenched in their positions, a simmering lifelong hatred that would linger on in stalemate until one side moved house or died. And that clannish thing too: hate one member of the family, hate them all, as if they were all the same.

'I suppose you'll want to know where he is? Your grandfather?'

But Aldo already knew the answer, the house had told him at first glance. Stalemate broken. The neighbours had outlasted him, war of attrition won.

'We're very sorry, Aldo,' they said. 'It's a terrible shame.'

Yes, he thought, I believe you. I'm sure you think it's *such* a terrible shame.

'Where did they put him? After he died?

'San Michele. Next to Luca.'

'Good,' said Aldo. 'Well, you know what I mean . . .'

'Can we offer you a coffee?'

But he knew they didn't really mean it, wouldn't really want him in their house. So, yes, let's have a coffee, just to annoy you, you hypocrites.

The neighbours drank their coffee in a hurry, looking increasingly towards the door as they did so. So, thought Aldo, time to bring up the goats.

'Your goats . . .' he said.

'Oh, yes . . .'

'They'll have to leave.'

'At such short notice? But they need shelter.'

As if goats had rights!

'I need shelter too. They'll have to go.'

'But, Aldo, the house is unoccupied, has been for years. We've acquired certain rights.'

'That takes twenty years. We all know the law.'

'But it was unoccupied, it was going to waste.'

'Well, it's occupied now. I'm moving in.'

And he stood up and thanked them for the coffee and slammed the door as he left.

He walked back into the house and saw the goat was still in the cupboard. He chased it out of the room and it ran off down the garden. Then he went upstairs to sort out the other one. It was standing in the far corner by the window and it shat on the floor when it saw him.

'Fuck off, Mister Goat! Off you pop now, get out!'

But off he did not pop, Mister Goat. It just stood there and looked at him, chewing on nothing. Then it shat some more.

'I said get the fuck out of here!' Aldo yelled, and he ran at the thing. It hurtled towards the window, tried to exit through the aperture, pushed itself half through, then forced itself back into the room and stood there looking at him again. So Aldo ran at it again and up it went, onto the bed and down the other side, then through the door and he heard the clatter of its hooves and then the banging as it fell down the stairs. He ran down after it and chased it out into the garden and it ran over to where the other one stood beneath the pair of stunted trees.

'Keep out of my house!' he shouted. 'And get off my fucking land!'

But they stood by the trees and watched him, all quizzical again, and the neighbours were all on the doorstep, jabbering.

'What the fuck are you lot looking at?' he said, and he banged the door as he went back inside. And so Aldo moved in, and after eight years away put a roof over his head. He unpacked his one small bag of possessions and placed beside the bed a worn-out photograph of a girl in a ballet class in Leningrad. That night, Aldo lay on the bed in the upstairs room and stared at the ceiling until the wooden beams disappeared into the gathering dark and the island fell silent but for the chirruping of the insects in the long grass outside. And then, sometime between midnight and dawn, there were footsteps outside, the footfalls of a large bear of a man tracing a dotted line in the dew. Unseen in the darkness the man placed a bunch of fresh flowers on each of the slight elevations that lay beneath the back window of the house, and when he pushed his boat back off into the night, the goats wandered across to the unmarked graves, nibbled at the fresh green leaves, and chewed the red and white heads off the blooms.

The next morning Aldo set about tidying up the house, removing the rubble, sweeping out the dust and restoring the furniture to its rightful place. He could do nothing about the broken panes but the gentle summer breeze brought welcome disturbance to the air. He went down to the boat at the end of the garden and tried the outboard, but it was rusty and seized and the rotten wood of the boat caved in when he stepped on it. He walked up the main street and bought some bread and fruit at a shop and he went back and ate at the table in the downstairs room. He thought about the elevated price of what he had bought and he counted the money he had left. The resettlement allowance wasn't going to last him very long and soon he would have to find a job. He decided to try again at the boatyard. If there was no work for him there, he would ask around at the market and in the bars and restaurants that proliferated in the narrow streets and alleys all over town. He caught the *vaporetto* to Venice, stopping off at San Michele to find the place where his grandfather lay in the ground, and his thoughts turned to his father, lying in an adjacent grave. And then, inevitably, he thought again of Fausto Pozzi.

'One day he'll pay for what he did to you, Dad, I promise you that,' he said, and he left the cemetery in tears and got on the next *vaporetto* to Fondamente Nuove.

He went to the trattoria to look for Fausto Pozzi but it was still closed.

'Earned enough money for one day already, have you, Fausto?' Aldo whispered at the door. 'No need for the long hours that you made Luca work?'

He continued over the bridge and along the quayside to the boatyard, but the man there had nothing to offer and told him not to come back.

'Everyone's looking for work now,' he said. 'There's no need to bother me again.'

Aldo walked the streets for hours, waiting until the trattoria opened, and he sat on the wall beside the bridge and watched as the customers came and went, and he paid particular attention to the whereabouts of Fausto Pozzi, gazing in through the windows at him, and as Fausto locked up for the night and headed off towards San Marco, Aldo followed unseen and unheard. He gradually reduced the distance between them and as he did so he felt the knife in his pocket, pricked his finger with the tip and gripped the blade. But then he turned the next corner and Fausto had gone and the only footsteps were somewhere behind him, so he withdrew his hand from the knife and went back to Fondamente Nuove and waited for the *vaporetto* back to Burano.

He returned to the boatyard the following week anyway, despite what the man had said, and the week after that too, but there really was no work and finally the man chased him away, and every evening Aldo waited near the trattoria and followed Fausto Pozzi unseen. On more than one occasion he was close enough to kill him but he became uncertain at the moment of truth, and so the knife remained in his pocket and Fausto Pozzi remained on this earth.

Aldo trod his steady daily path around town, looking for work at the bars and market stalls, and he finally found a part-time job filling sandwiches at a bar near the railway station, but it was only for a few days and they didn't pay him what they had promised, and so he complained too forcefully and was soon back on the streets. His enthusiasm drained away and he returned each night to the house on Burano, dodging the fare on the *vaporetto*, and he counted his few remaining notes and coins and slept beside the photo of Katerina in the warm summer air in the half-ruined house and woke again to shout at the goats and to take the *vaporetto* back to Venice to recommence his search. Each day the piece of bread he ate was smaller and staler than the one he had eaten the previous day, and each night his sleep became shallower and more troubled. And then his money ran out altogether and he faced a choice between the life of a scavenger and that of a criminal, and he chose the former as a more gentle slope into the abyss. The first time that he went looking in the bins, the looks of disapproval caused him to flee back to Burano and he remained there for several days until hunger drove him back to Venice with renewed purpose, turning over the rubbish more methodically this time, and the rewards were correspondingly greater and soon he mapped out a regular route, equipped with his sacks and his bags, and he returned to Burano each evening with enough scraps to keep him fed for a day or even two, and occasionally with half-broken ornaments with which he would adorn the window-sills, and one day he found a serviceable picture frame in which Katerina's photo could sit safe behind glass. And on another day he returned with a couple of rickety café chairs with tall curving backs which he placed by the window that looked out across the garden towards the lagoon, and he would often sit there late at night and imagine that the beach at the end of the garden was the beach by the lakeside in Russia in the spring of 1943, and that Katerina sat in the chair beside him and that Viktor was somewhere out of sight upon a wooded hill, but then he would see the chair by his side was empty and the night was silent but for the lapping of the waves and the incessant bleating of the goats.

As each day passed, Aldo's beard grew longer and his eyes more distant and he became more attuned to this new way of life. Each day, before he set off towards Venice, he would pluck a flower from the garden and place it in a small chipped vase he had found near San Marco, and he would wipe the glass of the picture frame with his sleeve and replace it on the nail above his bed, as a religious man might clean and replace a picture of the Madonna. He often saw a street musician with a violin in Campo Santo Stefano, and he would sit and listen and rub his hands together to try to keep them warm against the cold and the damp of an accelerating autumn, and each day when he returned to the house it was slighter colder and less hospitable and the wind that blew in through the broken windows was less tolerable, and each morning the number of flowers in the garden was diminished until finally, one day in October, there were none. And so the flower from the previous day remained in the vase for more than a week, until it was no more than a clock of brown petals clinging to the stalk, counting down the dying days of the year with each falling petal.

By late autumn the bins around the markets were full of rich pickings that remained in edible form for longer than had been possible in the oppressive heat and humidity of summer. The discarded fruit and vegetables now lingered for days before mould ate them away from inside. The apples were the best, plentiful at this time of year and perfectly acceptable even when half-gone and smelling of cider, unlike the citrus fruits which fermented swiftly beneath the rubbish, turning foul and bitter. Aldo usually searched the bins under the cover of darkness now, hiding his face behind his lengthening beard and unkempt hair as he scavenged around the fringes of society. He had been doing this long enough now to have become something of an expert in the anticipated pickings of the various neighbourhoods. He would always start in Cannaregio, arriving on the *vaporetto* at Fondamente Nuove and passing the old family home first of all. Then he would cross the Canale Grande via the bridge near the railway station and cut through Santa Croce and Dorsoduro, passing the boatyard where the gondolas lay with upturned hulls, then on to the hated door of Antica Locanda Fausto before crossing the bridge at Accademia and on to San Marco. From there he crossed Piazza San Marco and continued along behind the Basilica into Castello, finally turning left again to head back to Fondamente Nuove with his bags full of rubbish. The whole circuit could take several hours, the exact time depending on how often and for how long he stopped to contemplate the landmarks from a previous life that littered his route. He considered it a working day, no different from any other job, requiring the same dedication and commitment if you were to make a success of it. It was certainly not a lazy man's choice of occupation, walking several miles a day in order to cover all the best spots. Of course, calling it a *choice* of occupation would not be strictly accurate, but he had come to accept the daily routine in the same way that a shopworker or a desk-bound civil servant might accept their daily commute and their day-long imprisonment behind a counter or a desk. And at least he was able to spend the whole day outside in the fresh air to which his time on the steppe had accustomed him, and the long hours of walking eased his mind. His working day had shifted with the seasons, summer's early evening run now giving way to a more manageable late-afternoon trawl as the winter nights drew in, and on dull days dusk came in mid-afternoon and Aldo was able to leave the empty shell of his grandfather's house on Burano a little after two, catch the *vaporetto* to Fondamente Nuove, and start work as four o'clock shadows filled the alleys. On one occasion, close to his old home on Fondamenta della Sensa, he saw a vision of Katerina walking towards him along the quay, and he paused and watched as the vision passed him by, its head turned towards the canal, and as the vision's footsteps faded away he nearly turned in pursuit, but he knew that it was futile and that even if a vision was capable of recognising a man, it would evaporate in his arms if he tried to detain it.

He was usually home before midnight, and on the rare occasions that he missed the last *vaporetto* to Burano he would find a place on a bench in the public gardens towards the eastern end of Castello. Beside one of the churches along this route there was a convent where the nuns would offer him a bowl of soup or a small brown bag of their homemade biscuits or a slice of warm *pizza bianca*, its top dusted with salt. And there was a café in the ghetto where the owner would sometimes offer him a coffee and slip him a sandwich or half a loaf of bread, although there was a tacit understanding that he would not linger for long on the premises. He always saved the bread until he reached Campo Santo Stefano, the spot where the old street musician often played the violin, and Aldo would sit and listen to the music and pick at the bread until all that remained were the crumbs at his feet over which the sparrows would quarrel in the dust. As he watched the man play, the music brought back memories of late nights at Casa Luca, of recitals in the church near the Rialto, of Isabella, and of course of the house suspended somewhere in time beside a lake in the shimmering heart of Russia, but all these memories merely accentuated everything that he had lost. Aldo would sit and listen until, tired of playing, the old man would put the coins he had gathered into his pocket, place the violin back in its case, and disappear beyond the far end of the square and over the bridge at Accademia. After the man had left, Aldo would head back to Fondamente Nuove and wait for the *vaporetto*, his heart sinking each day a little further into the mire.

As October lengthened into November, the daily round became a grind. Perhaps it was the worsening weather, the heavy mists that formed during the night and shrouded the lagoon for days on end, or the heavy squalls that blew in and drenched the rooftops and filled the gutters to overflowing, or the floodtides that rose through the streets and sent the inhabitants up onto duckboards and the rubbish floating across the squares, but whatever the cause, the decline in Aldo's spirits was outwardly visible and relentless. He began to miss days, convincing himself he was too ill or tired to do his round, and he would lie in the top room of the house on Burano as the roof let in the rain, and he picked at the bits and pieces he had saved from the previous day and then went out for a walk among the houses, and the kids playing football against the back wall of the church would call him names and kick the ball at the back of his head as he walked away. He would shout at them and then return to the house and sit by the water's edge in the rain and listen to the voices of the water birds as they swirled overhead in the mist, and then he would go inside and wait for darkness so that he could sleep fitfully until dawn. His wild beard and hair mapped his descent down the slippery slope of desperation and he reached the point where he gave up hope of ever fitting back into the life he had once had here, reconciling himself to a permanent role as scavenger and outcast, almost a beast, less than a goat, floating like rubbish on a rising tide of resentment. He knew his descent into squalor during the war was unavoidable, but when arriving back home his aspirations had grown. Of course he had expected to encounter some initial difficulties in readjusting, but he had assumed these would be temporary. After all, he must be some sort of hero, just for surviving, for making it back from the Russian front where tens of thousands of his comrades had been lost – almost ninety per cent of them, he had heard. So surely there would be people now to support him, to love him, for him to love, and some sympathy for the returning soldier trying to pick up the threads of his life and stitch himself back together again. But instead he found a changed society that had suffered too much to be interested in his plight, and nothing that was left of the life he had known, no one to help him, just the bare walls of an empty house on Burano commandeered by goats that had to be forcibly removed so he could shelter between its crumbling walls and watch his life fall apart all around him.

The Violin

Venice, November 1950

Aldo sat on the bench in Campo Santo Stefano and watched the old man with the violin. He must be well into his seventies, Aldo thought, dressed in simple clothes of brown, black and grey, his face pleasant and serene as he nodded at passers-by and then took up the violin and teased out a tune. Aldo watched him, his own empty hands fidgeting with the meagre bag of rubbish he had dragged around all afternoon. He twisted and turned it in his lap, looked inside at the contents, the rotting fruit of several hours' work. His head pounded, his feet ached, and all he had to show for his efforts were two florets of cauliflower, a handful of green leaves of uncertain origin, a squashed tomato and a husk of brown bread containing a variety of seeds that had largely been pecked away by the pigeons. He looked again at the violinist and noted the courteous nods of recognition he received from passers-by. A young couple stopped to listen and the music brought a smile to their lips and they walked off laughing, leaving a few coins in the old man's case. Aldo looked at the people on the benches around the square, chatting and laughing in twos or threes. Then he looked at the bench on which he sat, on which no one else would sit except for an old lady who perched like a nervous bird at the far end for a few seconds before looking at him, standing up, and hurrying away. The old man transferred the coins from his case to his pocket and replaced them with the violin and walked off in the direction of the bridge at Accademia. Aldo stood up and followed him across the bridge, then into Santa Croce and the labyrinth of alleyways and canals towards San Polo. He kept a discreet distance and the only footsteps were those of Aldo and the violinist, but as

Aldo tired, and the idea that had begun to form in his mind took flight, he turned away, disgusted at the thought that had made him stray so far from his normal route. He went back to the house on Burano and yelled at the goats and lay down on the bed and curled up and shivered in the November chill.

He stayed there until dawn and all through the next day and the following night. He woke at last in the late afternoon to the sound of heavy rain falling on terracotta tiles from leaden skies. He rose from his bed and walked under a steady rain towards the quayside and caught the *vaporetto* to Venice. This time he did not pass by the house on Fondamenta della Sensa and he skipped his usual stop-off at the café and the possibility of a gift of bread, and instead he headed straight for Campo Santo Stefano, already resolved to carry out the deed that was creeping up on him unseen. But damn it, when he reached the square the violinist was not there so he sat on the bench opposite the statue and waited as the rain turned to drizzle and then to a vapour that thickened into mist. Then he heard footsteps, familiar footsteps now, the sound of the violinist arriving, and Aldo observed him carefully as he got himself ready to play. He sized up the man's frail and stooping frame, the narrow shoulders and the crooked limbs. He looked down at the shoes which must once have been elegant, a polished shiny black with fresh new laces and sharp-edged heels, but now cracked and curling around the edges. Aldo listened to the music and recognised several of the pieces that he used to play in recitals before the war, the adagios of Albinioni and Mahler and Camille Saint-Saëns' *The Swan*. He watched until the man packed away his instrument and walked off towards Accademia, the usual route. Aldo stood up and followed a little way behind him, through Santa Croce and towards San Polo, and the streets were populated only by an occasional passing figure in the fog, and the violinist turned each corner a little way ahead of Aldo, but with each corner the distance between them diminished until they were separated by just a few short steps, and when the man turned around he raised his hand for protection but Aldo's fist smashed into the side of his head and the man fell to his knees and looked up at him.

'What do you want from me?' the man pleaded. 'What do you want? I have nothing.'

'I have less.'

The second blow knocked the man clean into the canal. The violin clattered across the quay, falling out of its case. Aldo picked it up and put it back inside. Then he hurried off up the alleyway and was lost in the fog.

He woke the next morning to the full of horror of what he had done. He looked at the ceiling and tried to persuade himself that the previous day could not have happened, but it was no use, reality could not be denied and the damning proof stood propped on a chair in the corner by the window where Aldo had left it the night before. Aldo lay on the bed for the rest of the day, shifting with the cold, alternately turning his back on the violin and then fixing it with a cold hard unblinking stare until his eyes grew tired and the light darkened, but then he would blink and the room and everything in it re-emerged, and the violin still sat propped on the chair near the door and seemed to be considering him silently. Aldo stood up but the violin sent him cowering back onto the bed and he lay there again until he needed to relieve himself, but the violin still would not let him past and so he was forced to urinate through the broken window into the garden below, where the goats regarded him with indifference and the neighbours, fussing about on their porch, had their suspicions further confirmed. Time waxed and waned until Aldo was no longer sure how long he had been in the room under the withering gaze of the violin, but he was certain that the sun had come and gone several times when the wind outside began to rise, rushing in from the east, across the sea and the spit of land bordering the lagoon, then across the marshes where the ducks sought refuge among the reeds, and then it came hurtling in through the broken windows. It swirled around the room, lifted Aldo's hair, howled down the stairs, banging the door back and forth as it departed. The violin twitched in the wind, the ghosts of notes lifting up and blowing around the room as the storm set off an orchestra of noise and the branches of the trees clashed together hard and brittle outside and the slamming door banged out its percussive rhythm. Aldo rushed past the chair where the violin sat, and he propelled himself down the stairs and then out through the door, assisted by the wind that was shoving at his back, and he rushed down to the beach, throwing off his clothes as he ran, and he plunged into the cold water and swam out into the darkness until his feet no longer touched the silt beneath him. Then he stopped and looked around and realised that the night was calm, the trees were still, the moon shining down and illuminating the house and the thin mist that was lifting off the waves.

He swam back to the shore and returned to his room, slowly ascending the stairs, his breath still hard and rasping, but now from exhaustion, no longer from fear. The violin still sat on the chair and he felt it observe him as he came into the room, but its gaze was no longer one of reproach and accusation but of triumph, and when Aldo picked it up and took the bow and ran it tenderly across the strings, its voice was clear and sharp and beautiful and it wrapped him in something like hope or even forgiveness, or what he imagined or hoped that forgiveness might be. He played all the pieces he knew and his fingertips, no longer accustomed to the bite of the strings, became grooved and tender and he placed the violin back on the chair and took a mirror and an old razor and a pair of scissors down to the beach. He hacked away at the long growths of beard, shaved off what remained, and saw a face that he had long forgotten looking back at him. Then he cut his hair short and gathered it all up from where it had fallen and cast it onto the black lagoon. He washed his face in the water and scratched away at the pig on his arm, pushing and pulling at its features, but it would not be removed and it looked at him, hurt and confused, perhaps even betrayed after all it had done for him, so he kissed it goodnight and returned to the house and slept until mid-morning. Then he took the *vaporetto* to Venice as usual, but this time he did not carry with him empty bags for the collection of discarded vegetables and fruit, but instead the violin. In Piazza San Marco he stood near Caffé Florian and a dam broke and the music that had lain dormant within him for years flooded out, and the tin that he left on the ground rattled its own

accompaniment as a coin or two was tipped in by passers-by and
Aldo nodded and smiled and occasionally gave a small considered
bow as they went on their way. He played until his fingertips were
red raw and blistering, and when he went to collect his tin he was
surprised by its weight and he tipped the coins into his hand, and
there were so many that some of them spilled onto the ground and
rolled away across the square.

The Outcast

Isabella opened the bedroom door and stepped out onto the landing. The smell of cats hung stale and yellow in the air but she barely noticed it now after two years of living in the house of Madame Leroux. She crossed the landing, squeezing past the empty suitcases that were piled against the wall, and set off down the stairs. It was no easy task in the gloom to negotiate the stacks of books that lined the steps, but they were rarely moved and she knew the path between them well, only stumbling when drunk, especially troubled, or otherwise distracted. On this particular morning she was, unusually, none of these. She wasn't sure to what she should attribute the unaccustomed lightness of her mood, but she put it down to the change in the weather. The onset of autumn, the leaves loosening their grip, the layered mist above the canal, did not so much cause a lifting of her heart as a feeling of belonging. She would wake in the cold grey light of her room, most often unaccompanied, unlike in the old days, and would dress without paying any great attention to her appearance. She would take a deep breath before leaving her room, holding it in for as long as possible and preferably until she was out in the street and away from the nocturnal perfume of the house's feline inhabitants. Quite often, as she hurried towards the front door, she would be apprehended by the lady of the house. Madame Leroux had left Paris sometime in the 1920s, travelling around southern Europe by bicycle and by bus, finally finding herself upon the shore of the Bay of Naples. She had made her way up the spine of Italy, happily frittering away a significant portion of her large inheritance before arriving, as she had always intended, in Venice with sufficient funds to purchase a small house and to deposit a hefty sum in the nearest bank. She then spent several months recovering from the rigours of her months on the road before relaunching herself into her various passions. Age had since tempered her and now, nearly thirty years on, she contented herself with the custody and protection of the local feline population. She was never quite sure how many of them lived under her roof at any one time – they came and went as they pleased – but the ones that lived in the streets nearby were no worse off than the ones that sheltered within her walls because each evening she would take her leftovers on trays of cardboard down to the square in the heart of the ghetto and the cats would twist their bodies into unearthly forms in greedy anticipation, wrapping themselves around Madame Leroux's legs as she lowered the tray to the ground, and every morning, after she returned from the fish market by the Ponte di Rialto, the scene would be repeated and the cats would breakfast on the scraps she had collected from the fishermen. When Madame Leroux's return to the house in the morning coincided with Isabella's departure, they would exchange pleasantries in the hall and Madame Leroux would let her gaze linger upon Isabella's departing grace as she hurried off down the quay towards Strada Nuova and the shop where she spent her days dispensing fine food from behind the delicatessen counter – *prosciutto di Parma*, its tastier cousin San Daniele, smoked *scamorza* cheese and the oozing white freshness of *burata*, wrapped in long green leaves and tied with a stem of grass.

Recent years had not been kind to Isabella and she regarded her thirty-seven years with weary eyes, bearing her body home each night on legs drained hollow by the drudgery of work, but she still possessed a handsomeness that teetered on the brink of beauty, a flicker that shone through the dreariness that had replaced the decadence of her youth. Her life had become mundane: days of unfulfilling work followed by nights rarely punctuated by the thrill of the unknown, and the unknown therefore never had the chance to grow into the comforting and the familiar. Even now, five years after the war ended, people who had known her then remembered her above all for her last and least forgiveable indiscretion, and many who had not known her at the time had since been made aware of it by those who considered it their duty, if not to guide a lost sheep back towards the path, then at least to alert others to its wanderings. Even now she was aware of whispers and disapproving looks with which people stabbed her in the back as she went on her way. A nun had once placed a pale hand upon her as she passed.

'Why do you do these things?' the nun asked her, squeezing her arm and smiling. 'God doesn't want you to do this. God doesn't want it.'

'Of course He does,' said Isabella. 'Otherwise He wouldn't make me.'

'Bless you, my child, for you are a sinner.'

'Bless me, for I am merely following God's will, and my own.'

She had spent time with friends after the scandal, and then a short time on the street before Madame Leroux took her in like one of her cats and gave her a room at the top of the house, rent-free, and all in return for nothing but her gratitude and the knowledge that she had helped to save another stray. And she had also helped Isabella to find the job she still held at the small supermarket off Strada Nuova, and even now she took nothing as rent but the offcuts of cheese and ham that Isabella brought home from the shop each Friday evening and the pleasure of her conversation and her company.

In the evenings after work, Isabella would leave the shop and drop in at the bar a door or two down the street, owned by her friend Michele, and she would knock back a glass or two of red, then take a detour through the eastern end of Cannaregio and into San Marco. She would stroll through the streets and play a game with herself, scoring a point for every former acquaintance she passed and an extra point for any who acknowledged her presence. Occasionally she would recognise an old lover and one or two of them still stopped to talk, and for a short time she could pretend she was back in her heyday of 1940 or 1941, but then she would return to the house in the ghetto and the smell of the cats, and she would spend the evening reading books on the stairs by candlelight or discussing with Madame Leroux the relative merits of Sartre and Rimbaud, and as the evening drew on the old French woman would allow herself a modest flight of fancy and imagine Isabella's elegant head next to hers upon a pillow in the night and she would look intently at the younger woman as the side of her face was lit up by the flames of the fire in the grate, but she never actually rose from her chair to embrace her, to quell the burning she felt inside, and instead she bore the cruel flame of unexpressed desire long into the night.

And then one evening in early December 1950, as Isabella idly counted former acquaintances and lovers in the streets round San Marco, she stopped to look at the multitude of sculptures, fashioned by the glass-blowers of Murano, that sat on the shelves of a shop on the corner of the square along from Caffé Florian. In the window, among the garish dolphins and sailboats and other unnecessarily colourful creations, a long black glass gondola, simple and dark and beautiful, floated on its fragile shelf of glass. She remembered the gondola that still lay tied up to the jetty behind the house she had shared with her husband not far from there, and at that moment she became aware of the sound of a violin from further along the square and she turned to look and saw the tall thin figure, motionless but for the slow jagging of the elbow and the tripping of the fingers, and she retrieved his music from the depths of her memory. She wandered across, stood a little way back and watched him as he played and then, as he finished his piece, she gently placed a coin in his tin.

'Thank you,' said the man, and he bowed as she took a couple of steps back.

She looked at him, and he looked at her. She saw straight away that he recognised her and that he understood – where she had been and what she had become – and she recognised the same thing in him.

'Isabella?' he said. 'Is it really you?'

'My dear Tintoretski . . .'

'Oh, it's so good to see you,' he said, lowering the violin and taking a step towards her.

'Is it really, Aldo?'

'Really, Isabella, really. It's so wonderful to see you. You can't imagine how good it is.'

'It's good to see you too, Aldo. Honestly it is. Where the hell have you been all this time?'

'To hell and back. And to heaven somewhere in between.'

'Same here, more or less.'

She smiled at him, something different to what he had ever seen in her before.

'Listen, shall we go somewhere?' he said. 'For a drink, I mean. One of the bars on the Zattere?'

'Sure. Anywhere's fine by me, you know that.'

On the way they passed Casa Luca, or rather they passed by the place where Casa Luca used to be. The door was closed but the curtains were held open by elaborate lace bows.

'This was Casa Luca,' Aldo said, glancing in through the sparkling glass of the window, all freshly cleaned. 'My father's old place.'

'Yes, Aldo, I remember it.'

'Look what the bastards have done to it,' he said, almost out of habit, an instinctive reaction, synapses grooved by repetition, then a closing of his fists. But then the thought juddered to a halt and retreated back along the synapse from where it had come, and so he did not walk over to the door and throw it open and call out across the room towards Fausto Pozzi, did not shout and swear and hurl elaborate threats as to the inevitability of revenge. The death of the street musician had, it seemed, devoured his hatred.

'Come on, let's go,' Aldo said to Isabella. 'There's nothing for me here any more.'

They carried on down the quay towards the Zattere and found a table outside a café.

'So, where do we start?' said Isabella when the waiter had gone.

'At the beginning, perhaps?'

'Oh, but that would take far too long. Let's start at the end and work backwards. And we'll miss out the boring bits.'

'Have there been any?'

'Well, of course, one or two. Not for you?'

'Sure. But when you spend years on the steppe, just waiting for time to pass, you get used to nothing much happening. And most of what does isn't worth talking about.'

'You can tell me, Aldo. If you want to . . .'

'I thought about you plenty, you know.'

She turned to look at him. 'During your time there? On the steppe?'

'Yes, on the steppe. In the gulag.'

'The gulag? Oh, Aldo, I'm so sorry. I had no idea. I would never have imagined.'

'Imagination is a wonderful thing, you know. Sometimes in the prison camp I felt freer than I ever did on the outside. Nothing was real, so I dreamt up anything I wanted. But now here I am, back in reality again, and so I have to deal with all the memories.'

'They can't all be bad memories,' she said.

'I have both.'

'But which are strongest?'

'I don't know.'

'You must.'

'But how?'

'Close your eyes, Aldo. What do you see?'

'An angel.'

'An angel?'

'An angel in the snow.'

'That sounds like a good memory,' she whispered. 'Now open your eyes.'

He opened them and he saw her face close up to his now, her eyes darkened by the disappointments of her life but still showing him something he had never expected from her. Her lips moved a fraction, just enough to touch his own.

'Close your eyes too,' he said, and she closed them and he studied for a moment the tiny wrinkles that edged the heavy lids, and he noticed the flickering of the eyeball beneath and the slight trembling of the lashes and a barely perceptible lifting of the brows.

'What do you see, Isabella?' he asked.

'Nothing.'

'There must be something.'

'Nothing.'

'Open your eyes, dear.' He brushed her lips with his own.

'Kiss me again,' she said. 'But kiss me with your eyes this time, not just your lips.'

'I can't. My eyes belong to someone else.'

'After all this time?'

'Yes, after all this time.'

'Your angel? Your angel in the snow?'

'Yes.'

'Then just kiss me with your mouth.'

He kissed her long and hard and felt her mouth melting into his and her thoughts mingling with his own as they embraced, eyes closed in the cold, and the waiter hovered in the background with another bottle and when they opened their eyes their glasses were full again.

'You meant more to me than the others, you know,' she said.

'Really? How could that have been?'

'Do you always need an answer?'

'No, not any more. Nothing makes sense, remember?'

'I taught you that,' she said.

'Yes, you taught me that.'

'Maybe that's why you meant more. You were untouched.'

'Are you trying to embarrass me again?'

'I didn't mean it like that, stupid. You're still untouched now.'

'I don't feel that way.'

'You are. You'll always be that way. That's why you're different, different from all the others.'

'And you?'

'Me? Untouched?' she said. 'You *must* be joking.'

The bar closed and the waiter politely dislodged them from their seats and they wandered away along the canal past the boatyard and towards Accademia.

'So where are you living now?' Aldo said as they stood upon the wooden bridge and watched the gondolas passing by beneath.

'Do you remember that first night?' she asked, ignoring his question as if deciding whether to answer it. 'We came along this way, remember, under the bridge in the fog?'

'Of course I remember. I was absolutely terrified.'

'Of what?'

'Of you, of course.'

'Terrified of me?'

She bared her teeth and lifted her hands and drew back her fingers in imaginary claws.

'You were a little intimidating,' he said.

'I was just testing you,' she said. 'You haven't told me where you're staying now either, you know.'

'Oh, on Burano. It was my grandfather's house but it's a bit of a shell now. I share it with the neighbours' goats – they let me in now and again.'

'I share with an old goat too, in the ghetto.'

'That's a lot nearer than Burano.'

'Yes, I suspect you might be right about that.'

'And I think I've missed the last *vaporetto* home now.'

'Well, that sounds like a good enough excuse. Just promise you won't think any less of me when you see the place. It's not like where I lived before. And ignore the smell.'

The house was silent when they arrived and the only shadows that moved in the hall were those of the cats. They followed Isabella and Aldo up the stairs and when the bedroom door closed they rubbed themselves against the frame and purred at the sound of the soft tender voices that drifted into the hall from Isabella's room. Inside, the two shadows of their former selves wrapped themselves in the cool shroud of the sheets and felt again the touch of warm flesh and they held onto each other long afterwards in the chill of the room. She kissed his hand and ran her lips up along the veins until her lips came to rest on the wild eyes of the pig, its face unfaded on his arm.

'You've still got your pet pig, I see?'

'Of course. How am I ever going to get rid of the little bastard unless I scour him off with a knife? He's sleeping now, though. Too much work for him these last few years – sometimes I think he's the only thing that got me through the war alive.'

'And your darling angel in the snow? She must have helped.'

'You're not jealous, are you?'

'Fuck you, Tintoretto.'

'I was only joking.'

'Where is she now, anyway, your little winged creature?'

'I have no idea.'

She stopped herself. 'I'm sorry, Aldo, I shouldn't make fun of her. I know I'm no substitute.'

'Don't say that.'

'Well, am I? Remember the rules.'

'You're more than you ever thought.'

'You haven't answered my question.'

'I know.'

'That's all right,' she said, but her voice gave her away.

'I thought you didn't believe in those things,' he said.

'I didn't. But it's been a long road, these last few years. A long, long road. I surprised even myself. I never realised I could do it, you know. Remember how I made fun of you? I had no idea.'

'Who was he?'

'His name was Walter. A German. I met him during the war, of course. When else would I have met a German? They were in Venice a long time, you know. They sent him away once, but he came back. And then when the British came they all left, and he went too and I've heard nothing since. That was five years ago. And of course no one round here understood. I suppose that's not surprising, with my reputation, but it really was different with Walter. But they had it in for me all the same. You know what they did to us? I mean, there were others like me, of course. You know what they did? I so wish I could make them feel what I felt, when they took me out into the street and scratched and kicked me and hacked and pulled at my hair, shaved my head like they were shearing a diseased sheep. Neighbours I'd had for years. The women were the worst, you know, I don't know why. Maybe they hated me already. I suppose I'd fucked half their men.'

She laughed.

'And then my husband threw me out. After so long, begging him for a divorce, all that duplicity, he goes and kicks me out for falling for a man of the wrong nationality, a man who should have been my enemy. What a husband, the fucking hypocrite.'

'He never deserved you.'

'That's what he said in the end.'

He stroked her hair, blacker than the darkness, as smooth and as long as he remembered it, swallowing up his hand in its softness. They kissed, a gentle kiss of mutual understanding, and listened as an orchestra of cats purred their lullabies outside the door.

'I'm tired, Aldo. I'm so tired.'

'Sleep, then, Isabella, sleep. And sweet dreams, my dear . . .'

He stroked her hair in time to the slow contented purring of the cats until her breathing deepened and slowed and then he too loosened his chains and invited the night to anaesthetise him, and it drugged his eyes with its softness and its love. Several hours later Isabella was still beside him, watching him as he woke.

'Thank you for everything,' she said.

'For what?'

'For making me feel like someone again.'

They caught the *vaporetto* in mid-afternoon, as soon as Isabella had finished her shift at the supermarket, the sky vast and empty as they cut across the lagoon, past San Michele and Murano and on between the buoys that marked the channel between the sunken banks of sand. They reached the powder-blue house on Burano as the sky began to pale in the east.

'Well, this is it,' said Aldo. 'Home, sweet home.'

'Nice place. Where's your family now, anyway?'

He shook his head. 'They moved to Rome a while back, it seems, when I was away.'

'To Rome? Why on earth to Rome?'

'Family duties. It seems my sister's husband is from there. Never met him, myself. A lot can happen in eight years.'

'And you haven't been to look for them?'

'Not yet. I will, of course, but I really haven't got the money for the trip. That sounds a pretty lame excuse, doesn't it? But, Isabella, I've barely been able to eat these last few months. I couldn't possibly pay to go to Rome and back, and the hotel and all the rest.'

'But you have to try, Aldo. I'll help you out. How much do you need? What are friends for, after all? Please, you have to go and look for them. I don't have much, but I'll lend you what I can.'

They sat on the beach until it was dark and then they went back to the house and up the narrow stairs. Aldo lit a candle and placed it on the chair by the door. It flickered in the breaths of air that slipped in through the broken panes.

'It's cold in here, Aldo. Haven't you got any blankets? And you've been living here since you got back?'

'Since July. It was warm enough in the summer . . .'

'Yes, but look at your windows. There's almost nothing left of them.'

'Blame the goats.'

'Goats?'

'Glass-chewing bastards.'

'Oh.'

'Isabella, for a long time I had nothing. Less than nothing. I was a beggar, you know. You wouldn't have recognised me, hair down to here, a great big beard. I was a mess. No one would offer me work, so I used to come back here every night, then back to Venice every afternoon to look through the bins for something to eat. But then I found the violin, and things have been better since then, with the money I get from playing in the street.'

'Aldo,' she said. 'It's too cold here. Let's go back to the ghetto. You can stay with me again tonight. And I'll lend you some money so you can get this place sorted out. And so you can go to look for your family in Rome.'

Pantheon

Rome, December 1950

Aldo boarded the train to Rome and Isabella saw him off and the train jolted out of the station and over the causeway towards Mestre. He closed his eyes and listened to the rhythm of the wheels and when he opened them again the train was crossing the northern plain. He fell asleep and woke as they were passing through Florence, the terracotta tiles of the Duomo lit up by the winter sun. The train reached Rome in mid-afternoon and the capital's December air was no warmer than in the north and Aldo pulled his coat tight around him and lifted the collar as he left Stazione Termini and walked across the forecourt and past the rows of taxis and buses. He set off down the Via Nazionale, a broad, straight artery pulsing with life, cars and buses ferrying people to and fro and pedestrians swarming across the streets and pavements, in and out of shops and buildings, restless atoms in the city's beating heart. Aldo stopped to catch his breath.

'Which way to the centre?' he asked a man at a newspaper kiosk.

'Where do you want? Piazza Spagna? Piazza Venezia? Pantheon?'

'Yes, yes, Pantheon, that's it.'

The man gestured down Via Nazionale and Aldo pushed his way along the crowded pavement, a steady stream of headlamps accentuating the dusk. He reached Piazza Venezia and Mussolini's enormous architectural monument to himself, the cars a rush of whirling light and noise round its base – ah yes, old Benito, Aldo thought. *Il Duce* and his fat fascist arse, as Luca used to say. He'd heard that they hung him by his ankles from a lamppost in the end, and he couldn't think of a better end for him, after all the man had done. A solitary traffic policeman stood stranded on his little podium in the middle of the square, waving his white-gloved hands here and there in a futile attempt at influence. Aldo turned down Via del Corso, then into Piazza Colonna and past the government buildings, then the streets narrowed and through a gap he saw great pillars holding up an enormous portico and the top of a domed roof just visible behind. He dipped his hand in the fountain in the middle of the square and washed the sweat from his face, then drank from cupped hands. He looked at the streets that ran up the slope on either side of the ancient building, and he remembered what Gianni had said about the view from his apartment, of the Pantheon in the rain and the ice creams that fell in the street as people hurried away, and he wondered about Gianni's family, and which of the old apartment buildings they might be in, and he thought about how much he wanted to be able to visit them now and tell them that Gianni had died a noble death, that he had fought bravely in battle and gone down like a hero, but then he was suddenly glad that he would never be able to find them, because they would see straight away that he was lying. So he stood and looked at the Pantheon in the half-light as thin white birds flew swirling overhead, and then it dawned on him that he had nowhere to stay. He went to the hotel on the corner of the square, peeling layers of ochre on its walls, but the price of a room was way beyond his means and so he headed back up Via Nazionale to the cheap-dive hotels that were clustered around the station, and later on he sat in his room and listened to the cars outside and the footsteps of other guests returning to their rooms along the echoing hall, the rise and fall of their voices, and the sound of a radio playing street songs from Naples. He woke early the next morning and made his way back to the old city centre but he had little information to help the police in his search.

'Come back in two days,' the desk sergeant told him. 'I'll see what I can find.'

But he returned to no avail. No record of their names could be found. He left the building and walked to Piazza Venezia, then up the steep flight of marble steps to the Piazza del Campidoglio. A wedding party had gathered there and the bride and groom were showered with rice as they emerged. Aldo turned and looked across the red-tiled rooftops that stretched across the old Tridente. He scratched at the spot on his leg where a bed-bug had bitten him in the night, a bite less potent than those of the fleas and bugs of Russia but an irritant and a bad memory all the same. His knees were stiff and aching, his feet were sore, he was hungry. His money would last only another couple of days. He placed his head in his hands and dragged his fingers back through his hair, then leant back and looked at the sky. A faint drizzle was thickening the air and he saw the wedding party scampering for the shelter of the overhanging balconies and the colonnades. He stood up and walked the short distance to the Piazza della Rotonda and looked again at the Pantheon in the pale afternoon light. A winter sun emerged from behind the clouds and he went inside and watched as a disc of sunlight traced its lonely path through the oculus and around the inner wall, and then the sun was covered up again and grey clouds scudded low and light rain fell through the aperture, the raindrops seemingly suspended in a perfect column in the air. Then he headed towards Campo de' Fiori and when he got there the market was winding down, the stallholders stacking their crates and calling out the final prices of the day, eager to be gone, the remaining fruit and vegetables gathered together in the corners from where the rubbish would be collected and the square hosed down that evening. Aldo sifted through a box of discarded bits and pieces, just a bad habit now, not exactly a necessity. A stallholder caught his eye, a probing look.

'Just looking,' Aldo joked.

'No problem, my friend. You can have a bag of the good ones if you want.'

Aldo took the bag, brimming with ripe tomatoes from the south, and thanked the man. As he turned he glimpsed a familiar figure disappearing behind the awning of a nearby stall. He rushed after her, looking around in excitement and panic for the rounded shoulders, the dark but slightly greying hair tied up in a bun. Then he caught sight of her again and he ran after her and laid an eager hand on her shoulder.

'Mamma! Mamma! Oh, my God, what luck! I thought I'd never find you!'

The woman turned, brushed his hand away, gave him a filthy look. The tomatoes slipped from his hands and splattered on the cobbles as he stumbled over his apologies.

'I'm so sorry, *signora*. I thought you were someone else.'

He walked quickly away, leaving red flesh and seeds on the street. His head was spinning now and he headed straight to the station. He sat on the platform for two hours, waiting for a train as the rain thickened into sleet and the temperature fell further and he rested his head in his dirty hands and looked at the worn-out shoes on his feet and noticed the remnants of the tomatoes that had stuck themselves to the leather. He closed his eyes and wondered what he would do when he got back to Venice. Where would he go? Who would he see? Unlike his longed-for return from the war, there was no sense of homecoming now, nor the all-consuming desire for revenge on Fausto Pozzi. The fierce will to survive that had sustained him throughout the hardship of his years in Russia – and his first months back in Venice – had been dissolving away with the recent upturn in his fortunes, and he sensed that its departure would leave a vacuum that could not be filled, the peaks and troughs of triumph and despair replaced by the numbing monotony of the plateau, a plateau on which everything for miles around was visible and yet there was actually nothing much to see, no anticipated future landmarks or waypoints by which to navigate his life, nothing except the occasional presence of Isabella blowing past him like tumbleweed in the night, unwilling to be detained on her way through the ghost town of memories that Venice had become for them both. And somewhere beyond the plateau, way out of sight beyond the eastern horizon where the birch forests rose, dwelt the possibility of Katerina, but she was a possibility that lived on only in memories and dreams, in a world devoid of time, a world freed of the minutes, hours and days in which we live and love and are condemned to find and then lose each other again.

Aldo looked at the station clock again. Still forty minutes until his train was due. Then he looked up past the station roof and he saw the dense flurries, the great downy flakes that were floating over the tracks, and he leapt to his feet and ran out of the station and into the open air and he looked up at the sky as the torrent of snow poured down, and he rushed off towards Via Nazionale. He reached the Pantheon and he hurried in under the portico and stopped in the doorway and watched as the snow fell through the oculus in a tumbling column from dome to floor, and Aldo felt his heart suddenly pierced with a cold white improbable joy. Gianni had been right all along. Sometimes it really does snow in the heart of Rome and the most beautiful thing one might remember, when sitting in the freezing mud of the Russian steppe in times of war, really could be the Pantheon, pure and white and ancient in a snowstorm. He spent the whole night walking through snow-filled streets and squares. He stared at his feet as he walked, kicking up the fresh snow, and he sensed the tramping of the others nearby, Gianni and Luigi and the sergeant, but when he looked up he saw that he was walking alone through the night and it was only their memory in whose footsteps he was walking, but they were with him nonetheless, and he lay down on a bench and slept in the blizzard and was happy. He woke as the first of the commuters were making their way to work. The sound of a hundred mopeds troubled the air and he got up and crossed the city and caught the next train back to Venice.

Letters

Venice, December 1950

Aldo returned to Burano and gave the house its first proper clean since his return from Russia in July. He found a couple of brooms in the cupboard under the stairs and swept out the house from top to bottom, then brought water from the lagoon in a bucket and scrubbed the floors with the stiffest of the brooms. He evicted the spiders from their cobwebs and turned over the mattress and dragged it downstairs and into the garden and beat it with a stick. The neighbours' goats wandered over in expectation of something novel on which to chew, then withdrew amid the clouds of dust when Aldo raised his stick at them. The next day Aldo woke with a renewed sense of purpose. He walked past the church and when the kids kicked their ball at the back of his head he kicked it straight back at them. He caught the *vaporetto* to Venice and went straight to the canal to the rear of Isabella's old marital home. Sure enough, there it was, the gondola, still tied up to the jetty just as Isabella had told him the previous week. He could scarcely believe it after all these years and he unhitched a nearby boat and pushed himself across to it, jumping out onto the jetty and into the thing, the old girl, even rougher round the edges now than he remembered her. Even the oar was still there, tucked away in the belly of the boat, and he picked it up and poled the gondola out into the Canale Grande, everything coming back to him so easily, as if it were meant to be. He passed beneath the Ponte di Rialto and as he rounded the bend towards Accademia he noticed a grey-haired man in a pastel-yellow jacket waving frantically at him with an umbrella as if hailing a cab. He watched the man for several seconds and, as the gondola drifted nearer, the woman at the man's side also began to wave, calling out across the short stretch of water that separated the quay from the boat. Suddenly it dawned on Aldo what they wanted, the mistake that they had made. Oh, what luck! Before they could change their minds, he turned the boat swiftly towards them, looking around to check that none of the officially licensed gondoliers were waiting at the pick-up point near the bridge. He swept in alongside the pair of tourists with a piratical swagger, barely resisting the urge to cackle like the brigand he knew himself to be. He looked at the pair of them and wondered what on earth the man was doing wearing a yellow linen jacket in wintertime. But the man's accent gave it all away – he was an American.

'How much?' the man asked in broken Italian. 'Half an hour? How much?'

Aldo plucked a figure from his head, then offered a second random sum for a whole hour.

'Oh, that sounds very reasonable, Ken,' said the woman.

'How long, honey? You want an hour?'

'Well, it is our second honeymoon after all,' she said.

Ken held up a single digit while mouthing slowly and loudly in English, 'One hour? Okay, one hour?'

'One hour, okay, one hour,' repeated Aldo, grinning from ear to ear.

'It looks a bit tatty, Ken,' the woman said as she was on the point of stepping aboard. 'The boat, I mean. Do you think it's seaworthy?'

'But we ain't going on the sea, honey.'

'You can't trust these goddamned Italians, Ken. I bet these canals are deep, and you know I can't swim.'

'Don't worry, honey. Just take a deep breath and relax and you'll float.'

'Ken, you sure know how to compliment a woman. Sometimes I wonder why I married you at all.'

'Too late now,' said Ken. 'After almost forty years. Well, shall we, honey?'

She nodded and looked at Aldo and smiled politely and he offered her his hand as she stepped aboard, and when she tottered he held her up and then sat her down on the bench. She was laughing at her own clumsiness and Aldo smiled at her in return.

'Silly me,' she said.

'Silly me,' Aldo repeated, a reasonable approximation, laughing as he did so. 'Silly me.'

'No, not silly *you*,' she said. 'Silly *me*.'

'Yes, yes, silly me,' he said, nodding vigorously, and she changed the subject swiftly to cushions.

'Don't you have any cushions?' she said. 'Cushions?'

She pointed to the seat and enunciated the word again with exaggerated deliberation and volume.

'Ken, he hasn't got any cushions.'

'Do you have any cushions? Cushions?' said Ken, stressing each syllable as if Aldo were an idiot, and the woman lifted her large bottom off the seat and made as if to place something beneath it in a way that made Aldo laugh.

'No cushions?' she asked again, slightly embarrassed now by his laughter.

'Ah, no, no,' Aldo replied in Italian. 'No cushions today, *signora*. Not today,' and he pointed knowingly at the sky.

The couple looked up, looked at each other, then nodded and smiled uncertainly. Aldo nodded back.

'What's he saying?' said the woman.

'I don't goddamned know,' said Ken, and Aldo pushed the boat away from the quayside before they could muster any second thoughts.

Right, thought Aldo, let's keep ourselves out of public view, no point in breaking the rules in front of everyone. He took them up towards the Rialto bridge, then cut into one of the narrow waterways that led into San Polo.

'Oh, this is so romantic, isn't it, Ken?' the woman kept saying, and each time she said it Ken nodded and smiled and patted her fat knee with his hand.

'We've been wanting to come to Venice for so long, haven't we, Ken? Ever since we were courting.'

'Were we ever courting, honey?'

'Oh, Ken, don't be such an ass. As if you don't remember. Say, do you think he could sing us a song?'

'Do these guys really sing?'

'Of course they do, dear. Betty told me all about it, when she and Marvin came here last year.'

'Oh, honey, Betty's full of bull. But I'll ask him anyway. Just for you.'

She smiled at him and he grinned back, raising his hand towards Aldo, snapping his fingers when Aldo failed to notice the gesture.

'Hey there, signore gondoliero. Can you sing?' said Ken, beginning to hum.

Aldo looked perplexed.

'Sing?' enquired the woman, letting out a few discordant notes, helping Ken out of his difficulty.

'Ah, sing?' said Aldo. 'No, no. Sing, no. Violin, yes.'

'Violin? Did he say violin? Fantastic!' said the woman, nodding so enthusiastically that it seemed the boat might rock in time to the weight of her approval.

Aldo rested the oar in the well of the boat and stepped down and sat on the bench opposite the couple and removed the violin from where he had placed it under the seat. He played the most romantic tunes he could muster as the boat drifted along the narrow canal, the notes echoing up and down the tall walls of the houses, then losing themselves in the sheets that were drying overhead. An hour later Aldo waved goodbye to the happy couple back at Accademia, stuffed a wad of Ken's notes into his pocket, enough to repay Isabella a sizeable chunk of the cost of his trip to Rome, took the gondola into a side-canal and tied it up to a pole. He set off towards San Marco with the violin, his step suddenly lighter than it had been for years. Isabella met him in the square when she finished work.

'I have something for you, Isabella,' he said.

He took the money out of his pocket.

'What's all this?' she asked.

'Your money.'

'You didn't spend much in Rome, then?'

'Oh, I did. I spent the money you gave me, nearly all of it.'

'So where's this from?'

'The gondola. I went back and got it today, and I . . .'

'The gondola? You sold the gondola? Are you mad? How could you sell the gondola?'

'Of course I haven't sold the gondola. I'd never sell the gondola. I took a couple of tourists out in it, Americans. Played the violin for them, a few romantic tunes . . .'

'And they gave you all that?'

'I know! Can you believe it?'

'Aldo, you little villain!'

'Rob from the rich, give to the poor.' He pushed the money into her hand. 'Give to the ones you love . . .'

She looked at him.

'Aldo, do you really mean that?'

He looked away.

'Do you, Aldo? Really?'

'Isabella, you've been so good to me.'

'Aldo, come on, it's nothing. Nothing at all.'

'If only you knew, Isabella. If only you knew . . .'

He tried to press the money into her hand again, but she pulled away.

'I don't want your money, Aldo.'

'It's not my money, it's yours. I owe you.'

'No, you earned it, you keep it. Pay me back when you can. And you might have more money soon anyway. There's a little shop down the street from where I work, the one next to the pharmacy. You know, where they sell wine from the barrel? And they're looking for someone to help out a few days a week, part-time to start with. I put in a good word for you with the owner, Michele, an old acquaintance of mine. He said you should drop by tomorrow at two.'

'Thank you, Isabella. Thank you yet again.'

'Forget it. And in the meantime, spend your money on some glass for your windows and some sheets for your bed. And then I might just drop by and see you.'

The next afternoon, Aldo was waiting outside Isabella's shop when she returned from her lunch break.

'Well?' she asked, half-smiling in anticipation.

'I got it! I got it! I start on Monday.'

'You got it? Fantastic! I knew you would, Aldo. I knew Michele would be good to you.'

Two weeks later Isabella visited the house on Burano. New panes of glass shut out the wind, impeded the cold, and the curtains that hung to the floor stopped the draught, and the sheets on the bed smelt fresh and new, and she woke the following morning in his bed, beneath the place where Katerina's photo was pinned to the wall. Aldo's new cockerel stood on the stump of an old tree outside and crowed in the dawn while chickens scratched and clucked around the kitchen door and Aldo went down and gathered up their fresh eggs. Then he boiled the eggs and took them upstairs in his bare hands, juggling their hot shapes as he got back into bed beside Isabella, and they shelled the eggs together and ate them beneath the sheets and then they kissed, hot yolk on their lips still, and then they took the boat back to Venice where Sunday crowds filled the streets and coins clattered into Aldo's tin as he played the violin in front of Caffè Florian.

It was some time since Aldo had last passed by the old family home on Fondamenta della Sensa and when he went there again in the darkness of a winter evening the house seemed abandoned and unloved. He stood on the small hump-backed bridge outside and looked at the walls of his old home. The shutters were open but there was no light inside and he went up to the window beside the front door and pressed his nose to the glass, peering through the gap in the curtains and into the room where his grandmother used to sleep on nights like this by the fire. A shaft of light from a street-lamp took the edge off the darkness and his eyes began to distinguish the outlines of grey shapes, the bare walls and bare floor and the empty fireplace. Aldo's heart skipped a beat – the house was empty! The new owners must have gone away, taking with them all their possessions and their memories, and Aldo's own memories, having sought refuge in the walls in the intervening years, came spilling out again in a rush. He looked up and down the deserted quay and pushed his hand against the window. It ceded slightly to his pressure so he shoved at it harder but was unable to force it open so he tried the door, seizing the handle, pushing and pulling this way and that, but it too would not budge. He ducked into the alley and looked up at a small window in the side of the house. He gripped the sill and pulled himself up and peered inside. The door of the living room lay open and he could see the hallway and the foot of the stairs beyond. He dropped once more to his feet, pulled himself up again, closed his eyes, and butted the glass with the top of his head. The windowpane shattered and he hauled himself through.

He could smell ash in the grate as he dropped into the room and he sneezed as dust from the floorboards got into his nose. The old house echoed with the sound of his footsteps as he moved quickly through the rooms, searching the drawers and the cupboards. On top of a wardrobe in the small attic room he found a cardboard box and he shovelled out its bundles of papers, sifting through them in the moonlight, invoices from Casa Luca and business letters to Fausto Pozzi and old holiday postcards from the coast. And then he found the photographs: his mother and father when they were young; men unloading boxes of fish at the market; Luca and Aldo with Massimo and his dad, their hands full of wild porcini mushrooms in an autumn glade; Luca outside the trattoria in the old days; the house on Burano, Aldo's grandfather beside the door and the neighbours' goats – a different generation of goats – grinning idiotically in the background; Aldo, aged ten or eleven, his violin in his lap; Aldo again, older this time, after a football match, his face streaked with mud and sweat and his body caked in filth in the rain, just as it would be one day on the steppe; another of Aldo, proud and tentative in his new uniform, by the bridge outside the house, the day before he went away to war; and finally a photograph of Luca and Fausto

Pozzi, both men huge and imposing and deeply serious as they leant their elbows on the bar in Casa Luca.

Aldo put the photos to one side and picked up a bundle of letters. He saw the official stamps and regimental numbers and he recognised his own handwriting on the envelopes. He took the first letter from its envelope and unfolded it and saw the date: 6th August 1942, a time when they were still hurtling towards the Don. He read the letter through, his words then still arranged in long neat lines on the page, like the lines of sunflowers that stretched into the distance under the heat of a Ukrainian sun. He read through the letters one by one, retracing in his mind the path of war in the east, digging up memories of all the things he had seen then and had wanted to forget. As the dates on the letters grew later, the words grew less legible, penned by a hand made unsteady by cold and by bombs. The last letter – 15th December 1942 – was barely five lines long, a quick note dashed off just before the Vicenza were pushed up to support the Alpini near Pavlovsk. And then the time for writing letters had gone and there would never again be a means by which to send them. No word for nearly eight years, he thought – no wonder everyone thought I was dead! He thought too of what it must have done to them back at home when his letters stopped coming, the absence of any news, no confirmation either way, just a gathering assumption that would one day have crystallised into fact.

He shoved the letters and the photos into the pocket of his coat and picked at a few small objects that lay in the bottom of the box, odds and ends from his adolescence, a spent cartridge from a hunting trip, a few hooks and floats and a cloth cap squashed flat. And then there was a sheet of paper, folded neatly twice, his name handwritten in large letters on one side, the letters of a woman's hand. He unfolded the page, luxurious heavy notepaper, the name of one of the better hotels in Venice embossed across the top in gothic font. The handwritten words were warmer and fuller than his own, written in a different language, a different alphabet, Cyrillic. His eyes passed quickly from the opening salutation to the end, and when he saw her name his hands trembled and he remembered the vision of her he had seen on the quay months before, how he had let the vision pass him by undetained. He held her letter close up to his face now and his breathing fluttered the page, and he read her name over and over again in a whisper, then his eyes darted back to the start and he consumed the words in a rush, trying to take them all in at once, a desperate hungry beggar opening his mouth wide for food.

Dearest Aldo

It's me. I'm here. I told you I would come, and I have. I've told you so many times, in every letter I've sent, that when the time was right we would meet again, that it would be in Venice, that I would come to this house and knock on your door and we would be together again, if perhaps only briefly. And I have kept my promise, Aldo. All through these five long years since they took you away I haven't heard a word from you, of how or where you are, or if you are even alive, but I never lost faith, I always believed. And now I am here, at your door. But they say you are not here, that they know nothing of you. How can that be? I have checked the address a thousand times on the map that you drew for me, and it is this house, undoubtedly it is this house, and now I have no idea where to look for you, but I still hope and I still believe and perhaps I will find you before I go. Perhaps I will find you at the bar – Casa Luca, I think you said it was called? I will ask for it and I will look for you there. I will be here in Venice for one more day and then I must leave for Milan, the next city on our tour. When I leave I don't know if I will ever be able to come back, but I will leave this letter with this family here and I hope that one day you will come back here and they will give you this letter, and all the others that I sent to you from Russia, and you will read my story and it will be like we have never been apart. And you must write back to me, you must tell me where to find you, because I hardly know where to look any more. Write to me at the address below. Write as soon as you can.

Katerina

Aldo sent the first of many letters to Katerina the following day, but in vain. Months went by and he received no reply and so he finally resigned himself to the thought of his letters, or perhaps her replies, residing like forgotten and lost little birds in the wire cage of anonymous pigeonholes in Italy or Russia or both, and so the bird that had unexpectedly sung up in his heart again stopped singing.

The Chief Inspector

The violin had saved Aldo, lifting him from the trench into which
he had fallen, providing the first few coins on his journey back to
dignity, drawing Isabella back to him too that first evening outside
Caffé Florian in Piazza San Marco, and now that he had been lifted
from the depths his reintegration into society gathered pace. He
rediscovered old friends, made new ones, people admired his skill
with the instrument, unaware of the guilt and the shame that his
possession of it entailed. He took to playing again in recitals in
churches where tourists liked to sit and listen to *The Four Seasons* in
Vivaldi's hometown, and Isabella would sometimes arrive unannounced and sit herself down in the shadows at the back, just as she
had in the old days, while Aldo sat on the platform at the front with
the other musicians. As he played, he often recalled the face of the
violin's previous owner, an involuntary memory dredging itself up
out of the canal, and for the umpteenth time he felt the fingers of
guilt wrestling with his own, trying to trip him up, to jostle his
fingers off the strings. At the end of the piece he would stand and
smile and nod in modest acknowledgement of the applause, and he
alone would hear the lone hand of guilt applauding in silence, ironic
and incomplete. And then he would see that Isabella was still at the
back of the church, and it would occur to him yet again that he did
not deserve her honesty and her decency, and he also knew that he
could never emulate her qualities now, because whereas his guilt
was real and weighed heavily upon him, all she had been guilty of
was a mere carnal exuberance, a taste for indiscretions of the flesh.

In the interval he followed the other musicians into a side-room where they would rest and retune and pass comment on any particular oddities or attractions among the audience. One evening in March, Aldo found himself sitting beside a newcomer, a cellist who it seemed had previously busied himself in other ensembles around the town. Aldo noticed the man's insistent gaze on the violin and he felt himself gripping it more firmly in his lap, as if it were a jewel and the cellist were a thief.

'That's an interesting-looking instrument,' the cellist said casually, and Aldo gripped the thing even harder. 'Where'd you get it?'

'Oh, it's been in the family for years. Bit of a hand-me-down, really. Tatty old thing, isn't it? Strictly sentimental value, but couldn't bear to part with it now. You know how it is.'

'Can I take a look?' the man asked, and before Aldo could reply the man was tugging it from his grasp. The man regarded it for a moment, cast a judicial glance in Aldo's direction, turned the instrument over, rubbed its back, sniffed the wood, turned it over again and ran his fingers across a small knot in the wood next to the bridge.

'It's strange,' said the man, 'but I'm sure I've seen this instrument before. An acquaintance of mine had one just like it.'

'Oh, one piece of wood can look very much like another,' said Aldo. 'They knock these things out by the dozen, don't they? Must be a coincidence.'

'Yes, must be. Strange, though . . .'

All through the second half of the performance Aldo felt the eyes of the cellist upon him and a voice from the past rising out of the canal. That night, even with panes in his windows and curtains down to the floor and new sheets and blankets on the bed, he felt an unusual chill in the room and he dipped in and out of sleep until dawn, rising early and arriving for work at the *bottega* earlier than usual, and he ruminated on the cellist's questions until Michele turned up as usual at half past eight on the dot. Michele, travelling trimly through his forties as if at least a decade younger, wore his copious dark hair slicked back tight against his skull and his eyes would twinkle especially brightly whenever one of the neighbourhood's young wives dropped by to fill her tall green bottles from his inexhaustible barrels of wine, smiling his special boyish smile for the ones who spoke to him most flirtatiously. Aldo had got used to him returning late from lunch, whistling as he breezed back in, his cheeks flushed with a subtle blushing of the capillaries. Aldo had been unaware of the reason for his boss's post-prandial unpunctuality until a forty-something widow who lived in the flat above the shop, her eye-shadow as black as her clothes, her nails as red as her lips, relieved him of his ignorance. Calling Aldo upstairs from where he waited for Michele in the rain, she brought him a glass of wine and a little plate of olives and sat herself next to him on the sofa. As he raised the glass to his mouth, Aldo noticed an imprint of her lipstick on the rim.

'You know why he's always late, of course, don't you?' she asked.

'Michele?'

'Yes, my dear, Michele.' She edged a little closer across the sofa.

'Let's just say he's enjoying himself. Somewhere warm and comfortable.'

'Yes, I imagine he is. How very sensible of him, with weather like this.'

'Oh yes, I can imagine it too. And he leaves you standing out there in the cold and the rain. When you could be somewhere warm and comfortable too . . .' She edged even closer. 'Do you have a wife, Aldo?'

'Why, are you offering?'

She smiled demurely but before she could answer he heard the chime of keys and the shop door opening downstairs. He jumped to his feet and placed his glass on the table.

'Thank you, *signora*.'

'Alicia, please.'

'Thank you, Alicia. You've been very kind, but I'm afraid I must return to work.'

He hurried out of the room as she placed another lip-print on his glass.

In the shop, the clip-clip of Michele's heels danced around the place as he busied himself with his bottles, the scent of *Acqua di Parma* following him in a little perfumed cloud around the room.

Then the door rattled open and a man walked in, short and stocky, hair trimmed short, his expression businesslike yet jovial, his jowls wobbling slightly as he walked. He marched up to the counter and addressed himself in a loud voice to Aldo.

'I'm looking for Aldo Gardini,' he boomed.

'You're speaking to him. How can I help?'

'Inspector Marchiori,' the man said, flashing his badge. 'Would you please honour us with your presence at the station sometime?'

'At the station? May I ask why?'

'I think it's best that we deal with the details in private. Tomorrow would be best. Two o'clock,' he said, and he turned and walked briskly away.

'I'll need to be back here by two-thirty,' Aldo called after him.

'We'll have to see. Remember, two o'clock. We'll be expecting you.'

The door slammed shut.

'Trouble?' asked Michele. 'Isabella said I wouldn't have any problems with you.'

'Don't worry, you won't.'

Aldo arrived at the police station the next day at two. Beyond the elaborate façade he found an interior that was practical and bland, tall walls and distant ceilings coated in uniform shades of grey, the floors a durable practical stone. He asked at reception and was directed upstairs to wait outside a door half-way along an anonymous corridor of the same uniform grey, lit only by a small window high up on one wall. Aldo sat on a hard chair and the minutes ticked by. Finally he heard brisk footsteps on the stairs and Inspector Marchiori marched along the corridor.

'Follow me, Signore Gardini,' he said and he opened the door and went into a small office. He sat behind the desk and gestured to the chair in front of it. 'Sit.'

The room resounded to his voice, nothing to stop the echoes but the desk and the chairs and a solitary metal cabinet. Inspector Marchiori flicked open a file that was in front of him on the desk. He looked at it casually, then raised his gaze towards Aldo.

'Now, I suppose you're wondering why you're here? Or perhaps you're not. Perhaps you already know.'

'On the contrary. I have no idea.'

Inspector Marchiori flicked further through the file, pursed his lips and made a loud sucking noise, as if struggling to ingest an exceptionally long strand of spaghetti.

'Do you have a criminal record, Signore Gardini?'

'Please, call me Aldo if you wish.'

'Thank you, Signore Gardini. I repeat, do you have a criminal record, Signore Gardini?'

'Of course not.'

'I see. No criminal record.'

'That's right.'

'Officially, or unofficially?'

'What do you mean?'

'We have no record of you in our files, but that doesn't mean you've never committed a crime.'

'I'm sorry, but would you mind telling me why I'm here?'

'You came of your own free will.'

'Because you told me to.'

'Full name?'

'Aldo Gardini. I thought you knew that? Aren't you going to tell me . . .'

'Resident in . . .'

'I'm sorry?'

'Where are you resident?'

'Burano.'

'Address?'

Aldo told him and he wrote it on the form.

'Occupation?'

Aldo looked at him with some defiance now, and just a hint of fear.

'Here, look, it's probably easier if you fill this in yourself,' said Inspector Marchiori as if suddenly bored.

He pushed the form across the desk and tossed the pen after it.

'I'll come back in a few minutes. Make sure you're finished.'

He left the room and Aldo sat for a few minutes in shock and then he quickly completed the rest of the form. An hour later Inspector Marchiori returned.

'Right, let's go, the Chief Inspector wants to see you now.'

He set off again down the corridor, Aldo hurrying after him.

'Look, I need to get back to work. I can't afford to lose my job.'

The policeman stopped abruptly and turned around, his face black against the sun that shone in through the window at his back.

'Signore Gardini, this is a most serious matter, most serious, and I would not be doing my duty if I did not deal with it most urgently. It is in all of our interests that we sort all this out as soon as possible so that we may continue our investigations into what is, I'm sure you would agree, the gravest of crimes.'

'What crime? I have no idea what you're talking about.'

'You will soon enough. I can assure you of that.'

He led Aldo up a couple of steps and through the open door of a large office. The windows were hung with red velvet curtains, the walls adorned with portraits of past luminaries of the investigative profession. The sole source of light was an elegant desk-lamp of green glass and brass, and in its dimly arcing glow sat the Chief Inspector. He was neatly dressed in a dark blue tie and blazer but he slouched back rather informally in his chair, his face lean and impassive, his forehead high, seeming to stretch way back over the top of his brow, his hairline receding with the years. What remained of his hair was slightly longer than one might expect of someone of his profession, the tight black curls glistening in the light. His eyes were illegible, possibly sad, and while Aldo presumed he never really smiled, he noticed that he had a peculiar manner of speaking, drawing his lips back as he gathered his thoughts, showing little flashes of teeth as he did so. So it was difficult for Aldo to know quite what the inscrutable Chief Inspector might be thinking, good thoughts or bad, or simply nothing much at all, but his brows evidently bore the weight of wisdom on their years.

'Sit down,' Inspector Marchiori said to Aldo, standing to one side as the Chief Inspector sat motionless behind his desk. The Chief

Inspector did not introduce himself and he left long seconds of silence for Aldo to sit opposite, shifting in his seat, trying to compose his thoughts. Aldo began to speak, the desk-lamp flickered, and the Chief Inspector leant suddenly forwards, cutting through Aldo's words with a voice that was polite, formal and exceptionally cold.

'Right, now let's keep this really simple. I'm going to ask you a few simple questions and I want you to give me a few simple answers, one simple answer to each simple question. Is that clear?'

Aldo nodded.

'Good. But before we really get started, I should warn you not to try to outwit me. No one ever has and no one ever will. Now, you play in one of these music ensembles, I believe?'

'Yes, that's right.'

'What instrument do you play?'

'The violin.'

'You possess your own instrument?'

'Yes.'

'A violin, you say?'

'Yes.'

'And how long have you had this violin?'

'A few years.'

'How long exactly?'

'I don't really remember. Quite a few years.'

The Chief Inspector looked at Inspector Marchiori and some sort of unspoken message seemed to pass between them.

'I see,' said the Chief Inspector. He drew back his lips and Aldo noticed for the first time the two gold teeth in the lower jaw, as if someone had punched the originals out of him sometime in the past. 'Let me ask you again. When did you buy it? I assume you did buy it, and didn't acquire it by other means?'

'No.'

'No what? No you didn't buy it, or no you didn't acquire it by other means?'

'No, I bought it.'

'When?'

'A few years ago, like I told you. I can't remember when exactly. Before the war.'

'Before the war?'

'Yes.'

'You're quite sure about that?'

'Of course.'

'In Venice?'

'In Rome.'

'You were alone when you bought it?'

'No, I was with my father.'

'He would be willing to corroborate your story, I assume?'

'My father is dead.'

'I'm sorry,' said the Chief Inspector, a matter-of-fact condolence. 'The rest of your family, then? They could confirm it, I assume?'

'I'm afraid I don't know where they are.'

The Chief Inspector raised his eyebrows.

'You see,' continued Aldo, 'I came back from the war last summer and they'd gone.'

'Gone?'

'I went home and they weren't there any more.'

'Oh, dear. How very sad, how truly awful. How long were you away?'

'Eight years.'

The Chief Inspector whistled through his teeth. 'An awful lot can happen in eight years.'

'I'm aware of that,' Aldo snapped. 'An awful lot *did* happen.'

'Please try to control yourself, Signore Gardini. This is not the time for displays of temper. So, you went home and . . . and nothing. So where are you living now?'

'On Burano. In my grandfather's house.'

'And you work at the *bottega*?'

'That's right.'

'For long?'

'Two or three months.'

'And before that?'

'I was unemployed.'

'So how did you survive?'

'I got by.'

'Yes, there's something of the survivor about you, I can see that. And you play the violin in the streets, I hear?'

'Yes.'

'Around San Marco?'

'Yes. How do you know?'

'I've seen you. I even put some money in your tin once or twice.'

'Thank you. Very kind, I'm sure.'

'Oh, don't thank me, it was purely in order to study you more closely. And you survived on small change for . . . for how long?'

'I have modest needs.'

'For how long? How long have you been playing? In the street, I mean?'

'A while.'

The Chief Inspector folded his arms and exhaled loudly and his junior colleague did the same.

'What did I say about the questions I was going to ask you? I want answers, simple ones. Simple questions, simple answers. Precise information. Ambiguity won't help you, my friend, so be as specific as you can. The more information you can give me, the quicker I can bring this matter to an appropriate conclusion.'

'I still don't know what matter it is that you're talking about. Is it illegal to play in the streets? If that's the case, I'll stop.'

'No, some people may not approve of people like you littering our streets, but I don't think you could call it a crime. Again now, how long have you been playing in the streets?' He raised an index finger in Aldo's direction and his gold teeth glinted. 'Careful now, be precise.'

'Since November. Or the beginning of December.'

The Chief Inspector lifted his finger again and Aldo stammered out a few more words.

'I can't remember exactly, I honestly can't remember. For a while the days all just blurred into one. It was a difficult time.'

'The beginning of December, then. Shall we say the beginning of December? I don't recall seeing you before then.'

'Yes, that's probably about right.'

'And you came back from the war in the summer, you say?'

'Yes.'

'The month?'

'July.'

'And you started playing this violin in the streets in December, the beginning of December. How did you survive until then? You were unemployed, you say?'

'Yes. I still had some of my repatriation allowance.'

'That can't have lasted long.'

'I eked it out slowly.'

'Did you stay with friends? Family?'

'My family aren't around any more. I told you.'

'Ah, yes, of course, I'm sorry. Friends? Do you have friends?'

'Yes.'

'And did you have any then?'

'Not so many.'

'Yes, I imagine, after so long away, surely you lost touch.'

'Most of my friends were killed in the war. But I suppose you wouldn't really know about that.'

'Perhaps not. But anyway, how did you get by? I'm genuinely curious.'

'I had to . . . I had to, you know, scavenge, scavenge a bit.'

'Scavenge? Scavenge a bit? What does that involve exactly?'

Aldo rubbed his forehead with a sweaty palm. 'Look, this is difficult for me.'

'Then don't make it more difficult than it has to be. What did this scavenging involve? It sounds rather elemental, primitive . . . rather uncivilised.'

Aldo raised his voice slightly. 'I had no choice. I was starving, I had to do what I could to get by. Look, it's difficult for me to talk about those days. It's not something I like to think about all that much.'

'Dark memories?'

'Not dark. Just unpleasant.'

'I'm sure. You must have been desperate.'

'At times. But you can get used to anything if you have to.'

'So you don't feel guilty?'

'Why should I feel guilty?'

'Just wondering . . .'

'I've done nothing wrong. My situation was none of my doing.'

'Your situation? None of your doing?'

'I had no choice.'

'We always have a choice. Always. For example, you could choose to stand up and walk out of this office now . . .'

Aldo shifted in his seat.

'. . . but of course we would then be free to bring you back here again, and we would simply have to start once more from the beginning.'

'So what fucking choice is that?'

'Watch your fucking language,' said Inspector Marchiori.

'The choice to contest your destiny,' said the Chief Inspector.

'That doesn't sound like much of a choice to me.'

'Perhaps we'll have to choose to differ. But the thing I do find difficult to understand is this . . . if your situation was so desperate, and I have no reason to suspect that it wasn't, why did you wait until the beginning of December to start playing your violin again . . . in the street, I mean?'

Aldo leant forward, rested his hand on the desk and stared the Chief Inspector in the eyes. 'How could you ever understand? Coming back from where I'd been, you can't just pick things up again where you left them. It's not that easy, it can't be done, everything was gone, all shot to hell. I had nothing left in me, and there was nothing left for me here, so what the fuck was I supposed to do? It was all gone and I was empty and I couldn't have played if I'd wanted to.'

'But after four or five months of . . . scavenging . . . you felt able to?'

'Those four or five months were considerably better than the preceding years.'

'So you didn't play at all? Until December?'

'No.'

'But you had the violin? You'd had it for years? A number of years?'

'Yes, I've already told you that.'

'So during the war, where was it during the war, this violin? You say your family has, well, disappeared, gone away, whatever . . . where was the violin all that time? I don't imagine you took it with you.'

'Are you making fun of me?'

The Chief Inspector shook his head and looked at Inspector Marchiori and laughed.

'Of course not, that would be unprofessional. But tell me now, where was the fucking violin all that time!?'

'Fuck you!'

The Chief Inspector stood up. Inspector Marchiori walked around behind Aldo and placed a hand on his shoulder.

The Chief Inspector enquired again, leaning closer this time.

'Signore Gardini, where . . . was . . . the violin . . . during the war?'

Inspector Marchiori rested a hand on Aldo's other shoulder too now and squeezed hard with both hands and then leant down and whispered in Aldo's ear, 'Where was the fucking violin, you little prick?'

'On Burano.'

'Where on Burano?' whispered the Chief Inspector, his face now close up against Aldo's, his fetid breath all over him.

'In my grandfather's house.'

'Where you now live?'

'Where I now live. Now get out of my fucking face!'

The Chief Inspector withdrew slightly.

'He must be an old man now, your grandfather.'

'No, he's dead too.'

'You're joking?'

'Of course I'm not fucking joking!'

Inspector Marchiori dug his fingertips in hard again.

'And whose is the house now?' asked the Chief Inspector.

'Mine.'

'Are you sure about that? A formal inheritance?'

'No one has told me otherwise.'

'Perhaps we should check it out for you, just to make sure everything's in order and all above board? There may be other claimants.'

'I don't see why that should be necessary.'

'We shall have to see. Anyway, we seem to have got a little sidetracked in all this excitement, and I know you're in a bit of a hurry to get back to work by . . . three o'clock, was it?' He looked at his watch. 'I'm so sorry, you're already rather late. We'll try not to keep you much longer.' He sat back down behind the desk and gestured Inspector Marchiori away to one side. 'So anyway, after the war, in July, when you came back . . . you went to this house on Burano and the violin was there? In a drawer? Under the bed? Placed conveniently upon a shelf?'

'In the kitchen cupboard.'

'The kitchen cupboard? A rather unconventional place for a violin, don't you think?'

'My grandfather was an unconventional man.'

'And you happened to find the violin, in this cupboard, but you just left it there for a few more months. Even though you needed the money, had nothing to eat, you didn't think of playing it for a bit of loose change now and again? So you could afford a loaf of bread?'

'Like I told you, I couldn't bring myself to play it. I didn't have it in me.'

'Oh, how very artistic. How very sensitive. And when you did decide you could play again, once you . . . had it in you, shall we say . . . was it in a suitable condition? After so long in the cupboard?'

'It was all right, I suppose.'

'But the strings, for example, weren't they a bit . . . a bit old, a bit dull? The sound can't have been the best.'

'No.'

'So I assume you changed them. The instrument sounded clear enough when I heard it.'

'You know about violins?'

'A colleague of mine does. Did you change the strings?'

'Yes.'

'So you bought new ones?'

'Er, yes.'

'From? Did you buy those in Rome too?'

'No, in Venice of course.'

'Of course. I don't suppose you still have the receipt? They did give you a receipt, didn't they?'

'Possibly not. I can't remember.'

The Chief Inspector shook his head. 'Bad form, very bad form. Assisting a commercial enterprise in the evasion of taxes.'

'They may have given me a receipt, I really don't remember.'

'You're getting all ambiguous on me again. How much did you pay for the strings?'

'I don't know. I can't remember!'

'For Christ's sake! Do you want us to be here all night? All right, all right, remind me, how long ago did you buy the violin?'

'A few years ago, like I said.'

'You're sure?'

'Yes.'

'How much did it cost?'

Aldo gave an approximate figure. 'I can't remember exactly – I told you, my dad bought it for me – but it was something like that.'

'Don't you think it's strange that you remember how much the violin cost several years ago, when you didn't even pay for it ... that's right, isn't it, you never paid for it? And you can't remember how much you paid for the strings just a couple of months ago.' He looked at Inspector Marchiori. 'That's quite strange, isn't it?'

'It certainly is,' Inspector Marchiori agreed. 'Pretty fucking implausible.'

The clock on the wall struck four.

'My dad always spent the same on our birthday presents,' Aldo went on. 'So I know more or less what it cost.'

'And where in Rome did you ... did he ... get it?' asked the Chief Inspector. 'Or perhaps you don't remember that either. You see, if you could give us the name of the shop, perhaps they could confirm your story.'

'After so many years? I don't think so. We got it in the market, anyway. Porta Portese.'

'How terribly inconvenient. Perhaps you could give us the name of the shop where you bought the strings in December? Or did you get those in a market too?'

'I don't know the name of the shop, but I can give you the address, roughly.'

'The address, roughly? That would be helpful. I'd also like you to bring the violin in sometime so my colleagues and I can take a look at it. Because, you see, I've been told it bears a certain distinguishing mark. Nothing too obvious, but rather difficult to duplicate. A knot in the wood, something along those lines.'

'According to who?'

'A colleague of mine. Quite an accomplished musician himself, as it happens. A cellist.'

He paused and drew back his lips and his teeth were suddenly visible again. Aldo stiffened in his chair.

'And the thing is, there's this case that's been puzzling us for, well, three or four months now, I suppose. Since the beginning of December, as it happens. There was a street musician, an acquaintance of this colleague of mine, the cellist – they'd got talking in the street once and had struck up a bit of a friendship, something along those lines. This man, he used to play in Campo Santo Stefano, the kind of thing you do now, I suppose, and he was there most nights and my colleague would stop for a chat on his way home and this fellow would let him try out his violin. And then for a couple of days the man wasn't there and my colleague thought he must be ill . . . it was pretty damn cold and who knows where this fellow lived . . . and then a body was found in one of the canals in San Polo, up one of the back alleys, right out of the way. And guess what? It was this man, and he'd been hit over the head. Well, we assume he'd been hit over the head – of course he may have fallen and hit his head on his way into the water. But the balance of probability, given the nature of

the wound, is that he was struck a heavy blow. By a fist, for example.'
He looked at Aldo's hands. 'And his violin wasn't anywhere in the
vicinity, it wasn't near the body, it wasn't floating in the canal . . .'

'Maybe he didn't have it with him that day.'

'But he took it everywhere, it seems. He was rather attached to it.'

'Well, maybe someone picked it up and walked off with it?'

'Without noticing the body?'

'You said the body was in the water.'

'Did I? Oh yes, of course. Perhaps it was out of sight. So we may
only be looking for a thief, or perhaps just an opportunist, guilty of
nothing more than picking up what he found without reporting it
to the police.'

'I still don't see what all this has got to do with me.'

'But of course you do. As I was saying, we may just be looking
for a thief, but the balance of probability is that whoever has the
violin is not just a thief but also, how shall I put this . . . well, yes, a
murderer. And the thing that is troubling me, Aldo Gardini, is that
this colleague of mine, an accomplished musician and a trusted
policeman of many years' standing, has told me, categorically, that
the violin you were playing the other night is the same violin – the
very same violin – that the street musician played. Now, if you had
told me that you'd bought the violin a month ago, six weeks ago, in
a market here in Venice, then I would have to accept that your
explanation was perfectly plausible, that the killer had perhaps sold
the violin on to you without you being aware of its dubious prove-
nance. But could you help me with this, my friend? Can you tell me
exactly how you managed to acquire that particular violin, that
specific violin, several years ago in a market in Rome?'

'No, I'm afraid I can't.'

'Then should I not doubt your story? Should I not think that
perhaps you did not acquire your violin – the violin – in Rome
several years ago, but rather in some dark back alley of San Polo in
early December of last year? Would that not be a safe assumption
for me to make?'

'No, it would not.'

'Could you elaborate?'

'I bought . . . my father bought . . . the violin . . . my violin . . . in Rome, several years ago, and a rather similar knot in the wood doesn't alter that fact. And if that's all you wanted to question me about, I suggest you find more evidence before you bother me with this again.'

'Well, of course we will be searching for further evidence. And as I mentioned earlier, we would like you to bring in the violin so we can take a closer look. Because in fact it's not just the knot in the wood that caught my colleague's attention . . . I may as well tell you his name, you know him already in fact, a newcomer to your ensemble – Inspector Galliani. Inspector Galliani also noticed various other characteristics in the wood. I have a full description here, if you're interested.'

He took a sheet of paper from his drawer, laid it on the leather-topped desk, smoothed it flat and leant over it. 'Let me see . . . a crescent-shaped scratch to the back plate, a slight discolouring of the neck . . . should I read you the whole thing?'

'That doesn't prove anything. He saw the violin last night. Of course he can describe it in detail. It doesn't mean it belonged to the old man, or anyone else.'

The Chief Inspector suddenly sat bolt upright. 'The old man? What makes you think he was an *old* man? Did I say he was an *old* man?'

'Yes, I'm sure you said he was an old man.'

The Chief Inspector turned to Inspector Marchiori. 'Inspector Marchiori, did I say he was an *old* man? I don't recall saying that.'

'No, I don't believe you did.'

'So, Signore Gardini, precisely how old was this old man? What exactly did this old man look like?'

'I have no idea.'

'You see, you may well think that none of this . . . evidence . . . proves anything. And indeed, between you and me, it may be true that none of this would stand up in a court of law, but the first step to solving a crime is to find the victim, and the second is to find the criminal, and the last step is to show beyond doubt that you have found him. Well, we have found the victim – I think we are all acquainted with him rather better than we would wish. And I'm fairly sure . . . no, I know . . . that I have also found the criminal. I know that because my colleague, Inspector Galliani, tells me so, and I know it even more after talking to you today. All that remains is the third step. All that remains is to show, to prove to others, that which has already been shown to me as clear as you are sitting in front of me now. And I know one other thing. I know that it is merely a matter of time, that you are no match for me and sooner or later you will be mine. But for now you may go. We will come and find you when we want you again, when we want to see the instrument. My apologies to your boss for keeping you so long. Good day, Signore Gardini.'

Aldo stood up and as he reached the door the Chief Inspector spoke again.

'You know, people think the dead have no voice, but I can hear them. All you have to do is listen, and they'll tell you all you need to know.'

Aldo turned and walked out. He was accompanied down the corridor by Inspector Marchiori, then down the stairs and out into the street where low cloud smeared the sky just above the rooftops.

Friday evening came, and Aldo had another appointment with the ensemble in the church near Campo Santo Stefano. As usual he met a couple of the other musicians in a café before the show. The violin sat on a chair next to him and Aldo's contributions to the conversation were abrupt and self-conscious and he wondered if the edge of his mood transmitted itself to the others and if they could possibly suspect the reason for it. But the cellist was not there – he had only recently joined the ensemble and was not yet a regular fixture – and Aldo hoped that the others knew nothing of the man's suspicions, but as the keeper of a dark secret Aldo still feared that far more of the truth might be known by far more people than was really the case, and he hoped that if the others noticed his cautious wary looks they would simply assume he was experiencing some banal domestic difficulty or a problem with money. He tuned into their conversation intermittently as it flitted from one subject to another. It turned to La Fenice, the great Baroque theatre in the heart of Venice.

'A pal of mine plays in the orchestra there, the finest in Italy,' said Bruno, the jovial second violinist. 'Probably the best in Europe, in fact, nothing like it anywhere.'

Another man shook his head and mocked Bruno's assertion.

'But you haven't even been there,' Bruno insisted, placing his glass of wine firmly on the bar.

'What about La Scala?' said another. 'Or one of the big ones in Rome . . . what do you call that one, you know, up by Largo Argentina . . . damn, my memory's going, I was there just last year.'

'But what could be better than Venice?' asked Bruno. 'What finer venue could there be? What did you see in Rome, anyway? Some second-rate rubbish, I bet.'

'No. It was very good. A ballet.'

'Ballet?' said Aldo, pricking up his ears.

'Oh, so you're still with us, Aldo?'

'Which ballet was it?' he said again.

'I didn't know you were a fan. *Swan Lake* – good stuff. They're in Italy again now, coming here next weekend, in fact. Bruno, you'll be able to see them at your beloved Fenice.'

'I've got my tickets already,' said Bruno. 'The Kirov – not very often they come this way.'

'The Kirov?' said Aldo. 'From Russia?'

'The very ones. From Leningrad. You want to go? You'll need to hurry – the tickets are nearly sold out.'

The following day Aldo was at the box office before it opened. He handed over the money and grabbed his ticket and pushed it deep into his pocket and went to work, and all through the day he checked his pocket, fifty or a hundred times, and he thought about Katerina each time he did so. Isabella dropped by at the *bottega* later that afternoon and Aldo filled a bottle of wine from one of the barrels and gave it to her. She held out her coins.

'Don't worry about that – just take it. Michele likes you, I know he won't mind.'

'Thanks, Aldo. Come round to my place after work?' she said.

'Sure. I get off at seven. Try not to drink all the wine before I get there. I've got something to celebrate.'

'Then bring another bottle. We can have a party.'

That evening Aldo knocked on the door and Madame Leroux let him in. He went up to Isabella's room and they sat on her bed and drank from the bottle.

'I hear you're in trouble, Aldo.'

'What do you mean?'

'With the police.'

'Oh, that. Who told you?'

'Michele.'

'Was he upset? About the police coming to the shop?'

'A little. Did you do it, Aldo?'

'Do what?'

'What they said you did?'

'Who told you what they said?'

'Michele.'

'And who told him?'

'The police.'

'What, they've gone and told him all about it? They've no right to do that.'

'Don't worry, Michele won't kick you out. I told him you hadn't done it.'

'And he took your word for it?'

'Of course. Michele and I go back a long way.'

There was a long period of silence.

'Have some more wine,' she said.

He took a long swig from the bottle.

'And the knot in the wood?' she asked.

'God, they don't keep any secrets, do they? The knot in the wood ... I don't know. There's this knot in the wood and it's supposed to be the same as on the violin this old guy had, but ... but I don't know.'

'You know, Aldo, if you ever need to tell me anything, I'm here. You know that?'

'I know.'

A little later they lay on the bed and Isabella reached her hand across Aldo's chest and stomach and then a little lower, but he did not respond.

'Too many things buzzing around in your head?' she asked.

'I suppose.'

'Then let me take them off your mind . . .'

'Not tonight, Isabella.'

'Is it this thing with the police?'

'Partly.'

'What else?'

'Katerina.'

'Katerina? Your Russian angel?'

'Yes. My angel in the snow.'

'What's up? Has she written back at last?'

'No, but she's coming to Venice next week.'

'Oh, my God. Are you sure?'

'Yes, Bruno told me. The Kirov are coming.'

'But is *she* coming?'

'Of course she is.'

'How do you know?'

'I just know, Isabella, I just know. And at last we'll meet again.'

Teatro La Fenice

Aldo flitted across Campo San Fantin, up the steps, and in through
the doors of La Fenice. He showed his ticket to an attendant who
ushered him from the foyer to the auditorium, past velvet curtains
trailing from ceiling to floor. The place was decorated in red and
gold, the gilt-edged tiers festooned with roses that filled the air with
their fragrance as the hum of the gathering audience swirled around
the huge brass chandelier high above, a golden bird trapped inside
its gilded cage. Aldo found his seat, just left of centre, just yards from
the stage, and eased himself into the unfamiliar softness of the chair.
He turned to look at the people around him, engaged in animated
conversation or looking through their programmes as the orchestra
tuned up their instruments and as the lights dimmed, almost imperceptibly at first, and the orchestra fell into silence, Aldo noticed
Fausto Pozzi just a few seats away. The Chief Inspector was sitting
right next to him.

The lights went out, the curtain rose, and the stage lights threw
the scene into the blue hues of night. White forms drifted through
the blue, floating in the pale light against a backdrop of imagined
trees and reeds and expanses of water that stretched from the back
of the stage into the painted infinity of the set, and Aldo was taken
back in time, back to a lake in Russia, back at last to the spring of
'43. He peered at the features of the dancers, searching for the face
he had held for so long in his memory, the face that had looked out
from the photograph he held in frozen fingers on endless days on
the steppe, the face that must have followed so intently the passage
of her own pen across the page as she composed lost letters to him

from Leningrad, the face that had crossed so many stages since they had parted. And then one of the dancers sailed higher, as if hung from invisible strings held by a hidden hand. Aldo watched her leap, her flight drawn out into an almost impossibly elongated ecstasy, all in white and suspended in the air, her head towards the audience, her eyes towards the sky. His mind went back to the first time he had seen her dance, that night on the beach by the lake in Russia, how beautiful she had been, and how she had talked about her dancing with such longing and such clarity, with no ambiguity about what she had ever wanted to do with her life. And here she was! She had fulfilled her dreams and he felt suddenly and deeply proud of what she had achieved and that he had once been her friend. As he watched her, his face wreathed in smiles, he imagined that she too might be looking for one solitary face, a face alone on a beach by a lake instead of a hundred pairs of eyes, and that the sea of faces might be condensed to just one – just one face looking back at her, just left of centre, just yards from the stage – and that when she saw him the weight of the intervening years would fall from her eyes and it would be as if they had never been apart.

Then his heart leapt as he saw her eyes fix on his – or at least he thought he did, willing it to be, reality and hope at last enjoined – and as the show ended Aldo dashed up the aisle as the audience burst into cheers and applause. He rushed to the side of the stage and in through a door to a corridor where people were going about their backstage duties, performers and stagehands and men gathering up tools and wires. He found a door that lay ajar and through the door he saw the ballerinas and there in the corner was a woman who looked just like Katerina, a shawl wrapped around her slender frame as she talked with the others, and then the sound of her laughter, just as he remembered it, but then someone was closing the door from the inside, and Aldo was reaching his hand out to the door, about to push it open, to put all his weight behind it and rush headlong inside, calling out her name, but he felt a firm hand on his arm and someone strong was tugging his arm away, asking him what the hell he thought he was doing, didn't he know this was a restricted area. Restricted area, like hell, he thought, I'm going through and nothing's going to stop me, not after everything I've been through, not after waiting so long. But the strong hand pulled him around and up he looked, into the eyes of his questioner, the glint of gold teeth, then the voice. The Chief Inspector.

'Signore Gardini, fancy seeing you here. Are you sure they're expecting you in there?'

'Get your fucking hands off me!' And Aldo raised a hand as if to strike at him.

'I wouldn't do that, my friend. You're in enough trouble as it is.'

'Then get off me, I'm going in!'

'I don't think our Russian friends would wish their stars to be disturbed when they're so tired, after they've shone so brightly on the stage.'

'But she's a friend of mine. Let me in. I must see her.'

'Yes, of course she is. A very dear friend, I'm sure.'

'Let go of me, I said. I met her in the war. Let me in! Katerina! Katerina!'

But the Chief Inspector held onto him and others were arriving now, Russian men whose duty it was to guard their compatriots from the temptations of the West. Aldo struck out at them, their voices setting him off, and once again he felt Russian fists laying into him, one more memory from 1943. He called out Katerina's name, pleading for her to come and tell them that it was true, that he *had* met her in the war and they had been dear friends and he must see her again, must be allowed to sit with her, one human being with another, both so dear to each other that they were never meant to be apart. But the door stayed firmly shut and he knew she could not hear his voice and he was dragged outside and the Chief Inspector called over a couple of off-duty officers to help him and together they carted Aldo away across the square. They took him to the police station and put him behind the iron bars of a cell. He sat on a wooden bench and waited. The hours passed and he listened to the footsteps of people coming and going through a door that lay out of sight down the grey corridor as evening turned to night and night turned to day, dawn appearing behind the small barred window high up on the facing wall. Finally he heard voices. Footsteps approached down the corridor and the Chief Inspector let himself into the cell. Aldo stood up.

'You can go now,' the Chief Inspector said. 'It seems there has been a misunderstanding.'

'A misunderstanding?'

'Yes, I'd trust Inspector Galliani's judgement with my life, but . . .'

'Galliani?'

'The cellist. But a small complication has arisen.'

'I told you so. I told you you were wrong.'

'I am never wrong. But his description of the violin seems to have been a little, how shall I put this? Well, a little flawed. Yes, a little lacking in accuracy. We went to your house, we searched it, as you might expect, we found your violin, a violin . . . in the kitchen cupboard, as you said . . . and there was no knot in the wood, no scratch, none of that. So for now you're free to go . . .'

He paused and Aldo felt him studying him as he did so, peering right into him, judging him again.

'. . . but of course we may discover at some point that you acquired this new instrument from elsewhere. Or perhaps you had an accomplice.'

'But that's impossible. Who could have helped me with such a thing?'

'Of course you would say that. Even you must have friends. But one day we will knock on your door again, and we will go through all this once more. But for now, without any evidence, I'm afraid I am temporarily unable to demonstrate the veracity of my convictions . . .'

'You mean you were wrong.'

'. . . and so you may leave.'

'Wait, I want to ask you a question first, if you'll allow me that?'

'Yes?'

'Why did you follow me backstage? Why on earth did you stop me seeing Katerina? What the hell did it matter to you?'

'Katerina?'

'The Russian.'

'Oh, Christ! You really believe there was someone there you knew? You must be even crazier than I thought.'

'But she was there! I saw her. Just yards away, after all this time. It was meant to be, and you stopped me, sticking your fucking nose in again where it's got no right to be.'

'I find your tone inappropriate. I could keep you here forever if I wished.'

'Could you? Do it then!'

'You're tempting me.'

'All right, all right. But tell me, what business did you have following me?'

'I was watching you, of course. You were of interest to me, after our conversation the other day. The story with the violin, all of that.'

The Chief Inspector pulled his lips back in thought. 'But, I'll let you in on a little secret, my friend. I'd become a little distracted, to be honest, thinking about this and that, as one does, and it was Fausto Pozzi who pointed you out, when you headed off backstage, otherwise I may not have noticed. He said you'd be up to no good, that I should go and see what on earth you were doing.'

Aldo sat down on the bench again and put his head in his hands, the pig on his arm stirring, opening its eyes, lifting its head. Aldo looked up at the Chief Inspector.

'Fausto Pozzi is a bastard. He'll pay for this. And he'll pay for the other thing too.'

'The other thing?'

'In the forest, years ago. Before the war.'

'In the forest?'

'My father, Luca Gardini. He was killed out there.'

'Oh yes, I remember it. A hunting accident, wasn't it?'

'It wasn't a fucking accident!'

The Chief Inspector rested a hand on Aldo's shoulder and squeezed it gently. 'Control yourself, now. You wouldn't want me to have to question you again.'

Aldo brushed his hand away. 'Where have they taken Katerina anyway? I have to see her.'

'There was no Katerina, Aldo, there can't have been. They all look alike, anyway, those communist girls – I wouldn't touch one with a barge-pole, myself. You just imagined it was her, someone you thought you knew. Wishful thinking, I suppose. That would be understandable after everything you've been through.'

'But it *was* her. I promise you, it was her.'

'Well, even if it was, she's gone again now, you can be certain of that. They left straight after the show, the last date of the tour. She'll be half-way home by now and I don't expect she'll ever be coming back.'

The Chief Inspector led him out of the cell and the door clicked shut behind them, the sound of someone closing the chamber of a gun. Aldo stepped outside into the street. He knew where he was going now. He knew what he was going to do.

Revenge

Venice, March 1951

Aldo retrieved the gondola from the jetty at Isabella's house and pushed it along the Canale Grande, under the Rialto and towards Accademia and then into the Rio di San Trovaso. Up ahead, next to the small arched bridge, he could see the lights of Antica Locanda Fausto and the tables that Fausto Pozzi kept for al fresco diners on the quay. The tables were empty, perhaps because of the weather – a typical late-spring afternoon had given way to a chill evening mist – or it may just have been the lateness of the hour. Aldo knew that very soon Fausto Pozzi would be locking up and lumbering off into the night, so he eased the gondola over to the side of the canal nearest the restaurant door and he waited. He had already waited far too long for this and he would make sure he went through with it this time, all the way, right up to the logical conclusion. The last of the customers emerged and Aldo watched them go, peering out from behind the carnival mask he had slipped across his face. He saw waiters retrieving the tables from the quayside, ferrying them inside and making snide comments about the customers they had served that evening as they did so. Then the waiters departed, scruffy sweaters and coats now where their white jackets and bow ties had been, and then the lights outside the restaurant were put out and the shutters were pulled closed and the lights inside were extinguished and Fausto Pozzi emerged from his hole.

'Signore Pozzi?' came Aldo's muffled voice from behind the mask, disguising himself well, no time for mistakes now, just wanting to get it done.

'Who wants to know?'

'Gondola, sir?'

'I beg your pardon?'

'Gondola?'

'No, thank you. I'll walk.'

'But I was sent to collect you.'

'Oh were you, now? By whom?'

'I don't know her name. She told me the time and the place and your name. That was all.'

'And where, may I ask, are you supposed to be taking me?'

Aldo noticed Fausto's voice lifting just a touch, perhaps a fatal curiosity taking hold.

'The Londra Palace Hotel. A fine venue, sir, for an appointment of this nature.'

'An appointment of this nature, you say? Of what nature might this appointment be, this appointment with this woman, this mystery sender of masked men in gondolas?'

'Please don't make fun of me, sir. I am only doing what I have been asked. I don't know her name, she's a visitor here, a guest in our town who wishes to repay you for your generous hospitality.'

'My hospitality? So I've met this mystery lady? Well, I must say I'm now rather intrigued.'

'I believe she may have dined in your restaurant – she struck me as the discerning type, a person of taste.'

'Well, yes . . .'

'She said she had found you most charming, that she would very much like to meet you again. But in a more intimate setting.'

Aldo watched as Fausto flicked back through the faces he had seen over the last couple of evenings. He knew that a man of lesser vanity would decline the offer, would see it for the ruse that it was and take his usual lonely route home across Campo Santo Stefano and along Strada Nuova. But Aldo knew that Fausto Pozzi would be unable to resist the lure, and he twitched it again.

'I must say, if you will allow me this opinion, that she is rather beautiful, rather tempting. I envy you, sir. In your position, I would be tempted myself, I would not hesitate a moment longer. And of course if I don't take you to her, she will be very disappointed. And I won't be paid.'

He gestured to the gondola with an outstretched arm and smiled beneath the mask as Fausto hesitated and then finally clambered aboard. Aldo stepped from the quay to the deck and took up the oar before Fausto could change his mind. Fausto sat on the bench and felt the cold of the canal rising into him through the wood and he watched as the man behind the mask turned the boat around and pushed it towards the Canale Grande. Then he leant back on the bench and looked skywards, running a series of improbable scenarios through his mind as to what might happen on his arrival at the Londra Palace. There had been one or two noticeably attractive visitors at the restaurant the previous night. One in particular had caught his eye, all salmon-pink in her evening gown – and that was just her tan – her fingers full of rings but none of them matrimonial. Fausto had sat with her for a few moments between her expensive main course and extravagant dessert and he imagined himself now as the nightcap he had omitted to offer her then. Clearly she had forgiven him his lack of chivalry and he imagined her greeting him in the Londra Palace lobby with the languid vowels of whichever exotic tongue came to her most easily, then leading him into the luxurious privacy of her room for charming conversation and a great deal more. As he dwelt on these possibilities, his fantasies reached new peaks of wild abandon, an abandon he knew had not existed in his reality for more than a quarter of a century and of which any real hope had been extinguished three years after the end of the war when the one person who had always maintained a firm if involuntary hold on his heartstrings had gone forever.

'I must say that's a very nice restaurant,' Aldo remarked as he rowed, interrupting Fausto's reverie.

'Which restaurant?' Fausto snapped, annoyed that the sense of mystery and anticipation that he had been laboriously constructing now lay ruined by the banality of the gondolier's unsolicited observation. The steady rain that fell now irritated him further.

'Which restaurant, sir? Why, your restaurant, of course, sir.'

'Yes, it is rather nice, isn't it?'

'It is indeed. My sincerest congratulations – I'm sure you deserve them.'

'I don't recall asking your opinion, though.'

'Well, I say *your* restaurant, but of course . . .'

Fausto recognised something in the voice now, an inflection. 'But of course *what*?' he said.

The gondola nosed past the jetty that served the Londra Palace and Fausto watched as the gondolier continued to push the oar through the water in his slow metronomic rhythm and the hotel slipped further away, a chaos of raindrops swirling through the bright lights on the quay.

Now Aldo removed his mask.

'You!' Fausto said. 'Aldo, what on earth do you think you're doing?'

'Well, I say *your* restaurant, Fausto. But of course I remember it in the old days, before it was yours. I suppose you remember those days too? How could you forget them?'

'That was all such a long time ago. A very long time ago!'

'Yes, it does seem that way, doesn't it? So many things seem such a long time ago now. And yet they still seem like they happened just yesterday. Take, for example . . .'

'Look, you've gone past the jetty! The Londra Palace is over there.'

'The Londra Palace? But why on earth would you be going there?'

'Let me out, I said!'

'Let you out? Here?' said Aldo, gesturing towards the dark water that surrounded them. 'Well, if you're sure that's what you want . . .'

'That jetty over there,' Fausto shouted. 'Let me out over there!'

Aldo turned the nose of the gondola away from the shore, out towards the black lagoon. 'Which jetty, Fausto? I don't see a jetty.'

'That one, over there. Behind you!'

'Behind me?'

'Look, stop messing about. Turn this bloody thing around!' His voice was quivering now. 'Turn the boat around, I said! Pull in just over there. Look, just turn it around.'

'It's funny, isn't it?' said Aldo. 'Sometimes you can be so close to something, but for some reason you just can't see it. You're looking in the wrong direction, or it's too dark and your aim is wrong, or you just go temporarily blind. Or maybe someone misleads you, and the thing you're looking for, what other people see, just isn't there for you any more, no matter how hard you try. Or you mix it up for something else. Has that ever happened to you?'

'Turn this boat around immediately. I'm getting all wet.'

'You'll be a lot wetter when I've finished with you!'

'Come on, now, please, Aldo, let's be reasonable. Let me out at that jetty over there and there'll be no further consequences for you.'

'No further consequences? For me? Yes, you're certainly right about that, there'll be no further consequences for me. You see, Fausto, I have no vested interests now, nothing to gain from seeking favours, because I've lost it all. And as you know so well, your hold over people depends on their hope. They hope your power and influence – your relative power and influence – will smooth their path if only they can keep on the right side of you. But when all hope is gone, well, what's to be gained from creeping around after favours?'

'How could I have been so stupid?' Fausto muttered.

'I know,' Aldo laughed. 'What a mistake.'

'A woman at the Londra Palace indeed . . .'

'Yes, it's almost funny, isn't it? How could you ever have believed such a thing? Just a stupid dream, Fausto, that's all. Snared by your dreams. And I had dreams too, you know, a long, long time ago. But I was forced awake before they were fully formed, and now I have none, except the one I'm about to fulfil. Can you guess what it might be, Fausto? We're both alone out here in the dark, you and me, just the two of us, adrift out here in the dark . . . oh look, the lights are fading now . . . and both our dreams are lost. And when hope has gone, all that remains is the truth. Quite reassuring when you think about it, don't you think?'

'Get on with it.'

'And so, Fausto, we must face up to the truth, you and I.'

'The truth?'

'Yes, the truth – heard of it, have you? We both know you did it, Fausto. Out there in the forest. *Oh look, Aldo, a wild boar! Shoot it, Aldo! Shoot it when I whistle!* You must have taken me for a fucking idiot.'

'Your words, not mine.'

'You're the one to blame, Fausto, you're the guilty one, the one who fired the shot. The shot that killed him. You, Fausto, not me.'

'But, Aldo, it was your bullet. The police proved it. It came from your gun.'

'Like hell it did. You set me up, and you'll admit it if it's the last thing you do in the short time you have left on this earth.'

'You wouldn't have the guts. You wouldn't do it. You wouldn't dare.'

But Fausto's voice was soft and unsure now, barely audible amid the drumming of the rain. Even his face seemed to be dissolving away in the downpour, breaking up into pieces in the dark.

'Believe me, Fausto, believe me. We're going out to sea and once we're past the breakwaters there'll be no coming back. See the storm over there? The sea will be rough tonight. So you don't have long. Tell me the truth, confess to me, just this once, just to me. Wouldn't it be so much better to be forgiven by someone before you die?'

'You couldn't do it. I know you. You're not strong enough.'

'No, you don't know me, Fausto, not any more, if you ever really did. And it has nothing to do with strength. I killed an innocent man for far less than this, for no reason at all really. Does that make me strong? Of course it doesn't. And does the fact that I'll tip you out of this boat and push my foot down on your head make me strong, even if you deserve all that and worse? Or does it make me weak? So I'm asking you to help me, Fausto, help me to be strong, help me to forgive you, because it might just save you and I can't do it on my own.'

'Fuck you! Why on earth should I help you, after all this?'

'You see, Fausto! You see? You still don't believe me. But I'm begging you, please help me here, because otherwise you're coming with me, I swear you are, and I know you don't want to go where I'm headed.'

Fausto shook his head and opened his mouth again as if to protest but Aldo swung the oar and struck him across the head, knocking his hat into the water and bringing blood streaming from his brow. The rain swept the blood away but it rushed out again as Fausto tried to wipe it away with his hand.

'Admit it, you bastard! Confess, for God's sake! Tell me you did it, that you fired the fatal shot, not me. Take this guilt upon yourself, or I swear you're coming with me!'

Fausto cowered on the bench, an arm raised across his bloodied face. Aldo swung the oar again but the arm caught the weight of the blow and Aldo heard Fausto whimpering in the dark. Aldo drew the oar back again, high above his head this time, and Fausto raised his arm and screamed back at him, 'All right! All right! Stop! I'll tell you, I'll tell you everything!'

'Go on, tell me!'

'I'll tell you, I'll tell you, the whole damned story, just put down the oar . . .'

'Go on, then, I haven't got all fucking night.'

The oar twitched above Aldo's head and Fausto's words came at Aldo through the rain.

'I loved you, Aldo.'

'What?'

'I always loved you.'

Aldo let the oar fall by his side. 'What the fuck are you talking about?'

'You're mine, Aldo.'

'Have you gone fucking mad?'

'No, no, I love you, Aldo. I love you because you're mine. And that's all I ever wanted, something that was really mine.'

'Oh, shut up! I haven't got time to listen to this!'

'Luca didn't know. He never knew. God knows how I kept it from him all those years, how I kept it from you.'

'Luca?'

'God, yes, I wanted to hurt him so much, but I just couldn't do it, I couldn't do it to you, and I couldn't do it to your mother. I knew if Luca left her she would never be happy without him, that bloody Luca, and she would never be happy with me, and that's what I wanted after all, her happiness. So I let it be, I left you all in peace. I just couldn't do it to you, you and your mother.'

'Do what, Fausto? Do what?'

'She knew, you know, she knew. I begged her so often to come back, for years I begged her, but I knew she never would. Once she'd found Luca, I never stood a chance.'

Aldo sat down on the deck and held his head in his hands as Fausto went on and on, his voice unhinged and croaking as he tumbled out the words.

'I loved her, Aldo. Oh, Maria, I loved her so much! I waited all those years for her to come back to me, but I knew she never would.'

A look of deepest suffering traversed the face of Fausto Pozzi and he looked into the well of the boat. 'She would never have left Luca the way she left me . . .'

'No, Fausto!' Aldo bellowed. 'No, it can't be! She would never have had anything to do with a shit like you!'

'Oh, she had a lot to do with me, Aldo. We were close then, and you kept us close after that – our son, joining us forever – and you held us together even if she ignored and despised me, and I had to make do with watching from a distance and following your progress from there, trying to provide for you both, doing my best to make sure that idiot Luca kept you as well as I would have done if she'd let me. Did you never hear my footsteps behind you in the street? Didn't you ever turn around and wonder who was there, whose footsteps mirrored your own so precisely? Didn't you ever notice the way we walked, you and I, the same stride? Didn't you ever notice when you looked into my eyes that you were looking into your own? The nose, the mouth? We're both the same, Aldo, and you're a part of me. Like it or not, you are mine.'

'But it can't be true!'

'It is.'

'It can't be!'

'The way I protected you, tried to stop them from sending you away to the war. There were others who wanted you out of the way sooner. It would have been so easy for me to have you sent away, with the connections I had, to get you out of my hair, to stop your accusations about Luca's death.'

'My father's death! My father's!'

'No, Aldo! Your father is not dead. He's sitting with you here in this boat. Look at me, Aldo, look at me. Can't you see we're the same?'

Aldo looked into the little black eyes looking back at him, boring into his own, like looking down a coalmine at night. He saw Fausto's tears, the blood and the rain, streaming down the wild desolate face, the coarse hair around the snout matted with the dirt and filth of a lifetime at the trough, and it was as much as he could do to prevent himself from crossing over to embrace the broken man.

'Aldo, I swear to you, I swear it's all true. And there's more . . . that night in the woods, the gunshot – there was another one. Not just an echo, another man, another shot. You're right, have been all along, the bullet that killed Luca didn't come from your gun. How could it? How could anyone have believed that was possible, a freak shot in the dark like that? Your bullet's probably still stuck in a tree out there in the forest. Of course there was another shot, there had to be, someone with a clear view and a trained eye. The plan would never have worked otherwise. They sent us up there, they set it all up.'

'Who set it up?'

'They did. The ones who've been behind it all the whole time, behind everything. Behind Casa Luca, behind my other businesses. Where do you think I got all the money? I was a nobody, Aldo, just like Luca. I was a nobody from the shitty grey suburbs of Milan. But they took me on . . .'

'Who?'

'I can't tell you that.'

'Who Fausto, who? Tell me, for God's sake!' He raised the oar high above his head again.

'The police.'

'What do you mean *the police*?'

'The Chief Inspector. And the others, but the Chief Inspector was the big boss. He told me to sort it all out, to find someone who would work for me, who we could exploit. But he was always there in the background, the money was siphoned off. I got my share, of course I did, so did Luca. I'd have given him more, but it wasn't up to me. I'd have given him more just so you and your mother could benefit, so that you could be kept the way I'd have kept you. But it wasn't my decision.'

He smeared the blood across his face again and tried to wipe it from his eyes.

'Luca didn't deserve it, though, with his attitude. Call that love? He didn't do all he could for you, you know. And he wasn't even running the risks I was. If I hadn't earned enough for them they would have done me in, like they did Luca in – they still would do me in, I have to look over my shoulder all the time these days. But Luca was just too stubborn, that was the problem with him – too fucking stubborn, too fucking proud, and in the end they lost patience. I pleaded with him to see sense but he wouldn't, so I pleaded with them too, but they wouldn't change their minds. They never do. And so he paid the price for being stupid and stubborn and . . . honest.'

'But you didn't have to help them, did you, up there in the forest?'

'They'd have got him some other way if I hadn't helped them, and they'd probably have done the same to me too for not playing ball. Not that I was too distraught about his death, I admit that. But I know what it must have done to you, and to your mother. So after that I tried to ease off a bit, tried to protect you all, to make the business work better so that it would provide for you in a way it never could when Luca was involved. But they got greedier and greedier, they always do. They wanted more and more profit, they thought Maria would be a pushover, but she was even more stubborn than Luca. She said it would insult Luca's memory to change the way the place was run. So they sorted her out too.'

'Sorted her out? What the hell do you mean by that?'

'They're not in Rome, your mother and Elena. They're dead. They had them killed two years ago. And they'd have done the same to you too if you'd been around.'

'Oh my God, this is too much . . .'

Fausto stood up and shuffled across towards Aldo and pulled him into his arms. Aldo pushed him away and sat back down on the deck.

'I'm so sorry, Aldo. Your mother wouldn't sign over the restaurant, so they got rid of her. And Elena had to go too, or else she would have known. I tried to persuade them to go away for a while, to get out of the way, but she said I was just trying to get my hands on Casa Luca.'

'And the house? The people there said they bought the house from my mother. How did that happen, or did they take that too?'

'She sold the house first, nearly three years ago. She needed the money to keep Casa Luca going. They lived in the house on Burano after that, until . . . well, now you know. They're buried in the garden there, round the back, by the edge of the lagoon.'

'And you didn't even try to stop all of this?'

'I couldn't have, Aldo, I told you. They're too powerful. Once you're in, you're in, and they never let you out. There's no escape, and then one day they do you in, like they did Luca in, like they wanted to do you in if I hadn't talked them out of it, before the war and again when you got back – you gave everyone quite a shock when you turned up out of the blue, causing trouble again like that. And they'll do me in too. One day they'll come for me for sure and you won't see me any more, and you at least will know what's become of me.'

'And you think I'll care?' Aldo stood up and dipped the oar in the water.

'So what are you going to do with me now, Aldo?'

Then something scraped across the underside of the gondola and a small low island emerged, just twenty yards across, little more than an elevation suspended above the water, deserted but for a single windswept crooked tree.

'Get out, Fausto, before I change my mind.'

Fausto hesitated, then stumbled into the water and up onto the mudflat. 'You're leaving me here? But Aldo . . .'

'I don't want to take you with me.'

'Aldo, you think you've been wronged, but what about me? We've both been wronged, and we've both done wrong, and that makes us just the same. You're just the same as me, Aldo, just the same.'

'You know, Fausto, for so long I wanted to kill you, ever since that day in the woods. But before the war I couldn't bring myself to do it, and then for a long time I was simply too far away, and when I got back I was so confused. I lost count of the number of times I followed you through the streets at night, but for some reason I just couldn't do it. And now that I finally can, it just doesn't seem the right thing to do any more.'

He lowered the oar and began to turn the boat around. 'And one last thing. Why did you have to tell the Chief Inspector to stop me the other night at the theatre?'

'At the theatre?'

'Yes, at the theatre. There was someone there I needed to see backstage, someone who might have turned my life around. The Inspector said you'd drawn me to his attention, you told him I was up to no good.'

'I don't know what you're talking about, Aldo. He did that of his own volition. Honestly, Aldo, I swear to you it's true.'

Aldo paused for a moment, then started to row away. 'Farewell, Fausto!'

'Aldo, wait! Where are you going? Take me back with you and we'll forget all this ever happened.'

'How could we forget?'

'But what am I going to do here?

'Wait, Fausto. Just wait. Someone will come along eventually.'

'And you?'

'Me? I'm all done in. But look, do me one last favour, will you? The Chief Inspector, where does he live?'

'I don't know.'

'Come on, Fausto. Do this for me. I'll be doing you a favour in return.'

Fausto ran a hand through his dirty thinning hair and told him.

'Thank you, Fausto. Thank you. Now try to live up to what I'm about to do for you. Casa Luca is yours now, all yours. Just make sure you run it the way Luca would have wanted.'

Aldo pushed off and looked back at the island, barely higher than the water, just a single crooked tree and a single crooked man, floating on the waves in the dark. Fausto stood up and called out to Aldo, but he was already out of earshot. The storm was coming in off the Adriatic now, the first drops of rain coming down and lightning in the sky, the eastern horizon illuminated by bright flashes, an artillery barrage of memories, and the lagoon, streaked with light, stretched away as vast and cold and empty as the winter steppe.

Aldo found the house with little difficulty, in a narrow street in Castello. He waited in the rain until dawn, the silence in the streets finally disturbed by occasional passing figures, an old woman with a basket and a man with a stick, and then a small girl who wished him good morning and told him she was on her way to buy eggs, her smile making Aldo feel that his heart might break open and spill itself on the ground at her feet as she passed. But his heart was harder than that now, and so he waited outside the Chief Inspector's door and pricked up his ears for the slightest sound from within. Finally, he heard footsteps in the hall and the sound of the lock being undone and the door was pulled open. Aldo crashed inside, smashed the Chief Inspector's head against the wall, pulled him to the ground and slammed the door shut with his foot. Aldo knelt on top of the Chief Inspector, pinning him to the floor with his forearm so that when he spoke his words had to squeeze themselves out through the narrow gap that was left to them.

'Come to tell me something, have you, Aldo? Come to confess?'

'You were right,' said Aldo. 'The dead *do* have a voice, but I don't believe you can hear them. So I'll speak for them instead. I did it. I killed him, the musician, the old man. The *old* man. You were right all along.'

'I knew that already. I knew you were the one I was looking for.'

'And I was looking for you, I just didn't know it. But I know every-thing now, Fausto told me, the whole thing. Luca, and my mother and Elena – the whole lot!'

'What the fuck are you talking about?'

'Casa Luca, you and your mob, everything.'

'You stupid bastard! It's a trick, don't you realise? A trick!'

'I don't believe you, my sly cunning friend. Fausto has told me everything, the marksman in the forest, the second shot, from a police gun, not mine, the shot that killed Luca.'

'Ha! And you believe him, you believe Fausto Pozzi? Of course he would say that. He's a liar.'

'You're the liar. There was a second shot, I heard it.'

'Of course there was a second shot, of course there was, but not from this fantasy, not from this marksman lurking in the trees. How could that ever have worked? Not even I could have pulled off that one. The second shot came from Fausto's gun, that's obvious, always has been. But people believe whatever you tell them, and we covered it up – we covered it up, that's all. And the bullet *was* his, ballistics confirmed it, just as I thought. It was a personal thing, not business, he just took the opportunity when it came, a spur of the moment thing, nothing he had planned.'

'I still don't believe you.'

'And you think I care?'

But Aldo was doubting himself now. How could he have got it so wrong, leaving Fausto alive out there in the lagoon just when he had the chance to see to him, to see that justice for Luca was done?

'So you covered it up, then, Chief Inspector? You let me take the blame, left me to carry the burden all these years. Do you realise what that's done to me, how it's marked my life ever since? And more than that, you let Fausto off the hook. So you're just as much to blame, you're as guilty as he is.'

'It goes with the job . . .'

Aldo drew the knife from his pocket and held its point against the Chief Inspector's chest. Then he slid it into him, and as the blade went in, the fire in Aldo's eyes went out, and the Chief Inspector looked back at him as he held it there.

'Can you feel that, my friend? Can you feel what it's like, to be stabbed in the heart? That's for Luca, for what you did to him, and it's for my mother and sister too. And it's also for me, and for all the other poor bastards you and your kind helped to send away to war. You're right, Chief Inspector, the dead have a voice, and I can hear them now. Can you hear them too? They're talking to you, Chief Inspector, they're talking to you through me, and now it's your turn to suffer in silence.'

The Chief Inspector moved his lips as if desperate to speak but Aldo slipped a firm hand over his mouth and pressed his words back inside.

'In silence, I said. Suffer in silence, you fascist. You pig.'

Aldo felt the impact in his stomach before he heard the shot, the Chief Inspector's finger tightening against the trigger of the gun that he always carried inside the pocket of his coat. Aldo coughed and tasted the blood in his throat and saw little specks of it on the Chief Inspector's face. He pushed the knife in hard again and the Chief Inspector's eyes slid shut. Aldo stood up and threw the knife down and wiped his hands on a coat in the hall and stumbled back out into the street, clutching his abdomen. As the pain from his wound spread out from his belly, and waves of nausea threatened to overcome him, he staggered against a wall and let his head rest against the damp bricks.

'Fausto Pozzi,' he said out loud as his legs threatened to give way, his face pressed hard up against the wall now. Fausto, he thought, you bastard, you tricked me good and proper in the end, just when I thought I had you, lying about the bullet and its origin, about who fired the fatal shot, when it was you that fired it all along. And if you lied about that, you'd just as easily lie about Luca. All that stuff about my parentage, I knew it couldn't be true. But the Chief Inspector, he was a bastard and a liar too, so who to believe? And no time left to me now to find out the truth of it, not now, not in this state. Truth and justice, they were all I ever wanted, but I'll be leaving this world with neither of them now. And so you're going to get away with it after all, aren't you, Fausto? Just like you always do, you and the likes of you.'

But he could not let it go, not without a fight, not until his last breath had left him, so he stumbled along to where he'd left the gondola and he climbed unsteadily aboard, turning it around and pointing it down the canal in the direction of the lagoon and Fausto Pozzi. But he had gone barely fifty yards when his vision dimmed and blurred and his eyes blacked over and he fell into the well of the boat. He got up again, unsteady on his feet, poling frantically at the water with the oar, but then came a terrible weakness in his arms, exhaustion catching up with him. He knew he was never going to make it now, not all that way to the island in the lagoon. But someone had to know, someone must know the truth, so he turned the boat around again and inched it up the Canale Grande, under the Accademia and Rialto bridges, then up the side-canals and into the ghetto. He tied the boat up beneath Isabella's window and lifted the oar to tap on the frame. He saw Isabella's face behind the glass and she came down and let him in and he followed her up the stairs, past the books and the cats that littered the way, and he lay on the bed with his head in her lap. She bent down and kissed him, tasted the salt in his hair, felt the damp in his clothes.

'Aldo, my dear, where have you been?'

'Out in the gondola. The lagoon.'

'There was a storm last night.'

'Yes, I saw it. I've been out in it all night. I'm tired, Isabella, so tired.'

'You can rest now, Aldo. I'll take care of you, don't you worry about that.'

He looked at her as if suddenly confused, as if some sort of certainty had unexpectedly started to dissolve.

'You know, Isabella, perhaps you were the one. Perhaps you were the one all along and I just didn't realise it.'

'Aldo, that's ridiculous, I can't have been.'

'Why not?'

'I can't have been, that's all. What about your angel? Your angel in the snow . . .'

'My angel? Do angels really exist?'

'What do you think?'

'She seemed so real.'

'There's your answer, then. If she seemed real, then she was.'

He closed his eyes and she caressed his clammy brow. Then she saw the blood on his shirt.

'Oh my God, Aldo, what's happened to you? Let me fetch a doctor.'

'No, Isabella, don't go. I have to tell you something. I want somebody else to know, this secret mustn't die with me. Fausto Pozzi, he did it, I know that now, or I think I do. Yes, yes, it was him, it must have been. He killed Luca. And the Chief Inspector covered it up and later he did away with my mother and my sister and he'd have done the same to me. Tell the papers, tell them about their deeds, tell them to look for the bodies in the garden on Burano, beneath the window by the lagoon, where the wild flowers grow thickest. Will you tell them that, Isabella? Will you?'

'Don't worry, Aldo. I'll tell them.'

'And will you find Fausto Pozzi for me? Don't let him get away with it. Will you see that justice is done?'

'Yes, Aldo, I'll do that, I'll do that for you. I don't know how, but I'll find a way.'

'And try to find a way to take on Casa Luca. Call it Casa Isabella, if you want. I would like that. But Isabella, run the old place as Luca would have done.'

She nodded, uncertain now, he could see it in her eyes.

'Isabella, I mean it. Do it for me. Justice for Luca, and Casa Luca for him too.'

'Don't worry, Aldo. I'll do it. I'll do it for you, just for you.'

'Thank you, Isabella. And there's one more thing . . .' He swallowed hard.

'Don't worry, Aldo, I already know.'

'No, you don't. The old man, the street musician, I killed him. I'm so sorry, Isabella. I deserve no forgiveness for that.'

'Aldo, I already knew.'

'But how, Isabella?'

'I just knew.'

'But I don't understand why the police didn't pursue me further. They had me, they knew all about the violin, and then for some reason the story changed. They said they had the wrong violin. That mine didn't match the description. But it did, I know it did. It just doesn't any make sense.'

She stroked his hair and smiled. 'It makes sense, Aldo. Somebody swapped the violin. Somebody went to your house, broke in, found the violin in the kitchen cupboard, replaced it with another for the police to find.'

'But who? Who would have done that for me, Isabella?'

But he knew the answer.

She reached under the bed and pulled out the instrument and laid it on the mattress next to him.

'It'll remind me of you always,' she said.

'Is that a good thing?'

'Yes, dear Aldo. A very good thing.'

Isabella stroked the waves of his hair again, then wrapped him in arms that were at last more tender than voracious.

'Oh, Aldo, sweet child, how I've loved you, right from the start – I surprised even myself. If only I could have kept you from harm.'

She held him ever tighter and the pig on his arm blinked and closed its eyes at last, forever this time, and Aldo allowed his eyelids to fall across his eyes too, and his breathing slowed and his ears picked out the sound of a boat passing beneath the window and he followed the sound and let himself get on board and the boat carried him away into the beautiful heart of Venice.

Isabella sat beside the coffin as the gondola toiled through the waves towards San Michele, the rain cold and incessant as the gondoliers lifted the dark box out onto the quay and carried it among the graves. Isabella and the priest stood alone as the coffin was covered over while Fausto Pozzi looked on from further back, unseen among the tombs. Then Isabella returned to where the gondoliers stood smoking beneath the trees by the perimeter wall. They extinguished their cigarettes as she stepped aboard and they carried her back across the grey-green waves to Venice. When she had gone, Fausto Pozzi placed his flowers on the grass beside the muddying earth, turned his collar up against the cold, and stood for a long time alone in the rain.

Isabella went to Michele's shop and pushed the door open.

'I've come to let you know that Aldo won't be coming back.'

'No?'

'No. He's gone.'

'Gone where?'

'I mean he's gone.'

He saw her black clothes and the look in her eye.

'Isabella, I'm so sorry.'

He put an arm around her but she withdrew.

'Have a wine?' he said. 'For him.'

They drank from small squat glasses, Isabella taking a sip, then draining the dark red liquid into her mouth.

'Michele, I have to go.'

'Come back later . . . if you like.'

She looked at him. 'I don't think that would be appropriate on a day like this, do you, Michele?'

'Perhaps not,' he said, and adjusted his hair.

She turned abruptly away and walked back out into the bustling, seething street. She stopped a little way along, nearly turned back the way she had come, to look for Fausto Pozzi. But no, she thought, not now, not this day – there would be plenty of time for all that. Somehow she would find a way – she would find a way to sort out Fausto Pozzi, and then she would take on Casa Luca. But she wouldn't call it Casa Isabella, as Aldo had suggested, nor Casa Luca, as Aldo would really have preferred, but instead the name that Isabella felt to be most fitting, a final act of love: Casa Aldo.

And then she made her way slowly back to the house in the ghetto and sat on the stairs and wept while Madame Leroux whispered her name in the darkness of an adjacent room.

Barbed wire

Tambov, April 1952

Katerina stepped off the train and caught the bus to the village. Her footsteps were light and silent as she moved along the path that led into the forest. She walked for some time through the trees, then up the slope and down over the rocks to the lakeside and up and over the outcrop that led to the secret path, now overgrown with brambles and hawthorn bushes that sent white petals showering down like perfumed snowflakes in the warming breeze. Viktor's house stood at the edge of the treeline still, facing the beach, its broken windows looking out over the silver-blue waves that rippled to the shore from the other side of the island. Katerina knocked on the door and pushed it open. The room was covered in dust, cobwebs strewn across the beams, hanging in wispy grey beards around the place. The furniture was as she remembered it, the sideboard with the violins and the pickled vegetables, the stove in the far corner and the table with the three empty chairs in the middle of the room. She went to the far side of the room and opened the door to the bedroom and looked out through the window towards the lakeside, and she thought she glimpsed for a moment Viktor's silhouette on the beach with his nets and his boat, but when she went outside he was gone and the nets and the boat were no longer there.

As she walked back towards the path she saw a small cross that had been driven into the ground near the edge of the trees, the name of Koshka carved into its wood. She walked back through the forest, across the small clearing where the stream ran over pebbles and the footprints of wild animals lay fresh in the mud, and then on through the long grass where the mayflies would soon gather along the edge of the forest. The trees parted and she saw the watchtower a short distance away, its tall dark skeleton stark against the sky. She walked beneath it, past the open gate and the first of the bunkers, and she looked towards the side of the decaying camp, to the place where Aldo's stooping figure had been in 1943, staring into the woods. She quickened her pace, reached the spot where Aldo had stood and faced her. She reached out her hand again now, twisting it towards his memory, and this time there was no barbed wire to impede her touch, because time had rusted away its bloodied strands, and she stepped easily across its broken remains and stood where he had once stood.

She thought of what might since have become of him, how they had promised to write to each other, perhaps even find each other again in Venice after the war. And she *had* written to him – many, many times – but she had received no reply. She had even gone to his house that first time when the Kirov had toured Italy, had knocked on his door but the people there could not or would not help. And that other time, after that, when she had seen someone very much like him in the audience at La Fenice, just left of centre, just yards from the stage, and she had wondered if indeed it was him, come to find her, perhaps hurrying in afterwards to find her backstage. She had lingered longer than usual that evening before leaving, but of course he had not come. How could he have come? He would have been long gone by then, she was sure of that, lying in the Siberian earth outside some god-forsaken gulag in the east, another young life lost, a delayed victim of war just as Oleg had been. But she was a survivor, she knew that now, and she would live life for both of them, she would make the most of life's little leap, would leap for them too, lifting them up in her heart as she did so.

She turned and looked towards the woods, just as Aldo had always done. She saw that a small lake had lifted itself out of the ground in the years since the war. A spring breeze rippled its surface, shifting the reeds, and as she watched, fish flung themselves skywards, chasing after bugs. She put her hand in her pocket and felt the little wooden fish that Aldo had given her all those years before.

'It'll last forever,' he had said. 'And it'll bring you luck.'

And he was right. It had brought her luck – she had survived the war and had fulfilled her dreams, most of them anyway. And it had certainly lasted – it had lasted the test of time, just as her memories of him had done. The war was long gone and the prison camp had decayed, the woods advancing into it, nature taking things back and hiding what had happened there – but Katerina's love for Aldo had outlived it all, and it always would, tucked safely away in her heart.

Acknowledgements

Firstly, I would like to thank my agent, John Beaton, without whom this book would never have been published – without you, John, all the time I spent on it would have been wasted. Equally, I would like to thank everyone at Polygon – particularly Alison Rae, Neville Moir, Hugh Andrew and Jan Rutherford – for taking a chance on me, for their expertise and guidance, and for making this a much better book than it could possibly have been without them. Thanks are also due to David Robinson and designer Andrew Smith. And I would also like to thank my wife for her long hours of patience during the years in which I was writing *The Art of Waiting*, when there seemed little hope of it ever being published, when the time I spent on it should really have been ours to share.